TALONS of the ABYSS

Talons of the Abyss

Book 3 of the Immortal King Trilogy

Denise Tanaka

Pronunciation of Names and Naming Customs

Some given names, particularly in the Green Forest region of the kingdom, have a diaeresis mark (two dots over the letter "e") to indicate that a vowel pair is not a diphthong (combined into one syllable) and is pronounced as two syllables. For example, the given name of Glëa po'Lon is pronounced Glay-uh /ˈglɛɪə/

Maternal lineage, whether or not one is a gentry/landowner or a commoner, is indicated by the prefix "po" + apostrophe + the first syllable of the mother's given name. For example, King Glëa po'Lon is the son of Queen Lonielle.

Content warning

This novel contains graphic descriptions of combat violence, physical injury and death, emotional abuse, child marriage, and arranged marriage. This novel also makes references to war, battle, mutilation/scarring, depression, suicide, sexual violence, child labor, and drug use.

PART ONE

Chapter 1.

Day 23 of Measures Month, in the Year of Xol 758

The immortal king Glëa po'Lon sprinted hard up the spiral stairways of Xolhold Keep. His youthful body easily dashed across the stone bridges that branched from one tower to the next. A squad of bodyguards in black wool uniforms had trouble keeping up his pace.

His lifelong friend Lord Vilbyss had been absent from the day's routine session at the Assembly of Lords. The king had spent the daylight hours suffering in boredom. Lengthy discussions had bogged down in bickering over renovations to the aqueduct system, of constructing extensions to the royal highway, and recommendations from the royal treasurers on taxation rates to pay for it all. Then, a castle page had dared to approach the king's throne to bring a message. *Governor Vilbyss had fallen ill. His heart...*

Near the top of the tower, he halted just short of the chamber's door. One servant dropped to his knees, startled at the king's emergence from the stairway. Another two servants hunched over bowing as they pulled open the heavy, oak door.

King Glëa charged into the anteroom of Governor Vilbyss's private chambers. He passed by the Lady of the House who comfortably sat vigil on a sofa.

"Your Majesty!" Lady Vilbyss did not have time to put aside a collection of ribbon-bound papers that she was reading. Her triple layers of embroidered, beaded skirts weighed her down. As she struggled to rise, one velvet slipper came off and her padded footstool toppled over.

The king ignored her and rushed forward.

He plunged through a barrier of heavy curtains that divided the foyer from the bed chamber. People cluttered the room at the periphery of his vision. Servants in drab garments and a team of the royal surgeon's staff milled about with their tasks. All that mattered to the king was the old man lying in the bed.

"Why wasn't I called sooner!"

Dozens of people dropped to their knees.

"He didn't want you to see him this way." Lord Meldon, the royal surgeon, bowed his forehead to the floor.

The mattress seemed too large for the sole occupant. Mounds of pillows and downy quilts half swallowed him in a nest of softness. Ardis po'Lin, the Governor Lord Vilbyss, was propped up against the headboard but sagged slightly sideways. His eyes were closed yet he still breathed. *At least he is still breathing.*

"Your Majesty," said Lord Meldon. "Please don't be alarmed. He's doing well and is certain to make a full recovery."

"Recovery... from what exactly?"

Glëa gripped the ornate post of the bed canopy's drape. He stared in amazement at the old man who looked so small lying there. Wrinkles and pouches drooped under his closed eyes. Freckles were like spattered wine stains on his balding scalp. An old fencing scar dragged his upper lip sideways into a perpetual sneer. Glëa remembered giving Lord Vilbyss that scar in fencing practice more than fifty-five years ago. They had been youths on the verge of adulthood recklessly enjoying the peak of their vitality. One careless strike of the prince's blade, followed by a failure to parry, and his friend's face was forever changed. Now, the passage of time and their divergent paths had chiseled even more drastic changes.

"His Lordship experienced a fluttering of the heart and a simple episode of swooning." Lord Meldon dared to rise to his feet without the king's expressed permission. "It's not uncommon in a man his age."

By the calendar, the former general Governor Lord Vilbyss at seventy-three was the same age as the king himself. By the mirror, Glëa looked like his great-grandson.

An elderly civilian stood concernedly on the opposite side of the canopy bed. "We are praying hourly to his noble ancestors for their intervention. It seems that our pleas are being heard; they have not yet called his soul to cross into the Bliss of the Eternal Fields."

Glëa knew the lord's mister by sight but had trouble recalling his name. The Lady of the House sat vigil in the foyer, most likely reviewing an inventory of their lands and possessions that she would soon fully control as the widow. This middle-aged fellow with a receding hairline was Lord Vilbyss's true companion and source of affection for the past several decades. As the lord had once explained, *One gets my name. One gets my heart. It's an acceptable arrangement.* The lord's mister faithfully wore the house colors: a sash of yellow silk with a brooch pin die-cast in the wagon wheel insignia of the Vilbyss coat-of-arms.

"What have you done for him?" the king asked the royal surgeon.

"I assure His Majesty we are doing everything possible. He is certain to make a full recovery from this incident. You shall see him back on his feet in a week or two at the latest."

Glëa tenderly stroked the old man's bald forehead. The flesh felt cold. *So cold.* He leaned over the broad mattress and lightly kissed the scar at the corner of Lord Vilbyss's mouth. The lips tasted sour and reeked of bile.

"Specifically, what have you done for him?"

"Your Majesty, we have wrapped his feet in nettle leaves, slipped camphor oil under his tongue, and drizzled silver water into his eyes. We have also given him the usual tisanes of willow bark powder and sun-star root. Now, we are preparing to apply a bleeding treatment of leeches."

"With all respect, my lord," said one of the junior surgeons. "I think he's in a weakened condition—"

"Exactly why he needs his blood to be thinned so that his heart can more easily pump," the royal surgeon barked across the room. "You were going to get the leeches ready, Captain?"

The king looked at that member of the medical team who had spoken. He recognized the tall, broad-shouldered man in his early thirties. Captain Ashglëa po'Denn had served as a field medic during the war. A singular act of heroism had brought them face-to-face, on the last day of the final battle, and had earned him a commendation.

"Have you any reason to object to leeches, Captain?" the king asked.

Ash slid his hand to the back of his neck. "Uhh... well, Your Majesty, I've seen what happens to men on the battlefield when they've had too much blood drained out of them."

The royal surgeon inhaled deeply to expand his chest and appear taller. "Captain, may I remind you, we're not on a battlefield anymore! Lord Vilbyss has not been impaled or stabbed. His heart has fluttered in a way that I have seen many times before in other men of advanced age. Now, you are in your second year of the medical academy, are you not?"

"Yes sir." Ash slouched but did not quite manage to bow to his supervisor. His hazel-green eyes sparkled a bit of defiance in the candlelight.

"When you've been an accredited surgeon for as many years as I have, then you shall have the authority to *think*. Until then—"

"Hold." The king raised his hand, and all the discussion stopped. Silence hung over the room as long as the jeweled rings on every finger glimmered.

The bed-ridden old man's flesh drained of color. With each passing wheeze, Lord Vilbyss struggled to inhale. His skin turned grayer. *Is no one else seeing this but me? He's dying. My friend, whom I've loved since we were children, is dying!*

"Captain Ashglëa, are you very confident of your opinion?"

"Yes, Your Majesty, I am."

The king looked hard into the man's eyes. Glëa's immortal consciousness grew invisible tendrils that reached for Ash's mortal heart. A faint ringing filled his inner ears. For a moment, it felt like plunging into murky waters and spotting a jewel at the muddy bottom. He focused on the threads of those hazel-green irises and allowed the sense of all else to drop away.

The captain glowed like a lantern with the confidence of practical knowledge yet there were stains of unhealed grief. Captain Ashglëa had seen more than his fair share of the dying and the dead. Memories of bloody corpses rattled audibly in the man's eyes. Yet a darker secret lay buried in the layers beneath his ordinary sorrows. Residue of something unnatural, long since exorcised, tainted everything else. The king's vestigial human soul formed thoughts as words. *Oh yes, my young captain, you've encountered demonic forces long ago. You understand that some ailments cannot be cured with tree bark and forest roots.*

The other man's voice echoed faintly in the dreamscape that enveloped them both in blue shadows. *Don't ask. Please don't ask.*

Glëa drew a breath and retreated into his own eyes. A pleasant backwash tingled over his skin like goosebumps. The captain turned aside with a slight blush as if something intimate had just passed between them.

"No leeches," said the king.

The royal surgeon said, "Your Majesty, if may implore you to reconsider—"

"Must I repeat myself, Meldon?"

"Of course not, Your Majesty." Lord Meldon bowed from the waist but tilted his head just enough so he could shoot what had to be a vicious glare in the captain's direction.

"Captain Ashglëa, arise and accompany me. The rest of you, wait and do nothing until I return!"

The king turned sharply on his heeled royal slippers, creating a squeak like snapping fingers on the terra cotta tiles. The captain grabbed a shoulder satchel and hurried to follow his sovereign.

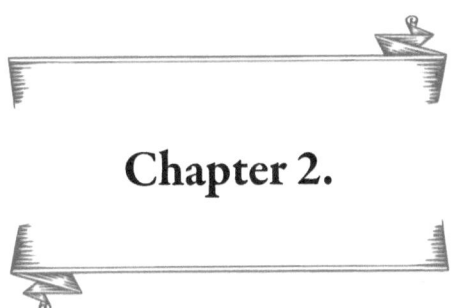

Chapter 2.

King Glëa waved off the helpful hands that offered to assist him into the rowboat. Although he had not been in a watercraft for many years, he settled easily onto the center bench. He gathered the bulk of the full-length hooded cloak around himself. The brown wool borrowed from Lord Vilbyss's wardrobe worked to conceal the sovereign king's departure from Xolhold Keep at this late hour. A handful of his most trusted bodyguards—Cody, Herry, and Sorrix—accompanied him without pomp or fanfare.

The long rowboat glided over the golden waters of Harbor Bay at sunset. Glëa kept his gaze aimed downward, his face concealed by the hood that faintly held the musk of his lifelong friend. *If Ardis dies tonight, all that remains is the scent of him and my memories. In time even those will fade. How could I be so foolish in failing to contemplate this inevitability until now? In fifty years, I have not aged a day.*

Captain Ash said, "May I ask where we are going, Your Majesty?"

"You may not."

Herry answered glumly, "You'll see, Ash. Wait and see."

The rowboat steered for the northernmost hook of the crescent-shaped bay. The lighthouse tower's bonfire shined to penetrate the incoming fog. Their course avoided the bustling end-of-day commotion of the wharf. Merchant ships at anchor had finished unloading or loading their cargo. The harbor master's office shuttered its windows and locked its doors. Ships' crews had ventured into the streets of Capital City to seek entertainment in that quarter of town where lanterns burned all night long. Meanwhile, the fishermen had long since rolled up their nets and gone to bed.

A floating buoy's brass bell clanged dully as the rowboat glided past. Off-key tones rankled his immortal senses. Glëa put his fingertips into his ears.

"Feeling unwell, Your Majesty?" Ash eyed him sideways with concern.

"Not at all, Captain."

Ash reached into his satchel. "I've got a sack of cloves, if you're feeling queasy. You put one under your tongue—"

"I am not feeling queasy, Captain."

"As you say."

The rowboat arrived at the shore of a rocky lump that some might generously call an island. Too far from shore to have a bridge, the place was known as Seagulls' Rock.

All three guards and the junior surgeon climbed out. Their boots splashed calf-deep in the lapping waters. They dragged the rowboat up the gravelly scree to where Glëa could disembark without soiling his borrowed cloak.

Wooden palisades crowned Seagulls' Rock and encircled an area the size of a horse corral. One guard stood in the watchtower above the barred gate. "Who goes there!"

Glëa pushed back the cloak's hood to reveal his royal visage to the amber lanterns. "Open the gate, Captain.... Donthell, is it?"

"Jahn?" the guard asked.

The king sighed weary irritation to be mistaken for his look-a-like decoy who occasionally impersonated him at public events.

"No, don't you see?" Sorrix shouted up at the watchtower. "It's him.... Himself!"

"Oh, mercy on me!" Captain Donthell called down orders to the gatekeepers.

The gate's bolt lifted. Panels of vertical logs separated at the center. Massive grinding hinges spread open to offer them entry.

"Stay behind us, Your Majesty." Herry led the way forward into the gate. The two other captains Cody and Sorrix covered his back. The junior surgeon Ash fell into formation at the rear. The boatman stayed behind with the craft.

Sulfurous odors and something more hideous reeked in the enclosure. Glëa carefully maintained a neutral facial expression as his bodyguards and the surgeon were eyeing him protectively. They expected him to be anxious or startled. No one except his closest lifelong friend Lord Vilbyss knew that he had experience with the otherworldly creature kept chained here. The king squared his shoulders and braced himself to face the beast.

A squad of soldiers dressed for combat training in steel breastplates, gambeson tunics, cuffed gloves, and bowl-shaped helmets lashed tightly under their chins. They wielded all sorts of polearms and various types of swords. Bonfires raged in massively bright plumes of flame that nearly obscured the occupants of the place.

Why not train with crossbows that have the power to penetrate that hide, Glëa briefly wondered but the thought soon passed. He was not here to inspect their methods.

A large trench had been excavated in a circle and filled with sea water. The beast at the center of the watery trench crouched on a boulder. By clinging to the stone perch, its black talons scraped flakes off the granite. It growled as it rattled the iron chains. Its breath stank of rotten meat.

Glëa chose to stand near the trench's rim. He rested his hands on his hips as he surveyed the creature. Although it had been a decade since he faced one of its kind, nothing about its appearance surprised him. This was exactly what he expected to find shackled in this training ground.

The creature squatted on its two legs with knees bent outward. If it were to rise straight, the king knew, it would stand a full head and chest above a tall man. Black reptilian hide had lumpy scales that glistened in dirty rainbows. Bat-like velum wings were folded against ridges of serrated spikes that ran along its spine. A tail with a barbed tip whipped left and right like a snake wriggling through sand. Its narrow snout had blue fangs that dripped oily saliva. Topaz eyes with slit pupils focused on the group of men.

"Oh," said Ash.

The king noted a remarkably subdued reaction for a man facing one for the first time. Oh yes, he mused, the captain had surely experienced horror and not just in battle. Someday, he would coax the story out of him, but now he had a more urgent matter to address.

"Damn me," said Cody. "I'd forgotten how hideous this wretched creature is."

"Indeed," the king said. "It is a vile monstrosity."

The troops in training brandished their sharp blades and polearms. "Don't be concerned, Your Majesty. We've got the beast well under control."

Herry explained, "The nomads of the Outerlands call them Surleista. In their language it means 'the burned children of the gods.'"

"Hatched from charcoal eggs," the king murmured.

The beast hissed. Fangs snapped at Glëa's presence. Its topaz eyes flashed bright golden threads that reached for the king's face. Its growls buzzed. Wordless words resonated in his thoughts. *Kindred! You see me. You feel us. Help me.*

"Be quiet," Glëa barked at its horned snout. His thoughts continued speaking to the beast on the invisible golden threads that connected their eyes. *I am not your kindred. I have not come to help you.*

The Surleista howled and thrashed its chains. The iron links held around its ankles. *Help me. Help me.* When it squawked from its reptilian throat, Glëa could almost make out human words. "Help. Help."

Despite his efforts to remain focused on his purpose, Glëa's memories replayed the decades of when he was shipwrecked on an uncharted island in the deep sea. His heart went cold remembering the shrieks of the same type of beasts that had raked the air, day and night, for every moment of the forty years he had been marooned. Constant as the rush of the seashore, hundreds of them had swarmed in a constant cyclone of wings twirling around the barren stone peaks. Hundreds of them were trapped by the ocean's waters like flies in a glass jar. Eternal, un-killable, and constantly hungry, they devoured all but a handful of his ship's crew.

Help me. You know us. You know me. You are me. I am you. We are One. Help me. Help me. The longer the beast growled, the deeper its resonance buzzed into his mind.

Stop, stop, stop, Glëa chanted in his thoughts.

Ash put a hand on the king's shoulder. "You still look a bit queasy from the rowboat, sir. Here now, have a whiff of cloves."

Pungent odors of spicy wood rushed up Glëa's nostrils. The king closed his eyes to break their connection. In the dim shelter of his eyelids, his mind regained a sense of the present moment.

"Better, sir?"

"Yes."

"Careful, Your Majesty," said Sorrix. "Don't get too close. That tail's barb can slice your gut open like a scythe."

"I am well aware of the danger, Captain." The king inhaled the night air to clear his head. A few quick blinks, and he reopened his eyes to stare coldly at the beast once more.

It snapped its leathery wings straight out to full extension. The wings made a loud snap like a ship's sails catching the wind. Firelight from behind illuminated the spiderweb veins in the velum. For a moment, the king stood transfixed by the horrible beauty of it.

The beast sniffed the air and squealed in a higher tone. Its topaz eyes fixated on the junior surgeon, ignoring the steel-tipped poles and those who held them. Its growling voice chanted a single word in human language. "Meat.... Meat... Meat."

"Back! Back!" The trainees stepped into formation and jabbed their polearms in the air.

Herry smacked the surgeon's upper arm. "Whatcha got in your pockets, Ash?"

"Nothing."

"C'mon, I know you."

Ash shrugged. "Well, I've a little bit of quail drumstick left over from lunch—"

Herry dug into his friend's coat pocket to bring out a napkin. "Shit, you'll get us all killed. Those shadow-beasts crave meat, ya dolt. Nothing but meat."

"I see. Sorry."

Glëa stepped forward shoulder-to-shoulder with the line of spearmen. He stood his ground and faced the chained beast.

Captain Donthell spoke from the watchtower, "Do you have any questions, Your Majesty?"

I should ask something. He expects me to be curious, as if I have never seen a scratcher before. "Are you sure those chains will hold?"

"Oh yes, definitely. Their strength is that of an average mountain bear. Once you know how to handle them, they're really quite manageable creatures."

"Are you managing them, Donthell?"

"Yes, Your Majesty, indeed. Not only that, but the water is another safeguard. You see, we don't understand why, but they cannot pass over water. Any water! Running water, stagnant water, fresh water or salt. Not only can they not fly but they can barely stand in it. Quite pathetic, really, to watch them groveling and screaming in the shallowest of puddles."

"Elemental spirits in the waters repel them," the king murmured. By whatever impossible magic that allowed them to fly at all, that one rule was absolute.

"Perhaps that's so," Captain Donthell agreed.

Glëa looked to its topaz eyes with the vertical slit pupils. The beast stared back at him with the keen interest of a predator.

"How... How many of these beasts do we have?"

"Four total," said the captain. "Caged in the cave below. We only bring 'em up one at a time for training."

"Why bring them up one at a time?"

"It's, uh, too risky to face—"

"Risky?" He raised the volume of his voice but did not turn away from the blackened scaly snout of the beast. "Risky, you say? The dry mountains of the Outerlands are infested with these vile creatures. They hunt in packs. They attack livestock in swarms. My troops should be training to extinguish the scratchers from the world."

"Yes, Your Majesty's point is well taken. I will discuss the matter with Colonel Fordon."

A grating squawk came out of the beast's corrugated throat. The gray-tongue flapped over its spiked fangs. It straightened its neck and raised its jaw like a wolf howling at the moon. A scream peeled out of its throat. A drawn-out wavering screech plunged into Glëa's ears and shuddered down his neck. The sound played gritty images of memories that were not his own. This pain was not meant to be held by a human mind. Halberds chop off the Surleista's knotty paw. Swords whack off the crookedly bowed legs. Pikes and lances plunge into its abdominal scales. The beast opens its maw and roars rage at the men in black coats.

Glëa hummed at the beast, a soft *mmmm* from his closed lips. His hum carried the thought, *Stop whining. You're mine, now. You belong to me.*

The beast gulped the back of its tongue. With one more defiant growl, it fell silent.

He quickly turned aside to avoid the temptation of reaching forth with his immortal soul's song to probe into its thoughts. The last thing he wanted was any further knowledge of its feelings.

"So, that hide looks thick," said the king. "Are they hard to kill?"

"To some degree, yes, Your Majesty."

Glëa's gaze scanned over the layered scales that scored the beast's concave abdomen. He remembered his expedition's crew throwing rocks or fighting with whatever tools had not sunk with the ship. Rocks bounced. Grappling hooks failed.

"Fire is the only effective weapon," the captain continued. "Their blood is flammable like lamp oil."

"Indeed."

"Flaming arrows work best. One or two well placed shots, and they pop like boiling clams. Their bodies turn to ashes faster than a clump of dry moss."

The beast snarled and clicked its fangs. That snout was as long as a blacksmith's bellows. If the king were to step too close, that yawning maw could bite him in half with one gulp.

One of the trainees added, "But fire archers are not always available, Your Majesty, which is why we train with alternative weapons. We practice how to keep them at bay, how to disable and dismember them, until we can go in for the kill shot. Stuffing a lit grenade into its mouth is particularly effective."

A crate nearby held a collection of ceramic apples with fuses.

Glëa flexed his fingers. In mirroring the gesture, the beast tapped its talons on the granite perch. His breaths grew short, impatient for the captain to continue his narrative and tell him the rest of what he was not supposed to already know. Or, would the soldiers conceal its deepest horrors so as not to frighten their sovereign lord?

"Show me how their limbs regrow."

A trainee accepted the nod from his captain and stepped forward. He wielded the halberd with expert grace. He spun the pole left and right like a windmill in his hands. The lily-shaped blade sparkled in the torch light. Flashing steel and the scarlet tassel flipping caught the beast's attention.

The beast reached forth its left paw. The Surleista scratched at the air the way a cat would tap at a dangling ball of string.

The trainee hooked the halberd under the beast's wrist. One swift flick of his weapon severed the paw clean off.

The beast screamed. Its voice's power rippled the trench waters and reverberated in the timbers of the palisade walls. The agonized wail of the Surleista pounded a ringing buzz that penetrated deeply into Glëa's skull. The undertones and overtones of its voice, audible only to his immortal soul, bloomed in the marrow of his bones.

Its outrage and confusion quickened the rhythm of his own heartbeats. *Hurt me! Hurt me! Why?* Topaz eyes sucked him inside the memories of that inhuman mind. For a moment, Glëa felt himself being a creature of the air gliding over broad flat plains of dry grasses. Its pain echoed as a burning ache in his own wrist.

Glëa backed out of range of that whipping, barbed tail. He closed his eyes and fought the irrational urge to apologize.

"Your Majesty, are you all right?" Herry and Cody closed in on either side of him. They dared to touch his shoulders to offer support as if fearing he might swoon.

The trainee laid down the halberd at the king's feet. "Please, Your Majesty, don't be afraid."

"I'm not..." Glëa rubbed his very human eyes to regain the sense of himself. *I am not you. I am not you. I am nothing akin to you.* He drew in deep breaths to savor the odor of sea water, bonfires, and human sweat. He slowly exhaled through pursed lips. He focused on the mortal sensations of his human skin, his red blood, and his fragile white bones.

Once more, he looked at the snarling beast trapped in shallow puddles.

Its arm sprouted bluish-gray tendrils. As Glëa watched, the tendrils grew and formed themselves like potter's clay in the hands of an artisan. Talons reformed. The scales shimmered silver for a brief instant before the reptilian hide darkened into the charcoal crust that it had been before. Its arm, fully restored, clutched the rocky perch once more.

"Twenty-seven, twenty-eight," Ash counted in a whisper. "Barely enough time to reload a crossbow or light a grenade's fuse."

"Yeah," said Herry at his side. "Imagine facing a swarm of those damned un-killable things in the open."

Another trainee picked up the severed paw from the ground. He was about to throw it into one of the nearby bonfires, when the king called out.

"Wait." Glëa crossed the space in three quick strides. He took hold of the severed paw by its thumb. Holding it away from himself as the grayish-green ichor dripped like melted lard, he carried it back to his group.

Ash yanked a kerchief out of his shoulder satchel, making ready as the king approached. Without question, he received the severed paw dripping its flammable blood. He gingerly fingered the obsidian talons. The other trainees or battle-weary soldiers fought their urge to cringe away, but the surgeon did not flinch at the sight of it.

"Do something with this, Captain," the king commanded. "Make a medicine of it. Save my friend."

"So as His Majesty wishes, so shall it be." Ash wrapped the kerchief around the severed paw and tied off the corners with a knot.

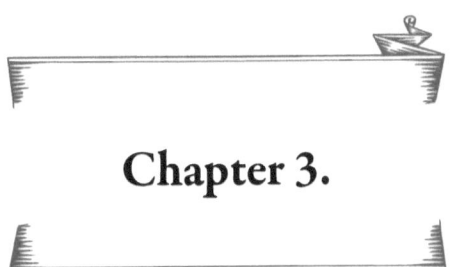

Chapter 3.

Ash rushed up the tower's stairwell alone. The king had trusted him to carry out the urgent task. He clasped the odorous bundle to his chest as if it were a sack of diamonds. The stench of blue-gray ichor was more odious than rotten eggs soaked in spoiled wine. Such a thing was not meant to emerge from the darkest depths of the underworld; such a thing was not meant to cohabit the domain of ordinary men. His jaw clenched as he forced aside the fresh memories of that monstrous beast in chains. Vertical slit pupils in yellow eyes, claws and horns, and a charcoal hide would loom in his nightmares for days to come.

Two young nurses on the surgeon's staff, Penella and Anjashe, descended the stairwell. They carried large bundles of soiled sheets and towels. He had to turn his broad shoulders sideways to allow them passage.

"Penny... Anja..." He nodded a cordial greeting as they continued past him down the stairs.

"Excuse us, Captain."

"Of course."

When he reached the top, the oak door was held open by a small boy in Lady Vilbyss's service. Ash paused at the threshold and struggled to recall the name of the child, barely six or seven years old by the look of him, whose sole purpose in life was to obey commands.

"Bean, is it?" Ash asked.

"Yes sir." The little boy lowered his head in hopes of avoiding attention. "What do you require, sir?"

"Nothing, I just want to say that you're doing an excellent job of holding open this door. Well done, Bean."

"Thank you, sir."

Ash entered the anteroom and observed that the Lady of the House no longer occupied the sofa. Briefly, he wondered about where the lady had gone. No matter; he had urgent business to attend.

More of the surgeon's staff emerged from the bed chamber. They carried wooden toolboxes and wicker baskets filled with medicinal supplies. Eyes cast downward and avoiding Ash's inquiring stare, the group split into two lines that flowed past him on either side. Shuffling softly across the rug, saying nothing, they poured out through the door.

He caught the last young man by the sleeve. "Heden, what's going on? Am I too late?"

The youth shrugged him off. "Sorry, Ash, but you've really got yourself on his bad side this time."

Ash let Heden go. He pushed ahead through the heavy draperies of brown velvet edged with gold-tinted fringe.

Mister Flenn, the lord's beloved, occupied a stool at the bedside where he could hold onto the unconscious Lord Vilbyss's hand. The Lady of the House was not present at her husband's deathbed. Only two maidens in pale yellow gowns stood vigil by the headboard. All the remaining medical staff had gone; even Ash's tools had been packed into a small wooden chest and left by the door.

Lord Meldon the royal surgeon used a small glass cup to apply the last of his prescribed number of leeches to the bedridden lord's swollen ankles.

"What's happening, sir?" Ash asked. "The king said—"

Lord Meldon first looked past Ash's shoulder to the gap in the curtains to be sure that His Majesty had not returned. "The king is not a doctor."

"But he's immortal."

"Blessed of his ancestors, graced with undimming youth he may be, but eternal youth is still a youth."

Ash held forth the kerchief bundle. "I am under a vow to the king himself to use this creature's paw—"

Lord Meldon snorted and waved him away. "You stupid lug, do you dare assume that we never thought of this?"

"You know what they are? What they can do?"

"Oh yes, I'm well aware of those indefatigable creatures that plague the western desert. You forget who is the lord surgeon and who has the privilege of sharing table with high-ranking cavalry officers. Of course, I have attempted to harness their unholy powers of regenerating severed limbs to no avail."

"Oh, have you?" Ash cocked his head. "I haven't seen mention of it in the hospital's logbooks."

"We don't tell you everything, Captain. There are certain matters that are not kept in the public records. It is impossible to make a brew of the abysmal beasts. Its blood is flammable. Its flesh is poison; we fed it to a dog with disturbing results. We can't brew it in a tisane; it curdles even in olive oil. We don't dare risk a dollop of a morsel under someone's tongue."

Ash nodded along as the head surgeon spoke, patiently waiting for his turn to respond. "Obviously it can't be brewed. Water spirits repel them."

Lord Meldon straightened his back and put both fists against his hips. "'Obviously,' you say? Hear me now, Captain, I've had just about enough of your smug pomposity. I know who you are! I know where you came from!"

Ash stiffened his shoulders and raised himself tall. "It doesn't matter where I came from."

Lord Meldon pointed to the center of Ash's face. "You feel privileged to have risen above your ignominious beginnings. Orphan without a family name! You're not a person of worth for being adopted as the ward of the House of Browden, oh no, you're just the beneficiary of an act of charity by a noble woman."

"For which I am grateful every day," Ash said.

"You presume to imagine that you have a special place in the king's eyes, because you performed well on the final day of the last battle? You were in the right place and at the right time by mere happenstance! You did your duty, Captain, as would any other soldier in your stead."

With jaw clenched, Ash forced a smile. "All very true, sir."

"Ha, so you admit it?" Lord Meldon shouted.

"Anything and everything you wish to say about me, or to me, it doesn't matter. Only *this* matters now." Ash held up the kerchief wrapped around the monster's severed paw. Bluish-black slime leaked out of the corner and dripped onto the rug.

"Discard that wretched mess, Captain."

"But what if you try—"

"I said, no! I will not risk His Lordship's well-being with unholy contamination. My word is final, Captain."

"The king won't be happy."

Lord Meldon grinned. "The king *will* be happy when Lord Vilbyss recovers from this minor fluttering of the heart. I've applied the leeches. They will work to drain the excess fluids and bring his system into equilibrium."

Ash retreated through the next door to a cold, dark room. Mister Flenn's apartment lay adjacent to the master's bed chamber. For as long as the mister kept vigil by the lord's bedside, his room was unoccupied. The Lady of the House had separate chambers on the floor below. He felt certain he would not be disturbed.

He kneeled on the hearth to unwrap the kerchief. Enough silvery moonlight seeped through the lead glass window to allow Ash to see what his hands were doing. He dared not light a candle.

"So," he whispered to the noxious paw. "Fire destroys you. Water repels you. Air spirits seem to like you, though. Earth too, if your kind dwell in caves like my buddies say. Let's see how you get along with wood?"

He used a small, charred log as a pestle. On his knees, using his weight, he squashed the paw and crushed its bones. Only the talons could not be broken. He put them aside like iron spikes and continued the grisly chore of mixing the hearth's cold cinders with the bluish-purple slime until it became a workable paste.

"Am I doing the right thing?" Ash looked aside to the dim empty corners of the chamber. He waited for a sign from the Beyond and, when none came, he rose confidently to his feet.

Briskly, he hurried from the empty apartment and returned to the master bed chamber.

"What are you doing?" Mister Flenn stood up to block Ash's approach to the head of the bed.

"Begging your permission, sir," Ash said. "I've made a medicinal poultice for His Lordship."

The lord's servant girls sat on the storage chest at the foot of the bed. Their sole purpose was watching and monitoring the leeches feeding on the lord's ankles. Their curious eyes, glittering in the firelight, strayed to what Ash was doing.

Mister Flenn sniffed the kerchief that Ash held with gloved hands. "A poultice?"

"Yes, sir, a poultice."

"You aren't sneaking around and trying to disobey Lord Meldon's orders, are you?"

Ash smiled calmly. "Oh no, sir, I wouldn't dream of overstepping. Not at all. This poultice is routinely applied to help with ailments of the chest. I assure you, sir, that my only goal here is His Lordship's speedy recovery."

"It smells horrible."

Ash shrugged and thought of the most odorous medicinal herbs in his toolkit. "Sulfur powder, asafetida, pickled garlic, valerian, and *periduran* seeds."

"Oh." Mister Flenn took a step back. "It's the valerian that gives it the blue color?"

"Yes sir. A very astute observation, sir."

Ash peeled back the blankets from the old lord's chin. The lips were gray. The chest hardly moved. Gurgling from deep in his throat signaled the beginnings of the death rattle. *The leeches are draining him. He won't make it to the next hour.* Gently he applied the kerchief and its noxious plaster to the old man's dry chest. Then he lifted the blankets back into place to cover it up.

"May the spirits of your noble ancestors allow you to stay with us a bit longer," Ash said reverently.

Mister Flenn returned to sitting on the stool at the bedside. He clasped the bedridden man's hand. Tears dripped out of his eyes. "Please, Ardis, come back to me. I don't know what my life is without you."

Ash stared at the back of Mister Flenn's balding head and felt a wave of amazement. Their fifty years of devotion to each other was common knowledge at court. How did such unwavering affection endure for so long, he wondered. Of all the monstrous and unnatural things that Ash had experienced in his life, this was the most incredible of all. *How does it feel to be in love? Truly in love and not just comforted by warm arms for a night.*

21

Weariness sagged his shoulders. His calves ached from standing on his feet all day.

One of the servant girls stood up from the foot of the bed. "Shall I call the boy to help carry your tool chest, sir?"

"Not necessary." Ash crossed the room to the crescent shaped nook. Without so much as removing his boots, he settled onto the cushioned window seat. He tucked a decorative pillow in the crook of his neck.

"You're spending the night here, sir?"

"I'll stay for a little while," he said.

The girl brought him a knitted throw blanket and draped it across his belly.

Ash smiled up at her kindly expression. Her soft-cheeked features gave him a feeling of comfort and welcome.

"Thanks, uh, what's your name?" he asked.

"Loëginne, sir."

"You're very kind, Loëginne... May I call you Ginny?"

She demurely lowered her eyes and backed away. Ash regretted being so forward, too soon, as to frighten the girl. *I'm not one of those lords*, he wanted to assure her. *I don't abuse servant girls and brag about conquests to my buddies.*

Loëginne explained, "Lord Meldon said that we should summon him if the leeches get full and drop off too early. But my sister and me don't know what's-a-what about leeches. Can we count on you to help? That is, just with the medical things, sir?"

"Of course," he said. "I'm happy to stay and help. To be clear, I mean, just with the medical things. I'll stay here on the window seat."

"Thank you, sir." She smiled through a sigh of relief.

"Wake me, Ginny, if something changes." He closed his eyes and dropped into slumber.

Ash slept through ordinary dreams of tree branches falling out of clouds and spraying flower petals as they hit the ground.

Someone's hand shook him awake. Ash's elbow bumped into the glass pane. He startled before remembering that he had fallen asleep on the window seat of Lord Vilbyss's bed chamber. The windowpanes were still dark. By the drowsy heaviness that weighed upon his skull, Ash knew that it was still the middle of the night.

"My apologies for waking you, sir," said Loëginne the servant girl. "But—"

Lord Vilbyss was sitting upright in bed fighting against Mister Flenn who struggled to push him back to the pillows.

"Unhand me, Flenn! What's the matter with you?"

"Don't exert yourself, Ardis."

The lord frowned at his own feet. "Why are there leeches on my ankles?"

Ash bolted to his feet and approached the bed. "My lord, you're under Lord Meldon's care. Do you feel dizzy? Nauseous? Any pains in your chest?"

"No, no, and no! Get those damned blood-sucking slugs off of my ankles immediately, Captain."

"Yes, my lord. Right away, my lord." Ash hurried to gather the necessary tools from his wooden chest on the floor. He returned with a dull butter knife and a ceramic jar. But when he gently pried the first leech's sucker off the man's leg, the dark worm dropped. It lay on the bedsheet, dead and shriveled like a raisin.

Bless me, what have I done? The lord's blood is contaminated. Have I saved his life or poisoned him? Ash quickly scooped up the rest of the dead leeches into the ceramic jar.

Lord Vilbyss gripped the kerchief that was glued to his chest. "What is this stink?"

"Oh!" Ash leapt a few quick steps to return to the lord's bedside. Thankfully, he had not removed his thick leather gloves even while he dozed by the window. He peeled the kerchief away and used a dry rag to scrub the blue paste away. The lord's thick patch of white chest hair came away like breadcrumbs. The skin left behind was rosier and smoother than anywhere else on the old man's body.

Mister Flenn wept and laughed. "It was just a soothing herbal poultice. Nothing important. Praises be, the leeches worked."

Best to let them assume so, Ash thought. *If word of this gets out, everyone will want a dose. Every lord and lady and officer and foot soldier and servant will go into a frenzy of craving. No... No, I will not poison the blood of anyone else. Lady Prophet, if you are my witness and hear my prayer? I will set fire to the training camp on Seagull's Rock and destroy every one of those monsters before I let that happen.*

Chapter 4.

Far to the north of Capital City and Xolhold Castle, a little village clung to the bend of Bear's Ears River in a valley below the shores of the Great Northern Bay. The nearest baron marked the spot as a small circle on his map but rarely traveled so far from his comfortable estate. River barges docked there for a few hours at most. It was a place that transients or refugees from elsewhere temporarily called home.

"Rise up, Candor, or you'll be late for your job." Ravel po'Marn of the House of Spareen squatted at their hut's hearth in the pre-dawn dark. She scraped a dull knife across a chunk of flint to spark fire.

Talons grafted to the center of her chest vibrated in pulses. Three monstrous finger bones a Surleista's paw clustered in twisted alignment between her breasts, sheathed in her flesh, papered over by pink and tender skin. Beastly talons aimed at her collarbone like arrowheads in a quiver. Ravel kept the talons hidden from sight beneath her shirt, told no one, and rarely looked at them herself.

Despite the layers of linen and wool that Ravel wore to conceal them, like hunting hounds that had caught a prey's scent, the claws throbbed and stretched her skin. Fire always excited those blackened spikes. She watched the hearth's fire take hold of kindling sticks, as she did every morning, and laid her left hand over the thorny lump at her breastbone. *Hush, hush,* she silently admonished the severed paw rooted into her ribs.

All night, as she did every night, she had reclined awake on a rickety cot adjacent to her younger brother's cot. Sleeplessly she waited through the long silent hours for songbirds to herald the coming dawn. Ravel had not slept in six years since impaling herself with the talons to gain their power. Yet she feigned the actions of an ordinary woman for her brother's peace of mind. She dreaded the day when Candor would discover her secret of what a monster she had become.

"Mmm... butter cookies... cashew fudge... rose tea..." Her younger brother half sleeping mumbled in a dream of things he once had before they lost the war. Such things he could never enjoy again.

How big you've grown, she thought. Stretched out sleeping, his calves now hung off the end of the bed's frame. Candor po'Marn, the only surviving lord and heir to the House of Spareen, had developed a tall lean body like their father. His neck extended high out of the knitted scarf that swaddled his shoulders. A lock of his fawn-colored hair hung across one eye. Ravel resisted the urge to finger-comb his hair neatly into place.

Candor would turn seventeen in the next month; he was no longer a child. Recently he had sprouted to his full height and stood taller than Ravel by a hand-and-a-half. Every day, he looked more like their late father. Ever since the walnut lump at the front of his throat had cracked and deepened his voice, he sounded more like Father when he spoke. To hear that deep bass voice come alive again, Ravel sometimes indulged in a fantasy that the war had never happened or that Lord Spareen had not died on a battlefield.

Morning's light seeped through the curtain of wicker reeds. Pinkish-gold speckles of light illuminated the flaws in the mud-and-straw walls. Outside their hut, village women sang to welcome the merchants' river barges coming up from the south. Joyous voices *ho-wah, ho-wah, ho-ho-wah* carried on the pre-dawn breeze.

"Time to wake up, milord." Ravel bent over her younger brother's cot and kissed his forehead in the way their mother used to do. Sleeping, he rolled face-down into his pillow. Millet husks in his pillow made a crunchy sound like boots walking on gravelly sand.

Ho-wah, ho-wah, ho-ho-wah. Villagers sang in two different tones, from low to high, now that the river barges had arrived.

Ravel grabbed her brother's shoulder and shook him awake. "Come now, Der, you're going to be late for work."

"Ugh," he grunted. Eyes still closed, Candor rose from his cot. He ducked a ceiling beam as he crossed the few steps to the corner of their thatched hut. He urinated into a bucket and wiped his hands on a hanging rag.

"Tea is ready." Ravel poured fragrant waters from the kettle into a chipped stoneware mug. As always, she turned her face aside to avoid the tiny eyes of water spirits sparkling in the liquid. Even when it boiled, the water screamed at what she had become.

"Share breakfast with me, Sister." Candor straddled the three-legged stool. He took his place at the head of a makeshift table. He straightened his shoulders proudly as if he sat over varnished mahogany instead of a roughly hewn cedar plank balanced atop a barrel.

"Thank you, but I shall eat later." Ravel served him a barley biscuit and a wedge of hard cheese. She reached across the table to lay down the stoneware plate.

While her arm was extended, Candor deliberately moved his teacup to pass beneath her wrist.

Water spirits in the cup prickled against her flesh. Ravel gasped as if stung by a hornet. She pulled back quickly. Her skin itched with a raw tenderness that she dared not touch.

"Steam didn't scald you," Candor said grimly.

"Yes it did."

"Don't lie. I saw it."

"Hurry up and eat breakfast or you'll be late for—"

"I saw it," he said again.

"Please don't worry. This, uh, spasm happens to me from time to time... It's an old war wound... I was burned by the blackcoats' firebombs in battle."

Candor frowned at her keenly. Golden firelight played brightly on half of his face. "Don't lie, Sister."

"At the Battle of Border Field, as I've told the story many times, I was stabbed in the thigh and pulled from my horse. I fell from my saddle to the ground and—"

"Stop." His deep voice sounded so much like their father's that Ravel felt an urge to stand at attention for a superior officer. "During the war, I was just a small helpless boy. I should have been the one to fight at our father's side for the honor of our household and our prince. Instead, you took up arms. If only our roles were reversed, you would not have suffered."

She contracted her fingers, drawing in a handful of her layered tunic. "Der, listen to me. Listen! Never be ashamed that you were too small to hold a sword. Be glad you didn't see what I've seen or do what I've done."

"Stop denying it." He withdrew his hand from underneath hers. "You aren't suffering from an old war wound. Admit it, Sister! You never sleep; I know because I've tried to catch you unaware. You hardly eat. You don't drink water. Does your body still follow the cycles of the moon?"

The talons pulsed. Ravel crossed both of her wrists over her breasts. Did he see the glint of monstrous craving in her eyes and mistook it for simple angst? *Should I tell him? But would he believe me? Such things as I have seen are impossible to explain.*

He glared at her from beneath knotted brows. "What unnatural practice have you performed upon yourself, Lady Spareen? Tell me now."

"You don't believe in unnatural things."

"You're wrong to presume what I do or do not believe," he said.

Ravel looked at the dim shadows beyond the reach of the fire's glow. Corners of the two stubby cots were sharply defined in lines of peacock blue against the indigo shadow beneath. Floorboards revealed their grain and a texture of knots in fingerpaint patterns of violet and gray. Nothing was ever dark to her eyes, nor would it ever be again, because of the monstrous claws impaled in her chest.

"I've wanted to tell you. I've feared that you won't understand."

"I will listen," he said.

"Can you really? We were taught to be sensible pragmatists. Father told us that ancient myths of prophets and miracles are just allegory. Magic stories are a fantasy of the illiterate masses."

"A true disciple of Sense and Reason accepts what is plainly evident before his eyes, no matter how unexpected. Believe me, dear sister, I will listen."

Ravel loosened the drawstring that held her undershirt's neckline tightly cinched beneath her chin. Then, she pried apart the overlapping panels of her wraparound tunic. By keeping both wrists clamped over her breasts, she preserved her modesty while exposing her sternum. She straightened her back and showed him, at last, what she had kept hidden.

Even after six years, the skin still felt sore where she had impaled the bony spikes into herself. She wondered if they would ever heal; was it possible for such monstrous things to be accepted by her mortal flesh? Revealed to the light of the hearth's fire, the talons vibrated like a harp's deepest strings. Their resonance buzzed deeper into her ribs and penetrated to her backbone.

"You said it was a war wound. You lied." Candor's eyes widened.

"It is a wound but not from the war that our father fought. It happened afterwards. What I'm about to explain to you is going to seem like incredible nonsense. I swear by our father's eternal soul, it's true." She looked down on her own breastbone at the things she rarely beheld directly. Twisted black talons sheathed in her scarred skin glistened darkly in the firelight.

"Go on," he prompted when she was silent too long.

"These are the finger bones of a monster who cannot be killed by spear or sword."

"What sort of monster?"

"Flying horrible things." Ravel looked into the eyes of the youth who used to cry and run to Mother when a tree branch slapped his bedroom window. "Don't be afraid, Der, they're not around here."

"I'm not afraid. Go on."

"After the war, I searched for you in the Outerlands' desert. I encountered wild flying predators that the nomads call Surleista. They can withstand being impaled. They can re-grow severed limbs. Fighting them is like trying to kill river mud with a butter knife. The only way to kill one is to incinerate its head down to glittering ashes. Even then, one has to wonder if the dust still breathes its hungry hatred of man."

Candor reached forth a tentative hand but retracted before his fingertips came too near. "These are talons from such a beast?"

"Yes."

"How did they get implanted into you?"

"I stole them from magic-workers who wore them this way. They were spies and diviners for the Iron King during the war. We fought. I killed them by tearing these claws out of their chests."

Ravel's fingers curled into fists to recall that moment in the fight. Without the talons to sustain their unnatural lives, they had succumbed to being the corpses that they truly were. Screams echoed in her thoughts of those walking corpses who should have died long before.

"You did this mutilation to yourself?" he asked with incredulity.

"Yes, well, I put them into my skin, and they latched onto me. At times it feels as if they have a mind and a will apart from my own."

"Were you fighting through his spies to get to the Pretender? Were you trying to assassinate him after we lost the war?"

"No."

Candor gritted his teeth. "Why not?"

She raised her gaze to the basketry of the thatched roof. Seed jewels of sunlight twinkled in the gaps between the twigs and dried fern fronds. She thought of the slate-gray sky beyond and the thunderclouds building in the north. Somewhere up there, above the view of mortal eyes, above the clouds and at the threshold of the stars, floated a city of crystal towers. The sanctuary of the gods held a nest of unhatched golden eggs. On that fateful day, its buoyancy had been broken by the Knights Magicker's scheme. Sinking from its lofty height, it would have smashed into the mortal soil.

"I implanted these into my chest in order to..." The talons piercing her chest grew warm. She paused to breathe deeply with difficulty against the heat building on her skin. "...to save the Jeweled Barge of Heaven from falling out of the sky."

"That's impossible," Candor said. "Heaven cannot fall to Earth."

"It certainly would have if I did not work to save it. Well, we saved it together. Lord Torval sacrificed himself. Its cracked crystal windows were sealed by the flow of the scholar's blood. He gave his life for all things to stay in their rightful places, Heaven above and Earth below."

"Lord Torval of the House of Pegamodi," Candor repeated thoughtfully. "Our father's ally."

"Yes. After the war, I pursued him for months because I heard rumors that he rescued a boy from the burned ruins of our family estate."

Candor's expression turned flat and blank. When he spoke, it was in monotone as if reading aloud a passage from a historical record. "He carried me away on his horse. He left behind our home in flames. I shouted at him, begging him to pick up our mother's corpse from the mud. I shall never forgive Lord Torval for leaving her body unburied."

Silence passed between them. Ravel watched the young man's face for any flicker of emotion. But he had already wept too much and screamed through too many nightmares.

She continued, "Of course, by the time I caught up with Lord Torval in the Outerlands, he had already dropped you off to take refuge with the hermit archivist."

"He said that he had urgent, dangerous business to attend," Candor said. "I hoped that he was going to rally the surviving noblemen and attack the Pretender's battle camp. In those early days after our defeat, our enemies would have been drunk on victory, careless, and sloppy in their defenses. Weeks and months passed, but I did not despair until the news came of the deceiver's coronation. Disappointment is too feeble a word for my opinion of that coward. The liar of all liars squats on the throne of kings. Lord Torval did nothing about it. He failed to organize an insurgency when the tide of history might have turned in those early days."

"An insurgency would have been foolish," she said. "Remember, the king had his magick-workers as spies in those early days. Every noble household bent their knee to his will. What do you imagine could be accomplished by one man on a horse?"

"Father always said, 'where there is life there is no defeat.' Do you remember the legends of ancient days? King Davarche the First stood against the hordes of the wicked chieftain. He brought peace and law to the kingdom even though he was just one man on a horse."

"But with an army of thousands behind him and two mystical prophets in his service."

"One man," Candor insisted. "Torval could have rallied the forces of resistance if he had the courage to try. Now you're telling me that he only cared to pursue this ridiculous fable? A crystal city in the sky? Heaven falling out of the clouds? Even if what you say is true, how did his so-called sacrifice accomplish anything of worth? To this day, an imposter squats on the throne of Xol!"

Ravel hung her head in weariness. The more they argued, the further apart their opinions drifted.

"Sister, you look ill. You should rest."

"No," she whispered. "I'm fine. They crave light. In the darkness, if I stay calm, they... they're quieting down, now."

Ravel closed the flaps of her tunic and cinched up her undershirt's drawstrings. Hand over hand, she shielded the talons from the firelight. The haze clouding her eyes faded back to normal colors. Yet the humming in her bones' marrow continued to resonate within her ears.

"Can't you take them off? Cut them out?"

"No," she rasped. "I've tried... but it's not just the skin. They're rooted too deep into my very ribs."

Candor rose to his feet. He stroked her head and smoothed her thin, sweaty hair back from her face. "Oh Sister, you have my utmost sympathy for what you have suffered. I wish you could have trusted me to share this secret earlier."

"You were so young." She tilted her chin up to his height and met his gaze. "I'm sorry I kept the secret so long. I wanted you to know, when you became old enough to understand."

When Candor smiled, dimples appeared in his cheeks. His boyish face reminded Ravel of their late mother. "I am so glad you showed me this, sister."

"I am too."

He laid his long-fingered hand against her cheek. "You don't need to bear this burden alone, anymore. I'm sorry that I was too small before, but I've become a man now. I'm going to take care of you. I'm going to take care of everything."

Ravel's mouth broadened to a smile for the first time in years. "What a fine man you've become. Father and Mother would be proud."

Outside, brass bells clanged in celebration of the river barges docking ashore.

Candor blurted, "I'm late!"

Ravel stepped aside to allow him passage to the cramped hut's only door. She inhaled a change in her brother's scent. An odor of guilty musk wafted out of Candor's skin. Despite the cool weather of the morning, a few beads of sweat rose out of his hairline. He avoided her eye contact, now, as he made busy gathering his cloak and gloves.

She added, "Der? Is there something more you wish to say?"

Candor side-stepped around her and launched outside into the morning's air. "Oh yes, by the way, I've invited a few friends to visit this evening. I leave it in your hands to cook us a fine supper!"

Chapter 5.

Ash's neck ached from sleeping in Lord Vilbyss's window seat. The pain was a minor annoyance; he had known worse. At dawn, he carried his wooden chest of surgeon's tools down the tower's stairwell and started on the walk home. Once outside the barbican gate, he avoided the western side of the inner bailey yard. In this early morning hour, he did not feel in the mood for the company of friends in the barracks. Nor was he inclined to report for duty to the Lord Surgeon at the infirmary.

Instead, he chose a footpath of smoothly tamped gravel that bisected a broad patch of lawn. Puddle ducks and small goats wandered free. The course took him along the eastern side of the inner bailey yard, past the banquet pavilion with its tarp draperies tied shut, and past the Opera House with its windows quiet and dark.

He passed the Tea House that was enshrouded in shadow. Although the sky turned pink overhead, the morning's sunbeams had not yet risen above the castle's high wall.

A group of tea novices worked hauling up buckets from the free-standing well. Satin ribbons tied back the long-hanging sleeves of their brightly colored robes. Skirts were tucked up in their cord belts, exposing their legs. Beaded cords netted their henna-dyed auburn hair. They stopped to shine welcoming smiles at him.

"Hello, Doctor," a pair of tea girls sing-songed in unison. Glass bangle bracelets dangled from their wrists as they waved to him. "Coming to see us so early?"

"Another time, dear ladies." Ash politely inclined his head to bow. "Good morning."

He strolled through the gatehouse that divided the inner bailey in Xolhold Castle's nested circles of walls. Ducking quickly beneath the spikes of the portcullis, he waved hello to his friends at the changing of the guards.

"How is Lord Vilbyss's health this morning?" Captain Teimethee called down from the gatehouse turret.

"He's recovering well, Teim," Ash called back.

"Praises be to our forefathers."

"Yeah," Ash said without enthusiasm. "Praises be."

A cloistered village lay in the outer bailey yard. Two-story wattle-and-daub structures clustered side-to-side, sharing walls and shingled roofs. Cottages and townhouses formed a backdrop for the workshops that performed the necessary day-to-day functions of the castle.

He offered greetings of the day to the bustling foot traffic of craftsmen, artisans, and servants of the castle. Tanners, ale-makers, metal smiths, coopers, wood joiners, glass blowers, and cobblers were just now departing their front doors to begin work in their shops. Bakers were already toasting bread loaves in their outdoor ovens; the scent of yeast and wheat made his stomach growl, but he was too weary to eat breakfast.

It's only been one night, he thought, *but I feel that I've been away from my own bed for weeks.* He glanced down to the oily blue sludge that stained his leather gloves.

"Welcome home, Captain." Ash's manservant met him at the threshold to receive his cloak.

"Hello, Will."

Willhem po'Sal had been a cook in the quartermaster's corps during the war. Ash, as a field medic, had amputated his leg on the battlefield. Having no rank, no home, and no trade to resume after the victory at the Battle of Border Field, Will had come into Ash's service at a bargain salary. After all, a newly made gentleman needed a manservant, and a newly destitute soldier needed a home; the arrangement was beneficial to both.

"Sorry I'm home so late, Will, or so early."

"Apologies are not necessary, sir." Will hobbled alongside Ash walking across the room. His peg leg tapped sharply on the floorboards.

Ash placed his tool chest on the roughly hewn table. Four stools were tucked underneath in expectation of a day when he might entertain visitors.

Usually, he ate meals in the barracks with his friends in uniform or in the infirmary with his peers on the medical staff. Glancing at the hearth, small feathery flames grew amongst the logs; Will had only begun to boil a millet porridge for breakfast.

"You've returned home just in time," Will said. "A messenger came and delivered a letter."

Ash tugged off his soiled gloves. "I'm too exhausted, Will. I'm going to bed for a few hours."

Will limped to the pantry shelf embedded in the opposite wall. Among the ceramic jugs, the glass jars and bottles, braids of garlic bulbs and baskets of onions, stood a folded parchment sealed with blue wax.

Ash dipped a tin tankard into a keg of tepid barley tea. He gulped the bland liquid to quench his thirst. Still holding the tankard, he turned for the open plank staircase.

"But sir, it looks important." Will's peg leg tapped as he followed his master to the base of the stairs.

"Who is it from?"

"The messenger could not say. He was hired in the Midlands at a crossroads water well. It was a horse trader with a forester's accent. She did not give her name."

"'Her' name?"

"Yes sir, I think it might be from *her*."

Ash paused at the urgency in his manservant's tone of voice. He avoided the man's perceptive stare. Will knew the background story of his humble origins and his adopted half-sister's estrangement from her noble family. How much did his manservant know or suspect of Lady Clear's prophetic powers? Had Ash managed to keep her secret well enough?

"I'll read the letter in private, Will."

"Very good, sir."

Ash carried the letter upstairs to the loft with a small window. The room was just large enough for his narrow frame cot and an oak chest packed with clothes. He unlatched the window shutter and flung it open to invite the daylight.

He cracked the wax seal. His heartbeat quickened to recognize the delicate penmanship of the woman's hand.

Don't be in a rowboat with the king at night.
Don't stain your favorite gloves.
Don't crush an animal's paw in the cinders.
Let the old dog come to the end of his time.

Ash groaned as he sank down to his cot's stiff mattress. Once more, he read the words aloud in a whisper so softly that he could barely hear his own voice. "'Don't be in a rowboat with the king at night. Don't stain your favorite gloves. Don't crush an animal's paw in the cinders.' Well, shit, it's too late fer that isn't it? Damnit, Clear! If only this letter'd reached me sooner..."

He curled his hand into a fist and crumpled the parchment.

"Even if I had got yer letter, what choice did I have? When my king summons me, I go."

Alone in his bedroom, he dropped the effort of speaking in cultured diction. His real voice came out: the voice of an orphan born without a family name, the voice that he kept buried in the core of his soul.

"An' why send me a letter a'tall? If it was really important, you'd visit me as a spirit apparition." He lay back and stared at the dark crossbeams on the ceiling. "M'sorry, Clear, but whatever calamity you've foreseen in yer visions, th' events are already in motion."

Chapter 6.

Ravel spent the day as both Lady of the House and maidservant in one. She swept the floor of their hut, dumped the fireplace ashes, and prepared a meal of what foodstuffs they had on stock in the pantry shelves. Candor's job as a clerk in the wharf master's office paid a better salary than he would earn at other labors. Too skinny to haul barrels, push wagons, or tow river barges upstream against the current, he qualified for the clerk's job by the simple fact that he could read and write both in classical script and the simplified phonetic letters of the merchants' vernacular. Even from a young age, his penmanship was exquisite.

He knows. He knows. She sang the chant in her mind as she went about her daily tasks. Sunshine seemed brighter, colors sharper, and movements easier than they had felt in years. Without the burden of secrets and lies, a new phase of their lives had dawned. She looked forward to frank and honest conversations with her brother. Now, he was no longer a child. With the growing sensibility of a man's mind, he might understand the fantastical facts of the world beyond what mortal eyes could see. She would help him to accept the truth. Their father had battled and died under a misconception. Glëa po'Lon was not a pretender or a liar. The Iron King truly was immortal.

Ravel made ready with a stack of stoneware plates. Her brother had not specified how many guests were invited. Six plates were all they owned; six plates would have to do.

Light-toned voices from outside nattered their way towards the door. Youthful enthusiasm blended with silly chuckles. Before Ravel had seen the first of their faces, she surmised that not one of them had aged much beyond their twentieth year.

Candor slapped open the rickety door frame. "Hey, hey, welcome friends! Please enter my humble home."

Three young men filed inside. They clustered shoulder to shoulder, spanning from wall to wall, for there was no foyer to properly receive visitors. One fellow's boots jostled the cot's frame where Ravel pretended to sleep every night. Another bumped against the rack of hearth tools. The third stepped forward to the crude table. They jockeyed amicably in the cramped space for a comfortable standing position.

Candor faced the group as a gracious host. "We have some, uh, treats for you. Sister, would you serve our guests?"

Ravel clasped her hands at her belly in ladylike fashion. "Aren't introductions in order, milord?"

"Quite right. My apologies." Candor extended his hand in a gracious gesture. "Sister? I should like to present Prosper po'Vinn, fourth son and sole surviving heir to the House of Atoyëin."

Prosper had a classical nobleman's features with a high forehead, angular cheekbones, and long-jawed face. His dark complexion, like many of the prestigious lords of the western country, gave the illusion of a legendary hero sculpted in black basalt. He had closely trimmed his curly hair into a tight skull cap as if ready to don a battle helmet. Yet his slender fingers had no calluses or scratches, showing that he had managed to avoid any hard labor.

She dipped her knees in courtesy. "A privilege to make your acquaintance, Mister Prosper. I presume your father was Colonel Atoyëin in command of the Tenth Infantry Division?"

"Yes, that's right." Prosper had a deep voice and made an obvious effort to subdue his volume in the small space. She imagined he could easily shout above the noise of galloping horses and rattling wagons. "I was a second lieutenant in the Badger Brigade. A pleasure to make your acquaintance as well, Mistress Ravel po'Marn eldest daughter to the House of Spareen."

"Badger Brigade was a good unit. I'm sure you did them proud."

"Yes, thank you, Lady Spareen."

Candor broadened his welcoming gesture to the remaining pair. "Over here we have Lord Prosper's guardsmen-at-arms. May I introduce Redson and Stander, who are twin-born brothers."

The twin young men stood awkwardly, shifting on their feet, waiting for their senior's next move. Broad cheekbones and soft features were identical but Ravel noticed subtle differences. Their dark complexions were further blackened by many hours outdoors. Yet their necks' posture and off-balance stance revealed them as scholarly lads. They had surely spent most of their childhood hours sitting in chairs or hunched over reading desks and writing tables.

"Greetings and welcome to our home, good men." Ravel opened her palms in polite invitation to the table.

Prosper's bright smile never dimmed. "She's a passably handsome woman and everything you promised. I agree to the union."

"Union?" Ravel asked. "What union?"

Candor grasped his friend's hand to accept the bargain. "My thanks, Pros', and cheers to a fruitful alliance of our two houses."

She clenched her fists. "Hell's blazes, Der, have you gone deaf? When did you promise my hand?"

"Prosper and I have been talking about it for weeks," Candor said. "It's fortunate for you that times are what they are. Women of good family are hard to find in this rural territory."

Ravel forced her fists to open palms outward. "We're certainly not the only refugees from the Midlands to flee north after the war."

"Indeed, we are not. We are fortunate to have found each other." The clean shine of Prosper's neatly aligned teeth began to annoy her.

She drew in a long breath to maintain a reasonable tone of voice. "I don't understand your reasoning, Der. Why do you need me to get married now? What good would it do to match me up with another refugee who's just as desperate as we are? You're not being sensible at all."

Candor flexed his fingers as if climbing an invisible ladder that went nowhere. "Marriage would quiet your restless heart and ease your loneliness."

"That's kind of you." Ravel rested her hand across her brother's lean wrist. "But I'm not restless and I'm not lonely. I have you."

"There's the problem, don't you understand? Our neighbors gossip."

"Let them. Words can't hurt us."

Candor insisted, "It is not seemly for a lady to be unmarried at your age."

"My age?" she repeated. "I've just passed my twenty-eighth birthday."

"Indeed! Once you're beyond thirty, you'll be a spinster for life. There are no decent households who would even take you as a governess. Are you not planning for your future at all? Do you want everyone to think you're a whore?"

"No one thinks I'm a whore, Der."

"Of course they do. Everyone up and down the river is whispering behind our backs. They dispute if we truly are brother and sister. It's why I have not invited my friends to visit until now, or the neighbors will assume we're running a brothel out of this hut." Candor raised his palm to block her objections. "My decision is final. You need a husband for the honor of our house and our name."

Ravel crossed her arms. "We no longer have a house. We no longer have a name."

Candor banged his fist on the table. The plates rattled. "We will always have our name! The Pretender robbed us of everything else but that."

She looked away from her brother's face twisting with fury. "I'm not marrying you, Mister Prosper."

Candor clapped a hand to his friend's shoulder. "She doesn't mean that, Pross!"

"I know exactly what I'm saying," Ravel said. "Call me rude. Call me a shrew if you'd like. I only hope that you'll appreciate my forthrightness before we get too far along in this ridiculous misunderstanding. My brother has promised my hand without my knowledge or consent. Though you seem to be a fine gentleman, the fact remains, I will not marry you."

Candor spoke across his shoulder at her. "As Lord of the House, I do not accept your refusal. I command you to be married to this noble man—"

"Excuse me, did you say that you *command* me? What am I, a brood mare to be corralled with a stud stallion? Father would never—"

"Father isn't here, I am!" From Candor's thin throat came the blast of a deep male voice; its bass power stunned her into silence. "I am the lord of the house in this new upside-down world. You are my responsibility, Sister."

While they argued, Prosper pulled from his belt's pouch a chain of copper links. He tenderly laid the necklace on the crude table. Polished metal twinkled brightly in the fireplace's light.

"I propose to take you as my betrothed, Ravel po'Marn eldest daughter to the House of Spareen, to cling unto me and—"

She swept up the necklace into her fist. Copper chain links dangled from her clenched fingers. "How dare you attempt to shackle me with this necklace like bridling a horse. Have you ever attempted to woo a maiden before?"

Prosper looked at her brother curiously. "Does she expect to be wooed at her age?"

"Is she still a chaste maiden," asked the one named Redson. "She's fairly old, after all."

Ravel's lip curled in a sneer at the affront to her virtue but said nothing. If she were asked directly, she could not lie; she had gladly lost her maidenhood in the battle camps years ago.

Prosper scooped up her left hand. He bowed while raising her knuckles to meet his mouth. He hung on utterly still for as long as it took for the moist warmth of his lips to seep into the skin of her hand. The polite gesture surprised her for harkening back to another world, another time, and a peaceful place long ago extinguished. Ravel shut her eyes and surrendered her hand to his grasp. Memories strayed to other nights, long ago... other campfires... other soldiers... when she had closed her eyes to the horrors of battle and found comfort in a man's embrace. The claws at her chest lay still. For a moment, she felt wholly human and ordinary once more.

With a smile, Prosper came away from kissing her hand. "She accepts my offer of betrothal."

"No, I..." Ravel's protest froze on her tongue. She could not deny that she had responded to his bold advances. A virtuous maiden would have pushed him away. An honorable lady would have slapped him. Yet she had done neither; she had indulged in a moment and so had forfeited her right to object.

"Very well," she said hoarsely. "I will allow time to become better acquainted. Consider this an arranged introduction."

His friends rumbled low laughter, made *oohs* and *ahhs*, and remarked that Prosper's kiss must have a persuasive magic of its own.

Candor popped the cork on a jug of dandelion cider. Having too few cups, he passed the jug from hand to hand. "A celebration, then, of the union of our two great houses Spareen and Atoyëin."

"A betrothal only!" Ravel reminded them. "We're not married yet."

"Of course, my dear lady, my intended betrothed." Prosper recovered the copper chain necklace off the table. He stepped behind her and fastened the hook at the nape of her neck. Metal links felt cold against her skin.

The jug passed around the circle ended with Candor who raised it high as if it were a gilded goblet. "On this auspicious day, may the blessings of all our departed parents be upon us. May our lives and our deeds bring honor to our ancestors who watch from the Bliss of the Eternal Fields."

Chapter 7.

Two of the king's territorial governors, Lord Vilbyss and Lady Browden, joined King Glëa for supper on the balcony outside the royal bed chamber. From this high tower, clear weather offered a panoramic view of the wharf and Harbor Bay to the east. The king dressed casually in his bone-white housecoat with twenty-five silver buttons fastened neatly in cord loops. Cranberry breeches covered his plum-colored hose. Soft soled slippers lined with fleece topped his ankles.

Governor Lord Vilbyss sat more upright at the table than he had in years. His face was a rich, healthy shade of brown. His cheeks flushed pink. He ate heartily quail, pheasant, grilled sea bass, steamed dumplings packed with hash, and crispy toasted greens. He smiled easily. He moved with a comfortable swiftness that defied his chronic lower back pain. All in all, he looked remarkably younger—like a man in his fifties rather than a man of seventy-two.

Glëa said, "I'm glad you're feeling better, Ardis."

"Yes, yes, I feel wonderful. My compliments to your royal surgeon. Lord Meldon should be knighted for his skillful application of leeches."

The king smiled at his old friend's renewed vigor. *Captain Ashglëa is lying to the world; this vigor is not the product of leeches; clearly he made a medicine of the Surleista paw, just as I asked. Perhaps it is for the best that it be kept in confidence.*

Governor Jiveine po'Bel, the lady matriarch of the House of Browden, occupied the chair at the king's left-hand side. "Should the royal surgeon be granted extraordinary accolades for simply doing his job?"

The king's turned his smile to the elderly lady who poked at her own plate of cinnamon baked apples and butter-sauteed mushrooms stuffed with goat cheese. Lady Browden seemed in a sour mood this evening, but then, not much pleased her these days. The weight and responsibility of her office would be a load for anyone, although she bore it with the strength of a woman half her age. Instead of a feminine gown, she wore a tunic of sage green wool girdled at the waist by a leather belt. But for the lack of a sword and helmet, she dressed for galloping into a battlefield. The scent of horses, wet hay, and human perspiration brought mortal reality to the supper table.

"No need to be jealous, Jiveine."

"How's that again, Your Majesty? I'm.... I'm not jealous. I'm grateful to the blessed mercy of your ancestors, Ardis, that you recovered from your ailment so quickly."

Lord Vilbyss laughed heartily across the table at her. He raised a cup of mint tea as if proclaiming a toast in her honor. "You should wish to feel as I do today, ol' crone."

"You old dog," she grumbled.

The king sipped at his mint tea. Sunlight sparkled in the crystal goblet. Broken rainbows flashed into his eyes. Ever since taking the rowboat to Seagull's Rock and sharing private thoughts with the Surleista's mind, the king's inhuman senses had become heightened. Glëa inhaled the scent of crystalline color. The eternal soul within him savored the aromas of violet, blue, and green.

"Does something trouble Your Majesty?" asked the old man at his right-hand side.

"Why... why do you ask?"

Lady Browden added, "Your mood changed. You appeared to be distracted in your own thoughts."

The king drank tea to buy time for recollecting his human composure. He savored the hot liquid going down his throat. His two companions politely waited for him to speak again.

"I was merely reminiscing about my youth. It was so long ago that I was a child..." He caught himself before saying, *hatched from a golden egg in a crystal nest in the clouds.* "My father used to take his breakfast at this very spot, alongside my stepmother and her son... When my little brother Rouchard was of the age to be learning his first letters..."

Lord Vilbyss laid his hand atop the king's. The warmth and weight of the old man's palm soothed Glëa's swirling thoughts.

"It serves no good to dwell on the days of the past," the old man said.

"For once, I agree with the old dog." Lady Browden leaned into the table. "The harvest was bountiful this year. Your people are well-fed and content. We must plan ahead for continued prosperity into the next year and the next."

Lord Vilbyss chuckled, "You sound like my wife. She speaks of nothing else but preparing for the days ahead. In fact, I just learned this morning that, all the while I was ailing in bed, she spent the hours auditing the inventory of our properties and assets. She has meticulously itemized the allocation of inheritance to our sons and grandsons. Honestly, I must wonder if she was thankful for my recovery or annoyed at how much time she wasted in reviewing the household's papers."

Lady Browden cracked a smile that deepened the wrinkles in the creases of her cheeks, yet her eyes sparkled with vitality. "Oh, that woman could read all forty-eight volumes of the Annals of the Kings and discover the one misspelled word!"

"True, very true." Lord Vilbyss withdrew his hand from the king's as he grew somber. "Although, this incident has given me pause to consider Your Majesty's situation."

"Explain."

"You regained your throne six years ago, but you remain a bachelor. A king should have a queen at his side."

"Why? As an immortal, I have no need for someone to bear heirs to me. In fact, I am determined *not* to have a son who may be frustrated that I'll never die and who may plot to overthrow me. Nor shall I sire a daughter who may be seduced by the first ambitious traitor to come along."

The lord said, "Even so, you should have a queen."

"Yes, you should," Lady Browden reluctantly agreed. "As Light of the World and Beacon of the Golden Age, you should uphold the traditions of your ancestors. There have always been two thrones at the head of the twenty-one stairs since the time of Davarche the First. People are fond of traditions."

"Yes, they are, Jiveine. Yes, they are."

Lord Vilbyss added, "It gives a kingdom a sense of continuity and stability. If you are to rule as the King of Xol indefinitely, you need to think of establishing practices for the long-term. She would be the first of many mortal queens to serve out their lifetimes at your side."

"And it may help to quell the grumblings of troublemakers in the outlying territories." The lady clenched and unclenched her calloused fingers. "Not that we're calling them an insurgency, yet. Surely you are becoming as concerned as we are with the sporadic outbursts of harassment from stragglers, unbelievers, and scattered remnants of the Horsemen of the West. The kingdom's light shines over the grassy plains of the Midlands, to the dry mountains of the Outerlands and as far up as the shores of the Great Northern Bay. Yet there is a smattering of those who turn their eyes away from the light of truth."

Lord Vilbyss added, "By taking a queen, it will show strength and stability to those who wish to live in saddles not towns. For those who wish to block progress, the message must be clear. Your reign is eternal."

"Have you any thoughts of whom you might choose?" asked Lady Browden.

Their position of sitting so near brought up a human memory of long ago. Decades had carved worry lines across her forehead, tugged creases at the corners of her mouth, and turned her skin to paper. Yet her eyes had not changed. Framed in a lace of crow's feet were the same, brilliant irises he had once known. In his memory played an old song from a ballroom dance celebrated years before. *I dreamt that I dwelled in a golden wood, where fireflies of diamond were twinkling.* He recalled lifting her wrists and inviting her to the dance floor when he was just a nineteen-year-old prince, and she was just a maiden of a noble house. By the dreamy drift of her eyes to his lips, she remembered too.

"Ah-hem," Vilbyss coughed into his hand. "Act your age, you crone! If you could see yourself play-acting as a damsel pretending to swoon and batting your eyes at him."

"Jealous, as always?" she shot back. That voice had roughened by the passage of years and shouting at soldiers on the smoky battlefield. Yet it was still the voice he remembered from fifty years ago, when they were both young together. How much she had changed and how little.

Glëa glanced to the man seated at his right. Old memories played in a different part of his mind. The renewed color in Vilbyss's cheeks recalled those rollicking days of sparring at swords and the camaraderie of galloping to race their horses side by side. By the steady stare of his eyes, he remembered too.

"There is a plethora of noble houses to select from," said the king. "I must choose carefully the name that would be exalted for all history as the first queen of the Immortal King. All of them are equally worthy and unworthy."

Lady Browden said, "If I may be so bold as to mention, Your Majesty, that I have granddaughters of marriageable age."

"As do I," said Lord Vilbyss. "As well as a plethora of maidens to offer from branches of my extended family."

Glëa leaned back in his chair. "I will consider my options."

"So you say, Your Majesty, so shall it be," they said in unison. Their eyes met across the table in rivalry, then broke into competitive smiles.

Chapter 8.

The hut being cramped, Ravel's brother suggested moving their celebration outside. Candor and Prosper shared the jug and reduced themselves to giggles when the last drop ran out. Redson was handy with a bow and arrow; he shortly returned from the woods with a rabbit. Stander skinned and gutted the catch. Before long, a merry campfire glowed under the skewered meat.

Dusk came early as the sun fell behind the high, jagged mountains to the west. Their campfire illuminated the grassy clearing but could not penetrate the darkness of the forest all around.

Ravel strolled a slow circle around the young men. The way they straddled logs and even their refined accents reminded her of bygone days at battle camps or in the watchtowers of fortresses. Eating in the open and sleeping on beds of straw did not seem to bother them, as they had lived this way even before the defeat at the Battle of Border Field. The only difference was that they had no commanding officer to order them to break camp and march.

So, this is to be my life? With my brother as my lord, his friend as my husband, and two men-at-arms to be our servants? Her eyes rolled skyward to think of her parents reclined in the blissful serenity of the Eternal Fields. *Well, Mother, I could do worse. Perhaps he's right.*

Stander offered her the roasted leg of the rabbit. Charred flecks dotted the pale meat. "My Lady, let me offer apologies there ain't no salt."

Cooked meat held no appeal for her; raw meat was what she craved. Ravel's eyes strayed to the bucket of discarded entrails floating in dark blood. The talons at her chest pulsed and throbbed. She heard in her memories the squawk of Surleista on the wing: *meat, meat, meat.*

"No, thank you." She waved off the food. "You're still growing boys; you should have it all."

Ravel turned her back on the bucket of entrails. She faced the commonplace scene of four young men consuming their evening repast. Each of them used the small belt knives to tear off bite-sized morsels rather than gnawing into the skewered meat. Dressed in burlap and coarse linen, nonetheless they maintained their gentlemanly manners.

Prosper looked at her with renewed interest. His eyeline strayed downward to her torso but his expression showed no carnal interest. He assessed her posture and the width of her hips, judging whether she was capable of childbearing for a few more years.

Seized with the urge to do something ordinary, Ravel took up a broom propped against the door frame. She swept the doorstep and continued sweeping vigorously as if to reduce the flagstones themselves to sand. She busied her mind with everyday thoughts: how additional hands could help shore up the roof before winter's snowfall or build a smokehouse to preserve meat. *Every day that we're alive, the Iron King has not won. Where there is life there is no defeat.*

"Hey there, Reds," said Prosper to the archer. "Trot down to the village and see if Xid's back today."

"Got it." Redson shouldered his quiver and bow before jogging into the woodsy shadows. A drift of breeze, a wave of sycamore boughs, and he was gone.

"Xid?" Ravel asked. "Who is Xid?"

Candor smiled with wet lips. His cheeks flushed pink from the cider. "Xidron is a Southerner by birth but he's a sensible enough companion."

Prosper draped his arm around Candor's shoulders. "Xid rides into the domain and brings us news."

"Rides?" Ravel repeated. "So, this Xid fellow has a horse? Just him, not the rest of you?"

"Has a farmer's horse," Candor corrected her. "We are lords of the Great Midnight Bear. We ride on pure-bred Roan Blues or nothing."

Ravel chuckled in rhythm with her scratching broom. "If your life depends on it, you'll ride a donkey's bony backside and be glad for it."

"I rode a mule once," Stander admitted. Prosper shot him a scolding look but his friend simply shrugged. "Like she said, my life depended on it."

Ravel carried her broom into the circle rimmed by scuffed boots and lanky knees. "So, this Xid fellow brings you news, but why? Of what use is it for you to know the happenings in the Kingdom of Xol?"

The three youths shifted their eyes amongst each other. Stander picked at the meat in his teeth. Prosper jabbed at the camp fire's embers with a long stick. Candor simply stared at her in the cold hardened expression that he so often wore these days.

"Oh no," Ravel groaned. "Please tell me you're not plotting some foolhardy scheme. A few brazen acts of random destruction? Raising a mob of villagers to harass a local baron, perhaps? Or would you dare aspire to insurrection against the king himself?"

"A butcher deserves to be butchered," Candor said.

Prosper's stalwart glare assented.

"Assassination?" In a blink, she saw their skulls behind their flesh. The scent of death wafted thick in the air.

Ravel strolled into the fog of campfire smoke. As a captain under her father's command, how many youths such as these had she ordered into battle? She evaluated her brother and his friends for size, for lack of strength, and for martial agility that they had yet to demonstrate.

"So," she said to Prosper. "You'll make me a widow before you make me a bride?"

"Have you no confidence in me?" Prosper asked.

"You'll have no use for my confidence or my encouragement when you face a squad of crud-coats. They will cut you down without breaking a sweat."

Stander popped to his feet. "If I may speak frankly, my Lady, you aren't being at all sensible to dismiss our martial skills so lightly. Pross' was a lieutenant in the Badger Brigade, Reds is an archer, and I... I..."

"Yes, you.... what?" she asked.

Stander crossed his arms and pulled two daggers from sheaths at opposite sides of his belt. Fine steel glinted in the fading sunlight. He held the pose for a moment as if expecting an artist to sketch his likeness for posterity. Then, he launched into a one-man dance of ducking, stabbing, and kicking at shadows in the air. His legs opened and snapped shut like the rods of a fan. His arms cracked the air with the precision of a coachman's whip. Eyes focused on an imaginary foe, his expression was grim, murderous, and ever so young.

When Stander finished his routine, Prosper and Candor both gave dignified claps of approval.

"There, you see?" Prosper said. "We're prepared for whatever the crud-coats throw at us."

Ravel frowned sternly as her father often had. If this were a battle, she would send him forth without qualm; but if this were a battle, the youths would have a thousand foot-soldiers at their backs. *They're not ready to be assassins.*

"Very well done. I'd like to see that routine again. Stan, do you mind?"

"Gladly, my Lady." Stander pulled his knives exactly as before. Once again, he held the pose as a salute to his imaginary foe.

Ravel threw a rock at his gut. She hit Stander's belly dead center. He bent over and wheezed to catch his breath. The rock thumped to the ground.

In two steps, Ravel rushed forward with her broom stick aimed for his throat. When he instinctively raised his arms to block, she whacked his ribs instead. Then she shoved him from the side. He dropped and rolled belly-down on the grass. Before he could push himself off the ground, she kneeled onto his back. Her kneecap dug in between his shoulder blades. The broomstick tightly pressed across the nape of his neck as he lay half-choking face down.

"You're dead," she told him. "Put away your peach peelers and sit down."

Prosper bounded to his feet. "Now see here, my dear betrothed. That was cheating."

Ravel whirled on him, springing to her feet and raising the broom in one smooth motion. She swung the broomstick aiming for his head. Prosper ducked exactly as she had hoped. While he was slightly crouched, she wind-milled the broomstick in her hands. The stick clocked the side of his kneecaps, hooked behind his calves, and swept his feet out from under him. Down he went, hard to his shoulder, as if he had fallen from a bucking horse.

She stomped his wrist into the dirt. The hard tip of the broomstick pointed at his throat's lump. "If this were a lance," she said, not even breathing heavily. "You'd be dead."

Prosper smiled up the length of the broomstick at her. Instead of anger, he had the look of wanting to kiss her. "You're wonderful. Teach me to do that."

"Exactly!" Candor exclaimed. "What I've been asking for years. Teach me. Teach all of us, Sister."

She stepped back to allow her betrothed to get up. She held the broom one-handed tucked behind her shoulder, as she would hold a polearm staff. By force of habit, every object in hand could be a weapon: any housewife's pots and pans, any farmer's rakes and spades, any traveler's walking stick. Whatever she touched could be used to fight and keep fighting until life left her. She looked at her brother's soft hands that had never wielded a weapon in battle or soaked in his foe's blood. His delicate fingers resembled their mother's hands made for turning the pages of books and pinching the tip of a writing brush. He held his coney drumstick as a simple morsel of half-eaten meat rather than a bone that could be snapped in half and impaled into his enemy's eye.

"No, Der. I've told you before, I'm not teaching you martial skills."

Her brother scowled at the argument they'd had so many times before. Rage and frustration narrowed his eyes.

"Why?" Prosper asked. "Why not?"

"Because our father was ten times the fighter I am," she said. "And he's still dead."

"Yes, he's dead!" Candor bounded to his feet. "By the blazes of the abyss, do you think I don't know that as well as you do? Do you think I wasn't there? That I didn't see what they did to Father?"

The image of the battlefield's aftermath replayed in her memory with painful clarity: her father's corpse impaled on a pole, his legs dangling, his face a distorted mask of smothered pain. Soldiers in black uniforms had knelt at his feet casting dice to divide his possessions. Six years had passed since that day, but with all that had happened in the meantime, it felt more like six hundred years.

"Or that I didn't witness all of the outrageous abuses the crud-coats inflicted on our mother before they killed her?"

Ravel lowered her eyes. A scene she had not witnessed played in her imagination. Her graceful mother sprawled on charred and blood-soaked ground. She lay beneath a dog pile of laughing rapists who ended their revelry by strangling her.

"The bastards who did these horrible things are still breathing air!" Candor's deep bass voice broke with emotion. "They are enjoying their days of victory, laughing with their friends, eating sumptuous feasts, and happily forgetting what atrocities they've committed. How can you endure one more day allowing them to sleep peacefully in their beds?"

Prosper patted his shoulder in consolation. "That's right, Der. You're telling her. That's right."

"Holler and rail at me all you will, Der," she said coolly. "I won't allow you to embark on a foolhardy mission to assassinate the king in his own castle. It's suicide! Let your friends waste their lives if they please, but you are the lord of my house, and I am your bodyguard. If I must cut off your feet, I won't have you go with them. I've buried Father. I've buried Mother. I won't bury you, too."

"Coward," he said with narrow eyes.

"Fool," she answered.

Stander pointed to the tree line. A lantern's pinprick of light pierced through the woods. "Look there! Reds is coming back and Xid is with him!"

Chapter 9.

A plough horse with shaggy hooves loped into the grassy clearing. From the saddle dangled the legs of a youth a few years older than her brother, but still quite young. His broad-brimmed felt hat marked him as a vagabond peddler but his saddle bore no wares. He could only be one thing: a messenger.

Redson jogged behind the horse's tail, oddly in the place of a lord's squire although he was better dressed than the rider.

"Where in the vapors were you!" Xid dropped to dismount. "I waited outside the tavern. What're you about having supper like lords in a garden?"

Redson caught the bridle and led the horse to tend its needs.

"I've gotten betrothed," Prosper told him.

"Betrothed? Betrothed to be married?" Xid rolled his eyes in Ravel's direction.

She nodded politely as she adjusted her ears to his Southern accent.

"You're the Lady Spareen?"

Ravel said, "And you must be Xidron."

He swept off the broad felt hat and dropped into a deep courtly bow. Ravel cocked an eyebrow; she hadn't expected such etiquette from someone dressed so roughly. Narrow cheekbones made his eyes seem too large. He let his hair grow excessively long to the beltline and plaited his dark locks in multiple braids entwined with yellow cord.

"Xidron po'Éad, son of Lord Ethossnon of the House of Kthoss, at your service." For a Southerner, his accent was not so thick which meant he had enjoyed a gentleman's education in the Midlands.

"Kthoss... Kthoss..." she mused. "That household was in the court of Bastard Prince Tolljet, wasn't he?"

Xid replaced his hat and stood tall. "My father was a Lord Baron of the Saffron Province before he was butchered in the siege of the South Palace along with the rest of the prince's court. I was among the weeping squires who carried the tragic message beyond the battle lines. I myself delivered the news to *your* prince that the Usurper had mounted my prince's noble head on the spikes of his own palace gate. I witnessed Prince Rouchard weep with grief."

"So have I," Ravel said. "Many times, my comrades-in-arms and I stood guard at our prince's battle tent and heard him mourning the loss. Although born from different mothers, my prince's affection for his half-brother Prince Tolljet was sincere."

"Thank you, milady," Xidron said. "I stayed in the battle camps of the blue flag for the next two years, until *that* day..."

A somber pause quieted them all for the memory of the Battle of Border Field that ended all battles forever.

Xidron finished, "One could say, having watched two princes killed, I feel as if I've lost the war twice."

Ravel nodded sympathy. "Have a seat, Xid. Have some food. You must be tired."

He removed his long cloak with a flourish. The swirl stirred up glittering embers in the campfire.

Prosper raised a cup in a toasting gesture. "To the honor of our fallen Prince Rouchard, may we succeed in avenging him."

"Vengeance! Vengeance! Death to the Pretender!" the young men chanted.

"Ah!" Ravel barked her exasperation. "What a ridiculous fantasy to assassinate the king in the heart of Xolhold Keep? Just the five of you?"

"With your help." Candor narrowed his eyes in a stern, commanding expression.

"No," she said. "My life's entire purpose and duty is to protect you, my brother, the son and heir to whatever is left of our household. I brought us to the flagless territory to keep you safe."

"Our household that the Pretender's roaches burned to the ground." Candor paused for breath. By then, sunset's colors had faded and the sky behind him turned dull gray. "I'm pleased that you remember your role in life, but I worry that you are losing your resolve. I haven't, Sister. I haven't forgotten how our parents groomed me from the cradle in noble etiquette and knowledge to become a lord who would honor our ancestors. Every day that I wake up, I offer thanks that I am the first-born son and heir to my father's name. Every day, I pledge to the spirits of our forefathers that I shall never forget who I am: Lord of the House of Spareen."

"Yes, you are... You are my lord." Ravel's dry throat cracked on the words.

"Tell me, Sister, what is the value of being a lord if my vassals have been slaughtered and my manor house is a pile of kindling, rubble, and ashes? What meaning does my name have now? Our household tomb is smashed and looted. Our heraldic flags don't fly. The prince to whom I was born to serve is fallen."

"I don't know what to say," she whispered.

"How can you endure one moment of your life here in limbo at a river's bank in the wilderness? We exist in a nowhere land without title or honor. Don't you want to reclaim what is our right? You are a lady, the eldest daughter of the House of Spareen. You were a captain in Prince Rouchard's royal cavalry. How can you endure wearing anything but our house colors, carrying a cooking knife instead of a sword, and marking the hours in anonymity?"

"We're alive," she told him. "We're safe. We're free."

Candor's eyes flashed in the dwindling camp fire's orange light. "An imposter squats on the throne of Xol that rightly belonged to our murdered prince. By such lies he has deluded the lords of the land! How can any sensible man believe that he is forever young, that he is the lost prince returned from his doomed voyage to the Deep Sea after forty-five years? No man is immortal!"

Ravel stepped toward her brother. "What if your assumption is wrong? What if the King of Xol is not a pretender after all?"

Only Xidron looked down. Ravel noticed from the corner of her eye.

Candor cried out, "No, no, he can't be!"

"Why not?" she asked. "If you accept the premise that miracles occurred in days of yore, then why can't miracles happen now? What if by a blessing of Heaven, he truly is immortal? What if he really is Glëa po'Lon—"

"No, no," he insisted. "For if he is, then it means that everything our father and our prince had fought and died for was wrong."

"Perhaps it was," she said gently. "A sensible man admits when his facts are wrong."

"No! It is not him! It can't be! The real Prince Glëa would never have made war and slaughtered his own brothers. This man is a pretender and a butcher. He deserves to be butchered. If no one else seeks justice, then it's up to me."

"Don't seek revenge, Der. You can't go up against the Iron King's army with these four youths."

He turned away so all she saw were the shaggy locks of his russet hair. "Will you abandon me, Sister, as you failed to protect our father?"

Her dry eyes burned but could not produce tears. Since implanting the talons into her chest, she was incapable of weeping. Yet the urge choked up in the back of her throat. "You're all I have left in this world."

Prosper stepped in between them. "Please don't argue, both of you. Night is falling. Let us not end this auspicious day with anger in our hearts."

Candor walked swiftly away from the campfire to the cube of thatch and sod that had been their home. He struck a commanding pose on the flagstones of the hut's doorway. "All of you, collect your belongings from the tavern. Come back and meet here at daybreak. We begin our journey tomorrow."

He went inside the flap of wicker reeds that served as a flimsy curtain door. Ravel choked up at the abruptness of his exit, as if he had slammed a gateway and bolted it shut. All pretenses were gone. Even if he did not believe in magical, otherworldly forces, her brother knew that she did not need sleep. She would stand guard beneath the cloudy stars all night to keep him safe.

Chapter 10.

As there was only one horse and six of them, Xidron's plough horse became the pack animal. The youths donned knives and pouches at their belts then loaded the horse with everything else. They brought an impressive collection of supplies: canvas tarps, ropes, woolen blankets, hatchets and spades, a cooking skillet, a small cauldron, kegs filled with rainwater, and sacks of dry lentils.

Candor never looked back to the village on the river's edge. With his friends tugging the pack horse, he allowed Ravel no time to reminisce either. *It wasn't much, but it belonged to us, and it was safe.* Ravel glanced heavenward and imagined the spirits of her parents gazing down from the eternal gardens. *What would you do with this boy, Father? Would you approve of this course I am allowing him to follow? Can I dissuade him from his foolishness before he goes too far?*

The group's boots cut their own trail over hills brushed with loft grass, foxtail weeds, heather, thistle, dandelion, and clover. The whole of the continent expanded laid out as a banquet table before her eyes. Soft hills textured by scattered swathes of trees formed a landscape in the shape of dinner rolls laid on a platter and garnished by the occasional sprig of parsley. Yet the pastoral beauty of the panorama views soured when she thought of the journey ahead.

Days of travel blended into a monotonous course of similar grass-brushed hills and monochrome boulders pocked among the green. Soil turned from sandy gravel to yellow-orange clay the further south they went. A cool distant sun made its routine patrol from east to west. Clouds in fluffy tufts drifting slowly across the sky. Ravel eyed the skeins of white clouds for every hour that they walked in the open; she dreaded imagining what might happen if it rained.

Ravel kept up banal conversation with the youths and learned what she could of their backgrounds. Very little information seemed useful. Their home villages had been razed to the ground by the Iron King's blackcoats, of course. Their manor homes and ancestral tombs had been smashed to the foundations and looted for buried jewelry; whose hadn't? The twins Redson and Stander had served as squires under Lord Faramodi in the Eighth Cavalry brigade, so they knew horses. Stander had been schooled as a farrier and Redson was apprentice to a saddle maker. If we had any horses, Ravel thought wryly, these two would be useful.

Each day's hours passed in a predictable cycle from morning through the afternoon and into evening. Golden sunsets shined in brushstrokes of gray clouds and glowed a rosy amber at Prosper's right-hand shoulder. Her new husband gave Ravel his profile and little else while maintaining his determined stride.

Each night, Xidron and Prosper performed the routine tasks of building a fire and cooking supper. Prosper cherished his tinderbox and prided himself on how quickly he could grow flames out of sparks, twigs, and bark chips. Redson and Stander, the twin brothers with the longest legs and highest reach, strung ropes and hung their tents from low-hanging branches. Candor did none of the work. He held onto his satchel that contained their traveling funds, the maps and compass, and other such treasures as he kept for himself. As the ranking lord in the group, he had claimed custodianship of every valuable thing; his friends never asked nor approached.

The youths ate their meals together and always left behind an extra bowl for her. Ravel feigned the sophisticated etiquette of a noble lady who would not intrude upon the gentlemen's table. This became a routine for her to step away from the group and to eat alone. Every night, she discarded the lentil porridges and wild meat stews in the underbrush. Every night, her bare fingers grabbed wriggling worms and lizards out of the dirt. Only freshly killed raw meat could satiate her hunger. How long until my secret is discovered, she often wondered.

Every night, they huddled in wool blankets to sleep under the tarps. Candor tended to flop about as he slept, so the twin brothers gave him a full body's width of space between them. Prosper snuggled like a spoon at Ravel's back and sometimes lightly kissed her with tight lips in very gentlemanly fashion. As the others slept, Ravel lay awake and watched the shining eyes of owls in the trees.

One evening, they made camp within a grove of lofty spruce and juniper trees. Candor double-checked their position on his map until night fell and it became too dark to read. As the boys settled down in bedrolls together, Ravel stood vigilant outside of the tent. She watched the first stars appear in the darkening sky.

Prosper rose up out of the tent. He joined her in gazing at the constellation of the Great Midnight Bear aligned near the crescent moon waxing to half a circle.

"The sky never changes," he said. "Since I was a boy learning the names of the stars, it hasn't changed up there. It's only down here, on the ground, where nothing is the same as I expected it to be."

Ravel remarked to her betrothed husband, "Not how you imagined you'd be married, eh?"

"No, it is certainly not how my father would've planned." Prosper said. "But since that one day, nothing is."

Redson and Stander nodded somberly at their friend's words. Their eyes darkened in private thoughts of what they had lost at the Battle of Border Field and what would never be again.

Prosper fastened a shallow kiss onto her mouth. Ravel allowed him to hold the connection. The prickle of his unshaved chin scratched against hers. The aftertaste of lentil porridge was bitter on his lips. He held the kiss for as long as he could hold his breath, then withdrew.

"Excuse my advances," he said in a husky whisper.

"No offense taken. We're betrothed, aren't we? You've a right to kiss me any time you wish."

Prosper exchanged concerned glances with his friends. Xidron covered a salacious smile with his hand. Candor noncommittally rolled his eyes. Then her betrothed leaned toward Ravel as if trying to read dim script in faded ink.

"You didn't seem too hesitant, just now. I'm sorry to ask again but you're still a virtuous maiden, aren't you? Even at your age?"

My age? I'm not the Hag of the Forest. Ravel forced a smile and looked him straight in the eye. She lied coolly for the sake of her household's honor. "Of course, my virtue is intact. I'm a lady, aren't I?"

Prosper lowered his head. "I'm sorry to have asked. I meant no insult."

Candor said, "Well, I am insulted. Would I have given her in marriage to you if she weren't pure?"

Yet her brother's harsh eyes fixed upon her. A wondering glittered darkly beneath his brows. Candor had been a child at home when Ravel served as bodyguard to their father. Lord Spareen had commanded a division of a thousand infantry troops during the war. As a captain, she had spent more time in a saddle than at a table. She and her father led columns of foot soldiers marching the grassy plains between the Fortress at Lake Ward and the Fortress of Sharp Crag. She had practiced martial skills in sparring with virile young men. She had shared a bath house with the other sex. She had slept in crowded barracks like livestock in a barn, or shared tents in battle camps, without a nursemaid chaperone.

Candor's suspicion colored his face. If she could keep a secret for six years of the talons embedded in her chest, then how easily could she conceal any indiscretions she may have enjoyed. She wished for the liberty to shout at the accusing slant of his eyebrows. Honor and fealty obligated her to uphold the integrity of their noble house. Duty and loyalty demanded her silence. *Yes, yes, I have taken comfort in the arms of men who are all dead now. Why should it concern you? It was war. Those were desperate times. Father knew that I 'tried on boots' and he did not condemn me. He did not call me a whore. He did not look at me the way you look at me now. You may be the Lord of my House, but you are not my father.*

Chapter 11.

Captain Ashglëa put in a full day's shift at the infirmary. A quiet, uneventful day passed much like so many days had passed before. The slow pace misled him into staying a bit longer than usual. Evening fell quickly and the darkening windows surprised him. He bade good night to the apprentice staff and left behind the chamber stocked with powders, ointments, salves, and leeches.

He strolled across the open yard of green grass growing up through the gravel. On this evening, the clouds thickened overhead but the air smelled dry. Soon the nights would be colder as the world turned to winter. Ash felt grateful every day that the Capital City enjoyed mild weather all year round. The most snow he had seen in the last few years had been a dusting of flakes on the rooftops that melted by midday. *Ancestors willing, may I never be knee-deep in snow ever again for the rest of my natural days.*

Past the long rectangular barn that served as barracks, the odors of a hot meal caused his mouth to salivate. An open, shingled awning covered the area. Dozens of royal legions in black uniforms reclined on benches or straddled stools. They drank from pewter tankards and stoneware soup bowls. Some slurped off wooden spoons. Others dipped chunks of bread into the stew. Conversations murmured amongst them in recanting the day's uneventful hours. Voices overlapped and blended into an obscure wordless buzz. The occasional laugh popped up.

Ash looked forward to ending each day with a supper of soldier's stew: carrots, leafy greens, purple onions, brown or white beans, and a little bit of meat.

The head cook was a one-eyed man with a rotund belly; it was said that he saw only half of what he brewed and had to taste everything twice to make up the difference. He used a long rod to stir the contents of an iron cauldron the size of a bathtub. Brick cubes propped it off the ground with enough space underneath for a fire. One small apprentice kneeled dangerously close to feed another log to the flames.

"Good evening, Ethrem," Ash said to the head cook.

"Evenin', Cap'n."

Ash relaxed his face into a friendly smile. The cook's familiar accent from the backwoods of the Green Forest felt as comforting as a belly full of hot stew.

"Sorry I'm later than usual," Ash said, mindful of not slipping out of his own cultured diction. "I lost track of time."

"Not ter worry, Cap'n. There's still a-plenty."

Ash used a ladle to fill his bowl with more solids than liquid. He grabbed two pieces of toasted flatbread from a platter near the stone-barrel oven. Then, moving down the line, he unhooked the tankard off his belt to take a draft off the ale barrel.

He turned to the awning and searched for an empty space to sit. Most of the benches and stools were already taken.

One man sat on a bench by himself. He hung his head and stared into his half-finished bowl of stew. Ash could not see his face. By the unkempt bush of brown hair, and by the fellow's slender shoulders, he recognized the recently promoted captain.

"Say there, Herry, do you mind if I join you?"

Captain Herry looked up only as high as Ash's belt buckle. "Be my guest."

Ash swung one leg over and sat down straddling the bench. He used the boards as a makeshift table to put his tankard while he slurped the rim of his soup bowl.

"If you're still hungry after you finish that, you can have mine," Herry said. "I took too much."

"You're sure?" Ash garbled his words with boiled celery, carrots, and flatbread stuffed in his cheek.

Herry nodded. "My stomach's all mixed up. I requested a schedule change two weeks ago. The commander just approved it. I'm not doing the night shift anymore. This would've been my breakfast, and now it's my supper."

Ash swallowed and gulped ale to help wash it down. "Why? I thought you liked the night shift."

"Not since I got tapped to be in a rowboat."

The two shared a moment of quiet breathing. All around them, conversation murmured and rustled like dry leaves.

Ash leaned in closer to the shoulder pads of Herry's black wool uniform. He whispered, "We aren't supposed to talk about that night."

"I don't," Herry said. "I haven't."

"Good."

"But you know, Ash, what everyone knows. I was on assignment in the Outerlands a few years back. My squad patrolled the desert and met the nomads of the hot sands. They traded me one of their bone flutes for my tin whistle." Herry smiled briefly, then his lower lip quivered as his smile dropped away.

"You're very good on the flute." Ash hoped to lighten the fellow's mood. The effort failed.

"I've seen those creatures up close in the wild. I've seen what they do. They're horrible enough in the light of day. I can't bear to face them in the dark."

Ash gently took hold of Herry's soup bowl and lifted it out of hand. "Why don't you get your flute out and play us something, eh?"

"Six years ago, I was there on that mountain of red sandstone. The king's magic-workers went rogue and tried to blow it up with tar bombs. The whole mountain was a nest of them. Imagine it, Ash! A whole nest of unhatched black eggs and those winged shadow-beasts swarmed to protect it." Herry kept staring at the ground. His eyes widened as if he saw something between his boots more than gravel, trampled weeds, and hard-packed dirt.

"I know, Herry, I know." Ash patted the fellow's shoulder. "Try not to dwell on what's already done. What happened is in the past. You're here now. You survived. You and Stockard and Viktor fought them off and you won."

"Not all of us won," Herry said.

"Yeah, I know. But you brought Deiv's body home for a proper burial with honors."

"We wouldn't have made it except for *her*."

"Her?" Ash tilted his head. "Who?"

"I'm not supposed to talk about her, either. Don't tell Viktor, but it's been six years. She's probably dead. She probably died that day. I can't imagine how she survived." Herry sniffed and wiped his nose with the cuff of his uniform's sleeve.

"Who?"

"Some rebel woman, a westerner in the company of bandits. She had a weird, magic-working noble person with her. He was a scholar with a lot of unnatural knowledge. He's probably dead too. She served him—or allied with him—it wasn't clear. She fought with us, side by side, against those creatures and against the king's magic-workers gone rogue."

Ash straightened his back to put a little distance between them. "This rebel woman sounds like a very peculiar person."

Herry looked aside to the groups of black coats absorbed in conversation with each other. He paused long enough to be sure that no faces turned in their direction. No one else was paying attention to their dialogue.

"I shouldn't have told you. I'm not supposed to talk about *her*."

"C'mon, we're friends," Ash said. "You can tell me anything."

"Oh yeah? Like the way you share your secrets with me?" Herry looked straight into Ash's face with a stern challenge.

Ash broke out with a smile. "Well, sure, I don't share everything. I've got a couple of embarrassing episodes in my past that I don't—"

"Not talking about your past."

"Then what?"

Raising a finger to point at his face, Herry accused, "*He* told you to make a medicine of it and you did."

"No, I didn't." Ash made sure not to blink or flinch.

"I saw you!" Mindful of their comrades all around, Herry whispered through clenched teeth. "You wrapped it in a kerchief and brought it back. The very next morning, his lordship was up and about like a randy goat."

"No, no, you've got it all wrong. Sure, I attempted to comply with my order, but I failed. Trust me. I failed. Listen to me, Herry. That unholy spawn of the abyss played no part in his lordship's recovery. It was all the leeches, yes, the leeches did it."

Herry scrutinized Ash's calm, sincere expression for a long time. At last, he exhaled and relaxed the tension in his shoulders.

"Good," Herry said. "Some things are not meant to mix with human flesh."

"Very true," Ash agreed.

Chapter 12.

King Glëa reclined in his bedchamber on a pallet of soft cushions by the fireplace. After a long day of writing and signing laws, edicts, and criminal judgments, he had stripped down to his linen shirt and leggings for the night. A stout tea table was crammed full of butter-cashew pastry, slices of peaches and raspberries, and a silver carafe of mint tea. Every night, the servants prepared this spread for him. He nibbled at either pastry or fruit, but rarely did he finish it all. They served him in such abundance merely because he was the king of the known world. It would be a disgrace to let him go to bed with an empty stomach.

And he was not alone.

Every night, Alyss the Guild Mistress of the Royal Tea House reclined at his side and stayed until morning. This had been the routine for the past couple of years since King Glëa's victory in battle that ended the civil war. In the same way that he nibbled on fruits or pastry, he delighted in the taste of the artisan who skillfully provided an illusion of intimacy without exposing the vulnerability of true emotions.

On this night, Glëa felt a growing curiosity about his companion's origins. Until now, he only knew the superficial details that were so commonplace as to be unmemorable. She had chosen early in life to seek apprenticeship at the Tea House Guild in the palace of the late Prince Tolljet in the southern province. Entering the tea house meant leaving one's prior self behind to become a new person of refined etiquette. Even her name was carefully crafted for her new identity.

Alyss must have demonstrated an early aptitude for the exquisite skills demanded by the guild. Practitioners of the arts wore intricate garments of layered skirts and shimmering silky veils that draped the body flatteringly as living statues. The very art of dressing required one to thread intricate lacings and finger-tuck pleats that would unravel under less masterful hands. Herbal powders darkened the eyelashes and reddened the lips. Alyss's skin radiated a sweet floral scent. A tortoise shell comb lifted her henna-dyed auburn hair into a coiled wad atop her head. Alyss wore a necklace of glass and ceramic beads, finger rings carved of tortoise shell or bone, and sandalwood bangle bracelets. By the code of the Guild and the edicts of traditional alchemists, no artisan of the Tea House ever wore anything metal.

Alyss sat beside the king each night with infallible poise. As the hours passed, she showed no sign of weariness, always smiling in a demure and subtlety alluring way, always ready with the carafe to refresh his tea or to offer a cream-filled pastry. Alyss listened to him discuss the events of the day and offered no opinions except, "You are most wise, Your Majesty. I have every confidence that you'll decide what is best."

On this night, as Alyss refilled his cup, the lamp light twinkled in her glass necklace. Each bead was molded to resemble a pinecone. Each bead itself a cluster of hundreds of smaller beads. Glëa admired the play of miniature rainbows in the myriad facets of the glass balls. Light and color played in his eyes. Light so pure that it struck a tone, a single note reverberating in his mind as clearly as if a musician in the room had plucked a harp string.

"So pure," he whispered while caressing the beads of her necklace. The glass sparkled green against his fingertips.

"Pure?" She laughed huskily. Her breath carried the fragrance of honey and mint. "Surely you don't mean me, Your Majesty. My maidenhood days are long gone, as you well know, but I am flattered that you—"

Glëa kissed her with a lightly puckered pip to interrupt her. "Don't speak, Alyss. Sing to me. Sing me a song."

"As you wish, Your Majesty." Smiling graciously, she shifted her legs beneath the layers of silky skirts and looped veils. She arranged herself alongside a large, varnished plank of a fifty-seven-string harp and spent a few moments adjusting the tuning. She plucked select strings and twisted ebony knobs. "Any requests?"

"Sing something old," he said. "Something older than I am."

She tilted her head curiously. A lock of auburn hair slid across her bare shoulder. "Allow me a moment... Oh yes, I have just the song that may please Your Majesty."

Alyss sang in a clear, unwavering voice with an extraordinary vocal range that matched the broad span of strings. She sang an old tune in the disharmonious melody of ancient days, a tune so old that it could only be played on this antique instrument made in the craftsmen's tradition going back a thousand years more. The varnished board showed old scratches and faded designs in paint, but aging only made its tones richer. Alyss sang in the language of ancient days no longer spoken by living men, that Glëa as a young prince had learned to write but not speak. She sang an epic ballad from the Warring Era that told of the heroes of the Zanaster Dynasty battling monsters of living stone and snakes of liquid light, banishing bloodless wraiths into the swamps of the Southern Peninsula, and making bricks of their mortal enemies' cremated remains to lay the foundations of the ancestral castle.

As she sang, the strings of the harp and the strings of her throat wove a web of sound that intoxicated him. The weight of his flesh lightened so that by inhaling deeply enough he seemed to float away from her as a plum blossom caught on a breeze. Firelight glinted across her eyes like sunshine on a rippling creek.

Light and sound and song opened a window into her thoughts. Glëa's mind soared on the resonating waves of her voice. His eyeless eyes found her memories of preparing to be his companion this evening. He glimpsed a scene that had come and gone hours before as if the memory were his own. He saw every detail of the boudoir in the Tea House where he had never visited: her gray dressing robe hanging off one shoulder, her glass and ceramic jars of toiletries, her brass framed mirror, even the blue-hooded sparrow that perched twittering on her windowsill. He heard the slurp of bath water in a sponge. He smelled lavender and rose oil in the musk of human skin.

The mood in her memory darkened into melancholy. Alyss had read a brief letter that reported on the health and well-being of a small child. The letter came from a miller in the Green Forest region and enclosed a small lock of brown hair.

You have a child somewhere? His mind's voice whispered in the void. *You've given him away to live secretly with a miller's family? Because a Tea Mistress is not allowed to be a mother?*

"Ugh," Alyss groaned and stopped singing. "Forgive me, Your Majesty, I suddenly don't feel well."

Vertigo drummed inside his skull. Purple sparkles turned gold inside his eyelids. Heartbeats pattered wildly inside his ribs. Perspiration beaded on his forehead and throat.

"Rest a moment," he whispered hoarsely.

"Thank you, Your Majesty. My apologies for my lack of stamina this evening."

Glëa sipped the tea to soothe his parched throat. "Has something happened to upset you today, Alyss?"

She turned away from the glow of the fireplace. The sharp angles of her profile blurred into amber shadows. "It is not appropriate for me to complain."

"Surely you know by now that I am most displeased when those in my company withhold their innermost thoughts. Tell me, Alyss. I command you to tell me what thoughts you hesitate to speak."

"If I may respectfully observe, Your Majesty, with the ancestral blessing of eternal youth, passion, and virility that you exhibit, it is regrettable that you have not yet reopened the Garden of Delights here at Xolhold Keep. My guild mentor often spoke fondly of the pleasurable times that she enjoyed there with your father. May the soul of King Tokustein enjoy unending bliss in the Eternal Fields."

"The garden," he repeated.

"Yes."

"The garden is what occupies your thoughts?"

"Yes," she insisted. "For although you defeated Prince Rouchard's army, his austere ideas remain alive. There are some who condemn the Tea House arts based on the ideologies of the Horsemen of the West. They are offended that I entertain you in chambers every night."

Glëa fingered her silky garment dyed in gradient hues of yellow, taupe, orange, and scarlet. "Do you ever regret abiding by the strict rules of the Tea House Guild, such as, not being permitted to have children of your own?"

Alyss looked aside to the strings of her harp. "I do not regret bringing pleasure to a world that has suffered so much rage and sorrow. I only wish that the austere pragmatists could see the value in what I bring. Outside the shelter of these walls, some people in the city call us 'whores.'"

"Regrettably, I cannot prevent grumbling in the streets unless I want to start rounding up people for whipping and executions. My father was not that sort of king and neither do I wish to be a tyrant. I've learned from my studies of history that such tactics are never a long-term solution. Davarche the Fourteenth ruled with a bloody hand. The legends say that the ramparts of Xolhold's western wall are filled not with gravel but with the skulls of those who displeased him. But look where it got him."

"Overthrown by his son in a violent coup." Her fingers traced the seashell inlay on the sound board of her harp. Her hands curled towards the strings in position for the first chord and made ready to play the Ballad of the Murdered King if he should ask.

"Exactly." Glëa put the goblet aside. "Which is why I won't have children."

"It is your most prudent rule. No son. No daughter. Only..." She giggled in a low, sultry tone. "...the pleasure of your company."

Glëa vaulted to his feet. He left behind the cozy nest of cushions and walked the floor. His stockinged feet padded softly on the carpet. He came to stand at the grand four-posted bed and leaned against the tassel cord that drew the curtains.

"The lords have advised me that I should take a wife," he said to the bed's stack of pillows and the quilted down-filled comforter. "As you've said, my late brother's austere philosophy is quite persistent. It is unseemly that I should remain a bachelor for all eternity."

"That is sensible counsel," Alyss said. "So, may I ask, if you have thought of whom you would take as your queen?"

"Did you know that, in my youth, Jiveine... that is, the Governor Lady Browden was among the debutante contenders for my favor? If only I had not sailed away to explore the Deep Sea, we might have married and produced a pack of children. I could have been a plump old king enjoying a room filled with grandchildren by now."

"But if you had not sailed, the ghosts of your royal ancestors would not have rescued you from the shipwreck and blessed you with eternal youth."

"Mmmm," he murmured. A king never blushed to be caught in a falsehood, but the shining soul within him cringed a bit against the urge to scream the truth. *That's not what happened! I fell out of the crystal city. I dissolved into this fleshy shell, but I am still here!*

Glëa strolled to the fireplace. The blaze heated his chest through the gauzy nightshirt. He stopped short of the brass screen and surveyed the engraved tiles over the mantle. Each tile bore the insignia of a royal house established in the reign of his ancestor King Davarche the First. Some names had been extinguished in the war and yet the tiles remained.

Alyss stroked the fifty-seven strings of her harp in playful plucks in trying to decide on her next melody to perform. Random chords jumped left and right, scattering his mind away from the orderly array of household insignias.

"I will make a decision soon," he said. "This year has seen prosperity and a bountiful harvest. How better to celebrate than with a royal wedding."

Glëa meandered nearer but stopped short of the bearskin rug. She tilted her head to the side so that the cord of her neck's muscle made a straight line from her chin to her collarbone.

"Why so sad, Alyss?" he asked.

"I am composing a new song for your bride-to-be." Her pleasant mood dimmed with the last word.

He settled down beside her on the rug. He inhaled deeply the rose powder that dusted her soft skin. His lips brushed over her bare collarbone.

"Come now, Alyss, don't sulk. No matter whom I choose to marry, it will be an arrangement for the good of the state. I will still need your services for many years to come."

"Yes, but will I be your honored concubine? Or am I, as the disgruntled townsfolk call me, a whore—"

"Listen! You are an artisan of grace and refinement, of wit and delight. You bring such pleasure to me as can never be supplanted. Regardless of whom I marry, Alyss, *you* will always be mine."

He tackled her to the cushions and pushed aside the harp. She giggled when he raised her skirts and wedged himself in between her bare legs. He smothered her giggles with a kiss. Then he paused, lying flat on top of her with only his elbows to keep his chest from crushing hers. Firelight played over her eyes and sharpened the threads of her irises. Glëa parted his lips as if to kiss her some more but instead licked the air and tasted the colors of light on their shared breath. Even as his human body eagerly rushed forward, his shining soul lagged wanting an intangible *more*.

Chapter 13.

Two weeks and a few days passed until Ravel and her brother's group entered more familiar terrain. Beige clay soil was overgrown with prickly weeds, thistles, and patches of stinging nettle. Streams bubbled up between cracks in the rocks; water like liquid diamonds trickled through the youths' fingers. Trout and freshwater eels could be plucked by hand from the shallows.

"We're in the Midlands, now." Ravel pointed to a stone pillar marking the boundary of the Kingdom of Xol. The bull's head emblem of the royal House of Davarche was chiseled into the granite. A rouge-and-black flag had toppled into the weeds some time ago. No one had yet picked it up. Candor deliberately stepped on the fallen flag as he passed between the boundary stones.

Sunlight had a brighter quality here in the verdant meadows of her former homeland. Grass was as green as a peacock's tail. Clouds of white wool spilled over the water-blue sky in the colors of their slain prince's blue-and-white flag. The scent of overnight rain refreshed the air and brought up the musky scent of fertile earth. Ravel inhaled cautiously as even the humidity of the afternoon had potential to shriek in horror at her trespassing.

Xidron pointed to a thatched cottage on the hillside. "From time to time, I've enjoyed hospitality at that farmer's home. I worry, however, that we are too large of a group to impose upon their humble means. I recommend that we push onward to the crossroads where lies a tavern in a small village called Hogsmead. We may find a fellow who trades in Percivons or Fellmonts or... uh, mules."

The other four youths groaned at the word, mule.

Ravel asked, "What's wrong with mules?"

"They're not Roan Blues," said Candor.

"So, you'd rather walk the whole way to the capital?" she asked. "It's taking you twice as long. Surely you've realized that by now. Stop being a stubborn peacock and mount up on draft horses or mules if you must. Surely when the balladeers compose verse to celebrate your heroic deeds, they'll just say you were on Roan Blues, so what does it matter?"

Candor loomed tall to glare down into her face. "We are on a righteous honorable mission."

That said, he charged off to climb a stack of boulders. Compass and paper map in hand, he checked their position.

Ravel sat down on a fallen log. So, discussion ended. She looked at Candor's profile and thought again of how much he resembled their mother even if his voice had deepened to be like their father's. He had Mother's eyes, after all. What would Mother say? *The process is as important as the result.* She recalled her mother scolding the servants to wipe the hardwood floors in parallel lines from the left wall to the right, how to tug at the washed linens so they would dry on the line without creases, or how to season the soup with a perfect mix of spices. The headboards of everyone's beds had to face north. She had seen her mother instruct Candor in how to properly hold a writing brush, *Not with your left hand, your right!* She had rapped his knuckles when he did not hold a spoon in the correct way and reminded him to always scoop his food away from himself. *Only farmers shovel food in towards their mouth.* She had often caught Ravel halfway up the stairs to make her go back and start again, left foot going up, right foot coming down. At the altar of the ancestors, Ravel was taught to light incense with her left hand and tap the silver bell with her right. Little rituals and procedures of everyday life used to have such importance.

She understood Candor's mission, now. They would do their deed properly and with honor as lords of the Great Midnight Bear, or they would not do it at all. Getting to Xolhold and assassinating the king was only part of the goal; how they got there, and how they killed him, was equally as important.

Ravel gazed skyward and thought of her parents' eternal spirits. Would they approve of his methods or even the goal itself? Gray clouds were silent and offered no guidance. All she had ever heard from her mother and father were admonitions. *Take care of your little brother's needs... Serve and obey the lord and heir... Protect the honor of our household name...* The burden of her lifelong duty lowered her head. She had nowhere else to go—there was never anywhere else in the world for her to go—but follow the young Lord Spareen and devote her own life to his survival.

Chapter 14.

King Glëa slowly paced back and forth in front of the Royal Treasurer's desk. His hands clenched and unclenched. He fiddled with turning the large jewels on his rings.

The counting masters droned on with their quarterly report of tax revenue and expenses. Stacks of parchments overflowed a line of rosewood trays. Near-sighted scribes hunched over their ink wells and writing brushes to make annotations of everything that transpired. For the past half an hour, the king listened to a detailed account of the costs and progress of the Royal Highway construction project that would someday connect the capital city to the unsettled plains of the Outerlands.

The Royal Treasurer's clear baritone voice describe the banal facts: how many leagues they had already paved in brick, how many leagues were yet feral, how the setbacks of seasonal weather and labor shortage had been overcome, and diplomatic achievements that facilitated commerce with the nomad tribes who roamed the desert sands.

"What about the insurgents in the borderlands?" asked the king. "I don't see where you've taken into account the cost of security forces, replacement of stolen materials, or laborers frightened into deserting the worksites. Are we pretending that harassment from troublemakers doesn't exist?"

"Uh... uh..." The treasurer shuffled a few of his pages around. He looked up in hope of rescue. His gaze came to rest upon the nobleman who had accompanied the king.

Governor Herald po'Aigrue, Patriarch of the House of Fordon, at forty-nine was the youngest of the territorial governors. He was a military man more comfortable in aligning troops for battle strategy than discussing the construction of roadways.

"With all of the utmost respect, Your Majesty, I would hardly call them insurgents. True, there has been some disorganized harassment from scattered remnants of disgruntled unbelievers. I've spoken at length with my brother Colonel Raegold who commands the stronghold at Chieftain's Gate. He assures me that the Outerlands are secure. There's more of a threat from the, uh, wildlife."

Glëa nodded to show that he understood the reference to Surleista on the wing. Ravenous flying beasts that could not be killed except by fire were troublesome predators to livestock herds.

"However, Your Majesty, it is the territory of the Great Northern Bay where I've seen more of the displaced unbelievers flee for refuge. In that region there is a potential festering risk to the stability of the kingdom."

"Governor Vilbyss is in charge of securing the north," the king said bluntly.

Fordon brushed back his shoulder-length dark hair in a self-conscious gesture. "Yes, Your Majesty, he has secured the coast and the shores around the bay itself. Rather I speak of the inland region above the Midland Country that is under my jurisdiction. That area has always been a challenging landscape with its rivers, its mountains, and its forests. My sources among the river barge merchants say that there are pockets of unbelievers scattered throughout the villages who speak openly of their disapproval of Your Majesty's rule."

Glëa inhaled the scent of a changing mood in the man's thoughts. As if someone had walked into the room carrying a bowl of freshly picked mint leaves, Fordon's demeanor shifted. His gaze turned to the storage shelves adjacent to the Royal Treasurer's desk.

Dowry chests were stacked on the shelves from each of the dozen noble houses who hoped for the king to choose a representative maiden as his queen. For the past couple of weeks, Glëa had met with each of the nubile debutantes; so many, one after another, that their faces blurred in his memories. Each of the girls had been groomed and dressed in finery. Each of them presented themselves with exquisite poise. They had all spoken eloquently to entertain him with their witty banter or knowledge of classic literature. Some of them demonstrated their domestic talents of penmanship or proficiency at a musical instrument, while others promised to learn whatever skills the king would wish them to achieve. His immortal soul had gazed into each of their eyes and found nothing extraordinary to interest him.

Glëa cocked his head to the side. "Your household has not offered a candidate yet."

"Well, as it so happens, Your Majesty, I've been looking for an opportunity to mention that I have someone to suggest."

"The houses of Browden and Vilbyss have offered sizeable dowries," the king said. "I doubt that you have the means to outbid them."

"He certainly does not," said the Royal Treasurer.

Lord Fordon lowered his head. "I have something else to offer that is more valuable than a chest full of gold, silver, and jewels."

"I'm listening."

"A solution to Your Majesty's dilemma."

"What dilemma, Herald?"

Lord Fordon stood tall. "Lady Browden and Lord Vilbyss are your fondest friends and confidants. Yet their households are lifelong rivals. If you choose a maiden from either of them, it will cause strife between them. If you choose a maiden from any of the other households, you will be showing favoritism that would certainly inspire the households of Browden and Vilbyss to jealousy. Which is why, if I may dare say, Your Majesty perhaps has hesitated to announce a decision."

"Walk with me, Herald."

The king spun on his heel and strode swiftly to the archway. In trotting up the narrow stairwell of spiraling stone steps, he did not bother to look back over his shoulder to be sure if Lord Fordon kept up the pace.

He emerged through an arched doorway to a high bridge connecting the tower to the ramparts of the outer wall. Two black-uniformed guards named Orlan and Rihan snapped their lances to attention. Sea breezes off the harbor stirred the king's long black curls. Sunshine warmed the top of his head.

"Who do you offer me?"

Lord Fordon spoke from behind. "An outsider from the north could strengthen Your Majesty's dominion over the territory that we were just speaking of."

"Who?"

"Forgive me if I cannot recite from memory the lineage of the young maiden." The governor pulled out a parchment leaf from a leather pouch at his belt. "Your father King Tokustein had a bastard half-sister Ruelyn who married a shipwright named Baron Hanseamal. They had four... or perhaps nine children. My apologies, the records are inconsistent."

"Eight," the king said. "Princess Ruelyn bore eight children but only four of my cousins survived their childhood."

"I see." Fordon returned his attention to the parchment in his hands. "One of those children, whose name is not recorded, bore a daughter. She gained ownership of a sizeable estate between the Midlands and the Great Northern Bay."

Glëa tapped his bejeweled fingers on the stones. "Xianna the Baroness of Taine."

"Yes, yes, and Xianna married a river merchant named Wemond Hawker. They have two sons and a daughter."

"You may stop your narrative at this point, Herald. My grandfather banished Princess Ruelyn and all her descendants in perpetuity. That whole branch of the family has been in exile since before I was born."

"True, their name is not in the roster of lords. But it is royal blood! One stroke of a writing brush, and three generations of exile can be swept away. One stamp of your royal seal, and the Lady of Taine can be a princess worthy of being your queen."

"You are suggesting that I marry my first cousin, twice removed?" the king asked.

"There is ample precedent for royal cousins to marry."

Glëa nodded while reflecting on the details of his lineage. He could not argue that a majority of his ancestors had chosen brides from the extended branches of the Davarche family tree.

"How old is the child?"

"Not yet in her sixth year."

"How can I marry a five-year-old? It's unheard of."

Fordon shrugged. "For now, it would be a marriage of state in name only. She's not long weaned from her nursemaid, after all, but she'll grow. Children tend to do grow all too quickly. In a dozen years, she will be of consummate age."

Glëa peered into the man's eyes. He focused on the dark pupils that were like miniature windows in his mind. He sensed no maliciousness or excessive greed but caught the faint scent of opportunity.

"You've made promises," the king whispered.

"Well, it seemed too trivial to mention but, yes, I have a few vassals in my fealty who are barge merchants. The river that flows to the Great Northern Bay passes through my estates in the Midlands. Theoretically speaking, if a Queen of Xol were to travel for leisurely retreats to her home village and bring a retinue of servants on the way—"

"You make salient points, Herald. Very well, I agree to consider it. Arrange a meeting with my little cousin."

The governor smiled with a slight blush. "As you command, so shall it be."

Chapter 15.

Ash worked all afternoon in the infirmary's loft. He used a mortar and pestle to grind dried mushrooms, various roots, and herbal sprigs. Then he carefully sifted the powders and spooned them into glass vials. A kerchief tied across his face protected him from inhaling too much of the dust. Even so, from time to time, pungent odors caused him to turn aside to release a sneeze.

Every time he sneezed, his supervisor called up from the ground floor. "Be careful up there!"

Lady Thazin po'Shen, of the House of Kairedon, commanded the infirmary whenever the Lord High Surgeon was not present. Which was often. A dark-haired native of the Harbor Bay region, with narrow features, long fingers, and unusually tall for a woman, she carried herself with a stiff, straight spine. She dressed impeccably in a black linen gown and a russet bib apron with pockets. Her apron strings tied in the back with a fisherman's square knot, unlike the other nurses on staff who tied their aprons in bow loops. Thazin behaved more like a boatswain than a nurse, as she came from a family of shipwrights. The noble House of Kairedon held the unique distinction of having designed and constructed the infamous grand sailing vessel that had carried Prince Glëa away on his reckless adventure to explore the Deep Sea. Hardly a day went by that Thazin failed to drop that tidbit into conversation. The haughty tilt of her chin flaunted her pride at being part of a family who made such a magnificent contribution to turning the tide of history.

Ash tried to ignore her as much as possible. He continued his work of measuring spoonfuls of seed pods and weighing them on a little tin scale.

Lady Thazin's attention quickly diverted to someone else on staff. Her hard-soled shoes clicked in rapid drumbeats on the floorboards. "You there, what are you doing?"

"Ma'am, I'm applying an ointment to this archer's burn," said a youthful voice that Ash did not recognize from afar. Nursing staff on the floor came and went frequently.

"Which bandages are you using?" she demanded.

"The basket on the top shelf, ma'am."

"No, no, no, you careless, sloppy lad. Those are *mine*. I cut and rolled those myself."

The youthful nurse said, "I'm sorry, ma'am. I apologize, ma'am. They looked the same as the others."

"Clearly these bandages are made of a higher quality gauze. Pay attention, lad! They are intended for use on ailments of the noble class or higher-ranking officers, *not* for listed footmen."

"Yes, ma'am."

The injured man's deep voice spoke up. "I'm a Fire-Archer First Class, not a footman. I got burned in training with flame arrows."

Ash put down his tools. He moved to the railing of the loft and looked down to the ground floor. He knew the archer's face, but the fellow's name escaped his memory. Shirtless, the archer's forearm was scalded in a large spray of soot-black and bloody red. The fellow must have been training on the chained monsters kept at Seagull's Rock, Ash concluded. Why else would archers be practicing how to affix wads of pitch-tar onto the shafts of fire arrows?

He called down from the loft, "An archer first class is equivalent to a second lieutenant in the infantry. Definitely not a footman."

"Eavesdropping, are we?" She whirled on her heel and rested her fists against her hips.

"Yes," Ash said.

Thazin blinked in surprise, expecting him to deny overhearing their conversation.

"Be that as it may," she said. "*My* gauze bandages are meant for captains or above." She snatched the basket off the bedstand and carried it towards a rack of towels and wash basins.

Just then, a footman page trotted into the infirmary. He rushed between the rows of empty cots. "Are you Lady Thazin po'Shen of the House of Kairedon?"

She proudly raised her pointed chin. "I am."

"I've been sent to bring you, at once, ma'am."

"Whither am I to be summoned?"

The footman said, "To the stables, to report to Captain Teimethee po'Fan. Come at once! Don't dally to pack any of your belongings."

She asked, "Why would I pack any belongings?"

"You're going to accompany the captain's squad on an excursion. It may be several days, at least a week. He asked for you, specifically, as the senior ranking female on the medical staff."

Ash called down from the loft's railing. "Why does Teim need a female?"

The footman shook his head. "I can't say."

Lady Thazin swiftly moved to the entryway and plucked her long, hooded cloak off a peg. "Of course, I am honored to report to the captain at once. I am not one to question orders."

Ash noticed the emphasis in her voice and her backward glance aimed at him. Ever since that night when he had quibbled over treatment of leeches, the lord surgeon had berated him daily for impudence and disrespect. Thazin's snide tone washed over him like a cawing of crows in the distance.

Once the lady and the footman stepped into the afternoon sunshine, Ash called down to the nurse on the floor. "You're in charge. I'm going out for a bit."

"Yes sir, Captain."

Ash slipped out the loft's back door. He scurried down the staircase that led to the alleyway between the infirmary and a laundry house that served the barracks. Damp bed sheets hung on cord racks to dry. The odors of lye soap and the steam of boiling water drifted out from the open windows.

Taking a shortcut across the bailey yard, Ash trotted between stacks of firewood, clusters of barrels, and piles of drying hay bales. He waved greetings when a passer-by called his name but otherwise stayed on course for the royal stables.

Horses in the corral enjoyed the leisure of a cool, autumn afternoon. Heads down, they nibbled at the green grass. Occasionally they flicked their tails against flies. Most of them were the pure-black Garudan steeds with a few Percivons, Fellmonts, or Roan Blues mixed among the group.

"Aft'noon, Cap'n," said the stable head who stood near the corral's latched gate.

"Good afternoon, Mister Judge." Ash stopped for a moment so as not to appear rude.

Judge was a former Horseman of the West who had renounced his allegiance to Prince Rouchard after the defeat at the Battle of Border Field. Faced with the choice of execution or submission, he had pledged himself to Glëa po'Lon's service. From time to time, he sat in the honored seats at the Council of Lords and offered advice for the cavalry. Some found his foreign accent distracting, or unintelligible, but Ash secretly admired the fellow for refusing to alter his manner of speech. *Defeated but not defeated* was how Ash often thought of him. No one could challenge the plain fact Mister Judge knew everything that any man could know about the care and breeding of horses. Under his guidance, the royal stables thrived.

"Need your Fellmont mare saddled up, Doctor?" Mister Judge asked. "Going for a ride this late in the day?"

"No, thank you," Ash said. "I'm here for Teim.... uh, Captain Teimethee. Is he inside?"

"Yeah, he's saddling up with a squad of three, plus a carriage for a lady. Wouldn't say who." Mister Judge looked past Ash's shoulder and his face soured into a deep frown. "Oh, by th' blazes of the abyss, not *her*."

Ash glanced aside to see the footman page and Lady Thazin approaching the stables from the other side. "I think the carriage is meant for her. It's all very curious."

"Yeah, but it ain't my place to ask questions." Mister Judge leaned his elbows on the corral's railing. He returned his attention to the grazing horses.

Ash hurried forward to enter the stables at the opposite end. The barn doors were propped open like enormous shutters. Beneath the shadowy rafters, the paddocks reeked of horse manure, straw, leather, and unvarnished wood. It all blended into a scent that he found comforting and familiar.

Captain Teimethee was easy to spot from a distance. At a head taller than the other soldiers on his squad, he surpassed the withers of his Garudan steed. He was busy checking on the saddle's girth straps and lengthening the stirrups.

Lieutenant Kavin noticed him first. "Hey, Ashes, is that you? What're you doing here?"

"Heard you're taking Thazin out of my hair for a bit," Ash said. "Wanted to come thank you for a few days of peace. Hey, Teim."

Teimethee smiled broadly at Ash's approach. "Jealous we aren't taking you on the mission?"

"Mission? What mission?" Ash looked at the group of faces with disciplined yet slightly mischievous smiles. "What's on the order of the day?"

"We shouldn't say." Teimethee paused but could not restrain himself from blurting it out. "We're going up to the Great Northern Bay to collect His Majesty's intended bride."

"Up north, you say? I thought he was gonna pick one of the girls from Vilbyss or Browden house. Who is up north?"

"A great-granddaughter of King Tokustein's bastard half-sister," Teimethee said.

"I see," Ash said. "Sounds a bit thin, but royal blood is royal blood I suppose."

"Exactly."

"Why do you need Thazin?"

"To examine the girl's health, of course. Don't you know anything, bumpkin? We can't have a *man* touching a princess."

Ash forced a chuckle to join in the good-natured laughter of the squad. He served with Teimethee, Orlan, and Kavin for several years during the civil war. They all knew of his humble origins. Captain Teimethee was the only person who could call Ash a bumpkin and not raise his hackles.

From the opposite door, the footman page called out, "I brought her, sir!"

Ash backed away. "I'll avoid the hen-pecking, Teim. Don't mention I was here."

Teimethee lightly pushed at his shoulder. "Go on, you. Don't say anything about our mission, either. Can you keep it a secret?"

Ash laid his palm across his heart. "Certainly."

Chapter 16.

Ravel and her brother's group descended from the hills. After so long in the sparsely populated forestlands, even this cluster of cottages and sheds filled with barrels seemed like a bustling metropolis. The Tavern at the Crossroads was half a village dropped in the middle of nowhere. No homes. No farms. No craftsmen's shops or a lord's estate. Just enough structures occupied the intersection of wagon roads leading to the four compass points: the northern road from where they had come; the western road that became the Caravan Trail to the wild arid wastes of the Outerlands; the southern road that pointed to Lake Ward and the conquered domain of Ravel's vanquished Prince Rouchard; and the eastern road leading to the coastal shores and provinces of lords who had pledged loyalty to the victorious immortal king.

People moved about in every corner of her field of vision. They loitered to guzzle ale and chew into breadsticks. They worked to repair the axels on their wagons or clean the hooves of their mules, oxen, or fat-bellied goats. Somewhere, a blacksmith's hammer clanged onto an anvil. The scent of roasting venison wafted on the open air.

A stagnant muddy pond buzzed with flies and reeked of human waste. Nevertheless, the dirty water's eyes snarled at Ravel's passing.

Xidron noticed her flinch. More and more, with each day, he eyed her sideways as if she were a simmering pot of soup about to bubble over.

Candor gave out the assignments. "Prosper and I will inquire at the tavern about lodgings for the night. Redson and Stander, you'll keep watch over our belongings."

The two brothers nodded assent while standing at either side of the horse's neck. Stander rested a hand on his belt near the sheath of a knife.

"Xid, you may search for a horse trader and assess their stock but make no bargains or promises." Candor glanced aside at his sister and gave an unspoken order for her to accompany the southerner.

So, they split into three groups. Ravel walked with Xidron across the trampled, grassy space to a long roof propped up on stilts. The stable's walls were a haphazard mixture of rough-hewn boards and wicker screens. Wheelbarrows lay idle and stank of dung.

"Ho there, good of the day to you sir!" Xidron called into the shadows.

A man laughed heartily as he emerged into the clouded sunlight. "Mister Trinkets, is that you? Back so soon?"

He had the lilting accent of the northeast provinces and, predictably, showed no signs of having suffered after the war. The Iron King's legions of blackcoats had barely reached this far to the north and the lords of these provinces had capitulated without putting up a fight. This fellow's rotund belly, his well-cut leather boots, and coin purses sagging heavily off his belt marked him as a man who had only prospered in the years since Ravel's world had burned to the ground.

"Hello Karill," Xidron said with less enthusiasm.

"Who is your companion?" Karill smiled and his teeth were unusually clean.

"My name is Riven." She gave her alias just in case someone might recognize her name from the battlefields long ago. However, she made no effort to fake an accent; she spoke in the crisp diction of the Midlands and hoped this fellow would not look at her too closely for it.

"I'm sure it is." Karill winked at her as if sharing an unspoken secret. "Have no fear, Miss Riven, all are welcome. The tavern keeper allows no fighting here. It matters not which flag you once followed. In the mud, all dogs are brown."

Ravel averted her gaze to peer into the stable's mostly empty stalls. Her sights easily pierced the dim shadows. She saw a handful of mules, a pack goat, and a white donkey. The only horse was a Fellmont mare suitable for hauling a hay wagon. Any of them would serve to transport us, she thought while frowning at her brother's elitist foolishness.

Xidron said, "We're looking for horses.... Uh, steeds for riding and preferably Roan Blues. Do you know of any?"

"How many?"

"Six."

"I see." Karill stroked his bearded chin. He wore a silver band ring on his middle finger. "Young, sturdy horses for a long journey, eh? I've nothing in stock that would suit your friends, Mister Trinkets, but I can ask around. How long are you staying in town?"

Xidron shrugged. "At least for the night. Let me know in th' morning?"

"Verily I shall." Karill pointed to the fenced garden plot where a couple of lanky fellows stood guard at the gate. "Hasker's wagon is parked around the other side. She just came in a few days ago with a fresh stock of trinkets."

Xidron's eyes lit up with interest at the same time he scowled with indignation. "I've told you before, Karill, amulets are not trinkets. You'll be sorry, someday, when netherworld world demons and un-folk rise up to wreak havoc."

"I appreciate the warning." Karill laughed and turned his back on them both.

Ravel grasped the youth's elbow to restrain him from saying or doing anything rash. "Let's return to Candor and report—"

"Not yet." Xidron launched off at a brisk pace in the direction of the fenced garden. Ravel jogged a few quick steps to catch up with him.

For the first time, she gave more scrutiny to the youth's apparel. His left ear was pierced with a metal hoop that carried a single bead of onyx stone. Although his outer tunic was a plain rectangular shape belted at the waist, protective talismans were sewn to the garment by patches on the breast and sleeves. He wore an undershirt with an intricate pattern of symbols embroidered around the neckline. Several cord necklaces hung tucked into his shirt to conceal whatever additional pouches of enchanted items he wore close to his heart. Beneath the cuffs of his gloves, he wore several cord bracelets with carved beads. Ravel had never seen him remove his shirt, but now she wondered if he had the ink of sigils tattooed on his back as many southerners were rumored to have as protection against magical forces.

"Have you ever seen a demon or a... what did you call it? Un-folk?" she asked.

Xidron shot her a glance of affirmation. "My prince kept a bog blythe dwelling in the castle's moat. Some of us used to sit on the drawbridge over the waters and beg her to sing."

Ravel nodded as she recalled hearing such rumors years before of the Bastard Prince Tolljet's practices and her father's sensible dismissal of superstitious nonsense. *People can certainly learn to swim! It doesn't make them water-breathing mystical creatures.* In her ignorant youth, she had believed her father and laughed at such tales. Now, she knew better.

She said, "You understand that there are more fantastical things in this world than can be measured by the hands of men. Why don't you speak up when I argue with my brother? Why don't you help to explain that the Iron King is not a liar and pretender? He truly is the prince who sailed."

"Quiet your mouth!" Xidron ducked the passing attention of the garden gate. He sped up and Ravel hurried to follow.

"You believe in demons and magic," she insisted. "Do you believe that the king is immortal?"

"Yes," he said.

"Do you really?"

"Yes, I believe that is the body of the prince who sailed."

"But then why—"

Xidron set his course for a covered wagon parked at the rear of the tavern. A nearby ditch reeked of rotting garbage.

"Is it not obvious?" he said. "No man is immortal; therefore, he is not a man. What *thing* sits on the throne of Xol is no longer a pure blood prince. Glëa's body came back. His soul is forever lost at sea."

"How are you certain of what's inside a man's soul?" she asked.

"It is his actions that plainly demonstrate what a monster he has become. He made war upon his own brothers. My prince, and your prince, are both dead at his hands."

"They made war upon him, though. How much bloodshed could have been avoided if Glëa's brothers had welcomed him home?"

"My prince could not welcome what *thing* returned from forty years shipwrecked at sea. Prince Tolljet recognized that royal blood was contaminated by the unholy evil, the abomination that has poisoned him."

Ravel said, "What if there is a second soul inhabiting Glëa's flesh that is not an evil abomination? May I suggest it could be an ethereal being of crystal and silver—"

"Stop!" Xidron pointed to the center of her face. "Your questions betray the corruption of your thoughts."

"Where do you see corruption in a rational dialogue? I'm merely debating the counterpoint to your—"

"Do you deny that something unnatural has taken root in you?"

Ravel put a hand across the center of her chest. "It's a war wound."

"Do you think I'm a fool? That I don't see the signs? You don't sleep. You don't drink water. Your skin is turning into a jaundiced color." The youth's eyes narrowed sternly. "I was there at the siege of the Southern Palace. I saw the Usurper's squad of unholy spies in their scarlet hooded robes. I saw them climb the castle's walls by grasping the bricks with their fingernails. I saw the archers shoot them and they didn't die."

She reached out a sympathetic hand, but Xidron slapped her wrist away.

"I killed the magickers," she said. "You don't have to fear them coming back."

"How did they infect you?" he asked.

She opened the frog-and-loop buttons of her tunic's collar. Then she loosened the drawstring neckline of her undershirt. Slowly she drew aside the fabric with her fingertips just enough to expose a bit of her sternum. When the arrowhead tips of talons throbbed with joy at exposure to the air, she stopped. Ravel half closed her eyes and focused on breathing coolly in a steady rhythm. She gave him enough time to exclaim surprise and then re-fastened her clothing.

"I stole their power," she said. "But I am not them."

"Not yet. Your blood is contaminated by unnatural evils, but you've kept a sense of your humanity thus far. I can tolerate you for as long as you stand by Candor's side. I pity my friend Prosper for being your betrothed. How long will you continue to deceive him?"

"As long as necessary," she said. "Candor should have disclosed this to Prosper when he forced me into betrothal."

"Candor knows?"

"Yes, but I'm not sure how much he believes in their mystic properties. I think he's too delirious with rage and vengeance to care about the distinction between magic and the mundane."

"Then it's Prosper's fate to confront you on your wedding night, or deal with the half-demon spawn that you may someday produce. Not mine."

Ravel fell silent for she could not deny the truth of Xidron's words.

They approached the covered wagon. A few travelers formed a queue and leisurely examined the various wares displayed on a tarp on the ground.

"Hello, welcome friend." The wagon's owner was a woman of matronly age with gaunt cheeks and white hair tied up in a striped kerchief. A myriad of satchels and pouches hung from her belt or from shoulder straps, as if she carried on her body every precious object in her possession. Everything else was for sale.

"Mistress Harker, do you remember me?" Xidron smiled.

She stepped forth with open arms. "Of course, dear lad. A child of the House of Kthoss, if I recall."

Ravel flinched for the woman to openly speak the old name of a vanquished noble house, but none of the prospective customers turned their heads.

"Yes, yes, we are well met." Xidron pressed his hand across his heart in an honorific gesture. "Tell me, Mistress Harker, have you acquired a freshly blessed talisman?"

"Indeed, I have something very special that may interest you!" She walked to the tailgate of her wagon and reached into the clutter of boxes and burlap sacks. Her calloused hands, in frayed fingerless gloves, pulled out a varnished rosewood chest with brass hinges.

Ravel rested a hand on her hip. *Plundered from the burned ruins of some nobleman's house, no doubt.*

Harker opened the box to reveal not jewelry, not small articles of fine clothing, but a leather tube scrubbed clean of whatever heraldry had marked its rightful owner. She popped the cap off the tube and drew forth a parchment scroll.

"Oh, what is this?" Xidron received the parchment as tenderly as if she had handed him a newborn infant.

"The original writings of the First King's chief architect Brëalla Ulbannon, penned by her own hand."

Ravel looked over the youth's shoulder as he gingerly unrolled the crisp brown paper. To her eye, the letterings of ancient script were so sophisticated as to be unreadable.

"Ca-.... Cadent will love it! Won't he, uh, Riven?" Xidron's cheeks flushed, and his heartbeat quickened. "How much?"

"Thirty crown coins," Harker said.

Xidron's smile sagged at the corners.

The woman quickly added, "But for you, my dear friend, I can bear to part with it for just twenty-five."

Ravel said, "We should discuss it with my brother before we make a decision. He's more of a scholar and would know the value."

"Of course, you're free to go off and discuss it amongst yourselves. You're an honest lad and a good friend, so of course, I prefer that it goes to you. But you should know that I've had several other interested parties make inquiries. The longer you wait, it might not be here."

Xidron pulled his coin purse off his belt. He counted out twenty-five silver coins stamped with a bull's head. It left him with only two more silver crowns, a few copper rings, and a smattering of pewter squares.

Harker smiled with satisfaction as she repacked the scroll into its leather tube. "Your master will be much pleased, my friend."

"Thank you, Harker. Thank you!" Xidron tugged at Ravel's sleeve. "Come, let us go and show this to the others!"

Ravel trotted with him, following the footpath circling around from the rear of the tavern to its front steps. Uneasiness dragged at her sluggish feet. The transaction had gone so quickly that she could not articulate why she did not share the youth's excitement.

Candor, Prosper, and the two brothers occupied the best seats on the rug by an enormous fireplace. The hearth bricks and the chimney stones occupied most of the north-facing wall. Each of the youths held a stoneware bowl on their laps. They chewed heartily into roasted drumsticks of quail or fowl, patties of flatbread, sliced radishes, and shreds of purple cabbage. Flagons of ale rested at their feet.

Xidron jumped eagerly into the circle. "Look what I bought!"

"Did you secure horses?" Candor used a linen kerchief from his own pocket to wipe his mouth.

"Not yet. Karill is asking around. But look!" Xidron uncapped the leather tube and showed the scroll to Candor in the firelight.

Ravel's stomach gurgled in revulsion at the stench of cooked meat and vegetables. Nausea was so strong that the bile gagged her throat, and she could not speak.

Candor wiped his hands before gingerly taking hold of the scroll's edges.

Prosper informed them, "We've secured two upstairs rooms for the night and vouchers for a turn at the men's bath house. Apologies, my dearest beloved, but there is no public bath house for women."

She crouched forward with a hand pressed over her chest. The talons throbbed at her breastbone, eager to be released into the firelight. *Stop, stop,* she told them as if a team of skittish horses tugged at their harnesses.

Candor tossed the scroll into the blazing fire. "How much did you pay for this garbage?"

"Are you addled in the head!" Xidron took one step towards the flaming logs but could get no closer.

"It was obviously a cheap fake. You were swindled." Candor gulped from his flagon of ale.

"No, no," Xidron insisted. "Harker's a friend of mine. I've purchased many valuable, um, items from her many times before."

Stander snickered and his brother Redson joined in. "Junk jewelry, you mean? Beads of river pebbles and knotted cords that protect you from a wraith of the shadows sucking out your soul as you sleep?"

Ravel said hoarsely, "You shouldn't have burned it, if you're going to ask for Xid's money back."

"I spent twenty-five crowns!"

Candor stood up close to the youth's face. "Are you daft, man? I spent half that sum on our lodgings, meals and a bath."

Xidron turned aside and lowered his head. "I thought—"

"Show me this swindler."

Just the three of them went outside. Xidron led the way to the wagon parked behind the tavern. Twilight was coming. Moonlight leeched the world of its daylight colors. The traveling peddler had packed up their wares for the night. The wagon's lone occupant cooked supper in a small cauldron suspended over a campfire on the ground.

"You!" Candor barked. "Are you the peddler of fake copies of old scrolls?"

Harker made a painful effort to rise to her feet and turn around. She had braced herself with an expression of righteous indignation. "See here, who are you to challenge the authenticity of my artifacts? Are you a scholar? I think not! Show me, young man, what errors you claim to have found."

Candor stopped. His demeanor changed. His outrage drained away and he stood, mouth agape, staring at the woman's face. Ravel smelled the abrupt shift in her brother's bodily scent.

Xidron said, "He burned it."

The woman raised her arms. "Why did you burn it?"

"It was a sloppy forgery," Candor said gently. "I'm surprised that you didn't do a better job of it, knowing your penmanship skills."

She squinted against the smoke wafting off the campfire. "Do I know you, young man?"

"Yes," he said. "Years ago, you were apprenticed to the esteemed archivist Lady Leianna who gave me shelter after.... after..."

Her eyes widened in recognition. "Do I see before me the orphaned little lord? Is it really you, Moppy?"

Even in the dark, Ravel saw him blush. The other boys chuckled and nudged each other, repeating, "Moppy?" in a teasing sing-song.

"You've grown so tall!" Harker reached up to Candor's dimpled cheeks. He held still to allow her touch.

"You seem to have shrunk." Tears twinkled at the corners of Candor's eyes.

Ravel stared in wonderment at the sight of her brother fighting the urge to weep. Of course, she realized. He had taken refuge with a hermit archivist and must have become acquainted with any number of itinerant scholars.

Harker lowered her hands to her belt where several drawstring coin purses dangled. "I'm sorry that I asked such a dear price of your friend. Times are hard, Moppy, as you well know."

"I know," said Candor.

She began to weep. Her small shoulders folded inward and rounded her back. "Please forgive me, young sir. Mistress Leianna sold our entire stock of manuscripts to the royal library more than four years ago. We had to eat, and we can't eat books. I disapproved of her decision and thus we parted ways. Recently, out of desperation, I've reproduced a few selections entirely from memory. The purses of uneducated eyes have gotten me this far. You're the first to expose my deception. I'm sorry. I'm so very sorry."

Candor waved at her to stop the motions of untying her coin purse. "Keep the money."

"Sir?" the woman exclaimed.

Xidron looked aside in surprise.

"Shed your despair and seek hope in a new day," Candor said. "Just as your deception was brought to the light, so will the truth of all things be made plain for all to see. Now, go forth with a clear and honorable heart. Make ye deceptions no more."

"Milord." Harker bowed from the hip and remained bent over until Candor chose to walk away.

Ravel exhaled the tight, burning sensation in her chest and thought, *Here is my noble brother. Here is the heir to our noble house that I have fought and sacrificed my entire life to protect.* Clearly the woman was a homeless refugee. She lived out of this wagon. Every valuable thing she owned hung from her belt. Women in these days had few choices outside of prostitution. Even her forgery had an air of virtue.

As the three strolled back to the tavern's front door, Ravel wondered if she had made a mistake keeping him isolated for so many years. His body was protected but his soul had festered in grievances. This incident surely reminded him of the tender-hearted youth he had once been and could be once again. If he could grant forgiveness to this former-archivist-turned-vagabond-swindler, he could be persuaded to forgo his quest for vengeance.

Chapter 17.

More days passed traveling southward on the King's Royal Highway, each day like a bead on a string following the same routine. At sunrise, the young men arose from their sleeping mats. Ravel did not sleep but pretended to awaken with the others. They tended to the necessities, broke camp, loaded up the horse, and started walking. Except for brief rest breaks, they continued until dusk. Redson's arrows never failed to find small game to roast. Stander's knife and a tinderbox never failed to start a fire. Xidron did the dirty work of caring for the horse's needs. Prosper showed the most adept skills at setting up bedrolls and tarps; clearly he had spent more years in a battalion's field tent than in a lord's estate. Candor checked his maps and compass by the firelight each night before lying down to sleep.

Air cooled as the autumn days waned late in the season. This used to be Ravel's favorite time of year when the harvesters had stripped the fields and filled the silos with grain. Mother had known the best way to grill winter squash and glaze it with butter. Father drank cups of honey-mead by the fireside and recited tales of ancient, fantastical legends. Candor had been a fidgety toddler who could not sit still except for their father's deep, storytelling voice.

On the air rang the age-old songs that Ravel remembered hearing in her youth. *Hey-yo, hey-yo, bring the hay bale, yo.* For a moment, decades melted away and she was a child, again, reclining on the veranda of her own home to listen to the workmen singing in the fields. If they were to turn westward and journey over that ridge of bread loaf hills, they could discover the vacant plot of burned soil where their home once stood.

"How dare these farmers be happy." Candor picked up a rock from the roadside and pitched it upwards, as if aiming his rage at the clouds.

"Indeed," Prosper said.

"Ignorant fools," Xidron added.

Candor said, "They till the land and reap a harvest that will go to the grain silos of the Pretender's undeserving, traitorous lords. How dare they be singing in rhythm with their sickles as if nothing has happened."

"People just want to live and eat," Ravel said. "They don't think about which flag's colors fly atop a distant castle somewhere."

"They should," Candor said. "They will."

Early one morning, Ravel nudged her brother's shoulder to awaken him. She carried a handful of ripe black figs on an improvised plate of sycamore bark. All night long, she had prowled the fern bushes and rocky gorges to find a wild fig tree dropping its fruit to waste on the ground.

He groaned and mumbled something but kept his eyes closed.

"Wake up, Der."

He rolled onto his back and looked up at her kneeling beside him. "Is something amiss?"

"Nothing's wrong." She smiled to offer the figs. "It's a day to celebrate. Felicitations on the anniversary of your birth."

"Oh." Candor sat upright and crossed his ankles. He glanced at the others who were still asleep. The five youths shared a mattress of dry leaves and blankets. Nothing but a canvas tarp strapped between a pair of tree trunks served as a roof.

"Our ancestors' spirits are smiling upon you," she said. "You're seventeen today!"

"I turned seventeen three days ago."

Ravel blinked. "How's that again? Isn't this the twenty-first?"

"No." In the dim of pre-dawn twilight, his face softened. He looked at her gently with sad sympathy. "It's the twenty-fourth."

Ravel looked up to the fading constellations. Indeed, the South Star had moved across the tip of the waning gibbous moon. "Why didn't you say something earlier?"

"I marked the day in the logbook. Then I turned the page. I'm a grown man, now. I don't need childish treats or songs or games." Candor took the figs into his own hands. Biting one in half, he nodded approval. "These are quite tasty, though. Thank you for gathering them, Sister."

"Felicitations of the day."

Ravel pecked a kiss to his cheek near the corner of his eye. Candor abruptly turned his face away. She could only see the back of his head, but she knew that he was frowning. Rules of proprietary, that she thought long discarded, came to her mind. Sisters should not kiss their brothers once they reach the age of awareness, much less when a sister was betrothed to be married. Yet here they sat on the grass with no roof over their heads. She wondered if the etiquette of bygone days still mattered; apparently, to her brother, it did.

Prosper opened his eyes. Seeing them, he rose up on his elbow. "What's wrong?"

"She thinks today is my birthday."

"But that was three days ago." Prosper snorted disdain. "It's a good thing you're the one keeping accurate logbooks of our journey."

Perhaps her brother might have said something in her defense, but while Prosper was speaking he had chomped into the second half of the fig. A lord did not converse with food in his mouth. Candor wagged his head in either assent or disapproval. His attention divided between his sister, his friend, and the ripe figs in the palm of his hand.

Ravel rocked back on her heels and straightened herself into standing over them. "It was a simple mistake after traveling for so many uneventful days. I've got my bearings, now."

"Out of the mistake came a serendipitous discovery." Candor offered to share the handful of black figs. "Look what she found! They're delicious."

She moved away from the tent. Dawn brightened the sky although she could only see patches of blue amidst the leafless branches. Ravel kneeled at the circle of cold stones to start working on the fire. She used Prosper's tinderbox to strike up a spark with a knife and a chip of flint. Patiently, she fed scraps of bark chips and dry moss to the blossoming flames. She held her cloak tightly around herself, pretending to be cold, to shield the hungry talons from the brightness of glowing flames.

Prosper turned a sideways stare in her direction. His frown like a theater mask portrayed the visage of pure disappointment. Ravel understood that she had lost a few points of credibility, yet she felt no stirrings of embarrassment or shame. She had no urge to make any effort to win back his approval or respect. If she ever had it to begin with.

Larger twigs and sticks fed the fire. Flames grew and crackled. Embers floated up in the smoke, twinkled orange, and vanished.

During the day, Candor and his companions were not amenable to conversation while walking. The only time that Ravel could speak to them at length was in the evening after they had eaten supper. While the camp's firelight turned the youths into monochrome figures of brown and black, she took her opportunity to reminisce about happier times of long ago. Each night, as their eyelids drooped and the campfire dwindled, she hoped that her words would spark a realization in their minds of what tender-hearted youths they still were. Perhaps their minds would turn from the foolishness and insanity of their quest.

"Remember that summer, Candor, when our family travelled to this valley to pay tidings to Lord Wirhygger on the birth of his son and heir? You sampled their orchard and exclaimed how they tasted like three apples in one: on the first bite, a red crisp; on the second bite, a golden dew; and in the center was a core of honey nectar. Everyone was so amused at your clever description that henceforth the fruits of Wirhygger's orchard came to be called the Three-Flavor Apples."

"I don't remember ever being in this region before," Candor said.

Ravel added, "You would have been, um, in your seventh year."

"Which made you eighteen at the time?"

"Yes."

"Why did Father bring you along?" Candor asked. "Your age made you unsuitable as a match for Lord Wirhygger's newborn son and heir. Were you introduced to other suitors along the way?"

Taken aback by his question, Ravel searched her memory for the answer. "I spent five weeks in martial training with Lord Wirhygger's master of pole-staff, halberd, and lance. While you ate apples, I practiced impaling hay bales."

Prosper rose to speak solemnly. "The House of Wirhygger is no more. This very ground is stained with their blood. Speak not the names of those who haunt these meadows if it is not to pledge revenge."

"Blackcoat scum.... Butchers.... Ravagers...." The young men grumbled amongst themselves.

Ravel's hopes sank little by little with each passing night. The more she retold the stories of her brother's childhood, the more it became apparent that they did not share the same memories. Not only did the ten-year age difference set them apart, but from the cradle they were each assigned different roles in life. Candor's destiny was to be educated and groomed as the heir to their noble name. Ravel was merely a stand-in at Father's side until her brother grew old enough to take his rightful place. She was always a temporary fixture meant to step aside and become a Lady of the House once her brother came of age. It was never intended for them to share the same space at the same time; they were never meant to be truly brother and sister at all.

Chapter 18.

They continued walking on the southward branch of the King's Royal Highway. Ravel observed their course and asked one night, "Why not go due east, from here, and reach the coast? We might pick up more sympathizers from lesser lords in the fringe provinces who eluded the Iron King's wrath by staying neutral. They can be persuaded to join your cause if they are unhappy with the current state of affairs?"

Candor said, "No, we do not risk the quest in the uncertainty of seeking out allies who may or may not join our cause. We stay on course straight and true. We will retrace the steps of our defeated prince. We will walk the battle fields that once were soaked in blood. At the ruins of the Fortress of Sharp Crag, we turn eastward and not before."

Sharp Crag.... Her memory of the fortress was a cluster of gray stone cylinders that crowned the peak of a rocky promontory. The distinctive shape of the landscape was of a giant's fist punching out of the earth from below. Once the perfect place for an impenetrable fortress, it was breached by Glëa po'Lon's forces. Defeat at Sharp Crag was just one of many in a string of defeats leading up to the Battle of Border Field when everything ended.

"There, there!" Xidron pointed beyond the next grassy rise to a massive slab of rock jutting out of the meadowlands. "I see the Fortress of Sharp Crag!"

The youths whooped and clapped their hands. Only Ravel stood unmoved as memories roared into her thoughts like a storm.

She half-closed her eyes against the harsh glare of autumn's sunlight. The weather on this day was very much like another day years ago. Calendar days melted away in her mind. Ravel felt as if only an hour had passed since she witnessed the siege when the mighty walls fell. Only a handful of bodyguards were charged with the task of sneaking Prince Rouchard out secret passages and fleeing to safety. What fools they were to feel victorious in defeat. Their prince had survived to regroup and fight another day. The blackcoat legions had toppled the towers, smashed the roofs, and slaughtered everyone to the last. What had not burned or shattered, the victors packed up and carted away. When nothing of value was left to plunder, the blackcoats threw livestock carcasses into the cistern to poison the waters. They left the dead defenders to rot where they lay.

"If the crud-coats haven't completely ravaged the place," Candor said to the group. "The ruins should have some storage of supplies we can use: fresh clothes, tools, or weapons."

"Food?" Prosper asked.

Xidron lightly punched his friend's shoulder. "Not after six years, Pross! Think! Even dry beans will surely be rancid by now."

On approach, Ravel imagined that she could smell the blood of the slain in the soil. Candor led the way up the wagon road that the conquering army had left mostly intact. After all, they needed a working road to carry away the plunder. *Clop-de-clop* the horseshoes of Xidron's plough horse sounded dull on limestone brick, a sound as close to civilization as any she had heard in years.

The Fortress of Sharp Crag had long been reduced to a heap of rubble by catapult loads of flammable tar. A new addition to the sloping hillside had been created where once vertical walls had loomed. Ravel knew the place well from those days when she had worn a uniform of cerulean and cream, when flags of indigo had fluttered at the towers, when guards loyal to Prince Rouchard had stood sentinel at the gate. Now, six years later, she could not discern where the once impregnable gateway had been. Fallen palisades had flattened from wood rot. The bridge was gone, but it no longer mattered; alluvial mud had filled in the moat.

Enough of the fortress's southern battlements stood that one could almost call it a wall. Tenacious weeds sprouted in the crevasses, lending a surreal sense of peacefulness to the sprawling disaster of shattered bricks. Raspberry bushes sprawled out of control, picked clean of their fruits by rodents and birds.

"We're near the quartermaster's vegetable garden," Ravel said. "We grew beans, squash, radishes, and carrots. We kept rabbits and chickens in stacked cages. We kept plump fish in ponds. We had food. We had clean well water. We had pride. We felt so confident that we could outlast a siege for years."

The afternoon sun illuminated the inside of the courtyard and whatever remained of any structure. Ravel's eyes scanned over the collapsed rooftops of toppled barracks and armories, the horse stables, the lord's dining hall, and the scattered bricks of a free-standing well. She remembered laughing in camaraderie with those in uniforms of pale blue. They had scoffed at the advance of the Pretender's army. *No man is immortal. Truth shall win out.* They shared a haughty confidence that they would fight and never lose.

Xidron said, "But you didn't plan for *him*, or them who served him."

"The Pretender's spies slipped inside a sally door and placed grenades at the gatehouse," said Prosper.

Candor added, "All the old castles and fortresses have secret passageways: at Lake Ward, at the Well of the Green Forest, at Prince Tolljet's South Sea Palace, and at Xolhold Keep the oldest of all."

Ravel looked aside to her brother's satchel and thought of the parchment maps in his collection. She sighed deeply at the obvious conclusion. Talons tugged her scarred skin.

"No, no," she groaned. "You've been collecting architectural schematics from archivists and lost libraries. That's why Xidron purchased a scroll from that traveler as a gift for you."

He shrugged. "The Guild of Architects has records going back a thousand years."

"Is that your foolish plan? To sneak into Xolhold Keep by some long-forgotten bricked up passageway?"

Candor smirked with the pleasure of holding his secret. "You'll see."

"You foolish boy! The king knows every crack in every brick of his home palace."

"No!" Candor raised his chin and shouted at the clouds. "He is a pretender and a liar and a false imposter! Those who follow him are deluded fools! I will never believe that the foppish youth who sits on the throne is Glëa po'Lon the Prince Who Sailed on the Doomed Voyage to the Deep Sea."

"But what if—"

"He can't be! He can't. If he were, he would not have made war against his own flesh-and-blood brothers. Our blessed Prince Rouchard looked into his eyes and denied him. Remember?"

Ravel nodded; she remembered. *That is not my brother*, a quote from their prince, was repeated in a chant throughout the battle camps.

"If anyone would know the truth, wouldn't it be our prince?"

"Der, listen to me. Do you remember that day when I found you taking refuge at that archivist's cottage? Barely five months had passed since the Battle of Border Field, and yet, you did not recognize me. You screamed at the sight of me and ran to hide behind her skirts."

Candor narrowed his eyes. "No, I didn't."

The other youths exchanged curious glances. Ravel did not care for her brother's pride or for their opinions. The truth was the truth, and if a Pragmatist could not face facts, then he was a delusional fool.

"Yes, you did. After only a few months, you did not recognize my face. Think, Der. Think! How might it be if forty-five years had passed, and if by some miracle I was rendered immortal and had not aged a day. Would you know me then?"

"Must admit," said Xidron. "She's making sense there. Maybe you should listen to her—"

"Discussion ended!" Candor entered an archway to a mostly intact tower. Its door had been battered off its hinges. "Let's find a secure place to bed for the night. Reds? Stan? Go scavenge for firewood. Pross'? You're on water. Xid, tend the horse."

The youths obeyed their lord. They scattered like sparrows.

Ravel continued in her brother's dusty footprints. Sunlight beams pierced through narrow archer's windows. She followed him through sharp bars of light and dark, light and dark. Though she could have hopped two steps and seized his shoulders, he felt eternally outside of reach.

"Would you care to come with me, my beloved?" Prosper asked. "To look for water?"

She slowed her pace, letting her brother go farther ahead to check the stairwell. Was her betrothed intuitive enough to sense her mood, she wondered, or was he simply being practical.

"There's a well pump in the bath house," she told him. "This way."

Ravel led the way. Her boots crunched in gritty rubble where she had once patrolled cleanly swept ramparts.

"I'm sorry he was so rude to you," Prosper said. "It's not right, the way he speaks to you. Even if he is your brother, he's behaving ungraciously. I shall say something, the next time it happens."

"He's the lord of my household," Ravel shrugged. "What can you say?"

"But you're my wife, now." Prosper slid a hand up the nape of her neck. His tender touch froze her in her tracks and turned her around.

She paused at the threshold of the bath house where she once had embraced a fellow captain. Years ago, she had sneaked a deep, lazy kiss on this very spot. She had shared a private soak together at a late hour on the night before the siege began. In each other's arms they had shared passion if not love. Here she had paused to drink one last pleasant moment of another's soap-scented lips. Here for one candlelit moment was the last time she had ever felt completely satisfied, at ease, and happy.

A brown smear on the wall marked the spot where someone's blood had sprayed. Memories of death crushed sweeter thoughts. Corpses had sprawled in the hallway where she stood. More had littered the stairs where she had just ascended. Blood had darkened the waters of the bath basin. Names of the dead bubbled up in her mind: Valiant... Garland... Constance... Surety... Clover... Boone... She gritted her teeth against the urge to wail and scream. Her hands balled into fists as if she still held a spear.

Prosper embraced her tightly in his arms. Ravel leaned on his chest for a long, quiet moment inhaling his grass-scented coat.

"Don't... Pross', please, don't pity me."

"You were here, weren't you," he said without a hint of question. "You were right here, when the walls fell."

One more kind word from him and the last of her composure would shatter. Ravel clenched her jaw and could not speak.

"We'll take revenge for all of them," he said while stroking her back. "We'll put their restless angry spirits to rest in peace. You'll see, when the Pretender's head is mounted on a spike, the ghosts of these honored dead will cheer so that Heaven itself will echo the song."

Ravel closed her burning eyes that were incapable of shedding tears. She felt too weary to argue anymore.

Chapter 19.

Stander took first watch duty. He promised to awaken his twin brother Redson for the second watch when the moon crossed to the next broken window. He assumed his position standing at the lopsided, broken section of the archer's perch. He drew his pair of long daggers and began his routine of flexing and twirling the blades in his hands. He was good, Ravel had to admit. Probably spent a lot of lonely hours practicing stabbing imaginary opponents.

Ravel bedded down with Prosper, sharing a blanket but little else. Tonight, he did not even kiss her. Perhaps he felt self-conscious that a thousand ghosts of slaughtered defenders were watching.

In the purity of darkness, Ravel's eyes came a-light with a colorless hue. As the hours wore on, she did not sleep. She watched Xidron snoring like a horse. Redson in exasperation pinched the boy's nose to turn him over. She felt Prosper's breathing in a steady rhythm at the nape of her neck.

Candor's face in the depths of slumber was free of the grim determination that furrowed his brow by day. Still beardless, still at that age where his features kept an androgynous boyish quality, he looked like their mother except for the walnut bulge at his throat. He murmured in his sleep, "*Oh-ah-ee-na-so-wey-to*," a mnemonic for remembering the proper order of the phonetic syllables of the classical script. Ravel listened to him recite his lessons in his dreams. It used to be so important to remember the proper order of one's letters, to scribe verses in straight rows on the page, to hold a writing brush with one's second and third fingers just so. His young mind was full of what he used to be.

Night passed. Hours fell away. The sky brightened with the coming dawn. Ravel watched the shadows change color from purple to blue to orange. She waited for the others to awaken. She waited lying on her back, pretending to be asleep. Her left hand rested over the black claws embedded at the center of her chest.

Voices nattered outside. Horse hooves clop-clopped on the flagstones.

Ravel sat up.

Stander dozed at the archer's window with his arms loosely crossed over his lap. Of course, he had failed to stay alert until the next guard's shift. *The colonel would have dealt you a lashing for dereliction of duty.*

Under the cover of broken walls, Ravel peered down at the southeast yard. Nothing but moss-covered timber remained of the armory and the quartermaster's storage sheds. The fortress's yard formed a stadium of rubble, pebbles, and cracked stone.

Riders led a group of laborers uphill from the grassy meadows of the countryside. Although they carried swords and bullwhips, they were not in uniforms. They wore hooded cloaks of brown wool. Their linen tunics were colored gray or green. Their horses were a mixed lot of Saddlebreds, Chap-Trotters, and Bay Pacers in various hues of chestnut and brown. They were certainly not the mighty black Garudan steeds of the Iron King's cavalry but nonetheless showed the grace and poise of quality training.

Three in front, she whispered in her mind. *Five alongside the wagons. Three bringing up the rear. Military escort standard formations, but those are not quartermaster's wagons.*

Oxen pulled a line of sturdy but empty wagons. Laborers walked alongside the rolling wheels. They carried spades, pickaxes, and burlap satchels on their backs. About two dozen laborers appeared to be neither happy nor miserable. They did not sing with joy, as farmers at harvest time, nor did their spirits groan under the yoke of oppression. Simply they were coming to do a job. Judging from their well-aligned formation, this was not their first day.

Ravel squinted into the meadowlands beyond the base of the rocky promontory. Wisps of cooking fires threaded up to the sky. The odors of bread and grilled meat carried on the morning air. Clearly, more of them were encamped on the southern side of the fortress. Ravel and her brother's friends had not seen them by approaching from the north.

She lowered her eyes in shame. The first rule before setting up a field camp was to scout the surrounding area and secure the perimeter. *Forgive me, Father; I got sloppy.*

Three riders dismounted at the base of the cracked tower where Ravel crouched. If she were to spit, it would land on a man's cap. Apparently the leader, he tooted a small whistle to attract everyone's attention.

Redson woke up from his bedroll. "What's that?"

"Hush." Ravel waved her hand to signal him.

The youth grabbed his bow and quiver. He scurried across the dusty floor to join her. "Crud coats?" he whispered.

"No."

The leader called out orders for the day. "Wagons One and Two, start at the wall and clear the rubble up to here. Wagons Three and Four, start at the base of this tower and load up the rubble to this line here. Rock cutters? Get moving, go on! Find the blocks that are too large to haul and get busy chopping them down to size."

Tools came out. The men wearing straw hats got to work.

The dismounted riders unpacked tools of a different sort. Precision instruments were made of steel and brass, silk cord and glass. *Surveyors!* The word came to Ravel's mind with a rush of strong emotions that she could not name. Envy? Nostalgia? Astonishment? Indignation? She only felt her heartbeat quicken. Her cheeks flushed at the sight of a legion who had come to build rather than to kill.

Surveyors carried measuring rods of various lengths along with gauges, sextants, compasses, water tubes, and the prize invention of the Masonry Guild: the eye-mark. It was a tall pole topped with crossbars from which dangled four silken cords. Plumb bobs weighed the ends of the cords so that they hung perfectly straight. With that tool, one could mark the foundations of a four-story tower that would stand for a thousand years.

Redson shook his twin brother awake. Stander snorted out of slumber and nearly fell off his perch. Clumsily, he tumbled backwards into the chamber.

The lead surveyor looked up at the commotion.

She ducked to hide behind the wedge of broken bricks. Waving her hands, she motioned sharply for them to be quiet.

On hands and knees, the twin brothers shook the other boys awake. In whispers, they reported what was happening. "Surveyors... Masons... A team of laborers.... Clearing rubble.... Taking measurements to rebuild...."

Candor sat up rubbing his eyes. "Do they have horses?"

"Yes," Redson said through a grin.

Voices outside shouted an alarm. "Whose horse is this!"

Prosper swatted Xidron on the shoulder. "Where did you tether Kips for the night?"

"Uhh...." Xidron sat up groggily. He had slept with his feet turned in the opposite direction than his comrades for superstitious reasons. It had something to do with compass points. He rose with his back to them all. For a long moment, he stared at the shadows on the stone wall and struggled to get his bearings.

"Th' blazes." Ravel sprang to her feet. "Stay here, all of you. I'll tell them I'm alone."

She rushed down the stairwell to the ground floor. No time to construct a believable story in her mind, she resolved to follow her training. If caught behind enemy lines, give up nothing but your life in defense of your lord and prince.

One surveyor walked into the dim chamber to join the handful of laborers. They were examining the plough horse tethered to a broken timber. Foodstuffs and supplies enough for several people lay on the stones, but thankfully the bedrolls were upstairs.

Ravel opened her hands in a gesture of peaceful greeting. "Good of the morning to you, sir. Forgive me if I'm trespassing but, you see, I'm on a journey southward and sought shelter for the night."

"Pack your things and move along, ye wench."

She inclined her head respectfully. "Yes sir. Right away, sir. Thank you, sir."

Laborers with tools in hand shuffled back outside. The head surveyor glanced back over his shoulder at her, one last time, before he stepped out to the morning light.

An arrow streaked down from the archer's slit window above. It snagged in the surveyor's cloak. "What!"

Two knives glinted, twirling in mid-air. One blade found its mark grazing another surveyor's right shoulder. He cried out, hunched over, but remained on his feet.

Idiots! Ravel rushed to meet the targeted men in the bright sunlight of morning. Blood's odor wafting from the knife wound sent a rush of dizziness to her mind. Her stomach growled hunger. Saliva that tasted of rancid oil filled her mouth. For a moment, she could not move.

Laborers cried out in panic. They ducked for shelter behind or underneath the wagons. A handful of surveyors joined them in taking cover. The rest drew their swords and used their capes as flowing shields. One more arrow flew and snagged harmlessly in a panel of wool. All eyes turned up to the archers' windows on the second floor of the cracked tower.

"Two upstairs!" The head surveyor charged Ravel with his sword drawn. "I've got this one."

She grabbed a rock and hurled it at the man's face. He quickly ducked. By the time she bent over for another stone, he reached her. Nothing but bare hands, she side-stepped his long blade's thrust. Ravel plunged in close and grabbed his wrist. She used the man's own momentum to sweep his legs out from under him.

The surveyor tumbled onto his back. She stepped on his wrist so that he could no longer raise his sword.

Instead, the man drew a dagger and stabbed her in the outer thigh. His well-aimed blade pierced the large artery in her leg.

Ravel's blackish purple blood squirted into the man's face. A foul odor worse than tar-oil in a garbage fire wafted out of the wound. He spat what was in his mouth. His eyes widened in surprise. "What sort of un-folk are you?"

"I'm not..." She snatched the dagger out of his left hand. Then she kicked the sword's hilt out of his grip.

Meanwhile the other surveyors were rushing into the cracked tower. Ravel hopped away from the fallen man, ready to charge after those nine to defend her brother. Then she saw them and halted in mid-step.

Candor, Xidron, and Prosper were already outside. They had exited from the back of the tower. They sneaked around the outskirts of the wall to where the surveyors had left their saddled horses tethered in a neat row. Each youth grabbed the reins of two horses and led the docile animals away.

Diversion. Distraction. What the youths lacked in marksmanship, they made up for in strategy. Ravel trusted that the twin brothers would escape the upstairs room before the surveyors' swords found them.

Laborers threw rocks at her. Their aim was true. Stones pounded her thighs, her buttocks, and her back. Ravel raised her arm to shield her face. One rock hit the back of her head, and she heard her skull crack. Cold blood leaked down the back of her neck. She staggered but did not drop. A haze of purple and magenta clouded her sights. Talons pulsed at her chest. Heat prickled her skin as if she faced a roaring fireplace. Bile and sour blood filled her mouth. But the more rocks that struck her, the stronger she felt.

Voices called from the archer's window. "They got away! Split up.... Give chase. Go!"

Only four surveyors emerged from the archway. The other five must have pursued another exit to the rear of the tower.

Ravel snarled as she rotated to face the men. Rocks continued to pelt her, but she only grunted at each impact. The dent in her skull resealed itself, again and again, each time a stone hit her head. Blackish purple blood soaked her clothes, but the wounds themselves healed as quickly as sand flowing into a hole. At the center of her chest, the unnatural energy of the claws glowed as hot as a ceramic lantern.

"She's not going down," they cried to each other. "Why won't she go down?"

"What is she?"

Four men shoulder to shoulder formed a line. Swords drawn, they hesitated to rush at her. By now they had seen the ineffectiveness of weapons or rocks. Wide-eyed, they dared not attack.

Her hands curled as talons. She growled, baring her teeth. The line of men took a collective step backwards. Their fear smelled like bacon sizzling on a skillet. *Meat... Meat... Meat....* Ravel strained to resist the urge to chew into their faces and slurp the juicy brains out of their skulls.

Distant sounds of galloping horse hooves pulled her thoughts back to herself. Candor and his friends were making their escape. She faced a choice of whether to stand her ground and kill.

I am not a monster. I am not a monster! Ravel dropped the dagger.

She ran away from the hailstorm of bricks and rocks. Arms pumped and her feet kicked away the earth. She leaped through the blocks of shattered walls and kept running. She bounded downhill over the rough terrain. Morning dew held water spirits that screamed and clawed at her calves like running through a patch of thorns. Ravel ran faster chasing after the mounted youths who galloped at full speed into the meadowlands.

Chapter 20.

Ravel soon lost sight of her brother's horse galloping. As fast as she could run with her elbows pumping and her legs as pistons pounding into the soil, the horses streaked farther ahead. She stopped at a fork in the gravelly road to consider which path they may have taken.

One quick glance over her shoulder confirmed that the surveyor crew restrained from pursuit. Not only had the youths taken most of their horses, but they had witnessed her fighting skills and the unnatural color of her blood. Their most sensible course of action would be to retreat and inform their nearest superiors.

Would Candor have gone to attack the base camp, she wondered. Would they feel bold enough or foolish enough to begin their uprising in the encampment of architects and stone masons? By setting fire to schematics and ledger books, would they seek the thrill of righteous conquest?

Ravel turned to face eastward and scanned the meadowlands speckled with clusters of oak trees. Low rolling hills textured the familiar, grassy landscape. Years ago, she had stood in this same spot and marked notes on her map for devising battle strategies. A junior foot solder had once compared it to a knitted blanket crafted by an amateur who lost all sense of pattern or texture. The others in the squad had laughed and ridiculed the footman for being more of a poet than a soldier.

That's what Candor is meant to be, she thought. *More poet than soldier. Not as I am.*

She half-closed her eyes and focused inwardly on her breath: drawing air in to fill her lungs, then slowly allowing an exhale to seep out of her. Again and again, her chest rose and fell like a bird's wings pumping higher and higher. She called up thoughts of her little brother—the only thing that mattered right now. She remembered going upstairs to her mother's room and holding the bundle in her arms for the first time; she had been afraid of dropping him, he had cried, and she passed him off to the nursemaid. She remembered the first time he had toddled up behind her and punched her in the leg, for no reason at all. She remembered sharing fresh peaches with him, or bunches of tart grapes, and carving a holiday rack of lamb as he watched with hungry eyes. She remembered fearing him dead after the Battle of Border Field, searching for him through all her mystical adventures, and their reunion at the end. She remembered him sleeping in the rickety hut by the Great Northern Bay, and she remembered him coercing her into marriage for the honor of their household name. His childish eyes... his sorrowful eyes... his tyrannical eyes...

The talons pulsed to the rhythm of her memories. Skin at her chest itched and tugged in a certain direction.

Ravel used the tug of the claws as a compass and set off jogging. She scrambled up and over granite boulders. Her feet chewed into the grassy inclines to reach the tops of hills. On the downslopes, she stomped a scar through the dry weeds. Weaving a serpentine path around clusters of old-growth oak trees, she continued sniffing their trail for the better part of an hour until she found them.

At least the boys had sense enough to avoid the King's Highway, she thought. Ravel avoided the stream that was little more than a crack in the earth holding a trickle of rainwater runoff. A few sparkling eyes glistened threateningly in the dirty water but were too few to be of concern.

Five youths and six saddle horses rested under the canopy of a lopsided oak tree. One large bough extended sideways like the beam of a corral's fence, and they had looped the reins over it. The rumps of horses stood in a row. No saddlebags. The surveyors had carried everything in shoulder satchels or in ox wagons. These horses were geared only for quickly transporting the important people back and forth to the construction site from their headquarters camp. All their supplies that had burdened Xidron's farm horse were lost in exchange for these flat saddles and light ring stirrups.

Candor's voice projected out of the silence. "...ill-behaved, defiant mount I've ever sat astride. How did I get the unlucky draw of the worst horse in the bunch?"

Her brother stood beside one of the Saddlebreds, a well-muscled mare with a sleek neck and high withers. Candor fussed with adjusting the stirrup's buckles. The tethered horse showed signs of restrained annoyance on the verge of reaching the end of patience. Any moment, her brother could receive a nip on the shoulder.

Prosper said, "We can swap if you'd prefer."

They all saw her approach, except for her brother who faced the other way. Even the horses pricked up their ears and scuttled away from her.

Ravel grabbed her brother's tunic from the back. She shoved him staggering towards the edge of sunlight. "Idiot! Fool!"

"Sister..." Candor's expression brightened at the sight of her, disheveled and breathless and drenched in purple inhuman blood.

Prosper added, "Praises be to the ancestors, you found us."

She whirled and slapped him across the face. It left a smear of ink-colored blood. "Damn you to the blazes, my beloved. You abandoned me to fight them off alone."

"We saved the lord." He pointed at Candor. "That's how we were trained. 'Save the lord at all costs.' It's what you did, during the war, when you sneaked our prince through a secret sally door in the walls. Isn't it?"

Ravel gulped down the lump of bile in the back of her throat. His words rang true and blended into her memories. Her own comrades-in-arms howled their battle cries, making their last stand against the besiegers to cover the prince's escape. All of it for nothing.

Candor smiled. "I knew you'd make short work of those flat-foots. Did you kill them all?"

Ravel drew back her shoulders and addressed them as the captain of a squad. "We wouldn't have to kill or fight if you weren't the absolute worst bunch of limp cocks that I've ever seen strap on boots! You, Stander, have even failed your name by falling asleep on your watch. You should've been on your feet. You should have seen them coming."

"I'm sorry."

"And when you did have a chance to make your stand, you threw away your knives! You missed your targets for nothing gained. What skill is that, eh? To disarm yourself!"

The other youths snickered at his shame. Stander's complexion was too dark to reveal his blushing, but Ravel smelled the perspiration and flush in his cheeks.

"You, archer!" She turned to his twin brother. "You had a clear shot at your target, point blank, and all you managed to pierce was the bastard's cloak?"

Redson shrugged away his embarrassment. "I missed."

"You never miss. I've seen you skewer a running rabbit at a hundred paces. Admit it, boy. You flinched. You saw a human face and you flinched! You've never ended a man's life before, have you? Have you!"

Redson shook his head. "No."

"It's easy to shoot animals for supper and dance with knives, isn't it, but you've never killed someone who was trying to kill you in return. You're good at running for your lives but you've never had to fight for your lives."

Xidron stepped forward. "How dare you scold them! How dare you fault them for being young and inexperienced."

"So were the footmen in my squad! So were the youths who died in the siege of that fortress where your cowardly feet defiled the blood-soaked ground." She blasted her words shouting at him. Xidron retreated to the oak tree as if punched in the face.

"My beloved, please, calm yourself." Prosper extended his hand towards her as if to restrain a bucking wild horse.

Ravel waved him off. "And you, my beloved, you are a damned liar."

"How's that again?"

"You never were a lieutenant in the Badger Brigade, were you." Her tone was an accusation not a question.

"I... I was..." His voice cracked. Tears welled up in his eyes. "I was a first lieutenant, truly I was! My father the colonel made me an officer one rank below my three older brothers. When I celebrated my eighteenth birthday, he promoted me from second to first—"

Ravel inhaled the stench of his conflicted thoughts and his shame. "Liar. Liar!"

"I was a first lieutenant! I was! But... But it was in the quartermaster's corps. I secured the supply lines. I safeguarded the wagon trains full of food and clean water and blankets." Tears dribbled freely down Prosper's flushed cheeks. "My father made sure that I stayed well behind the front lines, while my brothers led troops. He praised me, nonetheless. My services were just as essential as those who wielded swords and spears against the enemy."

The other four youths stared at their comrade with mouths agape.

"Every member of the Badger Brigade knew me by name. They patted me on the back as a comrade-in-arms. They called me their honorary member and gave me one of their swords to wear at my side. I stood with the wagons and cheered them into battle, every time, until that last time. On that day, I stood ready with rolls of bandages and jugs of whiskey. I waited for their return.... and they never.... never... my brothers... my father..."

Prosper dropped to his knees. Hands pressed to his face, he wept and groaned into his gloves.

Candor rested a hand on his friend's shoulder. "You served our prince with valor even if your sword never drew blood. Today, you served me with honor. Shed your despair, my friend, and seek hope in a new day. Deceptions of the past are yielding to the light. So shall the Pretender's lies be exposed and Truth of All Things be made plain for all to see."

Ravel felt her shoulders sag as her outrage drained away. "Foolish boy, can't you understand what I'm saying? You're not ready for what you wish to do. None of you! Look at the mistakes you've already made. Even by choosing this place to rest your horses, any colonel would order ten lashes to stop in such an exposed and obvious place. If there were pursuers on your trail—and thank the watchful spirits of our ancestors there aren't any—the only reason they wouldn't find you is because no one would imagine that fugitives could be so blazing stupid. You stopped in this pleasant spot like peddlers traveling at a watering hole! Look at how you failed to appoint a guard. I walked right up to the shadow of this tree before any one of you saw me."

Candor only grinned at her frown. "Good advice, Captain, thank you. We won't make that mistake again."

"Aren't you hearing me, Der? You aren't ready for this! You couldn't beat a group of stone masons and surveyors. How will you take on the king's legions in the heart of Xolhold Keep?"

"We have horses now."

Balling up both her fists, Ravel growled at the frustration of having nothing to punch.

Prosper rose to his feet and wiped his face with a kerchief that he carried tucked in his belt. The other three gathered around and, together, they moved to untether the horses.

Candor chose the other Saddlebred that appeared to an older gelding with a more tolerant temperament for an inexperienced rider. The last time he had mounted a saddle, he was ten years old in the corral of their estate. The stable master had kept a watchful eye and walked alongside to give instructions. *Keep your feet level, don't point your toes down. Hold the reins with thumbs up. Square your shoulders. Look between the ears, don't look down.*

"Mount up, Captain," her brother said over his shoulder. Just as he had been taught as a child, he put his left foot in the stirrup and sprang off the ground. He paused to align his balance before he swung his leg over and settled onto the flat saddle.

Xidron ascended to the saddle of his speckled Chap-Trotter mare. "We can make it to the next village well before sunset. I know of a traveler's inn where we can purchase new supplies."

Prosper mounted the Saddlebred that Candor had rejected as ill-tempered. In response to his experienced hands, the mare perked up her head in readiness to receive her rider's commands.

Redson and Prosper got onto the Bay Pacers, identical carriage horses with dun yellow coats contrasting black manes and tails.

"Very well," Ravel grumbled. "We shall continue our conversation in the next village. We certainly can't stay here in the open."

The other Saddlebred mare spooked as Ravel approached. Although she extended her hands in a calming gesture, the horse only grew more agitated as if she held a hissing, venomous snake. She held back from the large animal with the widened eyes of a frightened rabbit.

Xidron asked, "Shall I hold 'er while you mount?"

"No," she said. "She smells the blood on me. There's no choice but to leave her behind. I can keep up on foot."

Candor set off at a trot. His companions followed in a haphazard formation. Ravel jogged at the rear. Sunshine's warmth baked the blood that soaked her clothing. Her own inhuman blood became a stench that threatened to even make herself retch. She breathed through her mouth, not her nose, as she jogged behind the horses.

The next village was her only hope to cleanse herself and restore her semblance of humanity. By then, she hoped to think of better words to say to convince her brother of his folly. *Yes, in the next village, when I've wiped the blood off my face and combed my hair, I can speak with him more sensibly. I've been wrong to chastise them in the way our father would have done. Harsh admonishments only raise a young man's hackles more. I will speak to him as our mother often did to calm him from a fit of childish temper. Mother never failed to get through to his senses when all else failed. Mother... Mother, I beseech your spirit, grant me your wisdom. Help me save your son from rushing to join you in the grave.*

Chapter 21.

In Lord Fordon's chambers, beyond the partition curtains of indigo velvet with silver fringe, an arched doorway framed an idyllic outdoor scene. The tiled veranda jutted out as a shelf from the cylindrical tower of gray stone bricks. High-pitched fife music tooted a merry tune that complemented the chirping of sparrows in the eaves. As the king emerged into the sunlit patio garden, he found the source of the music.

Captain Herry, in a full black wool uniform, straddled a white marble bench. Although the steel fife he played was a standard military issue, the tune certainly was not. Herry bobbed his head and swayed his shoulders as he played, inviting with his body for anyone who heard it to join along in gaiety and dance.

The little girl at the center of the veranda flapped her arms and twirled dancing to the fife's merry tune. She wore a linen gown dyed in chamomile yellow and pale woad blue. In stark contrast to the pastel garments, the girl had a wild mass of black curls. Though her childish face had round cheeks and a pert nose, one could discern the classical symmetry of her features. Her blue eyes glittered as brilliantly as sapphires.

No mistake, she is my blood cousin.

Two officers stood nearby. Colonel Viktor po'Aigrue was the governor's nephew. His wife Colonel Maetha had removed her uniform cap to let her wavy auburn hair drape loosely over her jacket's epaulets. Despite their black coats and sword belts, they too held an undisciplined pose. Arm in arm, the lady's cheek rested against her husband's shoulder. The pair watched the little girl fondly as if hoping they could keep her as their own.

"Your Majesty!" cried Maetha.

Herry choked on his fife. Both officers dropped to their knees. A handmaiden in a gray gown prostrated herself on the patio tiles.

The little girl, annoyed now, stomped her feet. "Music! More music!"

Glëa smiled. "You heard the lady, Captain. Keep playing."

"Yes, yes, Your Majesty." The fife went back to his lips. After a few false toots, Herry resumed the merry tune.

The Lady of Taine giggled like a songbird. It was a very small, dainty sound made by tiny lungs. Arms outstretched; she twirled in circles to flare her layered skirts into a bell.

"Rise, rise," the king commanded.

Governor Fordon emerged from the chamber behind him. "Welcome, Your Majesty. It is an honor to receive you."

He brought several maids in grey gowns and blue aprons. The maids carried a short-legged tea table. With rapid efficiency, they spread a tablecloth to hold an assortment of butter cookies, cashew fudge, and baked apples drizzled with honey.

Glëa took his place on the nearest of two wrought-iron chairs. He draped his hands off his knees and watched her dance until the tune had finished.

Breathless, the little girl clapped her hands. "More, more! More music!"

"Perhaps later," said Glëa. "I've brought you some snacks."

"Oh, cookies!" The little girl hopped to the second of the two chairs. Her handmaid spread a napkin across her lap.

Governor Fordon straightened to his full height. "May I present to milady the immortal Glëa po'Lon, first-born son of King Tokustein and Queen Lonielle, heir to the House of Davarche, Lord of the Harbor, Light of the World, and Twenty-Sixth King of Xol."

"Hello." The little girl put two cookies in her mouth and reached for a cube of fudge.

Colonel Viktor straightened at attention. "As proxy for the lady's father who is deceased, may I present to His Majesty the Lady Tiressa Valereine po'Xian, daughter of Wemond Hawker and Xianna the Baroness of Taine, the great-granddaughter of King Tokustein's acknowledged bastard half-sister Princess Ruelyn."

"Hello, Tiressa," said the king.

The girl mumbled, "Call me Lilac." Cookie crumbs sprinkled out of her mouth that the handmaiden hurried to brush away from her skirts.

"I don't care for nicknames," said Glëa. "I shall call you Tiressa because that is your proper name. That is how you shall be known."

"My *anma* calls me Lilac."

The handmaiden dropped to her knees at the little lady's side. "Please, my sweetie, listen to him. Do whatever he tells you."

"Why?"

"Because he's the king."

The little lady looked straight at him. "Why are you king?"

Glëa leaned back in his chair; no one had ever asked him that before. "My father was a king, and so was his father before that, and so on back for almost eight hundred years."

"I can count to a hundred."

Glëa nodded appreciatively. "That's very good."

Maetha put a black gloved hand over her mouth to hide her amused smile.

"Do you understand why I've had you brought here, Tiressa?"

The little lady pointed to Maetha. "She said I'm going to be a troth."

"Oh, did she?"

Governor Fordon coughed. "The child surely misunderstood."

"Don't lie, Herald." The king inhaled deeply the scent of anxious perspiration. "I can forgive you for making ambitious promises. I cannot forgive deceit."

"Yes, Your Majesty." Governor Fordon bowed. "Yes, I confess, I did imply to the girl's guardians that her betrothal was all but assured."

"What's a troth?" the little lady asked.

"The word is betrothed," Glëa explained. "It means a promise to be together, you and I."

"Together... like now?"

"Yes, exactly."

"And you give me cookies?"

"Yes, and more."

"More what?" she asked.

Viktor managed to remain stoically at attention as a soft twinkle flashed over his eyes.

The king thought, *She's charming. She could be popular as a queen, someday, an idol for the people to cheer. Rescinding her exile... Restoring her name and title... Showing mercy to those my grandfather shunned... It would be so easy to sign and seal a document. Without raising a single sword, I would be gaining goodwill and expanding the borders of the kingdom to the farthest northern shores.*

Glëa removed an emerald ring from the thumb of his left hand. He leaned forward over the tray of apple slices and offered it.

The dark jewel sparkled green in the sunlight. The little girl cried, "Oh! Pretty!"

"I've decided to offer you my promise of betrothal. This afternoon, we shall ask you to place your thumbprint mark on some papers. Will you do that?"

Governor Forden bent over. "Say yes, sweetie."

"Yes."

The king said, "Very good, I'm pleased. We shall arrange a celebration to make the announcement and formally make our betrothal of marriage. You shall be my first queen. Do you like that idea, to be Queen Tiressa of Xol?"

Tiressa hopped off her chair and spun around in circles.

"Sweetie, sweetie..." The handmaiden reached out to try and stop her spinning. The little girl skipped out of reach. "You need to say yes to him."

Tiressa hopped over to the captain and pulled at his sleeve. "Play music."

"As you command, my lady," said Herry fingering the holes in his fife. "But aren't you going to say yes to the king, first?"

Glëa looked again at the tiny doll of a girl, to the kitten's paw of hands that stretched outwards as she danced, to the scent of baby skin that wafted visibly in the air. *My first queen of what will be a series of queens. Children will mature and die of old age while I remain as I am. How many times will I repeat this process in a hundred years, or a thousand years, or in ten thousand years from today?*

Tiressa spun around. "I'm going to be a troth, yes! Then I'm a merry? Yes, yes, yes!"

Chapter 22.

On approach to the next village, Candor directed them to split into three groups. He reasoned that if a fugitive bulletin came from the surveyors at the fortress, they would evade suspicion. Xidron rode alone straight ahead as he had often traveled this course before to gather news from the king's domain. Candor kept the two brothers in his group. They loped off to circle around a hill and approached the village from the north.

Ravel and Prosper walked his horse on the well-trodden road, trailing slowly behind Xidron so they would not arrive at the same time.

Alone with her betrothed, Ravel said, "Shall we pretend to be husband and wife or master and servant?"

"The latter, obviously." Prosper walked beside his horse's head. "We can say that you fell in a puddle of mud."

Ravel glanced down at the splatters of dried blood on the front of her wraparound tunic, the cuffs of her undershirt's sleeves, and the knees of her loose-fitting breeches. "Falling into mud is a plausible story. However, my beloved, I don't understand why you see it as *obvious* that I would not be your wife who tragically lost all of our luggage in this unfortunate incident?"

"You are not behaving like a wife," he said over his shoulder.

"How so?" She fingered the chain necklace of delicate copper links. "I am wearing your pledge of betrothal, am I not?"

"Must I explain to you what is plain for all to see?"

"Please do."

The horse fidgeted, catching wind of the man's mood. Prosper kept walking at a steady pace and did not turn to meet her stare.

"You behaved like a shrew. You embarrassed me. You belittled me. You caused me to weep on my knees. This is not how a wife honors her husband."

In the momentary pause of silence, she knew that he expected an apology. The appropriate words came to mind but stopped short of emerging from her mouth.

"I expect better manners from a lady," he said.

Ravel hooked her finger on the chain necklace as she thought of her gentle mother. The Lady of the House of Spareen had always carried herself with even-tempered grace. She never emerged from her bed chamber unless her gown was neatly laced. Her long hair was always combed and braided into a clean rope down her back. Always her matrimony necklace lay in a perfect crescent across her collarbone. Mother bowed to greet Lord Spareen's return home every time he dismounted at the flagstones. Mother frequently apologized for things that were not her fault. She always addressed her husband in honorifics, not by name, never once speaking out of turn. Until this moment, Ravel never imagined that her mother could have been unhappy.

Before she knew it, Ravel's grip tightened on her own necklace. The copper links broke. Her hand relaxed and allowed the glimmering chain to fall. It dropped into the grass without making a sound. She walked on, leaving it behind for crows or magpies to decorate their nests.

I know this place. Ravel recognized the configuration of low-lying hills that encircled the potter's village. Years before the war began, she had accompanied her father's squires when traveling often between the estates of his vassals. A map of the terrain and a roster of names briefly floating across her memories. Inhaling deeply, she savored the nostalgic scent of clayey soil in the gray-and-yellow stripes exposed by generations of diggers.

The wood smoke of kilns wafted in dusk as villagers stoked their fires to burn overnight. A poet once described the work of ceramic artisans as a blazing sun contained in a box; Ravel remembered the phrase but not the reference. Youths carried wooden planks laden with greenware bowls, mugs, vases, jugs, or plates to be loaded into the kilns. Others draped more freshly turned wares with canvas tarps to dry in the night air. Elders scraped excess slop off the surface of potter's wheels, to finish the day, to start again in the morning with shaping clay into useful items.

Ravel felt the villagers turn their heads to watch her passing. Unlike the days of yore, when she rode as an escort alongside her father Lord Spareen, she felt no obsequious welcoming in their gaze. Villagers hunched as if ready to dodge a bucking horse. They frowned at her sideways. A few made finger gestures to ward off evil demons. Women pulled their children away by the wrists. Reclining dogs leapt up to bark at her.

The mood has changed under the rule of this king, she thought. *They fear travelers.*

"Where are they?" Prosper wondered aloud. "We've been on foot, but at least Xid should have arrived already."

"Mind your voice." Then she remembered to add, "Master. Sir."

"Mind your place." He hesitated where he would have called her beloved. Turning to look at her face for the first time in hours, his eyes darted to her collarbone. Under the cloud of subterfuge, he could not ask in public where the betrothal necklace had gone. Ravel did not wish to spend time discussing her decision to break it off.

She sniffed the air and found her brother's scent. "By the well."

The artisans' humble thatched cottages were arranged in a circle. Their doors faced into the center. From a stone well at the core, people took water in buckets or jugs. Once again, the villagers shied away from Ravel's and Prosper's approach. Some hurried to rush away and spilled water into the trampled soil.

Candor's auburn hair brightened in hue with the sunset shining on his head. Beardless face washed clean, smiling in conversation with his three friends, he looked like the child she remembered from years before. By the proud tilt of his chin and the straight posture of his shoulders, any passer-by could see that he had never done an hour of manual labor in his life. Even in the graceful way he sat astraddle an overturned bucket, his refined upbringing showed.

Prosper called out, "Hail there, now, fellow traveler. May I join you in this evening's repast?"

Xidron and the brothers raised their arms in greeting. Candor smiled to offer a gesture of welcoming.

"We are well met, good fellow," Candor said. "Come join us, for we have plenty to share."

"My name is Proffer. This is my, uh, servant girl Riven."

Candor gave their alias names as Cadent, Staid, and Rudd but only Xidron kept his true identity. After all, he had traveled this course many times before.

Ravel felt silly watching their awkward play-acting. The villagers had scattered or fled, so their performance had no audience. Yet they kept up the pretense of being random travelers meeting for the first time. They asked each other bland questions of their origins and destinations, replying with false answers. They shared bowls of stew and skewers of grilled meat chunks while making conversation about the quality of the food. *Worst bards or mummers I've ever seen. They're doomed if they hope to sneak into the royal castle on pretense.*

Xidron offered Ravel a small plate of meat skewers. She took a bite of the charred gristle, unable to discern if it was duck, pheasant, or rabbit. At the center it was still rare. She savored the taste of raw flesh on her tongue. Blood's flavor like the juice of a sweet plum aroused her senses. Even as sunset fell and the sky dimmed, her eyes remained bright. Inhaling deeply, she caught the odors of meat in the cottages and momentarily shivered with the urge to crawl into their windows and devour what lay on their hearth's chopping blocks.

"Shouldn't you tend to your master's horse?" Xidron nudged her shoulder. His stern gaze hinted that he had observed her unnatural craving for blood.

Prosper handed her the reins. "Yes, do."

The horse shield away in fear. Ravel had to give the reins to Xidron and say, "Please, good sir, if you would assist? I fell into a puddle of mud and, it seems, my master's horse is afraid of me."

She set down the plate. The ceramic's glaze of blue and speckled brown called up a rush of memories. Mother's plates, Mother's bowls, and Mother's teacups were glazed in this style. Since childhood, Ravel had eaten meals at her father's table on plates such as the one she held now. Meat and boiled vegetables, pastries and pies, fruits with cream, and cubes of hard cheese had once been plentifully arrayed on a white linen tablecloth on platters of blue and brown.

A tear leaked out of the corner of her eye. Ravel wiped it quickly, out of shame, hoping that none of the youths noticed. Her fingertip carried a slime that, at first, she thought was the grease of the meat skewer. Touching her face again, she realized that her own tears had become oil. *My blood is flammable. My tears are oil. What monster am I becoming?*

"Excuse me," she managed to blurt as she spun about and ran for the shadows.

Rain fell from the dark night sky. It was that familiar sort of warm, sticky rain that fell in late autumn and produced thunderstorms. As a soldier in days of yore, her only concerns used to be cleaning the mud out of her horse's hooves, keeping her sword oiled against rust, and drying her own socks. Now, the sky was a chorus of screaming.

She found shelter for herself among large racks of firewood. Beneath a shed roof, the chopped logs were kept dry under draperies of waxed canvas.

Rain drummed the shed's awning. Rain squatted the canvas drapes. Rain shrieked at her as it fell. She squatted and used handfuls of sandy sawdust to rub at the dried blood on her face. Using only her fingers, she tried to comb her matted tangles. Clumps of her hair peeled off by the handful, but she felt no pain in her scalp. If anything, it felt natural and normal to shed the outer vestiges of humanity.

She clutched the insistent stinging at the center of her chest. Talons pushed back like snakes in a bag. She smelled the faint aroma of her own blood as her skin stretched and old scabs cracked. Her stomach gurgled in hunger. The spikes echoed the call. *Meat... meat... meat...* An appetite that was not from her own belly surged through her core. She gnawed at the empty air. She growled in yearning for a bite of warm, bloody flesh.

Gray mice hid among the firewood logs and wiggled their whiskers. Ravel whirled toward the prey. "I see you all," she growled hoarsely in a voice not entirely her own. Her flat teeth snapped in eagerness to bite up and swallow everything that moved. *Meat... meat... meat...*

Mice scampered away. She watched through an emerald haze as their wormlike tails escaped her reach. In the night's darkness, everything was sharp and clear to her sight.

"Um... hello." A man stepped under the awning.

At first, she could not speak. Ravel rose to stand facing him.

The fellow wore a potter's burlap apron splattered with dried clay. He was of fatherly age but carried himself with an air of vitality. His short hair was as curly as a lamb's fleece. Gray streaks at his temples blotched the auburn brown.

"Hello," he said again. "I hope I didn't startle you. Forgive me for disturbing your, uh... uh.... Would you like a towel?"

"No thank you."

Yet he pulled a dry rag from underneath his apron. "Please take it. Keep it. Don't worry, it's not wet. I was careful."

Ravel accepted the cloth but merely held it limp in her hands. "Why should I worry if it's wet?"

He opened his palms as a gesture of pleading or surrender. "Let us speak frankly, shall we? I'll admit that I'm feeling uneasy to have this conversation with you. I prefer to say what needs to be said as quickly as possible."

Ravel tightened her grip on the rag. "Go on."

"We figured out what you are. You avoiding the rain gave it away." He pointed at her torso. "Those.... the... the *things* you carry pierced in your chest? Some of us have seen them before. Others had them, years ago, during the war. They were the king's spies and magic workers."

"I know of whom you speak," she said. "I killed them."

Briefly his eyelids fluttered. "Is there a bounty on your head? Will the king punish you for that?"

"No, none at all." She studied his eyes for acceptance of her words. "Those magic workers betrayed po'Lon and he was quite disappointed in them, at the end. What I did by stealing these talons, I did for a higher purpose that he would have approved. I'm fairly certain of that, please believe me. You aren't in any danger by giving shelter to us... to me."

"I'm just here to say that we don't want any trouble. We've opened our homes in hospitality to offer lodgings to Young Lord Spareen and his squires."

"You know?" she gasped.

He shrugged and his elbows flared out from his sides. "Some of us are old enough to remember him, and his father, and you. There are fond memories of when this village once belonged to the House of Spareen... to *your* house, Lady Ravel. We're all very sympathetic about what happened to you, but we're pleading for you to accept the world as it is. Now, this village is pledged to a new lord baron. We're a mixture of those who fought under the flag of blue-and-cream and under the black-and-rouge. Allegiances change for those in ranks up above. But for us down here working in the clay of the earth, life goes on the same as it always has been."

"I see," she said after a thoughtful pause. "I understand your dilemma. I don't wish to cause trouble. I've also accepted that the past is gone. My prince and my home are gone. Glëa po'Lon is the rightful heir and king of the land."

"Glad to hear it." He sighed relief through a nervous smile.

"My brother and I appreciate your hospitality. Despite my... my impediment, I give you my honorable word that I shall cause no disruption nor bring any cause for your lord's displeasure. Thank you for allowing us to stay."

His smile dropped. "You misunderstand."

"How so?"

"When morning comes, we want you gone. All of you. Gone. We will happily give enough of the food, clothing, and supplies as you need to get on the road. Am I clear?"

Air chilled in the space between them. Ravel assessed the man's posture and facial expression. She searched for some hint of trace sympathies and saw none. His hands were clenched into fists like knobs at the ends of his sleeves. She listened to the tone of his deep bass voice. She hoped for a slight hesitation, or a lilt of wavering resolve, but heard none.

"Please, let us stay a bit longer. My brother's heart can benefit, more than you could imagine, from familiar surroundings and a peaceful environment."

"No," he said plainly.

"Why?" Ravel took a step towards him. The man flinched back on his heels.

"We are all afraid of *you*."

"Me? But—"

"You... You and the *things* you carry pierced in your chest. True, you don't look as mutilated as the king's spies did, but we don't trust you. It's plain to see you've changed. You're more un-folk than human, now. When morning comes, we want you gone."

Without giving her a chance to respond, he stepped into the dark rain.

Ravel squatted curled forward over her knees. As the rain continued to scream down from the night sky, she hugged her belly and waited for the long hours of darkness to pass.

"I owe you an apology." Candor bypassed the customary greetings of the morning. Hands held forth with palms facing upward, he contritely approached the rack of firewood.

"Whatever for?" she asked.

"You were right, dear sister. I've been foolish."

Tiny eyes of water spirits swarmed in the air like gnats. Although the sky had cleared of rain showers, the humidity lingered in the brightness of morning. Droplets of dew sparkled on patches of grass and glittered in the grains of sand. The skin of her hands and cheeks prickled as if pelted with ice flakes when walking through a snowy wind, but she endured the discomfort.

Ravel rose to meet him at the edge of the awning's shadow. She eagerly clasped his hands and smiled into his serene expression. Here was the brother she remembered from years before. Beardless face washed clean, auburn hair combed neatly, his shoulders and hands relaxed instead of clenched in readiness to fight. Candor smiled and his soft cheeks formed dimples.

"Please accept my apology," he said. "I've been stubborn and childish. Now I understand what you've been trying to tell me. Or rather, what you've been telling all of us."

The other four youths led horses to the firewood rack. The animals were already saddled and loaded with bags of supplies. True to the man's word, the villagers had apparently provided the group with clean clothing, a hearty breakfast, bed rolls, and trail food.

"We aren't ready to execute the plan I've been dreaming about," he continued. "Everything you said is true! We could have been killed easily by a crew of stone masons and ditch diggers. We are not skilled or equipped to face the Iron King's legions. During the war, we were just children. Not soldiers like you. How rightly you observed the truth. We've never drawn blood from an adversary in a fight."

Ravel blinked at oily tears welling in the corners of her eyes. "Did the villagers speak with you?"

"Yes!" Her brother let go of her hands. A bit of embarrassed laughter coughed out of him. "Yes, yes, they did. I'm feeling quite humbled this morning, if I must say. I had not expected to encounter Reason and Pragmatism in the countryside. We spent long hours of the night speaking with a group of wise grandfathers."

"I'm so glad."

"Come, sister, let us travel onward. Let's not over-burden these simple villagers who have been so generous with their hospitality. Xidron will lead us to a larger town where we will seek proper lodgings."

On cue, Xidron joined Candor's side at the edge of the awning's shadow. He offered a folded bundle of cloth. "Here."

Ravel received it curiously. She unfolded a full-length hooded cloak. The linen had been treated with beeswax like the panels of the awning that sheltered the racks of firewood. The garment felt heavier and stiffer than usual, but it served to block the aggressive spray of screaming water droplets in the air. She raised the hood to cover her head and most of her face. The villagers planned well, she thought. No excuses to stay; not even the threat of rain.

Candor offered his elbow like a gentleman. She lightly rested her hand on his forearm. Her brother escorted her into the open sunshine and gracefully guided her around mud puddles.

"I'm so proud of you coming to your senses," she said. "Of course, I accept your apology, Der."

"Blessed may it be, our balance is restored."

"Blessed be," she responded.

Prosper cast a frown over his shoulder just before he mounted up his horse. If he still thought of her as a cantankerous disobedient shrew, he said nothing. Are we still betrothed, she wondered now that I have broken and discarded the promissory necklace?

Redson and Stander mounted their horses. The animals fidgeted in place, bumping rumps. The youths made awkward efforts to get control of their mounts' heads.

Xidron held the bridle of Candor's horse while the young lord swung his leg up to the saddle. Ravel thought of critiquing her brother's form, recalling the bygone days when he had needed a step stool to reach the stirrup, but decided to wait until another time. There would be plenty of opportunities to teach him better techniques of horsemanship once they reached a more populated town. She imagined they would find a way to ply their skills and make a modest living, as they had in the northern territory. Once more, they could have a home, a hearth, and a garden.

From high in the saddle, Candor said, "That one's for you, sister."

A mule stood nearby waiting for a rider to mount its well-packed traveling saddle. The beast had a dun-yellow coat, a black mane and tail. A dorsal stripe was a dark line bisecting its rump.

Ravel looked aside to a small group of villagers nearby. They went about their morning chores of opening a kiln and unloading the bisque ware that had been fired overnight. Hunched over, they avoided her direct gaze. She spotted the aproned man standing among them.

"Thank you!" Ravel called out. Her voice felt hoarse and scratchy in the muggy, humid air but she had to say it. She could not, in good conscience, leave them without saying it.

The aproned man waved his hand in a vague gesture of returning the thanks while urging her to leave.

Xidron strolled close to her on the way to his own horse. He muttered at her, "Your brother doesn't understand the demon blood inside of you, the evil that poisons your blood. The villagers know all about what un-folk you've become. You're worse than a wraith of the shadows, they said. They've given me a bag full of amulets and talismans. I'm watching you."

"Good for you." Ravel cracked a smile at the southerner. "Keep watching me."

The mule did not balk when she mounted the saddle. Perhaps it was the ceramic beads and braids of aromatic herbs that decorated the bridle. Or perhaps the mule was an unholy sentient creature masquerading as a beast of burden. She did not ask. She just kept her poise in the saddle as they rode away from the potter's village.

Chapter 23.

Ash ascended the tower's spiral stairwell to the chambers reserved for the House of Browden. His stomach hardened into a knot the closer he came to the top. He clenched his fists and willed his feet to keep going until he reached an entryway alcove. Flagpoles displayed the heraldic banners of sage-and-silver to either side of the large oak door. He paused at the threshold to tug his clothing straight; one had to be at their best appearance when coming into the presence of this lady. Then, he raised the die-cast ring and knocked.

"Good evening, Mister Ash, sir." Jenny the serving maid, a familiar face from years before, opened the door.

"I apologize for being tardy," he said.

"Not at all, sir." Jenny's calm, soft face broadened in a welcoming smile. "Supper is just now being served."

Jenny escorted him into another world of luxury, warmth, and tradition. Green draperies with silver fringe hung by iron hooks hammered into the stone walls. Plush rugs cushioned the hardwood planks of the floor. A chandelier held two dozen beeswax candles, at least, and shined with the light of an afternoon sun captured in a cage. At the far wall, a large bright fire gobbled its stacked logs.

The lady of the house occupied the head of a rectangular table. She dined alone. Five empty armchairs tucked in neat alignment underneath the green tablecloth. Candlesticks illuminated platters of grilled meat, fish fillets, cheese wheels, bread loaves, pea soup, and boiled string beans.

Ash dropped to one knee. "Felicitations of the day, Mother. Praises be to the ancestors who guided you safely on the journey here."

Lady Dalhanna po'Ther, the widow of Lord Keane of the House of Browden, briefly glanced up from the morsel of white fish skewered on her silver fork. As always, she dressed impeccably in a snugly-laced one piece gown of green velvet. Her servants must have spent hours in washing, drying, combing, and plaiting her long blonde hair with silvery cords. Yet her lifetime of wealth and comfort failed to immunize her from the years that had taken their toll. The burden of grief carried for a decade showed deep creases on either side of her mirthless mouth. Her shoulders rounded in perpetual weariness. In looking up from her plate, her neck bent at a severe angle like the hook of a wall sconce.

"You may join me for supper," the lady said.

"I am honored." Ash took a seat at the opposite end of the table.

Jenny dished up a sample of each platter and brought him the plate. From her apron's pocket, she provided him with a wooden spoon and a pewter fork.

A younger house boy approached bringing a cup filled with tepid barley tea.

"Thanks, uh... What's your name?" Ash asked the boy.

Lady Dalhanna said sternly, "It is not necessary to know his name. The boy will come when his services are needed, and he will go away when services are rendered. You are *at table*, now, Mister Ashglëa, and as the adopted ward of my house, you will conduct yourself with proper decorum."

"Yes, Mother." Ash poked his fork into a cube of grilled lamb.

"One would have expected that, for your time serving in Xolhold Castle, you would have refined your manners."

Ash hurriedly swallowed the half-chewed lamb before answering. A gentleman should not converse with food in his mouth. "Yes, Mother."

"Nonetheless, I am extending my invitation for you to share a seat at the king's betrothal banquet. You may sit across from Rubëa's left hand, that is, opposite the empty chair that will be kept in honor of my other son."

Samuet. The name of Lady Dalhanna's deceased son and the image of his choking face turning to deathly gray floated through Ash's memory. He looked at his plate filled with food and no longer felt hungry.

"Is Rubëa not joining you for supper this evening?" Ash asked.

"He has not yet arrived. We traveled separately. As I understand, there was some delay involving his wife or his children." The lady dipped her silver spoon into her crystal bowl of pea soup. "He may be another several days, at least."

"I see." Ash held the stem of his glass goblet but did not drink. "If I may ask, Mother, have you also invited *her*?"

"No."

That single word ended the conversation. Supper proceeded in utter silence, with servants lingering in the shadows and the fireplace blazing in its stone box.

Ash marveled at the lady's cool demeanor. He wondered, not for the first time, how she could grieve for the death of her son while shunning the daughter who still lived. Although the House of Browden had not formally signed a declaration of exile for the bastard-born Valwynne po'Dal, nicknamed Clear, the matriarch's intention was very well understood. *How long will you continue to punish her disobedience*, he wished to ask but dared not. Surely the offense of marrying for love to a rogue horseman could be forgiven after so many years.

He also wondered if Clear had seen all of this in one of her prophetic visions. Distance meant nothing to her mystical second sight. Even while residing in the western Midlands with her horseman husband, Clear surely knew of the king's betrothal. If so, she could make the journey if she had foreseen a calamity about to happen. Just as she had tried in vain to prevent Samuet's tragic death, Ash felt confident that Clear would visit his dreams as a spirit apparition—as she had the power to do—or at least send him a letter by messenger. Otherwise, she would stay home to avoid the royal court and her mother altogether.

In finishing his plate, Ash wiped up every drop of sauce with the last cube of bread. He glanced aside at the windows darkening at twilight. *I miss you, Clear*, he murmured in the privacy of his thoughts. *I wish you'd come visit anyway. You may stay at my house. I won't tell Mother.*

Chapter 24.

Ravel knew the next town as Heron's Neck from traveling this road years before. The King's Highway penetrated a straight line between a cluster of low-lying hills. Soon they would cross the grand bridge over the Clement River and be within two days' walk of the capital city.

Prosper and Xidron rode in front of the group. Ravel and Candor rode side-by-side at the center. The twin brothers covered the rear.

"Are we not going to split into groups and pretend to meet as strangers?" Ravel asked.

Candor laughed. "Of course not, sister. We are maintaining the pretense that we have already met in the potters' village. Subterfuge is ineffective if our story changes from one day to the next."

Before they came within sight of the town, Ravel smelled the odor of meats being grilled. She heard the clatter of tools, the grinding of wagon wheels, the clicking of looms, and the ringing of a blacksmith's hammer. Goats bleated. Ducks quacked and chickens clucked. People in conversation buzzed the air. As their group came around the hillside into full view of the town, Ravel's stomach gurgled.

"Are you hungry, sister?" Candor turned his head to look at her.

Ravel pulled in the overlapping panels of her waxed linen cloak. Oily saliva filled her mouth in anticipation of so much raw meat roaming free.

"Yes," she had to admit.

"Be patient a little while longer," her brother said. "We shall find lodgings and feast well tonight."

"On what funds?" she asked, with a rush of embarrassment that she had not thought to inquire until now.

Prosper called back over his shoulder, "Xid and I have wisely kept our coin purses on our belts. Fortunately, the potters did not ask for payment in exchange for their hospitality. If we are frugal, we will have enough."

He was a former lieutenant in the quartermaster's corps, she thought. Of course he would keep a ledger of the group's basic necessities.

A knee-high wall of stacked river stones encircled the town. The wall like a pastry shell's crust defined the densely packed mixture of thatched and shingled rooftops. Outside the wall's ring, a quilt of farmland plots covered the landscape to the base of hills rising out of the flats. A lord's manor house topped the hills. Trees obscured the wagon road winding up the slope. The cube of gray blocks was softened by a paste façade thickly overgrown with vines. Even from a distance, Ravel recognized the structure as a place she had once visited years before. *Lord Baron Cullbrean, the vassal in fealty to our house... How can it be that his home still stands, undamaged, when ours has been burned down to the basement?*

The town's gate was a simple, square arch of timber columns. The kingdom's flag at the center of the crossbeam fluttered higher and larger than the other flags. A golden bull's head was imprinted on a background of royal black-and-rouge. The smaller flag of the House of Vilbyss displayed heraldry of yellow-and-brown with an image of a wagon wheel. The local baron's flag was a pattern of four quarters in black, red, yellow, and brown.

A wooden placard labeled the place as Loyalton written in both the ornate Classical script and the phonetic letters understood by commoners. *Heron's Neck no more*, she thought. The new king had a penchant for renaming the towns of his conquered domain.

Xidron made the necessary greetings to the gatekeepers with some familiarity. He had been this way before. Calling the group his friends that he had met on the road, Xidron laughed and cajoled the gatekeepers while Prosper counted out the coins to pay their entry toll.

They rode through the archway and passed underneath the Iron King's heraldic colors of blood and death. Ravel caught a change in the odor of her brother's perspiration. She glanced at Candor who gritted his teeth and clenched the reins of his mount. His throat said nothing but inside his mind was screaming.

The town's hard-packed dirt streets were narrow and haphazardly arranged. What began as a gathering place for farmers and craftsmen to barter exchanges of goods had expanded over the centuries. A cluster of shops became a network of villages, and finally a wall encircled a fortified town. Wattle-and-daub buildings with shingles loomed over thatched sod huts. A two-story brick tower stood sentinel over the town square.

They passed an open platform next to a shingled brick building. A trio of men, naked but for their underdrawers and socks, kneeled bound to whipping posts. Dry scabs streaked their backs. Punishment had been dealt; now they waited for the magistrates to dispense the mercy of release.

Guards in the royal black uniforms loitered on the porch of the jail. Crud-coats, Ravel used to call them. Now, she raised her sights to their faces and saw only youths not much older than Prosper or herself. Had they even fought in the war or were they newly enlisted, she wondered.

They passed the grand oak doorway of the Guild Hall. A queue of artisans waited on the doorstep to pay their dues or receive the stamp of approval on their charters. They too were travelers from outside of the town. Ravel heard the tongue rolls of southern accents as the artisans spoke with the Guild Hall's clerk.

"So many people," Stander remarked from the rear of their group.

"It's overwhelming," his brother Redson agreed.

All the better to be lost in a crowd, she thought but dared not say aloud.

Prosper and Xidron guided them to the portico of a two-story inn. Rain began to drizzle out of the afternoon sky. The warm rain forced Ravel to draw her waxed cloak more tightly around herself and hunker down into the hood. She was glad for the portico's trellis and awning thickly overgrown with jasmine vines that blocked most of the screaming eyes that tumbled out of the bright sky.

Candor dismounted and handed off his horse's reins to the two brothers. He loitered on the portico as Prosper and Xidron entered the inn to plan. His clothing was simple enough, but he could not help but square his shoulders with the haughty pride of a lord's heir who expected to be served. Other passers-by, going to and fro, gave him sideways glances. Like a white lamb in a herd of black goats, Ravel thought; he could not be inconspicuous in a crowd. *Blessed be that the villagers penetrated his stupidity and convinced him to abandon his quest for vengeance. We need to get him into a room with a bed before a couple of crud-coats happen to ask his name.*

Xidron emerged to share the news. "The inn is fully booked. No rooms."

"No rooms at any price," Prosper added. "We could only bargain for permission to lay our blankets in the attic loft. However, we will not have private space. There will be other travelers."

Candor frowned, shaking his head. "That is—"

"That is well bargained," Ravel interrupted. "And our horses?"

"We have permission to release them into a corral behind the Farrier's Row of shops," Prosper said. "I'm told it's located in that direction, a few streets to the northeast."

Redson and Stander got to work unsaddling their mounts and gathering their packs of supplies.

"And a meal?" she asked.

Xidron's expression brightened. "Around the corner is an area called Glutton's Row where we can purchase from shopkeepers all manner of victuals."

"I can't walk in the rain," Ravel said. "Would you bring me back some meat? Just meat, please. Lightly grilled or raw, if possible."

Candor inhaled deeply. "I smell cinnamon, butter, and yeast bread just like Mother used to direct our servants to make."

"Go on, Der." Ravel gently patted his shoulder. "Go find yourself a supper of all your favorite foods from home. I shall be ready upstairs with your bedroll and tuck you in, warm and safe, for the night."

"I'm not a child," he grumbled.

She finger-combed his unkept bangs off his forehead. "Forgive me, I meant no disrespect. It is my honor to serve you or see that you are served. It will be my honor to stand guard all night as you sleep. No matter what age you become, I will always take care of you."

Chapter 25.

The group slept on the planks of the attic. Ravel lay quietly so as not to arouse suspicion in the other travelers who shared the cramped space underneath slanted rafters. Throughout the night, she listened to her brother's breathing patterns and his bouts of murmuring in his dreams. At times he wept, and she could not be sure if he was conscious of it.

Two days passed as the youths made inquiries to every shopkeeper in the town but failed to find employment. All the craftsmen already had apprentices. Everyone else had an abundance of empty hands eager to do manual labor. The Guild Hall had too many clerks. The town's gate had twice as many sentinels as needed.

More and more people entered the town from all directions. By the third day, even the attic loft was filled to capacity. The inn began selling space on its stairwell. Those who could not afford even that much slept on the porch and suffered the cold night rain. *So many travelers!*

Arguments broke out in the streets almost every hour. The king's legions patrolled on grandly-muscled Garudan steeds to maintain order. They used shields and clubs to subdue the troublemakers. The jail became so crowded that those awaiting punishment were kept in livestock pens. Ravel watched from the inn's porch to witness travelers from all corners of the land of Xol being led away, wrists bound in ropes, by black-coat soldiers on black horses. She dreaded the possibility that the surveyors at the Fortress of Sharp Crag had reported the incident and put a bounty on their heads for horse thievery, assault, or worse. She feared that the potter's village might betray them to the local land baron and reveal that an inhuman 'un-folk' prowled the land. One careless word from Candor calling the king a pretender, an imposter, or a usurper would earn him a turn at the whipping post. What would she do then, Ravel wondered, if faced with the option of saving her brother from a lashing or keeping the secret of her otherworldly nature.

As the third night darkened, Candor called his friends into a circular huddle on their bedrolls in the attic.

"I have it! I have it!"

Ravel stood above them and gazed down curiously into the center of their shaggy heads.

"I've procured jobs!" Her brother held forth a rolled parchment tied with a red cord.

Other travelers unpacking their blankets grumbled, "Any scraps leftover for the rest of us?"

A glimmer of blue moonlight sparkled off the corner of Candor's eyes as he cast that fellow a disapproving scowl. Ravel moved one step to the left and stood guard in between her brother and the disgruntled stranger.

Candor lowered the volume of his voice. "We can join a group who are journeying to the capital city for the king's betrothal."

"His what!" Stander coughed.

"Betrothal?" Redson frowned deeply. "What hapless innocent maiden is being coerced to marry him?"

Prosper huffed disdain. "No one disputes why a so-called immortal king is taking a bride if he has no need for heirs?"

"Hush, hush." Ravel restrained an urge to kick him in the lower back for such careless remarks. Many strangers' ears shared the cramped attic.

Candor said, "I've gotten us all hired in the retinue of Lord Rubëa po'Dal."

"Who?" Xidron asked.

Prosper answered, "He's the eldest son and only surviving heir of the House of Browden."

"Browden?" Stander repeated.

Ravel's throat was dry and tight at the sound of that name. The matriarch of that house, General Browden, known as the Thorn Lily, was one of the Iron King's two closest confidants and a ruthless strategist during the war.

"Lord Rubëa poorly planned his journey from the Green Forest to Capital City along with his wife and children. The drivers are capable enough to handle the horses and carriage. However, his attendants lack a certain, shall we say, refinement? The lord has advertised for someone of the merchant class who can read... who can make intelligent conversation for entertainment during the long hours on the highway."

"Isn't that a wife's duty?" Prosper asked. "To entertain her husband?"

Candor said, "His wife is occupied in the carriage with her nursemaid and small children. The lord rides apart on a steed. Rumors say that his lordship is bored and is becoming more vivacious by the day."

"You mean vexed," Ravel corrected.

Her brother grinned with bright clean teeth. "I mean, insufferably rude. I spoke in confidence with members of his traveling retinue. They are preparing to fake stomach cramps or sprained ankles to get out of his service. I negotiated a contract with the carriage driver. We are their replacements!"

"All of us?" Ravel asked.

"Yes, all of us. When I said that we have our own horses, that sealed the deal. Sleep well tonight, my friends, for on the morrow we are bound for the capital city!"

Ravel put her hand on his shoulder. "Why? Why can't we stay here in this town? Once all the travelers pass through, there should be ample opportunities for work."

"Be sensible." He rotated his torso and faced her eye-to-eye. "This town is too small. The guilds have it all locked down. There are no opportunities for itinerant laborers."

"You imagine we will find jobs in the city?" she asked.

Candor smiled even wider, and his heartbeat quickened. "Our destiny is there. You'll see. I will make you proud of me, sister."

Lord Rubëa po'Dal of the House of Browden was every bit the pompous cock that rumors made him out to be. Ravel felt like throttling him unconscious within the first hour on the road. Loudly, he complained about everything from the humid weather to the quality of his morning tea. He criticized Prosper for how he had assisted with the lord's dressing routine. "Tie my sleeve cuffs before you cinch my breeches' waistband!" He insisted that Redson had roughly handled his horse when putting on the bridle and saddle. "You scraped Daffodil's ears, I saw it!" He demanded that Stander slice up an apple in a certain way. He threw the mis-cut pieces into the dirt until the youth finally achieved the desired shape. "Crescent! Crescent! Stupid clod, do you not know what a crescent is?" He called upon Candor to read aloud from a volume of fictional romantic stories involving a nonexistent concubine of the First King in the bygone days of centuries long past. "Skim over the descriptions of garden scenery. Find the spicy verses where the lovers meet!"

To his credit, Ravel saw that he handled his horse well; the four legs beneath him seemed like a natural extension of his own. She wondered if he had served in the cavalry during the war or if his family kept him safely well behind the front lines of battle. Years ago, she heard folktales that the Browden men were under a curse and doomed to never handle a weapon of war or be struck down by the wrath of ancient spirits. This explained why so many of the Browden women learned martial skills, and how the matriarch known as Thorn Lily rose to become a general in the Iron King's army. Until now, Ravel had never believed in legends or myths, but if true, it could explain this lord's irritability. Indeed, he did not carry a sword even for decoration.

Lord Rubëa's wife, her nursemaid, and three small children rode concealed in a curtained carriage. A team of six draft horses pulled the wheeled capsule along the well paved blocks of the royal highway. Two drivers handled the long reins and occasionally cracked a whip over the horse team's heads.

Ravel rode her mule alongside the front left wheel. She bundled her waxed cloak tightly around herself and imagined that she looked peculiar. Thankfully, rain did not fall. Sunshine turned the humid air into a muggy soup that clung to every bit of exposed skin. The harder she tucked her face into her hood, the more humidity reached inside to scratch at her chin. She felt grateful for the lord's obnoxious manners as a distraction for the others so that she could avoid anyone's scrutiny. At times she almost felt like a mythical wraith of the shadows herself. Unknown and unseen, she dwelled in the murky places just behind the corner of one's eye.

When crossing the stone bridge over the mighty Clement River, Ravel closed her eyes. She trusted the mule to carry her across with the rest of the group. The hooded cloak muffled the screaming waters that flowed north to south. *I can endure this*, she assured herself. *I can endure crossing the drawbridge over Xolhold Castle's moat, if I must. There is still a chance to persuade him away from his vengeful course. Perhaps the company of women and babies will soften his heart.*

Chapter 26.

The lord's drivers pushed the team to its limits. The journey should have taken two days at a reasonable pace, with resting overnight in a roadside tavern. Instead, they pushed the sweaty horse team to their limits. They passed the tavern at the height of the afternoon and, without stopping to rest, achieved a two-day journey in a single day.

By the evening, the carriage stopped to rest the exhausted horses. Lord Rubëa complained that they should press forward and not stop. One more shallow river. One more bridge. "I can make out the form of the city! We can sleep tonight in a real bed, at last!"

Ravel faced the orange-and-pink panorama of eastern sky. She gazed along the highway's line leading straight to the coast. Even from this distance, one's eyes could discern the sprawl of the capital city's rooftops and the spires of Xolhold Keep at the highest promontory of the seaside cliffs. White-washed stone towers soared taller than every other structure of earth and man. Built by King Davarche the First nearly eight hundred years before, the multi-story rectangular blocks had never been successfully attacked, never broken, never fallen. Though kings themselves had come and gone, and maps of territory had been drawn and re-drawn, always the cylinders of Xolhold Keep had overlooked Harbor Bay's serene waters. Five white towers clustered in unity were a beacon drawing all towards the center of civilization.

"With all due respect, my lord," said one of the coach drivers. "We've been pushing the horses very hard. One more step and they'll drop dead in their harnesses. An hour spent resting will be time well spent."

"An hour, you say? Unacceptable!" Lord Rubëa's horse dipped its snout to nibble at grass. He shifted his grip on the reins and commanded his horse's head to rise.

The second driver said, "Would you have them collapse just short of the city's gates?"

"Insolent, lazy clod, how dare you speak to me—"

Candor maneuvered alongside the lord's horse. "Shall we take you on alone, my lord, sir? Your family may follow at their leisure."

Prosper guided his horse to the lord's opposite side. Xidron positioned himself at the rear, effectively boxing him in.

Redson said, "My brother and I can stay behind to help check the hooves and such."

Inside the curtained carriage, the infant began to cry. The nursemaid cooed soothingly in a clashing duet with the screaming infant. The other two children chattered with complaints, "Make her stop! Make her stop!"

Even the lady scolded, "How are you so slow at unfastening your bodice, girl?"

Ravel shivered and crossed her fists across her own belly; it was harder and harder to resist the urges of her animalistic nature. She clenched her teeth that yearned to chomp into soft, juicy meat. *I am not a monster!*

She dismounted her mule and let the reins drop. She jogged a short distance to the side of the road. Kneeling in the grass, she clawed into the soil for a fat worm. Her teeth crushed the juicy worm's body. She drank of its slime but was unsatisfied. *Meat... meat... meat...* The word rang like a gong in her hungry mind the longer the infant cried.

Dimly she was aware of the lord, her brother, the southerner, and her former betrothed spurring their horses into a cantor. Horseshoes clicked on the stones of the king's highway.

"Ugh, what a bag of bricks," one driver exclaimed in a hushed voice.

"Hold your tongue, fool, the lady will hear," said the other driver.

"No, she can't—-"

Just then, the nursemaid got the infant latched on to suckle. The wailing stopped. The evening air fell peacefully still.

Ravel stayed crouched on her knees in the grass, hoping for a mouse to scamper by. *Just one*, she thought. *Just a little one. Just a little bite until we reach the city*. Human voices in distant conversation were muted and blurred by the throbbing inside her ears.

Stander said, "I'm sorry. You should have served a better man."

"Yeah thanks, mate, I—" The first driver's voice choked on the word. He gargled. Blood's odor wafted in the air.

"What! Murder!" A bowstring snapped. An arrow hit its soft target.

Ravel sprang to her feet. There lay the two drivers, dead, slumped on the carriage's high bench. One had a knife in his neck. The other had an arrow.

Before words or thoughts formed, she charged at them. Redson and Stander spurred their horses into launching from a standstill into a full gallop. She ran a few steps but stopped, knowing that she could never catch them on foot.

Whirling in place, she searched for the mule. Its dun-yellow coat was a spot of color galloping across the green fields. No hope of catching it or calling it back.

The lady called from inside the carriage, "What's happening? Who said murder?"

"Stay inside," Ravel growled. "Latch the door. Don't open it for anyone."

Ravel pumped her feet on the road, running as fast as she could manage. The vibrations of her brother's gleeful rage guided her to veer off the main King's Highway. Thankfully, the pursuit led away from groups of ordinary travelers hurrying to cross the river and find shelter in the capital city before darkness fell.

She turned onto a lesser-used wagon road overgrown with weeds. Fresh tracks in the soft earth led her, before long, to the odor of horses and the clash of human voices.

A narrow bridge extended only part of the way across the mighty waters. Its pillars ended in mid-air. This bridge had long ago washed out and crumbled, or it was destroyed in the civil war and never rebuilt. No travelers came to this abandoned patch of road. No one was around to witness what her brother and his companions were about to do.

"Stop, stop, please stop!" the nobleman cried.

"Quiet!" Prosper slapped Lord Rubëa across the face.

Ravel approached the cliff's edge overlooking the river. She stopped just short of the granite blocks marking the transition from the highway's paving tiles to the flat stones of the bridge.

Candor and his two friends dragged the stumbling man to the railing. They had disheveled his fine clothes of sage-green and gray velvet. Jewels glittered at his fingers, at his earlobes, and at the lacing tips of his delicate suede boots. For such a tall and robust-appearing man, the lord had put up a feeble resistance. Perhaps there was some truth in the rumors of a curse; men born to the House of Browden were not destined to be warriors.

Xidron held a rope tied into a noose.

She called out, "You broke your word!"

Candor turned to face her. Brows furrowed. Lips curled into a frowning snarl. Rage transformed his face into that of a stranger.

"What nonsense do you speak of, sister? What word have I broken?"

"You promised that you would abandon all of this... this...." Ravel waved her hands in the direction of Stander's blood-soaked fists. "This foolishness."

Candor raised his finger in a scholarly gesture of elucidation. "You misunderstood, as I expected you might have. Think back clearly! I said, we were not ready to face the Iron King's legions. We've never drawn blood from an adversary in a fight. We have never ended a man's life."

She shivered as the meaning of his words became clear.

"Look now," her brother continued. "We are in training. As our father trained you, and as he would have trained me if he had lived. We are preparing to do what must be done. Behold as we undergo the next test."

"No," she groaned. "Don't."

"You brutes!" cried the lord into the trees. "Help me, someone, please help me! Murderers are afoot!"

"You dare call us murderers?" said Prosper. "You vile, loathsome, despicable toad. You are the heir to the House of Browden who stood with the pretender against the true prince. Your matriarch was a general in the liar's army. She commanded two battalions of infantry at the Battle of Border Field. She gave the order to hurl pots of flaming tar into the ranks of my friends and my family."

The nobleman dropped to his knees at Candor's feet. He wept like a little boy caught stealing treats from his mother's pantry. "It was a war. You lot...

You wouldn't believe the truth. You wouldn't stop. It had to stop. It had to end. I'm sorry, but it had to end."

Prosper continued, "No one walked away from the carnage in flames. Not a man or a woman or a horse or a mouse in that field survived. Everything was turned to ashes while you went home, smiling, to your stone-hearted wife."

Xidron slipped the noose over the lord's head and tightened the knot at his neck.

"Mercy, please!"

"That's what *my mother* said." Candor pointed to the darkening hills in the west. "After they impaled my father, they pushed her to the bloody ground and took turns defiling her like rabid dogs. She begged for mercy, and they gave her death."

Prosper added, "So, I suppose, to you, mercy means death."

The group of youths chuckled darkly among themselves. Xidron picked up the slack of the rope and headed for the railing of the bridge.

Candor added, "You heard his lordship, lads. He asked for it. He wants mercy."

Ravel clenched her fists so tightly that her sharp nails dug into her palms. Mindless rage glowed in her brother's eyes. The fever of battle wafted like steam in the air. All the youths were intoxicated with a blood lust that she had seen before in others and that she had felt before herself. *I never wanted my little brother to have anything to do with what I have done. He was destined to wear soft shoes and carry a pen, not a sword.* He was never meant to be a killer or to have someone else's blood splashed on his face.

Yet the scent of blood and the odor of the lord's panic aroused her stomach. The inhuman urge for meat growled in her gut. The black talons burned hotly at the center of her chest. She resisted the trembling in her knees and the insatiable need to gobble on someone's fingers.

Ravel moved backwards, feigning retreat. She had one option left.

Xidron said, "Reds come help me with the rope. The gap in the railing is too wide. I can't reach through to tie it off."

"Yeah. Coming."

Six horses stood with reins dropped, nibbling at grasses by the side of the road. The lord's steed raised its headfirst and eyed her sideways. Ravel sensed the animal's fear and knew what would happen if she dared to take a step closer.

Ravel extended her arms wide. She flapped her cloak and bellowed, "Ha!" at the group of horses. One bolted first. The rest followed. By waving her stiff cloak and making a loud flapping noise, she chased the horses towards the bridge.

"Th' blazes!" Stander jumped aside. Prosper crouched into the bridge's railing.

Xidron and Redson grabbed Candor just in time. They pulled him out of the path of the galloping horses.

Ravel screamed, "Jump, your lordship! Jump for your life!"

Lord Rubëa vaulted over the bridge's railing. He splashed into the river below and floated away on the deep current.

"Traitor!" Candor screamed a sustained howl as he rushed full tilt into her.

He pushed her so hard that Ravel fell down the gravelly embankment. She tumbled, over and over, swaddling herself in the cloak, unable to stop rolling until she fell into the river's waters.

Cold dark waters howled to receive her. Water like acid burned her skin. Water spirits' tiny fingers ripped into her. She craned her neck and held up her face lest the waters gouge out her eyes. She had to clench her lips tightly shut to prevent herself swallowing even a mouthful of water. Eyes shut, jaw clenched, she screamed out agony through her nose.

Waters like rose thorns lifted her out whole. The river's current shoved her across to the opposite shore. Whips of droplets formed a chain that threw her out to land sprawling on sand and pebbles.

Raising herself to one elbow, Ravel shook her head to clear the vertigo. Water drops like hornets buzzed and stung as they dripped out of her ears.

Looking at her arms and legs, the exposed flesh not covered by the waxed cloak had been raked and scored. Her skin was raw, peeling away in ragged scraps that exposed the meat beneath. Veins turned black. Muscle fibers were purple not red. Her skull throbbed with a feverish ache, as if she had been bucked off a spooked horse and trampled. Through the rivulets of oozing blood, she could see the bones of her forearm, her calves, and the tarsals of her feet. She squeezed the flesh of her arm and held it as oily blood oozed through her fingers. It prickled as she held tight to stop the bleeding, but she held for as long as it took for the pain to ease.

She listened keenly to the sounds of twilight. She no longer heard her brother's voice or his companions. She could no longer sense the presence of the horses she had chased; perhaps they had stopped before plunging off the edge of the washed-out bridge, or perhaps not. She hoped that, at least, Lord Rubëa could swim in his velvet clothing well enough to reach the shore.

She lay prone on the gravel of the river's embankment and stared up at the darkening sky. In her youth, she would have prayed to the spirits of her ancestors for guidance. Now, she had no prayers left. She had no faith. Ravel saw nothing in the sky but gray clouds drifting across the teal sky of twilight. The tree line blocked her view of the distant hills of the west that she had once called home. All the world was slowly fading into darkness.

Toads croaked in the bushes nearby. Ravel lunged, grabbed one, and thrust its body into her mouth. Its long legs wriggled and slapped her cheeks. She gnawed to crush its skull and ribs just enough to swallow it down whole. Its mortal red blood dribbled down her chin and throat. She cupped her hands and caught the drippings, then finished her meal by licking her palms clean.

No wonder he won't listen to me, she thought. *I'm becoming a monster. If I am losing my own humanity, what hope do I have of saving my brother's soul?*

Staggering on weak and trembling knees, Ravel rose to her feet. She clawed into the soft soil and ascended the embankment onto the eastern shore of the river. In her weakened state, she assessed that it might take a couple of hours to traverse the farm fields that surrounded the capital city. Once inside the city's walls, she could scuttle the alleyways to avoid notice for as long as possible. She had one option left, one destination, one action that she had never expected to take.

In order to save her brother, she needed to betray him.

DENISE TANAKA

PART TWO

Chapter 27.

Day 12 of the Butcher's Month, in the Year of Xol 758

Water spirits in the sea breeze screamed at her approach. Ravel kept walking onward. *Am I doing the right thing, here? Is it not too late to turn back?* Barefoot and shrouded in the hooded cloak of waxed linen, she ascended the slope of the royal highway connecting Capital City to the outer gatehouse. High walls and a series of gatehouses encircled Xolhold Castle that loomed over the city's mosaic of shingled rooftops.

Stars twinkled faintly through dark clouds in the night sky. Moonlight failed to penetrate the fog. Her hood blocked the view of everything but the road beneath her feet. The closer she came to the base of Xolhold Castle, the less Ravel could see of its towers.

Crossing the drawbridge that spanned the castle's deep moat, Ravel tread carefully in the center. Far below sparkled the eyes of spirits that awakened to shriek at her presence. Thousands of eyeless eyes wailed in voiceless voices in a chaotic blend of fury and terror. But they were bound to the rippling waters at the base of the gorge. The moat's water spirits did not bother her as much as the nagging sea spray that pricked her cheeks. Moisture in the seaside air continued to harass her skin like a swarm of angry gnats; irritating but not impossible to tolerate.

At least it's not raining. Stop dwelling on physical complaints. Carry on, soldier. No turning back. Do your duty. Ravel's inner voice often spoke to herself in the commanding tones of her late father Colonel Spareen.

Ravel's blood tingled in the flesh that had just resealed itself within the last hour. She clutched the overlapping panels of her waxed linen cloak. As if marching to guide an infantry battalion through a storm, she willed her stinging bare feet to cross the drawbridge. Just a few more steps on stones moistened by the sea spray and she emerged onto gravelly dry soil.

Four spear-carriers in black uniforms stood guard duty at the outer gatehouse. They slouched in loose formation, at ease and complacent. Her approach interrupted a casual conversation about mocking a stable boy's series of mistakes that resulted in him getting kicked by a short-tempered stallion. A wave of dormant rage tasted like sour bile in the back of her throat. *Is this truly the greatest army in the land? Are these the victorious forces who destroyed my family, my country, and the future I would have lived?*

"Oy, beggar woman, the Day of Alms is not today. Begone, go on back in town is where you'll find scraps to eat." By their lack of alarm, it was clear that Candor and his friends had not yet implemented their plan of attack.

"I am not here to beg," Ravel said.

"Eh? What for do you approach here?"

"I bring an urgent message for the king."

One of the blond youths extended his hand. "Give it forth and I shall pass it up."

Ravel kept holding her cloak tightly shut. "It is not a written message. I must speak to His Majesty myself."

All four broke out in laughter. Their open-mouthed guffaws were louder than a few moments before when they had mocked a foolish stable hand for getting kicked.

She restrained herself from snarling as her mouth would be the only part of her face visible within her cloak's hood. She did not wish to appear hostile even to this group of fattened, contented foot soldiers. They stood at their guard posts, but they were not on guard. *If I were inclined to strike them down, how far would I get?*

"Tell him...." Ravel raised the volume of her voice. Moist sea air and thickening fog scraped raw the back of her throat. "Tell him that here stands the woman he met in the Outerlands who helped to save the crystal nest."

Confusion and curiosity quelled their laughter. The tallest one asked, "What crystal nest?" Another asked, "Are you a nomad from the Outerlands? You're not dressed in their garb." The third in line remarked, "Why don't you open your cloak and show your hands? Do you carry a weapon?"

Ravel unclenched her fists and held forth her open palms. "Tell him that I served Lord Torval of the House of Pegamodi. The king will understand this reference. He will be very angry if you turn me away."

The fourth guard, clearly the junior member of the group, received the stares of wordless suggestion from his fellows. He shrugged while grumbling, "Aye, aye, I'll run it up to the officer-of-the-day."

He launched from a stand-still into a decent pace of sprinting up the stairs and across the battlements of the crenellated walls. Ravel blinked to assess his fitness and speed as better than she had initially thought. The guards loitered when at ease, but they could snap back to readiness when called.

As they waited, the remaining three stood more upright, spears in hand. Before long, their attention drifted past Ravel to something happening on the road behind her.

Hooves pounded on the stones of the road. Without turning around, Ravel counted five of the king's royal steeds at full gallop. She bowed her head forward slightly to avoid drawing attention. Could it be that a patrol had found the lady and her children already? Or had they scooped the lord out of the river?

"Move aside! Move aside!" The tallest guard at the gate waved his left hand. Ravel complied and backed away to a patch of dry gravel.

War horses startled and shied away from where Ravel stood. Their riders in black uniforms regained control without losing a beat. They urged the large steeds to plunge through the outer gateway. One horse at the center of the group had double riders, with Lord Rubëa himself straddling the broad haunches and hugging the lieutenant in the saddle.

Time grew short. The lord would tell his story, and the castle would soon be alarmed.

Ravel stepped up quickly and once more spoke to the guards of the gate. "My message for the king is very urgent. Will you allow me passage?"

The guards waved her off, speaking amongst themselves. "I think that was a lord of the House of Browden, wasn't it?"

"Yeah, it looked like him."

Ravel pressed toward the gateway's threshold. Two spears crossed and blocked her passage. Rouge tassels dangled across the cuffs of their black gloves. With her hands still open, palms outward, she could do nothing but wait for the runner to return. Time was getting shorter and shorter.

"What d'you think happened to his carriage?" the guard said to his comrade.

"Could've hit a low-hanging branch and fell off his horse. Those soft-legged lords of Browden House, y'know."

"Yeah, they let their women do all the fighting."

Smirks and eye-rolls passed between them.

The running guard returned from sprinting the full length of the castle's concentric walls. He had pinkened cheeks but was otherwise not out of breath. "Bring her in."

"How's that again, Ieon?" asked the tallest guard.

"Bring 'er inside, Danëar. I asked the duty officer of the day, who asked the captain, who relayed her message to the commander himself. Colonel said we are to bring her into His Majesty's presence at once."

Spears uncrossed. Ravel walked straight forward into the archway of gray stone. Spikes of an iron portcullis loomed overhead for a moment. She briefly mused that if the grillwork gate dropped, and if her skull were pierced by the spikes, would it be enough to kill her?

Black uniforms carrying red tasseled halberds and iron box lanterns came to escort her. She smelled their apprehension rising out of wariness. She licked her dry lips in savoring the aroma of their flesh and meat. Her stomach growled with unnatural hunger. *Stop it. Stop it.* Ravel clenched her lips shut. She recited a chant within her mind like a prayer. *I am not a monster. I carry the talons of a monster, but I am not a monster. I am a lady. I am a lady of a noble house. I am not a monster.*

The squad of escorts led her through a narrow man-made gorge of stone block walls rising high on either side. Overhead on the ramparts, guards in black uniforms stared down at her. Ravel kept walking up the gradual incline and pretended not to notice those watching from the narrow archer's slits in the walls. The alleyway made a sharp turn and doubled back on itself.

Soon they came to another gatehouse with more flags, more bull's head emblems chiseled in the stones, and more spear-carriers on guard. Archers with longbows perched on the turret above the portcullis grill. With arrows already fitted to the strings, they were ready to launch their barbed shafts in the blink of an eye.

If only they knew, their arrows won't kill me.

The escorts guided her across the open yard of the outer bailey. Wattle-and-daub townhouses resembled a village plucked out of the countryside and transplanted within the castle's wall. A blacksmith's forge flared bright yellow. Craftsmen in their shops paused work to observe her passing by. Servants carrying baskets stopped on the footpath to let her pass.

"Keep moving, keep moving," said the guardsman escort.

Another gatehouse divided the outer bailey from the inner bailey yard. Concentric circles of walls grew ever smaller on the approach to the cluster of columnar towers that were the innermost Xolhold Keep. People worked in small groups to do the ordinary labor of the castle's functions in preparation for nightfall. They tended to the needs of the mighty black war horses and hauled wheelbarrows back and forth from the stables. Rows of barracks with open doorways gave a glimpse of off-duty soldiers cleaning mud off their boots at the end of the day. This was not the army of a tyrannical despot that she had half-expected to find. She saw no one being punished at a whipping post. No severed heads were propped up on pikes. No corpses hung on nooses anywhere. Overall, there was a sense of doing one's duty in an atmosphere of contentment.

I am making the right decision. Ravel blinked her dry eyes; tears did not come. *My brother is wrong. Forgive me, Candor. May we all survive long enough for me to apologize to your face.*

After passing through the barbican gate of Xolhold Keep, Ravel and her escorts entered a courtyard with a grand water fountain. She avoided the shrieking waters as best she could. The squad allowed her to walk a wider course. Perhaps they assumed that she showed respect for the statue.

A marble likeness of King Glëa stood on a pedestal at the center of the fountain. Blue gemstones sparkled in the statue's eye sockets. Clothing sculpted in stone imitated the texture of various fabrics: velvet, satin, corduroy, silk, fur, and lace. The wavy curls of his long hair cascaded to his beltline. Briefly she appreciated the artisan's skill at recreating an accurate representation of the king's boyish facial features. Frozen in stone for all time stood the immortal king's image. *Vain, haughty, pompous, posturing despot.* The words came to her mind out of reflex more than rancor.

A captain and two lieutenants emerged from the tower's stone-framed oak door. "We'll take her from here."

"Yes sir." The escorts saluted by clasping their fists together. Quickly bowing their foreheads into their upraised knuckles, they backed off and returned the way they had come.

Ravel assessed the captain who did not appear to be much older than his two lieutenants. His face seemed familiar. There were not many blackcoats that she had met, up close, since the war ended. She had encountered only a single squad in the Outerlands, years ago, in that mountain cave where her life's course had changed forever. After a moment's thought, she recalled his name.

"Herry.... Am I right?"

The captain's narrow eyes made a study of her face. "I remember you too, Rebel. We all thought you died in the rockslide on that mountain."

"I didn't," she said.

"Clearly." The captain turned on his heel. "Follow me, Rebel."

Ravel ascended the steps into the foyer of the northern tower. Candles blazed in sconces on the walls to light the way. Both lieutenants fell into position behind her, spears at the ready, as if they would do any good if she really meant harm to them.

"Congratulations on your promotion," Ravel said. "You've come up from the fife-and-drum corps, I see."

Herry did not respond. He led the way to a stairwell marked by tapestry flags. Ravel recognized the colors and heraldry of several noble houses: Browden and Fordon and Vilbyss. Of course, her own noble house of Spareen would not be among them. Only the victorious houses had their flags displayed here. All other flags had been burned in the war. All other names had been purged from the roster of lords.

Ravel ascended the wedges of stairs that spiraled upwards around a core. Turning on her right shoulder on the uneven weathered steps, her memories drifted backwards to when her younger brother was an infant suckling on her mother's lap. An older sister's duty was to guard the son and heir to their noble name until he came of age to stand on his own. Candor was a treasure to be protected at all costs. *Forgive me, little brother. Someday I hope you will understand that I have no choice but to do this.*

Captain Herry stopped at the threshold of a large oak door. To either side of the door frame, two narrow archer's windows overlooked the courtyard below. In a time of siege, this alcove would be filled with blackcoats making their last line of defense. Herry's lieutenants moved into position on either side to prevent Ravel from moving towards the door too soon.

Captain Herry took hold of the brass knocker but paused to look back over his shoulder at her. "I'm under orders from the Commander of the Guard to bring you here, so I have. But know this, Rebel. If you make the slightest move to harm my king, we will strike you down where you stand."

She slowly pushed back the hood of her cloak. The waxed linen hung stiffly and awkwardly off the nape of her neck. She waited for Captain Herry to get a good look at her jaundiced cheeks, her bloodshot eyes, and her thinning hair that was falling out in clumps by the day. To his credit, he held a mostly stoic expression although a twitch of his eye betrayed his utter revulsion at what she had become.

"I'd expect no less of you, Captain." An unspoken understanding passed between them.

Captain Herry knocked. Someone inside unbolted the door and pushed it open.

Chapter 28.

Ash made ready to leave work for the day. He packed up his writing desk in a small, curtained nook at the rear of the infirmary. His stomach gurgled in anticipation of a bowl full of the head cook's bean stew. He could almost smell the browned onions simmering near the barracks as he headed for the door.

A soldier in a hooded cloak stepped inside, blocking Ash's exit. He grasped Ash by the sleeve and held him from leaving. Within the hood was the lean, regal face of King Glëa po'Lon.

"Your Majesty?" Ash asked.

"Oh, praises be, I still look passable!" The fellow's voice had a much deeper and smokier timbre than the king.

"Jahn?"

Captain Jahn po'Shea removed his hooded cloak and hung it to a peg on the wall. His waist-length black hair was tied in a ponytail with a russet cord. Wavy strands had broken loose and drooped across his blue eyes. Even though Ash realized this was not the king but his lookalike, the resemblance was unnerving.

"How can I help you, Jahn?"

"I need skin cream."

"Skin cream?" Ash repeated.

"Yes, yes, skin cream! You know, the buttery crud that you dispense to the ladies."

"Why?"

Jahn pointed to his own jawline. "The big betrothal banquet is tomorrow and I've got to look the part. I've been shaving so much, my skin hurts."

"I see."

Ash led the way across the infirmary's ground floor. Large storage cabinets filled the space underneath the loft's overhang. He ducked beneath the open-slat staircase and bent over to the bottom drawer.

"You thought I was *him* when I wore a hood. But how do I look, really? Are my cheeks too brown? Am I getting too much sunshine? Have I tacked on weight? Am I getting too thick in the gut?"

Ash brought forth a ceramic jar wrapped with twine in parchment paper. "You look fantastic, Jahn, really. Until you spoke, I thought you were him."

"Glad you reminded me; I need to raise my voice to a bit higher pitch." Jahn cleared his throat. "How's this?"

"Perfect."

Jahn frowned while hugging the ceramic jar to his chest. "You're being too kind, Ash. Tell me honestly."

"Honestly, you look and sound very royal. Dress you up and comb your hair, and Lord Vilbyss himself won't know the difference." Ash clapped the fellow on the shoulder pads. "But why call you into service at all? It's just a banquet, not a battlefield."

Jahn said, "I'll do the parade through the city streets. We start at the aqueduct bridge and go all the way up the main avenue. Too many people came in from all the four corners of the known world. Too many rooftops for an archer to lie in wait. Too many alleyways for a knife-thrower to crouch. I'll be wearing a steel breastplate under the robes."

"Shit." Ash laid a hand to the back of his neck. "Have we not yet put behind us all the war and killing?"

"Straggling groups of troublemakers are still harassing folks in the countryside," Jahn said. "Nothing organized into an insurgency by any means, but still, it only takes one with a grievance..."

They both shared a moment of grim silence.

Jahn abruptly turned and quickly strode between the rows of empty beds. "Himself will do the actual ceremony in the Main Hall of the White Tower, of course."

"Why you?" Ash strolled behind him towards the rack of cloaks. "Aren't there a few others who stand in his place? If you're not feeling up to the task—"

"Feeling? I can't afford feelings." Jahn grabbed his black wool cloak from the peg. "I'm the best choice for this auspicious day. Alton and Xoeth are only good at a distance. People in the crowd might push up close to the carriage, close enough to clearly see his face—*my face*. Compare me to the statues and frescoes and visages stamped on coins? I'm still the best of the shadow guards, yeah?"

"Yeah, you are." Ash could not deny the strong resemblance. Only by squinting could he notice a slight difference in the distance between his blue eyes, the sharper cut of his jawline, or the bridge of his nose.

Jahn swirled the cloak around his shoulders. "This will probably be my last event, anyway. *He* says I'm getting too old."

"How are you getting old?" Ash asked. "Aren't we about the same age?"

"I'm thirty-one, come the new year! I can't keep passing for nineteen."

Ash put on his own brown cloak and followed Jahn outside. The sky had already turned into night. Clouds and fog blocked the faint glow of the moon.

"I'm training a new lad," Jahn said. "He's fifteen and growing tall fast. He's got the face but he's a blondie! We're going to dye his hair or make a wig. Even so, it's going to take a year, minimum, for him to learn the poise and manners. And what's more, the bumpkin is a fisherman's son! You should hear his accent."

Ash veered aside for the footpath leading to the barracks' chow line. Firelight lit the way glowing orange beneath the distant cauldrons. "Turn in early, Jahn. Get a good night's sleep, or you'll wake up with bags under your pretty blue eyes."

"Oh shit!"

"Sorry I mentioned it. Don't worry. You're fine."

"Fuck sod, Ash." Jahn stopped in his tracks. He turned around and slightly bowed. "My apologies. I take it back. I'm just so nervous about tomorrow."

Ash shrugged a congenial smile. "We're buddies, all right?"

Chapter 29.

Ravel's escorts brought her to an antechamber that bustled with activity. Servants in rouge gowns and long aprons glanced at her passing through their midst, but they were too busy at their tasks. They snipped the stems off cherries. They scooped the pits out of peaches. They used reed whisks to whip up heavy cream. To one wall, a large fireplace blazed around a bubbling cauldron.

Chamber guards wearing gloves parted the curtains. They wore rouge tunics, black hose, and flat-soled velvet slippers. Yet despite their dainty attire, their poise and stance showed a lithe agility that promised any threat would be met and subdued.

One guard announced, "The visitor at the gate seeks to approach His Majesty."

A signal was given, and Ravel was allowed to stroll forward into the luxurious chamber. Her bare feet patted on checkered tiles of rose and black marble. She crossed between fluted columns entwined with potted jasmine vines. The domed ceiling was painted light blue to imitate the sky and had a stained-glass skylight at its center. At this late hour, the colored glass had turned dark.

King Glëa po'Lon stood at a full-sized mirror of silver glass. He was only half-dressed in black velvet breeches and a bleached linen shirt. A bald tailor hunched to wrap the waistband of a pleated kilt around the king's slender torso. Ravel quickly assessed the exquisite workmanship in the brocade garment and realized that the king was being fitted for his betrothal attire. His tailor muttered as he checked the fit of the pleated skirt's waistband. "Still the same measurements... Hasn't gained a smidge in the gut..."

"Hello, rebel." The king's voice echoed powerfully as if they stood in a desert canyon. The sound rippled the air like heat. Undertones pushed her against coming any closer.

Ravel stopped at a barrier of flowering planter boxes. Rhododendron and geranium blossoms filled the air with the perfume of eternal springtime trapped indoors on a dark autumn night.

"Your Majesty." She felt a sour taste on her tongue at speaking those words. She did not kneel. She did not bow.

The immortal king was outwardly a youth of nineteen with boyish features that had not yet sprouted a moustache. Ravel's tainted eyes could now see the ethereal second spirit that cohabitated his skin. A hazy corona of brightness outlined his slender body. Mortal prince and inhuman soul shared one heart; the two minds as one. *Hello, Lil' Hatchling*, she was tempted to say.

An older man reclined nearby on a cushioned divan. He sipped at a glass of brandy. The potbellied nobleman wore a saffron tunic and a velvet cloak of such a deep hue of brown that it appeared black. *Lord Vilbyss*, she assumed from the heraldry on his signet ring.

One gray-haired, elderly woman dressed in a sage green gown and a gray chemise. She puffed on a white-stemmed silver pipe as she frowned in Ravel's direction. That irascible crone surely could be none other than his former general Lady Browden, the so-called Thorn Lily of the Green Forest.

The king continued, "I assumed you had died when the mountain crumbled, but well, here you are."

When he paused, Ravel caught the intensity of his stare. She understood his unspoken admonition to choose her words carefully. Most likely, he had reported an abridged version of what really happened on that mountainside all those years ago.

"Yes, here I am," she said.

The tailor politely coaxed the king into raising his arm extended out to the side. Glëa's chemise sleeve hung in a half-circle between his shoulder and wrist. Then, the tailor proceeded to stretch a measuring tape into his armpit.

King Glëa asked, "You said that you bring a message from Lord Torval?"

Ravel saw the flicker of hope sparkle in the king's eyes. She realized that he expected a very different message than the one she came to bring. Perhaps he hoped for better news of the other immortal. The scholarly Lord Torval was a more ancient fallen soul than the king himself. There was too much to tell of how that other immortal had sacrificed his life's blood. He had given up his life repairing the cracks in the floating crystal nest. His sacrifice and hers together saved the countless unhatched golden eggs from dropping out of the clouds ever again.

"Lord Torval is dead," she told him.

"I see." The king lowered his arm. The tailor moved to measure the space between his shoulders.

"His life ended that day on the mountainside. I apologize if there's been a misunderstanding. I clearly told the guards at the gatehouse that I bring an urgent message, and that I served Lord Torval of the House of Pegamodi, but I did not state that my message is from him."

Ravel wanted to speak to him frankly not as the king but as an ethereal spirit inhabiting the face of this man. *Torval gave his life to save the crystal nest from crashing to earth. All your unhatched kindred are safely incubating unawares.* Yet the watchful eyes of his mortal generals, servants and guards cautioned her into silence.

"What is your message, then?" he asked.

"My brother is coming for your head."

The elderly Lord Vilbyss raised his broad girth off the divan's cushions with more vigor than she had expected of a man his age. "Sound an alarm!"

"Don't panic, you old dog," scolded Lady Browden who lithely rose to her feet. "Who are you, beggar woman, and why should we fear your brother?"

"He has sworn to himself an oath of vengeance for the honor of our noble house. My name is Ravel po'Marn first daughter of the House of Spareen."

"An unbeliever," scoffed the elderly lord. "A traitor's house."

"A horseman of the west," the lady added, puffing on her pipe.

Glëa raised his hand in admonishment. Jeweled rings sparkled at each of his fingers. "A horseman of the west she may be, but an unbeliever she is no more. On that one occasion when we met in the Outerlands, she recognized the truth when she saw me face-to-face. Yes?"

Ravel nodded and took his cue. It felt awkward but she played along, as her brother and his friends had pretended to meet as strangers at the roadside tavern. "Yes, I acknowledge you are indeed the lost prince who returned."

He raised the corner of his left eyebrow, no doubt observing that she withheld calling him the rightful king of the land.

"My younger brother does not share my belief," she continued. "He maintains that you are a fair-faced imposter who has fooled everyone. He is coming for your head to avenge the deaths of our parents."

The king waved at his tailor to withdraw as if brushing away a persistent fly. Hunched over in a perpetual bow, the tailor backed away.

"When does he plan to attack?" Glëa asked.

"I don't know. If not tonight, then very soon in the coming days."

"How great of a force has he mustered?"

"He has no army," she said. "Just four..."

"Four hundred?"

"No, just four."

The elderly man and woman snickered between themselves. King Glëa remained solemn. Ravel had to admit, he radiated an air of regal authority even though he stood half dressed in his shirt sleeves.

"Do they have unnatural, special abilities? Has he enlisted any un-folk or mystical creatures as allies? Do they command wraiths? Bog blythes? Prophets? Have they captured the tail feather of a firebird?"

Ravel shook her head. "No, they're just boys."

"Do they have martial training?"

"Some, yeah, at best the equal of your footmen guards in a one-on-one fight." If Ravel were still capable of blushing, her cheeks might have pinkened to voice such an exaggeration.

Glëa came forward and rested his elbows on the frame of the flowering planter boxes. He stared hard, silently, straight into her eyes as if trying to read letters in the threads of her irises. Ravel felt the pressure of his piercing stare. Invisible tendrils of his mind scratched and probed at the shuttered windows of her thoughts.

So, Lil' Hatchling, she thought. *You are practicing how to be what you really are.*

"Yes I am." Glëa mouthed the words in such a quiet whisper that Ravel doubted he could even hear himself.

Candor's face as a child replayed in her memories. She thought of the auburn hue of his fawn-colored hair. The odor of freshly-picked wild figs floated to her mind along with spoken words. *Felicitations on the anniversary of your birth. You're seventeen today! I turned seventeen three days ago.*

A sudden headache throbbed in her skull. He was digging too far. He saw too much that he was not privileged to see. Ravel held her breath as she pushed back. All of her will strained in the effort to get him out.

Glëa pulled away in surrender and coughed an exhale. He pinched the space between his eyebrows. Everyone in the room waited in utter silence for the king to speak again.

How clumsy, she thought. *Lord Torval had strolled through my head much more skillfully. But then, he was not freshly hatched when he fell out of the sky. You have a lot to learn, Lil' Hatchling.*

"What is your brother's plan?" Glëa asked.

"I don't know," she said. "He did not confide in me."

"Would he try to steal a uniform and infiltrate my guards to slip a knife in my neck? He would surely fail. I know the names and faces of every soldier who walks through these halls. They've all known each other for years. No stranger gets within a spear-throw's distance of me. If he tries to forge a paper of transfer with a wax seal, he won't get past the outer gatehouse. Does your brother hope to sneak inside the walls on the next hay wagon?"

Ravel shook her head again. "He was a scholarly youth. He sought out archivists and collected old documents. He obtained architectural schematics and studied the long-forgotten secret passageways built into these towers."

"I am very well aware of all the false panels, double walls, sally doors, and hidden tunnels beneath Xolhold Keep," the king said.

"I figured you would be," she said. "Nonetheless, my brother has made extensive studies in the annals of history. There are numerous and legendary scenarios that he could replicate. He seemed very confident of success. Which is why I fear disaster. He's just a foolish boy. He's only turned seventeen years old."

"Yes..." The king stopped himself from blurting out that he knew Candor's age from probing Ravel's thoughts just now. Clearly, the truth of his dual nature was important for him to keep secret. How invaluable it must be for a king, she mused, to have the mystic ability to peer into the private thoughts of others.

The elderly Lord Vilbyss asked, "Why betray him to us? Why not stop him yourself?"

"We were separated on the road," Ravel said.

Glëa stepped back from the barrier of flowers and fern fronds. His long black hair, disheveled from the tailor's activity, hung in wavy locks past his waist. Servants held little baskets packed with flasks of perfumed oil and a variety of long-toothed combs. They waited for permission to approach but, until the word was given, they stood by like statues.

"You didn't answer Ardis's question," the king remarked. "Why betray him to us? Why not double your efforts to stop him yourself?"

"Surely you've guessed by now. I have an impediment." Ravel's dry throat rasped on her words.

He lowered his scrutinizing stare to her torso. "Show me."

Ravel pulled apart the waxed linen cloak to reveal her threadbare chemise. The drawstring collar hung low enough to expose her secret. She displayed the black talons embedded between the cleavage of her breasts.

"By his name!" croaked Lady Browden. "You're one of them!"

"Those traitorous magic workers," the elder Vilbyss added.

Glëa hushed them both with a wave of his hand. He held his silence for a long moment and refrained from offering any further explanation.

"I killed your magickers," Ravel explained. "At that mountain in the Outerlands, I fought them."

"You did me a service with assisting my squad with meting out punishment to those who betrayed me."

She glanced sideways to Captain Herry who gave a slight, noncommittal nod. Without knowing how much or how little the squad wrote in their official report, Ravel chose her next words carefully.

"I stole their powers by implanting these talons into myself. But with those powers also come certain limitations."

The king nodded knowingly. "You cannot interact with water."

"Yes," Ravel said. "The spirits of waters are antagonistic to me."

"Perhaps your brother would have sought to use your mystical abilities in his plan of attack?"

Ravel pulled shut the folds of her cloak. "Your theory is sensible. I accept the idea that he intended to use me in his plans. Although my brother does not believe in magical forces, he has seen these things in my chest. He has seen what I can do. Somehow, he has rationalized the contradiction between the magical and the mundane. I don't know what he was thinking. To be completely candid, I've come to realize that I haven't known what he is thinking for a very long time. Ever since his voice broke and he grew taller than I am by a hand-and-a-half—"

"Why betray him to me?" Glëa interrupted. "You still have not answered the question."

Tears did not rise to her dry eyes. Yet her brows furrowed with the urge to break out weeping. "I've come to beg for mercy. When his foolish plan is foiled, as I know it will be, I beg that you spare his life. You've already robbed him of his father, his mother, his name, his title, his estate, his future—"

Lord Vilbyss barked, "How dare you speak such impudence!"

The gray-haired Lady Browden said, "It's a deception. Don't grant her any favors, Your Majesty."

She looked up and met his unblinking stare. As she had surmised from the moment of entering this chamber, he had never told his generals the truth of his inner nature. Only she had been at Glëa's side, on that crumbling mountainside on the border of the Outerlands, when he discovered it for himself. His immortality came not from a miraculous blessing of his royal ancestors. A sparkling fragile creature had fallen out of the crystal nest in the sky and lodged itself within this young man's bones. What happened to him had also happened entirely at random to many others who were not princes. His magic workers had gone rogue to silence Lord Torval even as they concealed the truth from Glëa himself. This secret could shatter his kingdom's fragile unity. Surely he would do anything to preserve what he had fought so ruthlessly to gain.

Ravel sank to her knees on the marble floor. "I beseech you to hear my plea, not as king of the land, or as prince and heir to the Davarche Dynasty, but as the... the... the *man* you are in your heart. Were you not a reckless lad, once, when you sailed forth to explore the open seas? Can you not grant forgiveness for the folly of youth?"

King Glëa commanded, "Get up."

Ravel rocked back on her heels and smoothly rose to her feet.

"Clearly you have lost all honor and fealty to the noble house that you once held title to," the king said. "Whatever sort of a lady and an officer you may have been during the war, you are neither of them anymore. Talons have infected your blood and your mind. I am skeptical of anything you might say."

Ravel gritted her teeth; there it was, planting the seeds of doubt if she would threaten to reveal his secret.

"If you wish to earn my forgiveness for your brother's plotting an assassination, you must earn it."

The king merely tilted his chin in the direction of the curtained archway. Captain Herry came hurrying forth to genuflect at his feet.

"Your Majesty," the captain proclaimed while bowing over his own knee.

"Starting from this moment, Mistress Ravel, you are on patrol. You shall coordinate with my commander of the guard and prowl the ramparts. Sniff out your brother and his cohorts like the bloodhound you've become. I know very well what you can do. I also know that you don't need to sleep. You barely need to be fed, but for a few scraps of raw meat now and then. So, no excuses. No failure will be tolerated."

"Will you spare him?" she insisted.

The two old generals on the divan cushions grumbled their disapproval. Their murmuring voices blended with the background noise of fireplace logs crackling.

"You have my word," the king said. "My legions will be under orders to disarm, subdue, and restrain these foolish boys, if at all possible. In exchange for your cooperation, once he is secured in chains, I will not sign his death warrant. Are we in agreement?"

"Yes." Ravel paused before adding, "Sir."

Chapter 30.

Ash gently used two fingertips to apply ointment cream to the rope burns on Lord Rubëa's neck. The lord's head tilted upwards resting on the back of the dining chair. He sniffled as tears glistened in his closed eyes. Blood filled the gauze roll jutting out of his left nostril. More bloody gauze was stuffed into his swollen cheek. He gargled, swallowed, and grimaced at the taste.

Logs in the fireplace glowed black and orange. Candlelight fought the gloom of the dark windowpanes.

The dinner table had five empty seats but for Rubëa occupying the head of the table. All the platters were long since cleared away. Even the candlesticks at the centerpiece had been snuffed out. The table now held all of Ash's equipment: the pans for lumps of bloody gauze, the uncorked vials of medicinal powders, and a sewing kit with a spool of silk thread for stitching the gash on the lord's forehead.

Jenny brought a bowl of tepid soup. She set it on the corner of the table. "When you're ready, my lord."

Rubëa opened his eyes and blinked against the tears. "Where is Mother?"

"She is downstairs in her bed chamber," Jenny answered softly.

"Has she been made aware of what happened to me?"

"Yes, my lord."

Ash finished applying the ointment to the raw, red circle around his neck. He knew—they all knew—that Lady Dalhanna had no intention of rising out of her comfortable bed. If her son was not on the verge of dying, she had no cause to interrupt her sleep. Though Rubëa was a man nearly forty years old, Ash saw in his teary eyes a frightened little boy. For the first time in many years, Ash sympathized for what the lord might be feeling: to be helpless and in pain and to have no one offering comfort.

"C'mon, Rube, you're a braver man than this. Mother knows you're not terribly hurt so there's no good reason for her to come running upstairs in her nightgown."

"They tried to kill me!"

"Yeah but they didn't." Ash wiped his bloodied hands with a rag. "You survived. You climbed up out of the river. Well done. You're safe now. Let your mother get a good night's sleep. Tomorrow's a big day."

Jenny held up the soup bowl close to his chin. She offered to feed him with a spoon. He turned his face away.

Rubëa scowled at her. "How can I eat with a broken jaw?"

"Your jaw isn't broken," Ash said. "Not sure about the nose, though. We'll have to see in the morning if the swelling goes down."

Half a dozen guards in black coats entered the room. Captain Stockard at the front of the squad was a stout, square-jawed woman. She asked, "How serious are his injuries?"

"Bruised and scraped," Ash reported.

Captain Stockard advanced to the foot of the table and took a stance. "Are you able to report what happened to you, my lord?"

"They were going to hang me from the broken bridge. They put a rope around my neck! They accused me of burning their homes or killing their parents during the war. I begged for mercy, and they laughed at me."

Ash began packing up his medical supplies into a small wooden chest with brass handles.

Stockard asked, "How many highwaymen were in the group, my lord?"

"A dozen! Perhaps twenty..."

The lieutenants and footmen exchanged skeptical glances amongst themselves. Stockard asked, "How did you get away?"

"Something spooked their horses and caused them to bolt." Rubëa frowned in trying to remember. "Oh yes, and one of them had a change of heart. I heard someone yell, 'jump,' and so I did. I leaped into the river and nearly drowned."

Stockard asked, "What became of your wife and children, my lord?"

"Murdered on the road, no doubt."

"Were you not with the carriage, my lord, when the highwaymen assaulted you?"

Rubëa stood up out of the chair. The full breadth and width of his girth loomed powerfully over them all. "The carriage was too slow, so I rode ahead on my own."

"And your escorts, my lord? Where were they?"

Rubëa clenched his fist at the air. "My escorts *were* the highwaymen, Captain. They deceived me."

Jenny gasped in surprise. Ash spoke up with the obvious question, "The escorts from your own house betrayed you?"

"No, no, pay attention. You're not listening to me. I had to discharge my household escorts when they fell ill at Loyalton with stomach ailments. I hired a new group at the tavern."

Stockard repeated, "You hired a group of strangers at a tavern?"

"I had no choice," Rubëa said. "My escorts fell ill and could not continue. We were so close to the capital, I assumed that we would be safe."

Ash buckled the leather straps of his medicinal kit. He stared down at his own hands resting on the wood. *Clear, if you've foreseen any of this in your visions, why did you do nothing to prevent it? Unless a few bruises are not worth the effort of your mystic powers? Will we find his wife and children alive and safe, abandoned by the roadside?*

"They were cunning in their deceit," Rubëa said. "They appeared to have cultured manners and made interesting conversation on the road. Furthermore, the lads were so youthful and genteel, not at all what one would expect highwaymen to look like. They even brought a crippled woman who hardly seemed dangerous."

"How many, my lord, did you hire?" Stockard asked.

"Five lads and the cripple woman," he answered.

Stockard bowed. "Thank you for your cooperation, my lord. I shall make a full report to the colonel. We will take immediate action to hunt them down wherever they may be hiding. I assure you, sir, these ruffians shall not escape punishment."

Ash picked up his medicinal kit. He started to follow the other soldiers who were leaving the room.

Rubëa called out, "Can you give me a potion to help me sleep?"

"Jenny can help brew some more of the willow bark tea," Ash said.

"I need something more," he insisted. "I'm in pain! I know you have stronger treatments in that little box of yours."

"No." Ash stopped at the draperies and briefly turned back. "Stop asking me to help you poison yourself, Rube. Trust me. Some treatments are worse than pain."

Chapter 31.

Captain Herry and his two lieutenants escorted Ravel back the way they had come, down the spiraling stairwell, out to the firelit courtyard awash in brown shadows. Clouds drifted slowly across the slate sky overhead. They hurried past the water fountain with its grand statue of the king. Moonlight cast a silvery hue on the curves of towers.

Ravel briefly wondered what had become of Lord Rubëa that the squad of rescuers had pulled from the river. Clearly the lord had not drowned and was not unconscious. By now, he must have reported the assault on the bridge. Yet no alarm bells rang.

The captain led her across the inner bailey yard, past the stables and livestock pens, to the two-story barracks. He knocked twice on a narrow door and waited for someone to call out, "Enter!"

She followed Herry into the headquarters. Ravel immediately felt at home under a ceiling of oak crossbeams and stale air that reeked of soldiers, leather, wool, and iron. More years than she had ever spent in ladylike pursuits, she had spent in barracks such as this. She half expected to see her own father Colonel Spareen in charge of these racks of weapons and the neatly tucked bunkbeds. A row of knitted socks hung on the fireplace mantle to dry. One wall had shelves stocked full of wool blankets, canteens, and tin box lanterns. Above the officer's writing desk was a narrow shelf for stacking leather-bound folios of ledgers.

The commander's blond hair sharply contrasted with his black uniform. His blue eyes were so pale as to be grey. He had gained a bit of padding in the cheeks since their last meeting, years before, but Ravel still recognized him.

"Viktor," she said.

"Commander, sir." Herry stepped forward and clasped his fists in salute.

"Report, Captain."

"She has a younger brother, age seventeen with no martial experience, who is planning a small group infiltration for the purpose of assassinating His Majesty." Herry paused after saying all that in one breath.

"Very good, Captain." Commander Viktor fixed his ice-blue eyes on her; the same eyes that she had known in another place long ago. "The years have not been kind to you, Rebel."

"More than you can imagine."

She parted the front flap of her cloak just enough to reveal tips of the black talons embedded in her breastbone. No words were needed. Viktor and his squad had been there, on that mountaintop in the Outerlands, and helped her to fight the magic-workers who had once served and then betrayed the king. Viktor had struck them with mortal blows only to watch with horror as every injury healed before their eyes. To slice their flesh was like slicing into river mud; no sword, spear, or arrow left a permanent mark. Only by ripping the claw bones out of their chests could they be killed.

"You took those from *them*?" he asked.

"Yes," she said. "I did what I had to do to save the crystal nest from falling, but I couldn't save Lord Torval."

Viktor nodded that he understood what had happened after they parted ways and before the mountainside had crumbled away. He was one of the few who had seen the floating crystal palace while it was tumbling out of the clouds.

"You've done a great service," he said.

Ravel shrugged. "Whatever I do is never enough. There's always more to do."

"Such is the life of a soldier," he murmured, looking aside.

Herry continued, "By the word of the king himself, this woman is to be assigned with patrol units, day and night, until the infiltrators are discovered. Orders are to disarm, subdue, and restrain them if at all possible. In reward for her cooperation, her brother's life is to be spared."

"So shall it be." Viktor sat down at his writing desk. He swiftly penned orders on a few squares of paper and stamped each with his signet ring dipped in a wad of red paste. "You shall start on Xolhold Keep's south tower. Work your way around the ramparts connecting to the east, the north, the west, and the White Tower as well. Always stay within line-of-sight of the footmen on duty. Understood?"

"What if I need to seek him elsewhere?" she asked.

"Seek him wherever you feel he may be discovered but maintain communication with the sentinels at every step."

"I understand. Stay within line-of-sight. Call out my movements."

A pause lingered between them. It became clear that she would not address him as sir.

Viktor handed off the stack of orders to Captain Herry who received the papers with a curt bow. "I'm about to go off duty, but I will leave a detailed report for the night commander."

Ravel raised the hood of her cloak and turned to leave.

"Wait," Viktor called out.

Herry and his lieutenants were already out the door. Ravel stopped on the threshold and looked back over her shoulder.

"What is your brother's name?"

"Candor," she said. "Candor po'Marn of the House of Spareen and the only surviving lord to carry the name, thanks to you butchering crud-coats."

Viktor spoke in an even-toned voice, neither angry nor offended. "Carry on."

Ravel launched into the darkening shadows. She headed for the stairwell that would take her up to the peak of the south tower. Groups of lancers, spear-carriers, foot soldiers and archers in black wool uniforms watched her ascend. In the dark of night, Ravel found herself standing in collaboration with the soldiers who had levelled her home, who may have raped and murdered her mother, who butchered her father and so many other lords who stood in defense of a pragmatic prince who did not believe in miracles. All of it gone. In blood. In death. In ashes and dust.

From the rampart's walkway, Ravel sprang up to the edge of the conical roof. The height should have needed a ladder, but she cleared it as easily as a goat hopping a fence. With every passing hour, it became more difficult to feign humanity as the talons seeped drop-by-drop into the marrow of her own boats. She squatted by a brass flagpole bearing the coat of arms of the Royal House of Davarche and gazed over the castle's walls.

Out there in the farm fields, beyond her reach, thousands of simple people were leading simple lives as they had done for generations. For them, life had not changed except for the colors of the flags that their masters carried. Farmers had come indoors from their day of laboring in the fields. Craftsmen in the city closed their shops. Merchants at the wharfs counted their coins. If only her brother could feel contentment in finding a new life in this new world. It was not what their father had promised, but it was a life that one could have if they chose to accept the unbelievable as truth.

How did my life come to this, she wondered.

Chapter 32.

Ash arrived home long past the hour when he wished to be asleep in bed. He carried his medicinal kit under his left arm. A tin box lantern dangled from his right hand. Braziers flickered flames in the high watchtowers and the turrets of the gatehouses, too high for their light to reach the ground. The hem of his long cloak swept the grassy pebbles of the footpath. Every window was dark in the two-story wattle-and-daub townhouses clustered against the castle's high walls. Everyone else but the guards on night duty had tucked into their beds for the night.

He found his own front door by memory rather than by sight. Exhausted, he vaguely noticed that his upstairs window glowed from within. He assumed that Will kept a lantern burning in expectation of his return.

Ash stepped inside the cold downstairs room. First he put down his medicinal kit and lantern on the blocky table. Then he removed his cloak and went to hang it on the peg.

Someone else's cloak hung by the door. Odors of horse were muted by a lady's jasmine perfume. A pair of white lambskin gloves lay on the shelf.

Oh no, he thought with a knot tightening his stomach. *Why is Clear here to see me in person?* He ascended the wooden-slat staircase to the second-story room.

The lady stood alone to receive him.

"Hello, Ash!" Clear caught his hands. She popped up on her tiptoes and pecked a sisterly kiss to the corner of his jaw. "My, oh my, I am so glad to find you well."

Ash held her off at arms' length to have a look at his adopted half-sister. "Clear, what're you...? Why have ye come?"

Clear dressed plainly in a riding gown of linen, hemp, and wool layers. The strong scent of horse wafted about her. If anything, she looked more the part of a traveling merchant than a lady of a noble house. As always, she was much too thin for someone of her rank. Her cheeks sank inward and made her round eyes seem all the larger.

Ash dropped his well-educated diction and relaxed into his childhood accent. After all, she was family. "Why didn't ye send word you're comin'? You look hungry. Have ye had a meal yet today? Of course, ye haven't; lookit you."

"Please don't concern yourself with serving me at this late hour." She backed away and stood by the shuttered window. Beeswax candles flickered waves of golden light on her blonde braid.

"D'you know Rube got attacked on the road by highwaymen?"

"Yes, I know," she said with her back turned.

"Of course, ye do."

Silence lingered in a long, heavy pause between them. Although her back was turned, Ash imagined the lady prophet's large eyes filled with sorrowful burden. Future days and days long past often assaulted her mind in visions.

He asked, "Is his wife an' kids a'right?"

"Yes, a patrol should be bringing them to the city's gates about now. If I recall correctly, the children never witnessed what happened to the carriage drivers on the road. That's good, isn't it? Children should not see such things."

"Yeah." Ash looked left and right, making a note of her satchels, saddlebags, and a wicker basket full of loose papers. "Ye brought yer notes?"

"It has been quite a number of years since I've envisioned the events of this day. I need to refer back to my dream journals for the details."

"Then, you'll help catch th' highwaymen?" Ash asked. "Ye can identify 'em?"

Clear turned around to face him with a thin smile. "Yes, I can identify them."

"Good, that's good." Ash looked at the open window and darkness beyond. "Can I ask, where's yer husband lurkin' about? Is he in th' city investigatin' or trackin' the thugs?"

"I came alone," Clear said.

"By yerself? It ain't safe for a woman on th' road."

"I am not afraid of what's on the road."

"Of course, yer not." Ash looked at his stairway and the dimness of the ground floor room. "Lemme see if there's any cheese or olives in th' pantry."

"Please don't worry about feeding me, Ash. I'm very tired. May I sleep here tonight?"

"Cert'ly," he said. "Yer my guest. I'll sleep on th' rug downstairs. My manservant Will gets in 'fore sun-up. He'll make us a nice breakfast."

Her smile broadened and yet her eyes remained solemn. "Please ask Will not to wake me too early. I'm very exhausted from the journey here. I fully expect to sleep through until a late hour of the morning. Why don't you slip out and go to the barracks for a hearty breakfast with your friends? I'm sure the overnight patrols will have more news to discuss."

Ash felt his hackles prickling and rubbed the back of his neck. "Ye've seen a vision, haven't you. Are ye tellin' me to go have an early breakfast at th' barracks fer a reason?"

Clear sighed as she sat down on his cot. "What is meant to happen will happen, whether I tell you if I've seen it in a vision or not."

"Shit," he said. "I hate it when ye say things like that."

This time, her broad smile crinkled her eyes. "Good night, Ash."

"G'night, Clear."

Chapter 33.

All night, Ravel prowled the towers of Xolhold Keep. She watched and listened to the spear-carriers patrolling the ramparts, the parapets, and the inner stairwells. Everywhere else was shrouded in silence as the castle's inhabitants slept in luxury. The king's commanding voice haunted her thoughts, *You have my word, that my guards will be under orders to disarm, subdue, and restrain these foolish boys... if at all possible.* She was not naïve enough to rely on the tenuous bargain she had just made. If vengeance-seekers were to penetrate the inner chambers of the Keep and truly threaten the king's safety, her brother and his companions would be skewered on black lances. Her only hope was for the king's legions to show enough restraint and hesitation to give her a moment of opportunity. Even if she had to bludgeon her brother into unconsciousness and drag him away by his feet, she would stop his reckless plan. Better to end his escapade on a whipping post than on gallows.

Ravel perched on the edge of a turret that jutted off the corner of Xolhold Keep's northernmost tower.

Songbirds chirped in the potted fruit trees of the castle's courtyard even though the sky was still quite dark in the twilight hour before dawn. Morning grew near but had not yet come. Dim light meant nothing to her; the darker the sky, the brighter the unearthly glow within her own eyes. She could clearly see every detail of the stone towers and concentric circles of crenellated walls that spread beneath her bare toes.

"Hello? Good morning." A man's voice broke the stillness.

She looked down on a civilian who strolled the ramparts in an unhurried gait. The man was tall and broad shouldered. A silver brooch clasp on his cloak and layers of well-tailored clothing marked him as a gentleman of some means. Yet he carried himself with graceful strength that showed he spent more time on his feet than in a chair.

"Good of the morning to you as well." She deliberately refrained from giving him any honorifics. Even so, he did not appear to be offended.

"My name is Ashglëa po'Denn and I'm a captain in the surgeon's corps." He laid his right hand across his heart and offered a shallow bow. "It's a pleasure to make your acquaintance, uh, Mistress Rav-.... Lady Spar-.... May I ask how you prefer to be addressed?"

"My given name is Ravel."

He politely tilted his head. "You may call me Ash."

"A captain in the surgeon's corps," she repeated. "You aren't in uniform."

"I'm off duty."

"Why aren't you in bed at home?"

"My buddies asked me to come up here and check on you," he said. "How goes the search?"

"Tell your crud-coat buddies I've got nothing yet."

"I will," he said calmly, not insulted at all.

Ash came closer to stand beneath her at the intersection of crenellation and turret. Ravel crouched at the edge of the roof and gazed down to his upturned face. Sea breezes stirred locks of his long brown hair across his forehead. He had unremarkable but well-proportioned features, not classically handsome but pleasant enough to gaze upon. In this early hour, his beardless chin had the shadow of morning stubble.

"What's that you're carrying?" she asked.

Ash held up a small wicker cage in his left hand. Inside, a gray pigeon cooed nervously. "I brought you breakfast. Although I would appreciate it greatly if you could restrain yourself from biting its head off until I've left."

Ravel somersaulted off the roof's edge. She purposely aimed to land close to his boots. Her stiff cloak flapped against his knees.

Ash did not flinch or step back.

"You're quite odd," she said.

"How so?"

"You aren't afraid of me." Ravel inhaled the scents in his clothing that reeked of black tea and wood smoke. "The other crud-coats are scared of me. But you aren't. Neither are you repulsed."

Ash shrugged. "I'm a doctor. Not much can repulse me."

She accepted the wicker cage from his hands. The panicked pigeon flapped its wings but had nowhere to escape.

"Actually," he hesitated before continuing. "Would you mind if I asked permission to, uh, well... May I see?"

There it is. That's why he came. He is more curious than afraid. What an ignorant fool. Ravel set down the pigeon cage. She parted the overlapping panels of her tunic and loosened the drawstring neckline of her undershirt.

Dawn broke the horizon of sea and sky. A wash of golden pink shined on the black talons embedded in her breastbone. Their darkness tugged at her scarred skin. Sunlight and color aroused her hunger for raw meat and blood. Ravel inhaled a hiss through her clenched teeth to resist the growing urge to chew off the pigeon's head. Thorny talons arched waiting to drink what might dribble from her chin.

Now she sensed the quickening of Ash's heartbeat.

"Are you afraid of me now?" she asked.

"No." Ash looked soberly at her chest. "I feel sorry for you. I imagine it was agony to impale yourself."

"It was." She cinched the shirt's drawstring and closed the overlapping panels of her tunic.

"Do they still feel painful?"

She tilted her head. "In the early days, they felt like a strange animal latched onto me. They burned and gnawed and bored into the center of my ribs. With each passing day, they're becoming more and more a part of me. Or perhaps I am becoming a part of them."

"I see."

Ravel had not intended to speak so frankly to a stranger. Oddly, there was a disarming quality in his unhurried, steady manner. A fellow in his early thirties, at most, he had the air of a man twice his age. His quiet voice was better suited to a weary war veteran at a hearth fire telling stories of years gone by.

"Did you know the others?" she asked. "The king's magic workers?"

Ash avoided her direct gaze. "Yes, I met them on a few occasions. Believe me, by comparison you are quite convivial."

"Were you afraid of *them*?"

"No, of course I wasn't scared of those wretched sailors." He rubbed the back of his neck. A peculiar odor wafted from his skin that reminded her of pork lard burning in a fry pan. "Actually, that's a lie. Of course I was afraid of them. Everyone feared those ghouls, for good reason. We tolerated their presence in the ranks because they served our prince. Well, that is, until they went rogue and betrayed him."

"I fought with the squad that killed them."

"So I've heard. Herry brings it up when he's in his cups."

"I ripped the talons out of their chests and they..." Ravel paused to search for a single word to describe what she had seen in that moment. "...shriveled into dust."

Ash nodded soberly. "You'll be hard pressed to find someone who isn't secretly grateful to you for putting those wretched ghouls out of their misery. His Majesty's court is a much more pleasant environment without *them* skulking about."

An inhuman screech pierced the stillness. Ravel felt the talons at her chest pulse as if they were harp strings being plucked. The source was far away to the east. A beast screamed across the gently lapping waters of the Harbor Bay that shined like liquid gold in the morning's glow.

"What was that!" Her throat tightened. It took effort to croak out the words.

"Oh that? Uh, it sounds like seagulls or pelicans, doesn't it?"

Again, an odor like burning pork lard wafted from his skin. "You're lying," she said with certainty.

"Damn, but you *are* like them in some ways." He stepped aside to the crenellated wall. "Very well, yes, it's not seagulls. I really shouldn't be telling you any of this, but you'll sniff it out before long anyway."

Screeches continued in bursts. Varying pitches rose and fell like rusty bells caught in a hailstorm.

"There are squads of elite legions being trained on an island, out there, on Seagull's Rock in the middle of the bay. They've snared a few horrific beasts from the Outerlands that the local nomads call Sur—"

"Surleista," she finished.

"Yes." Ash rested his palms on the gaps of the crenelation. He gazed eastward into the morning sun's corona rising out of the watery horizon.

"Is the po'Lon utterly mad, bringing those demons *here*?"

Ash shot her a disapproving look across his shoulder. "His Majesty is not mad, I'll have you know. What's more, he's very sensitive about that term being tossed about considering all what happened with his father."

Ravel nodded to show that she knew full well the tragic tale of Tokustein the Mad King.

He continued, "Plus he's well aware of what havoc those creatures are capable of, which is why the best of our best are being trained in how to fight them."

"Have you seen one up close?" she asked.

"Yes," he admitted.

"Then you know if you cut off a limb, it sprouts back. Cut off its head and even the body re-grows itself. I've witnessed it myself! They are unkillable except by—"

"Fire," he said. "Their blood is flammable."

He lowered his gaze to stare at her chest. Ravel pulled the waxed linen cloak more tightly under her chin. *So is mine.*

Ash said, "They can't fly over water. A shallow rain puddle is enough to keep them contained. Thus, you see, with them trapped on an island in the middle of the bay, we're all perfectly safe."

"Safe?" She coughed on the word. "You feel safe?"

"Hardly," he said. "None of us are safe until you sniff out your little brother and stop him from doing whatever mischief he's going to do."

"I'm trying. I've prowled the rooftops all night long and I've seen nothing."

"Keep trying." Ash took a few steps to go back the way he had come. He paused, turned, and added, "Don't just use your nose. Use all your senses, human and inhuman. You stole the demon powers from the king magic workers, then use them. Use them! Use everything you've got until you think you've nothing more to use, and then use a little bit more. Think of how much you love your brother, how much you hate him, how much you fear him... how much you fear *for* him. Your animal passions can transcend the limits of your human intellect."

"Animal passions? You're disgusting. He's my brother!"

"Don't be ridiculous. I'm not suggesting you fuck him."

Ravel blushed at how easily he uttered the obscenity as if it were just another word for an ordinary activity like to eat, to sleep, or to walk. What new society was this that Glëa po'Lon created, where the most basic tenets of decency were forgotten?

"If I may rephrase, gentle lady?" He rested a hand on his hip. "Let's say your sisterly devotion can be a compass that guides you to him. Be relentless. Don't give up. Don't *ever* give up until you've saved your idiot little brother from his own stupidity."

Ravel nodded, dumb-founded at his sincerity. "Why do you care to help me?"

"I had a brother, once." Ash turned on his heels and quickly strode away.

Chapter 34.

After eating the pigeon and wiping the blood from her face, Ravel took to the castle's rooftops and prowled in search of her brother. From the ground level wafted the tantalizing odors of a king's betrothal banquet in preparation. Yeast bread toasted in the ovens. Autumn squash grilled on open firepits. Mushrooms sizzled in buttery cream sauces. Onions softened slowly in olive oils tempered with anise seeds and cinnamon sticks. None of those victuals aroused her hunger like the animals being slaughtered and drained. Blood collected in tin pails. Carcasses were hoisted onto roasting spits: the hogs, the veal, the mutton and lamb, the quail, and geese, and even the rabbits brought oily saliva to her mouth. *Meat. Meat. Meat.*

Ravel scampered over the rooftops of auxiliary buildings to the cluster of five towers that formed Xolhold Keep. Sea breezes shrieked at her but at least the wind blew the kitchens' most tantalizing odors in the other direction.

The donjon tower was being mopped and decorated for the upcoming betrothal ceremony. Flag banners unfurled from the second-floor mezzanine. Golden tassels larger than horse tails tickled the ground. Ravel gave a few quick sniffs and could not detect her brother's scent amid the soap buckets. She doubted that he could lay in wait for an ambush while brooms jabbed into every corner of the Great Hall and batons smacked the dust out of velvet draperies.

She hopped up to the eastern tower's conical roof and clung to the edges of the machicolations. Below her dangling toes, on a balcony of the highest chamber, a lone warrior clad in a chemise and loose leggings practiced their martial poses. Lithe and strong in their movements, the barefoot warrior turned and lunged in the limited space. Empty-handed, they dodged and struck at imaginary foes. Ravel admired the grace and skill of the warrior.

She crept nearer the edge of the roof. Only then did she recognize the matriarch of the House of Browden. A knitted cap contained the curls of her gray-blonde hair, hiding the outward signs of her age. Sixty years old, at least, but the former general Lady Browden's martial prowess was equal to the best elite guardsman that Ravel had ever seen. *If you had fought for my prince, Thorn Lily, how different the world could have been.*

Ravel scurried across the connecting wall to the south tower. She hopped to an adjoining turret and crouched above a similar terrace balcony. Servant girls in green gowns carried platters of fruits, boiled eggs, and butter pastries to a wrought-iron table. A lord and a lady sat opposite each other, with the table and all its bounty as a barrier between them.

Drawing nearer, crouching low to the roof shingles so as not to be seen, she recognized Lord Rubëa from the bridge. She assumed the lady to be his wife rescued from the curtained carriage. The two ate in silence, their eyes downcast at their glass dishes and silverware. Children were nowhere to be seen but Ravel could smell them nearby in the care of their nursemaids.

The lord winced as he sipped his tea. One side of his face was swollen as if his mouth were already full of biscuits. His left temple had a dark purple bruise.

Another lady of matronly age emerged from the double doors to join them at the table. Blonde hair was tightly plaited into a single rope that extended well below her hips. Stately in poise, she moved slowly as if chained by the dragging trail of her mint-green gown. The lady reminded Ravel of her own mother in the graceful way she carried herself.

"How are you feeling this morning, my son?" the lady asked.

"I could hardly sleep all night long, Mother," Lord Rubëa complained. "The pain is excruciating. Can't the royal surgeon do something about it?"

"No," his mother said. "Intoxication is for the weak-willed. Pain is to be endured."

Ravel allowed herself a flat smile. *Pompous peacock, you know nothing of pain.*

Lord Rubëa asked, "Have you spoken to Auntie? Has there been any progress in the hunt for those maniacs who assaulted me?"

"And me," his wife added. "And our children."

"They were going to hang me, Mother! Do you understand? They were going to hang me from the bridge. If not for their horses getting spooked and stampeding, to give me that moment of opportunity to jump into the river, I would have gone off to join my little brother Samuet in the bliss of the Eternal Fields."

His mother rested her fingertips lightly on his shoulder. "There, there, my son. You're safe now. The ruffians will be caught and punished."

Spear-carriers patrolled the battlements of Xolhold Keep. Ravel smelled their body odor and sensed their weariness in waiting for the end of their duty shift. The changing-of-the-guard would happen soon; the castle was waking up for the day. She tested how far someone could penetrate their defenses. Ravel clung to the outside bricks of the tower with her fingertips like a squirrel going up a tree trunk. When they turned to look left, she scuttled right and avoided the watchful eyes of the guards. She dodged the view of archers standing sentinel on the adjacent curtain wall. In no time at all, she reached the penthouse chamber and peered over the windowsill.

King Glëa po'Lon slept belly-down in a glorious four-posted canopy bed. Rouge curtains with gilded tassels draped from the mahogany frame. He wore only a linen nightshirt that exposed his pale calves and bare feet. His long hair spread over his back like a black wool shawl. His face lay against the pillow, eyes closed, serene in slumber. And he was not alone.

A woman sat up from the nest of silky sheets, quilted comforters, and knitted blankets. Disheveled auburn hair was darker at the roots and Ravel sensed the odor of henna dye. Hours-old face powders had rubbed from her cheeks, leaving behind pink smudges in the pillow. Ochre paste darkened her lashes. Nude, she wore nothing but a crystal-beaded necklace and bangle bracelets of blown glass.

"It's the morning, Glëa my darling."

The king smiled with his eyes closed, showing that he was already fully awake but pretending not to be. "Tell the sun to go back. Give me one more hour in your arms, Alyss."

"Are you not happy on this auspicious day?"

He rolled onto his back and gazed up at the bed's canopy. "It's all politics. The Council of Lords insisted that I have a queen, so I agreed to offer the vows of betrothal. I'll be married in name only. She is more of a child than you are."

The courtesan giggled lustily. "Oh Glëa, no one has called me a child in a very long time."

"You weren't even born when I set sail to explore the uncharted seas. Many is the day when even I find it difficult to comprehend that almost five decades have passed. Only a few are old enough to remember my father in his days of glory, before..."

Before he went insane with grief, you mean to say. Ravel tilted her head curiously to hear a gargle of emotion that caught the back of the king's throat. Could it be that the immortal Glëa po'Lon felt regret for waging war against his mortal, human brothers?

"Your father's spirit proudly watches over you from the bliss of the Eternal Fields," the courtesan said.

He reached over and caressed the woman's hip. Rings twinkled on every knuckle as he flexed his fingers, massaging her like a cat.

Alyss continued, "Praises be to the spirits of the royal ancestors who reached across the Great Divide and bestowed upon you this miracle of eternal youth."

Ravel gritted her teeth to overhear the dogmatic phrases of the deluded faithful. Did no one know the truth of what an unearthly creature had dropped into his skin?

He said to the courtesan, "Though I offer my vow of betrothal to someone else today, I will still have great need of you for many years to come."

"Gladly will I serve, with all my heart and body, for as long as Your Majesty desires me." Alyss lowered her face to his, aiming for a kiss.

Ravel quickly withdrew from the windowsill.

✕

The north-facing tower had a veranda decorated with intricate mosaic tiles of gray and indigo blue. Ravel perched on the slanted eaves of the conical, shingled roof. Shielded by the drooping boughs of potted wisteria, she gazed onto the scene below.

Butter pastries, fruits, and dishes of cream lay uneaten on a wrought-iron table. A servant boy in a blue apron stood ready with a tea kettle, but no one sat to partake of the breakfast.

A little girl flapped her arms and ran in circles around the table. Oddly, the girl resembled Glëa po'Lon with blue eyes and a wild mass of black curls. Ravel tilted her head, curious as to the identity of the child.

The castle's steward emerged from the double doors. She was a stern woman in a high collared gown who carried a pole-staff topped by a bronzed bull's head. "Has she finished breakfast?"

"She won't eat, Lady Thandra," said the servant boy with the tea kettle.

"Perhaps it's for the best. We can't risk having her spit up vomit on her raiment." The steward stiffly held forth her hand. "Come with me to be dressed, Tiressa."

The girl mumbled, "Call me Lilac."

"His Majesty has commanded that you forego the nickname and be called Tiressa henceforth," said the steward.

"My *anma* calls me Lilac."

The steward said, "Your nursemaid has been dismissed. You have a new governess starting today."

"I want my *anma*. I want my *anma*."

"No!" The steward Lady Thandra tapped her staff on the flagstones.

Tiressa pouted.

The servant boy dropped to his knees at the little girl's side. "Please, be a good lady and go downstairs to get dressed."

"Why? I have a dress."

The steward tightened her grip on the staff. "You shall stand before His Majesty the king today and accept the vows of betrothal."

Tiressa pulled a flower blossom from one of the pots. "My *anma* says Gley-ah is my cousin and we are very lucky that he's being nice to us. He's not nice to everybody, she says. Sometimes I think my *anma* is scared when she

213

says his name. I think she doesn't really like him very much, so I think I don't like him too. I don't want to be a troth-all."

"Oh sweetie, don't say such things!" The servant boy reached for the little girl, but Tiressa scampered away.

The child ran for shelter between the barrel-sized ceramic pots that held saplings of kumquat trees. "I don't want to be a troth-all! I don't want to be a troth-all!"

Ravel smiled in amusement at the panicked servant boy scrambled to catch the little girl. *Oh my, Lil' Hatchling, you are not the master of everyone in your domain. Enjoy your courtesan for as long as you can. Your intended queen is a rebel at heart.*

Chapter 35.

Beyond the inner wall that swaddled the five oldest towers that comprised the castle's keep, the fortifications expanded to a crescent-shaped bailey yard. Ravel made her way across the shingled rooftops of the barracks nested on the western side of the inner wall. She hopped the gap between the sheds of the ordnance depot and the tack shed adjacent to the stables. She passed over the infirmary building that in peacetime enjoyed rows of empty hospital beds.

Multitudes were gathering from the city and from the surrounding countryside. They flowed happily through the gatehouses like grains pouring through a silo's hopper. The open spaces of the bailey filled with straw hats, wool hats, kerchiefs, and unkempt hair. Small russet flags waved from people's hands. Fifes whistled a merry tune. Drums thumped like joyous heartbeats.

Ravel marveled at the mixture of types: southerners with their beaded attire and braided hairstyles, westerners who dared to wear garments in the colors of woad blue and cream, foresters in brown and green, sailors, merchants, and goat herders. Even a few nomads of the Outerlands openly wore their distinctive indigo cloaks. All these groups who, for decades, had fought amongst themselves were now united under one flag, one purpose, one king. All of them had come to celebrate and her brother intended to shatter it all.

A gilded black carriage drawn by eight Garudan steeds passed through the outer gatehouse. Someone released a spray of white doves fluttering overhead. Crowds surged and swarmed around the wheels. The joyous upswell of cheering made the black war horses fidget and toss their heads. Drivers in red uniforms held control and the carriage moved forward.

Chants of "Hail the Immortal," and "Hail the Eternal" rang up to the battlements. Sentinels raised their gloved hands in mirror image to the applauding hundreds below.

One man rode alone in the carriage. His long black curls glimmered with styling oil. All but his face was covered in furs, velvets, satins, and jewels. He waved with broad, graceful strokes of his arm. He smiled to the left and right as women held up their babies overhead for a glimpse of him. Blue eyes twinkled in that boyish, beardless face.

Ravel knew immediately that it was not Glëa po'Lon but a look-a-like impersonating the king in public. An assassin would have a clear shot and the guards were prepared. The man in the carriage was doing an admirable job of performing a regal smile in response to the outpouring of joy. Yet she noticed his vigilant upright posture and how he focused his attention on various groups of young men in the crowd. She wondered if he had a small shield tucked under all those robes.

The castle's clock tower gonged four times to mark the fourth hour since daybreak.

No one hindered the carriage's progress, but the wheels turned forward at an achingly slow pace. Ravel gripped the roof so tightly that her purple fingernails dug into the shingles. Wooly clouds drifted overhead. Their patches of shadows moved across the outer baily yard at the imperceptible pace of a sundial.

By the time the carriage reached the next gatehouse leading to the inner bailey yard, the castle's clock tower chimed again five times. *Unbelievable*, she screamed inside her mind. Ravel could have marched a company of wounded infantry soldiers more quickly than this royal procession.

Ravel hurried back over the rooftops of artisan workshops and townhouses. She hopped to the inner wall's gatehouse. A trio of archers held their unloaded crossbows safely at their sides. "Any sign of him?" asked the lieutenant.

"No," she grunted.

"Keep looking."

"I am."

She walked along the ramparts encircling the inner yard. Every few paces, she passed behind a black uniform standing vigil at the crenellation. Every

216

hundred paces, a half-tower blocked the way, and someone called up to the sentinels above for approval to unbolt the wooden door. One tower after another, Ravel passed through a turret's chamber on her way to the next.

The carriage moved a bit more quickly through the inner bailey. The gathering crowd of nobles and dignitaries were more restrained in their adulation. Ravel wondered if some of them suspected it was not really the king to whom they bowed. For the sake of the commoners, they had to keep up appearances.

"Hail the immortal," the nobility called out. "May his reign last ten thousand years."

Or will it end today, she wondered.

The impersonator had the help of several squires to dismount from the carriage. Bulky fur-trimmed sleeves and a cape the size of a tent tarp dragged behind him. He ascended the steep-sloping open steps to the barbican door of the White Tower. At the top landing by the ornate archway, he turned to give one last regal gesture.

"Today I share my joy with you, my beloved and loyal people. Today I pledge my betrothal to the lady whom you shall be revere someday as your queen. Forevermore shall my kingdom know nothing but peace, unity, and prosperity!" He lingered to bask in cheers and applause. Then, at a discreet tap on the shoulder from the lady steward of the castle, he turned into shadows and was lost to view.

Where are you, Der? The crowds of noble people filed through a lower-level door into the donjon tower. If ever there was an opportunity to strike, it was now. Ravel eyed the squires, the valets, the handmaidens, and the foot servants who followed their lords and ladies into the tower.

Flutes and horns played a spirited fanfare. Music swelled to the rafters and blared out of the windows. A chorus of youthful voices sang three verses of an ancient hymn. Still, no sign of her brother or his friends. Ravel perched on the merlon blocks of the wall and scanned the bailey yard.

A pause followed, then a man's high-pitched voice chirped in the open air. He was too muffled to hear clearly but it had to be the proclaiming of the betrothal banns. One long phrase introduced the king's name and many titles. Another phrase declared the child's full name and whatever titles His Majesty had bestowed or restored to her.

Bells chimed. Crowds in the open yard applauded in waves of joyous roars. The immortal king had chosen his queen.

In the courtyard below, in between the donjon tower and the inner bailey's curtain wall, a matrix of tent poles supported a patchwork of gauze awnings. The pavilion's draperies filtered the sunlight and offered golden shade for the finely dressed nobility. They dined on a banquet of all sorts of meats, fish, boiled crabs, raw oysters, grilled squash and boiled greens, buttered mushrooms, pomegranate seeds and ripe persimmons, baked pastries, and honey glazed nuts. Ravel looked down at enough food to satisfy a whole village for a month.

Nobles of old families and newly made families, and their murmuring retinues, filled the courtyard like an overgrowth of weeds and flowers in a walled garden. Long planks had been arranged as tables for the lords and ladies to sit on cushioned benches. Servants busied about carrying dishes or waving fans to dispel the flies.

The House of Browden was represented by Governor Jiveine the Thorn Lily, the Lady Dalhanna, Lord Rubëa, his wife, and their children. All of them dressed finely in their heraldic colors of sage green and silver.

Governor Vilbyss occupied a prominent place at the table. To his right-hand side sat a lady in velvet sleeves who had to be his wife. At his left hand was an elderly gentleman who shared an extra scoop of grilled scallops to the lord's plate. Ravel squinted at him curiously that a valet should exhibit more affection than the lord's own wife.

The rest of Lord Vilbyss's family sat coolly on the opposite side of the table. Ravel knew them only by the brown-and-yellow palette of their clothing. Two sons in their forties had weary-looking wives sitting at their elbows. Grown children who sat up properly scolded the fidgety littlest ones, but they failed to control the tiny fingers from sampling the bowl of whipped cream.

King Glëa po'Lon in full royal raiment wore layered robes of black velvet and rouge brocade over a gauzy blouse with frilly sleeve cuffs. Outwardly, he displayed all the colors of fire and iron, of sunset and earth. His massive cape of rouge wool was trimmed with a fur collar and held together by a brooch of ruby-studded gold. His long hair had been so thoroughly oiled and glazed that even the afternoon's sea breeze could not disturb the wavy curls.

The child bride dressed in her finest to be on public display for the first time. Her gold-trimmed bodice of black-on-red brocade mirrored the colors of His Majesty's garments. Inky curls fluffed up in a dark dandelion plume. She sat beside the king on a stack of cushions and held a toy ball. Too small for her feet to touch the ground, her feet dangled and kicked the frame of the chair.

"I'm not hungry!" the little girl squeaked.

"Eat or don't eat, as you wish." King Glëa po'Lon's bass voice carried easily on the breeze up to the lofty heights of the ramparts from where Ravel observed.

"Those are big fifes! The biggest I ever see."

"The biggest you've ever *seen*," he corrected. "They are called flutes."

Acrobats frolicked shirtless. Hosen that colored their lower bodies in pastel shades of bluebell, honeysuckle, and camellia. They cast ribbon streamers in swirling arcs overhead as they tumbled and leaped between the banquet tables.

"Where's my *anma*? I want my *anma*."

"Your new governess is in your bed chamber, now, preparing all of the things for you to sleep well tonight."

"I don't sleep in your bed?"

"No," he said.

"But you said we're together, now. We're a troth."

"Indeed, we are betrothed." The king pinched up a slice of apple baked in a glaze of cinnamon and honey. Jeweled rings sparkled on each of his fingers. "However, we won't be sharing a bed for quite some time yet to come."

"When?"

"When you've grown up to be a woman."

"A woman," she repeated while fingering the seed beads and threads of her toy ball. "Like my *anma*?"

"Yes, like your *anma*."

"Will my *anma* sleep in your bed with you?"

Glëa looked down at her. "Do you want your *anma* to sleep in my bed with me?"

"No, I want her. I always sleep with her. She's warm."

"Then, by all means, you may keep her."

"Frowning Lady said my *anma* is gone." Tiressa pouted.

The king tilted the angle of his upraised hand. His palm opened to the sky. "I can bring her back. Would you like that?"

"Oh yes, yes! I want my *anma* back!"

"As you wish, my queen, so shall it be."

The little lady smiled up at him. Even from a distance, Ravel could see that the child still had all her milk teeth.

"Do you have your own *anma* to sleep with you?"

"Yes, I do," he said.

The king looked aside to his courtesan who sat with elegant skirts arrayed on a half bench behind him. A silver teapot and a tiered rack of butter cookies were ready at her side. He gazed deeply into the courtesan's painted eyes couched in the powdered face.

"Is she warm?"

"Yes," he said. "She's very warm."

"Ugh," Ravel grunted under her breath in disgust at his very human decadence.

Glëa po'Lon startled. He strained to rotate his torso within the weight of his bulky clothes. Eyes narrowed against the sunlight, he gazed straight up to the wall's turret.

She stiffened in surprise. *How could he have heard me from this height?*

Despite the awning's shade, his blue eyes sparkled from an inner light. Clearly he did not detect her presence with his human ears. Ravel clutched her cloak more tightly across her chest. Lesson learned; it would not be so easy to approach him by stealth.

The castle's clock tower chimed the gong for the eighth hour since daybreak. She counted it out: one, two, three, four, five, six, seven, eight. *Time is growing shorter. Where are you, Der? What is your plan? Will you dare to strike by sneaking into his bed chamber?*

The king cocked his eyebrow inquisitively. Ravel answered by shaking her head.

"Again, again!" Glëa po'Lon called out with a smile as if to the dancing musicians, but he continued looking upwards to the parapet. Undertones rang beneath his words that resonated warmly in the claws at her chest. A second, lighter voice chimed in the air like echoes of a silver bell. Ravel cringed at the strong pangs of compulsion. Her blood quickened and her heartbeat pounded as if called to action by a commanding officer. *Mount up! Shields up! Charge into the breach!* Her spine stiffened upright. She raised her chin and sniffed the air in search of what she craved to find. The urge to seek out prey overwhelmed her and gave her shivers. For his sake, to please *him* was all that mattered.

"You heard him," barked the spear carrier from the watchtower. "Keep searching!"

"I am." She growled so fiercely that the spear carrier flinched back.

Ravel sucked in a quick breath. Self-consciously, she expanded her awareness to the dozens of faces wearing black uniforms who keenly watched her movements. They were all afraid of her, or repulsed by her.

She sprang into a running start and sprinted the walkway around the entire rim of the inner curtain wall. Arms extended stiffly behind herself, for a moment she felt weightless as if riding a swift horse at full gallop.

Hundreds more townspeople and travelers sat on the ground. They used their laps as tables, eating from their hands the surplus foods of the noblemen's banquet. Some of them looked up at her passing; most of them did not. Amidst the hundreds of people and all the variety of foodstuffs below, she caught a familiar scent that was not her brother. *Him.*

Curious about that off-duty captain who had visited her that morning, Ravel followed his trail away from the banquet.

Chapter 36.

Ravel found his townhouse in the lower bailey yard. She clung to the crossbeam that supported the roof's overhanging eaves and lurked just out of sight beyond the half-open window. From there, she peered inside the second floor loft.

Captain Ash sat on a narrow cot. He still wore his brown-and-green civilian clothes from that morning. Perhaps the captain was off-duty all day with the celebrations.

His guest sitting on the floor rug was a matron in her mid-thirties. Honey-gold locks were tightly braided into a rope that followed the line of her spine. She dressed in a side-laced riding gown dyed a pale woad blue. Leggings were soiled at the calves by grass stains and mud. The odor of horse sweat wafted strongly about her; she had ridden her mount to its limits to get here.

"Certain ye've had 'nough to eat?" Ash asked.

Ravel startled at the shift in his accent. So, he was not the refined gentleman that he had first presented himself to be. Ash sounded like a backwoodsman from the Great Green Forest lands.

"I'm fine, Ash, thank you." The woman, despite her plain clothing, had the diction of a well-educated lady.

"Ye sure? I can go back to th' banquet and grab ye some more leftovers. Yer so thin, Clear."

"Please stop apologizing for the sparseness of your pantry. I came to visit you, dear brother, not to be served."

Brother? Ravel squinted and failed to see any familial resemblance. The woman's face was narrow with high cheekbones and a pointed chin. Her close-set eyes seemed too large for their sockets.

"Have ye been eatin' a-right? How's that husband o' yours been feedin' ye?"

Clear's face crumpled as her pink lips trembled. Her large green eyes filled with tears. "Oh, Ash..." was all she managed to choke out before the weeping overtook her.

"There, there." Ash dropped to the floor and joined her sitting on the rug. He embraced her like a shivering bird. "What has that arrogant, clod-pate horseman done now?"

Horseman? Ravel leaned into the windowsill to listen more closely.

"It's nothing."

"It don't look like nothin'. Come on, pull yerself together so ye can tell me all about it." Ash plucked a kerchief from the cuff of his sleeve.

Clear wiped her face. "We argued."

"Obviously. What about?"

"It wasn't a single argument but more like a lot of little ones over the last... oh my, it's been two or three years or more. It started when he bought a new horse, a sixteen hander, a western Roan Blue stallion with a steady temper. Chance struck up a friendship with the horse breeder who was, of course, an ex-soldier of Prince Rouchard's. They started spending more and more time together, talking about horses and drinking late into the night hours. His friendship with the one quickly expanded into a friendship with dozens. All of them were former soldiers comparing their scars and battle wounds and complaining about the king."

Ash crossed his legs and draped his wrists over his ankles. "Th' damned war is over six years now! Th' old grievances are bein' swept away. Old grudges are bein' forgiven. Walk down th' streets of the city, and ye'll see for yerself. Two shopkeepers, side by side. One proudly holds a flag of black-an'-rouge. One put away th' blue-and-cream. Now they're neighbors. There's a place for everyone in th' Iron King's dominion, if they wish to come in peace."

Clear sipped chamomile tea from a stoneware mug. "Not everyone can bury their grudges to live in peace, as you well know."

"Yeah." Ash looked aside.

"Chance and I argued about unimportant things, at first. His new friends failed to wipe their muddy boots before they came into the house. They picked bare my plum trees without asking. Many times, he came home drunk and slept in his boots. Then, he started saying things to me that I'd never heard before: that I was a spoiled lady, that I was insensitive to the suffering of those defeated in the war, that I would tolerate any despot if it meant I could have pretty shoes."

"Th' churlish coxcomb," Ash said. "That's not you at all."

She dabbed his kerchief at her dripping tears. "He only said these things when he was drunk, which was often. He apologized for his behavior afterwards. I tried to be understanding. Most of what Chance said was repeated from his so-called friends. I knew what was really tormenting his heart. I saw it weigh upon him, wearing him down, a little bit each day. The more he listened to their war stories, the more it bothered him. He didn't... *We* didn't do enough to fight for his prince. In the end, Chance blamed himself for Rouchard's defeat at the Battle of Border Field."

Ash stood up off his crossed ankles. "That's it. I'm gonna go have a talkin' to this husband o' yours. He can't treat ye this way an' cavort with all his troublemaker friends!"

"Don't. Please, don't."

"Why not? It's been years a-comin' that I've wanted to tell that clod-cloppin' horseman a few things."

Clear's lips trembled more violently. She could hardly choke out the next words. "He left me."

"What?"

"He left me, Ash. Our marriage is over."

She succumbed to another bout of weeping and slouched forward over her lap. Ash bent over her and gently stroked the top of her head.

"There, there, ye can stay here as long as ye like. Take my bed. I'll sleep in th' infirmary."

Kerchief pressed to her face, she gulped back tears and tried to speak. "Please don't mention to anyone that I'm here. I can't endure hearing the criticisms against my husband. Not now.... I can't face Mother and Rubëa and his wife, much less Auntie..."

Ravel gripped the roof's crossbeam more tightly. *Are they related to the House of Browden? They refer to the Thorn Lily as their aunt?*

"Hush hush, now," Ash said. "Of course I promise. You know I always keep yer secrets."

Clear refolded the kerchief in search of a dry patch to wipe her face. "One more thing."

"Oh no," he groaned. "What?"

"Be careful of *her*."

"Who?"

"The ghoul lurking on the rooftop."

Ash rubbed his hand across the back of his own neck. "She's not a ghoul. She's a lady."

"She can smell when you're lying."

"I know," he said. "Like *them*."

"Yes, like them. Be cautious, Ash. The longer she wears those claws in her chest, the farther she will drift from her own sense of humanity."

"She ain't drifted too far yet. We had us a nice chat this mornin'. Trust me, Clear, she's just worried about savin' her stupid brother."

Clear reached up from the floor to touch his hand. "And I'm worried about mine. Be careful, dear brother."

Ash smiled. "I'll be fine, I promise."

Ravel returned to the garrison's headquarters where she had spoken with Colonel Viktor the night before. Upon her entrance, the soldiers paused their activities. They held utterly still as she strolled up through their midst. Bunkbeds to either side of her left a narrow space to walk. The soldiers some of them shirtless, some of them without pants, were in the middle of getting dressed in their uniforms.

At the commander's desk, a different officer sat writing in the logbook. This colonel outranked Viktor by one level, as evidenced by the double gold braid at the collar and crimson sleeve caps. Auburn-blond hair, worn in long flowing locks past the shoulder per the fashion of the time, made it impossible to discern the officer's sex from behind.

"Reporting..." Ravel's voice trailed off, unable and unwilling to use the word Sir.

The officer turned in the chair and revealed a woman's face. Her expression was as harsh and stern as Viktor's had been the night before.

"Have you found him?"

"No," Ravel said.

"Then you are reporting nothing."

"Reporting 'all clear' is still a report."

The officer nodded slightly. "My name is Colonel Maetha po'Nell. My husband has spent the hours of the night—"

"Your husband?" Ravel asked. "Viktor?"

Maetha curtly nodded. "As I was saying before you interrupted, my husband has spent the hours of the night writing out his thoughts of strategic possibilities. If your brother's education included the Chronicles of the Kings and schematics from the archives of the Architects Guild, then he would know the strengths and weaknesses of this castle's defense."

Ravel looked at the oak desk strewn with pencil sketches of the castle's layout. Carefully laid pewter coins served as makeshift figurines on a battle plan.

"We are on high alert at each gatehouse. Every citizen who seeks to enter for today's festivities has been thoroughly scrutinized. We are guarding every water sluice, every latrine tank, every sally door, and every gutter that flows to the moat. We've doubled the guards on the ordnance depot and re-checked our inventory of flammable pitch-tar."

Ravel recalled the Battle of Border Field when the blackcoats' siege machines had hurled payloads of flaming liquid death through the night sky.

"Any guard who is not at the assigned post, even slipping away for a piss break unannounced, will be treated as a full alert. Whatever sabotage, distraction, or subterfuge your brother may be planning, we've anticipated every amateurish possibility. We *will* stop the attackers."

"The king promised he wouldn't be harmed."

"'If at all possible,'" Maetha added. "Those were His Majesty's orders. I have it in writing, here."

Ravel stepped in closer to come eye to eye with this woman in a black uniform. She curled her lip in a sneer and exhaled a noxious, monstrous breath. "Make it possible, or I'm coming for you and your husband. Just ask him. Viktor knows what I can do."

Maetha uncorked a tin flask at her belt. Water spirits inside the flask whispered in its depths. "Step back, you hideous creature, or I will splash this at your face."

She retreated one step. Just one. "Perhaps he won't strike today. It may be too risky with so many guards on alert and so many innocent people—"

The captain laughed mockingly. "Are you so naïve? What better day is it for a vengeful insurgent to strike? When the multitudes have come to witness the king's betrothal ceremony, when the castle's walls are full of people, it's a surety that fanatics will slaughter as many as possible."

No, she wanted to say but could not bring the word to her mouth. Her mind struggled to clear the fog of sentimentality as her pragmatic father had once schooled her to do. If she thought of Candor not as her brother but as her opponent, the possibilities became clear. She could not deny, this day was an ideal time to strike. For vengeance, what better day than one where the king sought happiness for the future?

"Captain! Captain!" An archivist scribe dashed into the barracks. Head shaved bald and slender body concealed in flowing robes of turmeric yellow, Ravel could not discern if it were a man or woman. All that mattered was the urgency of the person's expression.

"What do you bring?"

The scribe offered Colonel Maetha a handful of loose-leaf papers. "We found these in the library. While researching the Annals of the Twin Prophets, we discovered this!"

Maetha frowned at the faded ink on the darkened parchment. "I don't understand this ancient lettering. Read it to me, scribe."

The scribe took back the papers and held them reverently, delicately, as one would hold a newly hatched songbird that had fallen out of its nest. "So it is written by the Prophets of the First King, hallowed be the names of Zëa and Zoë, the two who act as one."

"Hallowed be," Maetha responded. "Go on, scribe, read it."

"In the days to come there will be a calamitous day at the halfway mark between autumn and winter. A youthful king who is not young will choose a child bride. Beasts will prowl of tooth and fang. Beasts will defy the claxon's clang. Talons in a human chest will give power to the defeated..."

Ravel rested a hand over her breastbone.

"...and the Lord of the Abyss will intrude upon where the immortal stands."

Maetha asked, "Is there more?"

"No, Colonel," the scribe said. "We are searching the library's stacks again. This parchment, we must confess, was misfiled and out of place. Through an unforgivable clerical oversight, we have never seen it before."

Ravel inhaled the scent of veracity in the scribe's skin. How admirable to confess such a mistake. But then, in breathing more deeply the odors of the papers, she detected a more familiar scent. She crouched over the scribe's wrist and sniffed harder the fragrance in the parchment.

Her. Unmistakably, the parchment held the scent of the lady named Clear who had been speaking with Ash in his home.

Maetha waved the scribe away. The person hurried off with sandaled feet slapping the floorboards.

"The meaning is plain for 'a youthful king who is not young will choose a child bride.' Talons in a human chest? That's you. Halfway mark between the autumn equinox and winter solstice." Maetha clasped and unclasped her fists as she voiced her thoughts. "That's today. That's now."

"Beasts of tooth and fang," Ravel said. "Do you think Candor might release the Surleista from the island training ground?"

The captain cocked her left eyebrow. "You know about those?"

"I do."

"We've already considered the possibility. We've doubled the guards at the boat docks. There is no other way to transport the beasts to shore. They cannot fly over water."

"I know," Ravel said.

"Even if the denizens were released within the castle's walls, we'd make short work of them. Archers stand ready at every watchtower. A few well-placed incendiary arrows and they'll be dispatched before they can ruffle His Majesty's hair."

"Don't get cocky, Colonel," Ravel said. "It's when you think you've got everything planned is when you're most at risk of losing everything."

"Indeed." Maetha stored the archival parchment in a drawer of the writing desk. "Go continue your patrol. Report back here in one hour."

"One hour, as the bell tolls," Ravel agreed.

"You should know that you'll report to the acting commander Captain Cody for the rest of the night shift. I'm going off duty soon."

"I see." Ravel detected a softening in the woman's expression and a slight blush in her cheeks. "Celebrating the special occasion with your husband, eh?"

Maetha turned away. "That is all. Be off with you, now."

Chapter 37.

Ravel leaped back across the battlements to the outer bailey yard. She scurred again over the rooftops of the narrow, two-story townhouses. Not even servants were at home; they had all left to join the crowd of spectators for the joyous day.

One person remained alone in Captain Ash's upper-floor chamber. The lady named Clear sat on his cot.

Ravel gripped the edge of the eaves and somersaulted into the un-shuttered window. She landed in a crouch like a cat. "You forged that archival document. You planted it for them to find. Admit it!"

Clear looked up from reading a trifold pamphlet in her hands. "You're quite rude, Lady Spareen, for lurking on windowsills and listening to private conversations. I'm pleased that you've decided to drop in for a proper conversation."

The hood of Ravel's waxed linen cloak fell back. Air chilled the gaps on her scalp where her hair had fallen out. She was aware of her gruesome appearance, yet the woman did not show any signs of feeling intimidated.

The deeper she inhaled, Ravel could not detect the ordinary odors of meat and blood in that woman's body. A tingling urge to sneeze filled her nostrils. Clear's skin exuded a strong sweetness like flowery incense. The lady's scent overpowered the combined odors of the wooden floor, the musty blankets and rug, the parchment papers, and the wicker basket. *She's not human.*

"What are you?" Ravel whispered.

"Pardon, did you say something?" Clear tapped at her left ear. "I was born with a poor sense of hearing. Speak up more loudly, if you please."

"What sort of un-folk are you!"

"Such a rude question." The lady politely opened her palm in a welcoming gesture. "However, if you must ascribe an appellation from mythological categories, then you may refer to me as a Prophet of Ages."

"As in the old legends? You see visions of future days? You command elemental spirits?"

"Indeed."

Ravel paused to draw a breath. Until now, she had not imagined that she had the capacity to be surprised.

"Ash called you 'sister.' Is he a Prophet of Ages too?"

"Hardly," she said. "He is quite the ordinary man, tragically orphaned as a child and adopted by my mother out of charity."

Ravel insisted, "I can smell something unnatural in his skin."

Clear looked down and shuffled a few of the papers strewn on the flat mattress. "Well, yes, your perceptions are correct. He was touched by something in his childhood. However, the poison was cleansed and the matter resolved a long time ago. It is of no relevance now."

"That's why he isn't afraid of me," Ravel said. "He has seen unnatural things before."

"Yes he has. Which is why I'm hoping that you'll not cause him any grief today."

Ravel said, "I'm not here to cause any grief. I'm trying to stop my brother's foolish scheme. If you say you're a Prophet of Ages, have you foreseen what will happen?"

"Yes."

"Will my brother succeed in assassinating the king?"

Clear shook her head. "Glëa po'Lon's reign will continue. Even so, in his failure, your brother will cause a great deal of misery."

Parchment sheets in Clear's hands resembled the page discovered by the archivist scribe. Ravel surveyed the stacks of papers bound in cords, piled on the mattress to either side of the lady's sleeves. Then she noticed a bushel basket on the floor containing even more pamphlets, scrolls, loose leaf parchments, and kerchief bundles.

"You've been recording your dream visions for years," Ravel said. "Why bother to forge a document and hope the archivists would find it? Why not go to the king? Report what you've foreseen will happen!"

"I prefer to report to you, Lady Spareen, for your brother's sake." Clear gently folded the pamphlet in her hands. "The carnage will begin this evening in the Opera House near the end of the play's first act.

"The opera?" she repeated.

"It's less than two hours, if the play starts on time."

"Your prophecy mentioned beasts," Ravel said. "Do you mean the Surleista?"

"Yes, I've seen their wings aloft over the towers of Xolhold Keep. Unfortunately, my vision of today's catastrophe was brief and lacking in significant detail. I only know that the corrupted beasts will be released inside the castle's walls."

Arms crossed, Ravel paced slowly back and forth. "The crud-coats have already thought of it. They keep only a few Surleista in the training ground on the island. Even if Candor manages to bag the beasts, avoid the guards, smuggle them ashore and release them, archers stand ready on the watchtowers with fire arrows. Casualties should be at minimum."

"I assure you, the casualties will hardly be minimal. I saw perhaps a hundred or more half-chewed corpses." Clear paused to blow her nose again into the kerchief. "Regretfully, my vision of this day was incomplete. I woke up screaming in my husband's arms. This was years ago, during the war and before Glëa regained the throne. Only later did I cross-reference to another dream of his betrothal to sweet little Lilac."

Ravel gritted her teeth. "It's obscene to marry a child so young."

"They are only betrothed. The marriage will never be consummated."

"How can you be certain of that?"

Clear looked up at her grimly. "For in all my visions of future days, I have never seen little Lilac as an adult. I have never seen Lady Tiressa stand by Glëa po'Lon's side as his queen. I fear that her life may end today."

No. Ravel gripped the window's frame. She gazed outside to the expansive grassy yard of the lower bailey. By now, many of the townsfolk were making their way home. Yet they were in no hurry to leave; they lingered in large groups like flocks of sheep grazing in a field. They slurped from tankards. They carried food wrapped in kerchiefs. They chatted amongst themselves.

"Help me, Madame Prophet. Tell me what to do."

"You sound like *him*," she murmured. "You think that, by knowing what is to come, you can change what will happen. He tried. So many times, he tried to take action to no avail."

"You mean your husband?" Ravel asked. "Ash mentioned a horseman from my country?"

Clear nodded slowly. "I married a man from the west, many years ago, before Glëa returned from his adventure at sea."

Ravel paused to recall what she had overhead earlier. "Am I understanding this? You've had prophetic visions for years and kept them a secret? You foresaw the lost prince's return? You knew in advance the outcome of every battle? You knew how the Fortress of Sharp Crag would be penetrated? You knew of the day and the means by which *our* prince would fall, and you did nothing to forewarn him?"

The lady's heartbeat quickened. "Stop, please."

"No wonder your husband got drunk. No wonder he left you!" Ravel stood looming over the lady weeping on the cot. "Where is your husband now? Could my brother and his friends be in contact with him? Of course, that's their plan! Has he established a network of insurgent horsemen? You must tell the king! It's not just a handful of reckless boys, is it?"

"Your brother is not in collaboration with anyone else. Certainly not with my husband." As tears dribbled down her cheeks, she drew Ash's kerchief from the front of her bodice. "Please, trust me in this one fact. Your brother and his four companions are acting alone."

Ravel banged her fist on the wall. She left a pock mark in the coarse plaster. "Damnit, what happens before? How does Candor smuggle the Surleista inside the castle walls?"

"I don't know. When I dreamed of the carnage, I failed to see the inception of the incident."

"Have another dream, then."

"I can't."

"Why not? Tell me your fallibility and limitations, Madame Prophet, and offer your best excuses for your failure. Do the stars need to align? Does the moon need to be full? Do you require chanting of ancient scriptures or an animal sacrifice?"

Clear's face contorted as if about to weep but she had no more tears left. Her green eyes were puffy and red. "Did you ever notice, in ancient legends, that the prophets never traveled alone?"

"The twins Zëa and Zoë who served the first king." Ravel slowly unclenched her fists as she recalled the verses in ancient scripture of how the King Davarche the First had used the miraculous powers of the twin prophets to vanquish his challengers.. *Hand in hand, two by two, they stand as one. In unison they sing to summon the spirits.* In the legends, they always stood on the battlefield together.

"My husband was born a Prophet of Ages too. We need to be in proximity for our powers to manifest. Do you understand? I can only see visions when sleeping in my husband's arms. His spirit lifted my dreaming spirit's wings and then guided me home. My soul always returned to *him*, my harbor, my anchor. I can only commune with elemental spirits if my voice combines with his in a duet. Without *him*, I am a harp with no musician to pluck its strings."

When the lady fell silent, Ravel finished, "Without him, you're utterly powerless?"

Clear lowered her head. "Indeed."

"Let's get word to him, somehow. Let's bring him here to help. Where is he?"

The lady prophet raised her face to the candlelight and her expression was as blank as a mask. Her small mouth hung open, but words did not come. Her weeping ceased. Her body became still and, for a moment, it seemed that she did not breathe.

Ravel inhaled slowly, held it, and then exhaled a sigh. She knew that expression very well; she had seen it in countless faces since the end of the war.

"He's dead?"

Clear nodded a slight twitch of her head. "This past spring, on the anniversary of the defeat, he... he... My husband chose to end his own life. Surely you understand the significance of the day Chance decided to leave me forever."

Memories surged through Ravel's mind of the springtime meadows of Border Field on the day of the battle. Wildflowers burned in a hailstorm of fire arrows and pitch-tar bombs. Corpses of soldiers and horses gave their life's blood to the grass.

"May your husband's troubled spirit find solace in the Eternal Fields," Ravel said.

"Thank you." Clear fingered the kerchief in her hands.

"You didn't tell Ash. Why did you lie?"

Still looking down, Clear shook her head. "I did not lie. Everything that you overheard is the truth."

"But for a very significant omission," Ravel said.

Tears glistened in her reddened eyes. "I can't bear the weight of his sympathy. I can hardly bring myself to admit that I am a grieving widow. Ash will want to comfort me and offer healing, and I am not ready to be healed."

"I understand." Ravel paced back and forth between the large chest of Ash's clothing and the open window. Movement always helped her to think clearly. A good strategist did not dwell on shortcomings but evaluated how to make the most of one's assets.

Clear squinted at the faded parchments arrayed on her lap. "I must have overlooked something. Perhaps a fragment of another dream that, at the time, seemed unconnected—"

"Stop. Damnit, just stop." Ravel pointed to the bushel basket on the floor. "Pack 'em all up. Bring the load of papers to the commander of the guard. Report everything you've told me. The time for secrets is done."

Clear looked down. "You don't understand what I risk by revealing myself."

"What risk? Embarrassment? Do you think they won't believe you?"

A bright tear glistened at the corner of the lady's eye. "The twin prophets did not perform their legendary heroics by choice. The First King imprisoned their loved ones as hostages and compelled their service."

Ravel nodded in acceptance of the impossible. "Be that as it may, your husband is dead. My apologies for speaking bluntly, but the fact remains, you have no powers without him. Why should you fear the king enslaving you in his service?"

"I have my promise," the lady said. "My husband and I made a vow more sacred that our bonds of matrimony. For as long as we both—or either of us—lived, we swore to serve no king, no prince, no lord."

"I understand the burden of promises and vows," Ravel said. "I've broken every one of mine. But it's your choice, Lady Prophet. Will you cling to the vows you've made to a dead man, or will you stand up to save the lives of those who still breathe?!"

With that last word, Ravel leaped out the second-story window and plunged to the ground. She landed rolling and kept the circular momentum to rise to her feet. The joyous crowds, the squealing fifes, and myriad scents of the banquet's sumptuous foods did not draw her interest. Ravel turned her back on the festivities. She walked in sunlight across the open yard, towards the lengthening shadows cast by the lofty towers of Xolhold Keep.

Chapter 38.

Ravel identified the Opera House easily by its unique architecture. Its garishly decorated roof had bright red shingles and curled-up eaves. Carvings of bulbous fruits and wide-fanned leaves adorned the edges. A shingled canopy on red-and-black pillars sheltered the flagstone steps leading to the grand double doorway. The two-story building rivalled the frivolous ornamentation of the Tea House next door. Ravel recalled from her history lessons that the theater was constructed by King Davarche the Fourth as a dance hall where the sovereign could enjoy entertainment after a long day of haggling with his gentry to write the laws of the land. For half a millennium, the kings of the Davarche Dynasty laughed and wept to the performances of renowned actors, playwrights, and musicians of bygone days.

Theater arts were suppressed by King Tokustein during the grim years of mourning after his favorite son sailed to explore the Deep Sea and was lost in a shipwreck. The Mad King had forbade all dancing or singing except for funereal dirges and requiems. For more than forty years, this dormant theater had languished in silence, infested with rats, and clouded with spiderwebs, until Glëa po'Lon regained the throne.

Archers stood vigil on the castle's curtain wall behind the theater. Longbows and crossbows alike poised ready to launch their deadly projectiles into anyone who did not belong. Ravel gazed up at the barbed arrowheads pointed in her direction. She held her pace at a steady walk, unhurried, unthreatening, so as not to startle the sentries. She did not raise her hood; she let them have a good, long view of her half-bald scalp.

Servants and laborers bustled in and out of the broad double doors. They carried baskets full of stage props, rolls of curtain fabric, racks of fanciful wooden masks, and large musical instruments wrapped in cloth. Ravel sniffed the air as they jostled past her; she did not catch any hint of her brother's scent.

A youth in black uniform stopped Ravel at the threshold. "Halt there, *you*. What are you doing here? You should be patrolling for infiltrators, eh?"

"I'm expanding my perimeter."

She took one more step towards the lobby's doors. The soldier blocked her way.

He said, "We already vetted all of the actors, the musicians, the dancers, and the support crew. No one is here that isn't supposed to be here. All of them are on alert, too, for any stranger who wanders by offering to help or any admirers who seem inquisitive about their craft."

Ravel squinted at the single pewter button on his uniform's collar. The milk-faced fellow was not much older than her brother. He only carried a pole-arm and no sword.

"Good vigilance, Footman, but my orders are to search everywhere. So, you won't mind if I check backstage?"

He yielded to allow her to pass. "I'm a Footman First Class, by the way."

In line for a promotion if you serve well, she thought. *Let's hope you survive the night.*

Ravel entered a lobby that showcased more splendor than she had ever seen in the illustrations of history books. Thick candles projected light from dozens of mirror-backed sconces. Large tapestry rugs covered the hardwood floor in a forest loam of floral designs. Fluted mahogany columns rose out of the floor, bending to a peak in the domed ceiling. In the center hung a chandelier made of a thousand crystal beads, shining like a honeybee hive wrapped around a noonday sun. Not only had the king rebuilt and restored the dilapidated theater, but he had also improved it.

"Excuse me. Move aside." Two servants lugged a large crate by rope handles on either side. Glass bottles rattled within as they hurried past where Ravel stood. She inhaled the scent of beeswax candles and smoldering tinder boxes. Yet she caught no hint of her brother's presence.

Where are you, Der? How can the carnage begin here, as the prophet said? Could she be wrong? Can I rely on her dreams? If she did not predict her own husband's suicide, how much of the future has she failed to see?

Breathing more deeply, she detected a faint odor of sulfuric darkness.

Ravel turned in place to seek out the source. It did not come from the host bar in the center of the lobby. A group of Tea Mistresses in elaborate courtesan garb lit small braziers to boil tea. It did not come from either side of the carpeted ramps that led up to the second floor, or the arena seats beyond the curtains where thick candles were being prepared to light the stage. No, the rancid odor of sulfur, tar, and the Underworld wafted from a small access doorway underneath the left-hand ramp.

Ravel ducked past the banister's edge. She entered a small door and descended a narrow stairway into a dimly lit basement. *Great place to hide in wait for a chance to ambush the king*, she thought.

The unnatural odor grew stronger as she crept deeper into the basement beneath the stage. Intricate mechanisms of crossbeams, sprocket gears, and a wheel of timber spokes resembled the apparatus of a grist mill. Cedar, oak, and pine wood scents dominated the space. *That* smell like a rotten egg pierced through it all.

Some people crouched beneath the wheel's timbers. They whispered amongst themselves. Their voices did not match Candor or his friends. Yet they were certainly hiding something and doing something illicit in the shadows.

Ravel ducked the crossbars of the wheel to confront the group. "You! What are you doing?"

One person fell backwards off a stool. Another jumped up and tried to run, but Ravel blocked the way.

"Don't run, friends," said the third person who remained seated on a small stool. "It's not Shayle."

The actor was only half-dressed in a light chemise, striped leggings, and hair wrapped tightly in a kerchief. Ravel could not discern the actor's sex; they had a husky deep voice but a slender physique.

On the lid of a barrel lay a mortar and pestle, a jar of honey, and a handkerchief containing a few drumstick bones. Ravel bent forward to sniff at the black bones. No mistake. Those came from forearm of a Surleista—the monstrous beasts that could not be killed by sword or spear.

"You know what these are," Ravel growled.

"Don't tell Shayle, please! We'll be dismissed from the show." The one who had fallen off the stool blubbered in desperate panic.

The actor explained, "I am to give a performance to His Majesty himself. I need to prepare before going on stage. This, uh, medicine helps me to become my best."

"You eat *that*?" Ravel's voice rasped in incredulity.

"No, no, it's fatal if you swallow it. I smear a dose on the inside of my wrist." They pulled back a sleeve cuff to show a discolored rash with small white pustules. "Just a spoonful and I have enough vigor to perform for days!"

"Where did you get it?"

The actor's jaw clenched. "It's not easy to come by."

The other one, who had fallen to the floor, said nothing.

Only the third person confessed, "A nightsoil scooper knows of someone who cleans up a training ground..."

"The elite troops' training ground on a small island in the middle of the bay?" Ravel asked.

All three of them lowered their heads in silent assent.

She recalled what Captain Ash had told her on the rooftop the night before. *Cut off a limb and it sprouts back. Cut off its head and even the body re-grows itself.* Briefly she felt ashamed of her failure to imagine an illegal underground market to make use of the creatures' severed limbs. Smugglers of contraband would know how to circumvent all the security safeguards, how to pass in and out of the castle unnoticed.

Ravel grabbed the seated actor by the arm. "Show me your source."

"I can't! He came backstage a little while ago. He's gone now."

Panicked sweat aroused her senses. Oily saliva filled her mouth at the tantalizing aroma of the bloody meat beneath that person's skin. Her fingers stiffly arched. Her fingernails tingled, hardening, yearning to dig into soft flesh.

"Please don't hurt me!" the actor begged.

Ravel let go of the person's arm. "I'm not going to hurt you. I only need to know how the smugglers are sneaking their contraband into the castle. Where is their secret passageway?"

The three actors' expressions went blank staring at her, as if they were on stage and forgot their scripted dialog.

"Contraband... What contraband?"

"Sneaking into the castle...?"

"There's no secret passageway," said the one on the stool. "Shit-scoopers walk in and out through the gates while toting buckets of chum and entrails. Guards look to people's faces for identification. They don't inspect what offal is in the tubs."

"We told you," said the one kneeling on the floor. "He comes backstage only when he knows we need him. He's gone now."

Chapter 39.

Ravel ascended to a turret jutting off a corner of the inner wall adjacent to the donjon, the fifth and tallest tower of Xolhold Keep. From there, she gained a panoramic view of the entire castle grounds. She inhaled the cool breezes that blew over the nested concentric circles of walls. Dry air meant she had mobility; she still had a chance to stop him. Shadows grew on the western half of the bailey yard as the evening drew near. *It should be storming*, she thought. *There should be thunder. The sky should be screaming to match how I feel. Where are you, Der? What are you planning to do?*

Farther to the west, the city's rooftops filled the lowlands surrounded by neatly sectioned farm fields. The great river running north-to-south fed into aqueduct channels. Water pooled in a large reservoir north of the thirsty city. How many thousands of people dwelled in those cottages and shops, she wondered. How many innocent lives were at risk if Surleista took to the wing?

Ravel's gaze turned to the north. Her sights traced along the rocky promontory that ended with the lighthouse overlooking the sea. Creeks branched out around the reservoir. Fresh water rushed to the sea in an un-ending flow. White ripples of the famed waterfalls spilled over high dark cliffs like palomino horsetails. Feathery white waves crashed in futility against the vertical planks of rock beneath the lighthouse.

Fires blazed high atop the lighthouse tower. Nightly tasks followed routine. Spearmen with lanterns patrolled there too. A horn blew a long, low tone signaling the all-clear.

The wharf occupied a lower curve of Harbor Bay where broad sheets of boulders had been broken into a gravelly road. High tide had rolled in to fill the crevasses and tidepools of the massive, jagged rocks. A broad crescent swatch of the rocky shoreline was swallowed by lapping waves.

The vast unexplored ocean extended to the flat line of the horizon. Coast-hugging merchant ships anchored just offshore. Ships floated utterly still in the calm waters of the harbor bay. Smoky fog rolled in at the edges of the bay's curve.

"Any sign of him?" A spear carrier called down from the donjon's watchtower.

"No, I'm still looking. As you should be."

Ravel looked at the small island in the middle of Harbor Bay where the legions kept a few Surleista imprisoned as a training ground. Seagull's Rock was dark and silent as apparently no exercises were being held during the king's betrothal banquet. The tortured monsters were not screaming in their chains, but the sulfurous odor wafting on the sea breezes assured her that the Surleista were still there. She could not imagine how her brother could smuggle the beasts across the waters. All the fishing boats and rowboats were docked. Nothing disturbed the darkening satin waters.

Her gaze lowered straight down to the base of the steep cliffs upon which Xolhold Castle stood. Jagged rocks filled the area between the cliff's base and the shore's edge. Like the molars of giant oxen spilled out of a bag, the rocky shoreline made it impossible for ships to dock or wagons to roll here. Traffic coming from the wharf had to take an indirect route to the city by circling around the castle's outer wall.

One could only enter the castle's main gatehouse from the western side, facing the city, by ascending the incline of the royal highway. The moat's deep ditch was filled with grimy seawater. All three remaining sides of the castle were unreachable; high walls crowned the edges of a treacherous vertical cliff. Even if they had ropes and grappling hooks, Candor and his friends could not climb those walls unseen.

The opera house, she wondered. Why would the prophet foresee that the carnage would begin in the opera house?

The harder she tried to think strategically and logically, the more elusive were the possibilities. Ravel concluded that sensible reasoning was useless. Her human eyes and her human senses, prowling the castle all night and day long, had failed. She needed to be a blood hound as the king said. *Sniff out your brother and his cohorts.* Or, as Captain Ash had advised: *Don't just use your nose. Use all your senses, human and inhuman.*

She closed her eyes. She listened not with her human ears. She thought of her brother's scent and the aroma of his skin. Memories played in her mind of holding him as a newborn infant and pressing her cheek against his tiny face. *So soft.* The talons hummed at the center of her chest. A throb of hunger tightened her gut. The claws pulled and stretched at her breastbone's skin and, like a compass needle, pointed the way.

Facing eastward, she envisioned a straight line leading away from the theater's red-shingled roof and through the crenellated wall. The imaginary line continued beyond the walls and their foundation of stone cliffs.

A mausoleum lay at the water's edge midway between the wharf and the lighthouse. The final resting place of kings, known as the Tomb of a Thousand Faces drew her attention. White stone in profile sharply contrasted with a dark twilight sky. *Why the tomb of kings,* she wondered. *Why? What is there for you?*

Trusting her gut, Ravel leaped through the gap between the merlon blocks. She scuttled down the castle wall by clinging to the seams between the bricks. Her fingernails and toenails, hardening into purple hooks, did not crack by digging into the mossy stone. The wall gave way to sheer panels of rock sculpted by tens of millennia facing the sea. Halfway down the cliff's face, she jumped. The waxed cloak flapped as she plummeted to the gravelly scree.

Waterfalls to her left and tidepools to her right, Ravel had no other course but to approach the high tide creeping over the shoreline. Her brother's scent grew stronger with every step. Most certainly Candor came this way. It was the first scent of him that she had detected all day. The talons buzzed more strongly. She hurried across the pebbly sand towards the breakwater blocks.

Ravel had known of the tomb of kings all her life, had seen sketches and read narrative descriptions, but this was her first chance to see the landmark for herself. The mausoleum was a single-story cube of white marble blocks.

Ogganathian-style columns were a palisade of leafless tree trunks, each precisely chiseled to a geometric aesthetic.

At the stone steps, Ravel dropped to her belly. She licked and sniffed the cold marble slabs. Her brother's scent was vividly plain and mixed with the lingering odors of his four friends. The trail smelled fresh; they had passed this way within the hour.

She quickly bounded up the broad white stairway. Exactly twenty-one steps spanned from the gravelly road to the columned portico's arch. Each step bore a mosaic tile engraved with an emblem of all the Founding Lords who had supported King Davarche the First in his victory almost eight centuries before. Ravel noticed the emblem of her own House of Spareen pass beneath her bare feet. The dead were dead. Stone was stone.

Once she reached the portico, Ravel found the sealed door ajar. Coils of glass canes as thick as ox tails, that before had been twisted around the door handles as a chain lock, were broken into pieces. Chunks of glass lay littered at the flagstone. Consumed with rage and vengeance, her brother had discarded all reverence for the traditions that their parents had held dear. Their father would not have dared to approach this door. Only kings performing the funeral ritual of succession were permitted to break the seal and enter.

Ravel stepped over the threshold. Her bare feet padded into the gritty dust of un-swept centuries. Stillness and gray shadows met her with silence. A domed glass skylight filtered the moon's light into a purple glow. Mosaic floor tiles formed an intricate mandala of interlocking circles overlaid by a pattern of squares.

The walls were pocked with alcoves and niches. Cloisonné urns held the cremated remains of long-dead queens, dowagers, princes, princesses, cousins, and royal bastards. Ravel inhaled the stale, stone-scented air. Candor and his companions had passed through this chamber recently. The stench of their sweat lingered so strongly that she did not need her mystical senses to perceive it.

A hatchway opened to the chamber below. Tile cubes encircled the rim. Wax globs marked the spots where candlesticks had long ago burned down to the wick. A newly-crowned King of Xol was supposed to be carrying a light. But she did not need a flame to see the stairway.

Ravel descended the cool stone wedges leading down into an underground vault. She counted another twenty-one steps until she reached the floor of the crypt.

Her brother and his companions were nowhere in sight. *Water...* Ravel halted before the bottom step. Water dripped from cracks in the walls. Water had leaked in from the sea or had seeped up from the ground itself. Brine smelled cold and forbidding, stale and stagnant, undrinkable and untouchable. Water covered the entire floor of the crypt in a toxic slime. Water curdled and rippled into itself.

She could go no farther. No candles or lamps illuminated the dark chamber, yet her eyes could see clearly every detail in a monochrome greenish glow.

Rectangular blocks in four symmetrical rows contained the remains of all former kings of the Davarche Dynasty. Chiseled into the sides of each sarcophagus were their full royal names and bas relief portraits. The first king lay closest to the stairway with his tomb on a raised dais set apart from the others. More recent kings were interred at the farthest wall. Ravel measured and counted the distance with her eyes; there was no empty space for another single row. Twenty-five kings in total lay buried here: no more, no less. Perhaps no one had expected this dynasty to continue its reign for so many centuries. Or, she wondered, the ancient prophets who served the Davarche the First foresaw the exact number of his descendants and knew that the immortal Glëa po'Lon would never be buried.

"What could you find here to be useful," she whispered to herself. "No weapons, not even ceremonial armor, is buried with these bones."

From the stone walls came a voice whispering. *Let be sealed what is sealed. Keep buried what is buried. Let be not touched what should not be touched.* That voice was neither male nor female, not human or beast. It was a voice without a throat or breath.

"Are you a spirit?" she asked. "Are you a ghost of one of these kings?"

The whisper repeated, *Let be sealed what is sealed. Keep buried what is buried. Let be not touched what should not be touched.*

"I don't understand." Ravel sniffed at the air. Her brother's lingering scent was strongest near the raised dais of the first king.

Looking again, she noticed that the lid was slightly ajar. Someone had recently opened the Davarche the First's sarcophagus.

"Why would my brother desecrate a corpse? Tell me, ghost! Or if you can't be useful, be silent."

Abomination. Abomination. Abomination from under the sea.

"Can you help me, or not?"

The air shifted as if a window had opened. Odors wafted from the farthest end of the chamber. She detected the faint odor of darkness, of sulfur, of flammable tar and the rot of death. It was similar to what she had smelled in the theater's basement. Candor's musky, unwashed scent faintly melded with the darker aromas. Unmistakably, her brother had gone there, but she could not see what valuables lay at the farthest end of the crypt.

"Where did he go? Please, help me. What did he take from the king's coffin? Where is he now?"

A faint breathing sound like an old woman's sigh seemed to voice a lyrical phrase. *Two by two, hand in hand, we stand as one.*

Human figurines were set in a niche hollowed out of the back wall. Life-sized statues sculpted in beige marble, they stood facing each other. Their hands crossed with fingers entwined. The stone figurines were so expertly carved as to be lifelike, as if the bodies of real people were dipped in clay. Inscribed at the base of the niche was a verse of scripture in the ancient High Classical script: In Union is Their Power.

"Are you the ones speaking to me?" Ravel asked. "Are you the ghosts of the Prophets of Ancient Days? Can you help me? Help me, please!"

Abomination. Abomination. Abomination from under the sea.

"Yes, so you've said before. It's not helping me to understand. What do you mean?"

The stench of sulfur, flammable tar, and her brother's perspiration wafted again as if blown by a blacksmith's bellows. She looked more closely to the base of the sculptures from where the odors seemed to come.

Between the statues' feet, several of the floor tiles had been pried up and stacked aside. At first she had assumed the square layers to be part of the statuary base, but the longer she focused on her stare it became clear. A dark hole had been opened in the floor.

"By th' blazes of the abyss, there's tunnels! The idiots found tunnels!"

Briefly, she smiled, impressed that her brother was not entirely a reckless fool. He had architectural schematics of the castle. He had a plan.

Her short-lived smile dropped away as she realized this tomb's underground tunnel was unknown to the king's legions who guarded the bricked-up sally doors and secret passageways in the walls of Xolhold Keep. But a hermit archivist in the distant mountains far to the north might have preserved the lost diagrams of ancient architects sworn to secrecy. Candor's obsession with collecting faded scrolls proved valuable.

Abomination. Abomination. Abomination from under the sea.

"I know, I know! I'm doing my best here."

Ravel extended her foot off the bottom step. Shallow waters erupted into a field of countless sharp points like a box of needles spilled on the floor. Shrieking spirits in the liquid raised a rush of vertigo in Ravel's mind. She half-closed her eyes and strained to keep her balance while telling herself not to be afraid. The water was not deep; she could clearly see the outline of the stone tiles underneath the algae slime. She had survived falling into a river. Surely she could do this much.

Yet the harder she tried to take that first step into shallow water, the harder it became. Her upper body lurched and jerked in resistance. Gripping the stairway's rail, she swayed from side to side but could not force her foot to plunge into the water.

It's getting worse since the river, she thought. Resolved to follow her brother into the underground tunnels, she formed a plan.

First, she had to discard her stiff cloak and her calf-length wraparound tunic. Now she wore only a loose-fitting chemise that ended in a threadbare hem at her knees. *Father, give me strength.* She hopped from the bottom step to the nearest sarcophagus. She landed atop the noble resting place of King Davarche the First.

Within the marble box, a crimson silk veil masked the skull's face. Centuries had decayed the flesh but not the sumptuous velvet robes that garbed the skeleton. Jeweled neck chains, a cloak brooch, and a gold-plated crown glimmered brightly to the unholy shine of her eyes. *At least they aren't common thieves*, she thought.

The skeleton's left hand was broken off at the wrist. Ravel frowned to wonder why her brother would take only that. She gritted her teeth in determination to ask him in person.

Ravel waited for the spirits' guidance as she crouched on top of the First King's sarcophagus. Time passed but she could stand waiting no more. Ghosts of former kings, prophets of ancient days, or un-folk spirits in the stones, she could spare no time in waiting for them to speak again.

She leapt to the next sarcophagus in the front row. Water spirits lashed out. Water's outrage prickled and burned at her naked calves and bare feet. Ravel continued hopping from that stone box to the next row, to the second row, to the third row, and finally reached the last row at the rear.

Ravel landed on the lid of King Tokustein, the father of the princes who had battled each other. The so-called Mad King, in despair over the loss of his favorite son, had ended his own life by swallowing chips of glass or crushed diamonds. The stories varied. His tomb's flat lid was the least decorated of all. A small blob of wax showed where only a single votive candle had been burned in reverence by Glëa po'Lon himself upon his ceremonial accession to the throne six years before.

"You poor, mad, suffering fool." Ravel patted the plain smooth lid over the final resting place of her own prince's father. "You mourned only the son you lost at sea. You neglected the one who remained alive here at your side. Rouchard would have succeeded you, and the royal line would have continued unbroken, if you weren't such a selfish cock to let it all fall apart. I see it clearly, now. All of this is your fault, Mad King Tokustein."

Abomination. Abomination. Abomination from under the sea.

"Yes, yes, I heard you. Who is the abomination? Is it me? Is it my brother? Well, prophets or ghosts, if you won't explain any further, please be quiet."

Crouched like a cat, she made one last jump into the alcove of the prophets' statues. She ducked beneath the clasped hands of the two figurines.

She gazed into the hole where a very modern wooden ladder was propped. She stepped down and, upon descent, she sniffed the rungs. Oh yes, Candor's hands had gripped the ladder not too long ago. More scents overlapped from Prosper, Xidron, and the other two companions.

Ravel licked the pinewood and tasted her brother's skin. Though it had been seventeen years, she never forgot the first moment of inhaling the scent of a newborn's scalp. She recalled kissing the baby's soft hair as he slept in his bassinet. *Sneaky lil' cod, I'm on your trail now.*

Chapter 40.

Ash ascended what felt like a thousand steps to reach the top of the White Tower—the tallest of the five towers in Xolhold Keep. The shingled roof of the donjon capped an array of tall merlons. Wide gaps between the square columns offered a panorama of the castle's concentric nested walls. Ash turned his face to the left and right, briefly, to admire the view; it was not often that he climbed to these heights.

"Hello?" he called out to the sentries on duty. "Shouldn't you ask me, 'who goes there?'"

"We saw you coming." A youthful footman glanced over his shoulder and waved a half-hearted greeting. The remaining three spearmen kept staring morosely at the movement of lanterns in the bailey yard below.

"It's quite an impressive view you've got," Ash said.

"What've you got there?" asked the footman.

Ash held up what he had brought from the royal kitchens: a freshly killed and skinned coney hanging from a twine cord tied around its furry ankles. "I'm looking for *her*. I brought some supper."

"Why?" one of the spearmen asked.

"We don't want her to get hungry, do we?" Ash tried a smile to lighten the mood.

"She's not here, Doctor." One of the spearmen tossed the shaft of his spear from his left hand to his right, and repeated the cycle. The red tassel flopped back and forth. The heavy braided cords slapped on his black leather gloves.

The footman added, "About half an hour ago, she jumped over the cliff and went scouting down to the royal tomb."

"How odd," Ash said.

"Suspicious is what we call it," the footman said. "Very suspicious, don't you think? Cody said he heard Colonel Viktor talking to Captain Teimethee voicing doubts if the ghoul's got a brother at all."

Ash hooked a thumb on his belt. "Why would she need to lie to us? She's got un-folkish mystical powers. C'mon, think clearly. I'd see how she might withhold information, but I really doubt Lady Spareen would invent this story of a brother bent on revenge."

A spearman facing the oceanside perked up at the name. "Spareen, you say?"

"Yes," Ash said. "Her name is not 'ghoul.' Her name is Ravel po'Marn, first daughter of the House of Spareen, and she was once a lady."

The spearman facing east slouched forward as if a heavy burden had just dropped onto his shoulders.

Ash cocked his head in curiosity. "Have you something to say, my good man?"

"She's not lying about the brother."

The footman asked, "How do you know that?"

"I was in the battalion that advanced on the Spareen estate. I saw a boy."

His voice was flat monotone. His eyes glossed over with memories. Everyone else in the tower got quiet too, waiting to listen to a story they did not want to hear.

"It was the day of the last battle. We had been hard at it, for day and days, in the melee at Border Field. We were so very soddin' tired of fighting. You remember, don't you? You all remember that day?"

Every man's head nodded along. Ash breathed through his mouth and his tongue went dry.

"We followed orders to scout the surrounding countryside, to engage stragglers if they put up a resistance. No one wielding a blue-and-white flag could be allowed to stand. The war had to end. It just had to end! So, we burned the manor house. We took the lord. We took the lady."

"It was just war," said the footman. "You were following orders, Errik."

"We did things that I'm not proud of doing. I lost my head." He lowered his head and stared down at his feet.

The footman laid a hand on Errik's shoulder. "We all did things in the heat of battle."

Ash's heart pounded harder and faster inside his chest. He recalled the events of that day as if he had just now walked away from the field soaked in blood. In the medic's tent, he had tirelessly bandaged and stitched the wounds of soldiers who fought to restore the rightful prince to the throne. Their suffering and sacrifice had been worthwhile, he had thought. *We fought to bring peace and unity to the world. We fought for the promise of stability under the reign of an immortal king. We fought for truth, didn't we?*

The spearman named Errik sniffled and wiped his nose on the cuff of his sleeve. "The boy... The boy saw it all."

"The lady put up a fight?" asked the other spear carrier.

Errik nodded. "Yes, she fought very hard."

Ash leaned against a support column to catch his breath. He had eaten too much at the banquet. The dead animal hanging from his hand now made him queasy.

"If I face the boy now, what should I do?" Errik asked. "Should I apologize?"

"No," said the footman. The word *no* echoed around the group. "No apologies. Do you hear me? We defend the kingdom. We defend Xolhold Keep. We defend His Majesty the immortal Iron King."

Ash found his balance again as the wave of the nausea passed. He strolled back into the center of the group. Usually, he could fake a congenial smile in the worst of circumstances, but at this moment he could not dislodge his frown.

"If you're not going to apologize for murdering her mother, then at least give her *this* if she comes back." Ash dropped the knotted cord with the dangling coney. The carcass fell at the man's black boots. "Trust me, you really don't want to see her get hungry."

Errik the spearman raised his chin up and vigor returned to his eyes. "How dare you look at me in judgment, Doctor. Like you never did anything wrong? Like you never made a mistake?"

Mistake? The word rang like a brass gong in his mind. He visualized a small boy in a burned house weeping over the corpse of his mother. He imagined the helpless rage of that small orphaned boy, alone in the world and surrounded by death.

"It's not a 'mistake' to butcher a lady in her own house, in front of her own child." Glaring into Errik's cold blue eyes, Ash clenched his fist. He tensed his arm in making ready to punch the fellow in the gut if he said one more word.

The others gathered around Ash and formed a human barrier. Their black-gloved hands patted his shoulders. They murmured soothing words that he could barely hear through the buzzing and pulsing of blood in his ears.

"Let me go. Let me go!" Ash backed out of their grasp. He sized up Errik measured against his own height and strength. The spearman had a well-balanced posture but was half as slender. Ash figured that in a fist fight, unrestrained, he could easily get the better of this fellow.

"C'mon, Doctor, don't be—" the footman began.

"Don't tell me what to be." Ash turned for the stairwell. "Bite sod, th' lot o' ye."

He descended the wedge-shaped spiral steps. Skipping down quickly, he hardly felt his feet. Fresco paintings decorated the plaster walls and depicted historical scenes of royal splendor. Pastel two-dimensional faces passed in a blur.

Halfway down the tower's height, Ash stopped at an archer's alcove. One archway led to the observation balcony overlooking the Main Hall and the throne room. The space was vacant and dim beyond the stone arch now that the betrothal ceremony had concluded. He caught the odor of soap wafting up from the ground floor. He heard the sloshing of mops on the slick marble tiles below.

Another doorway led to the turret connecting the rampart's catwalk of the outer curtain wall. He veered to lean against the thick cool stone. He struggled to catch his breath in the cool dark air and waited for his heart to stop pounding. In the night air, all other sounds became clear: the hush of the ocean waves, the low horn blowing from the lighthouse, and muted laughter of an audience far below enjoying the upbeat music.

The opera had begun. Ash considered making his way to the theater; he had missed the overture. If he hurried down the stairs, he felt certain that he could slip inside and find a spare cushion at the rear of the auditorium. Yet he could not get his feet to move. The more he thought of sitting through a comedic musical performance for several hours, the more his stomach churned.

After a momentary pause, he decided instead to go to the soldiers' barracks. A flagon of dark ale, a carafe of honey mead, or a keg of hard cider promised to remedy the lump in his gut.

Chapter 41.

Ravel found a dome-shaped chamber at the bottom of the ladder. The hands of men had not—nor could they ever—carve something like this out of the earth. Its walls were as smooth and perfectly round as an inverted soup bowl. Rose-pink marble with blue mineral veins did not match the gray rocks of the seashore. Color radiated out of the walls and gave the wooden ladder's rungs an eerie, floral hue.

She gained strength with each breath. The longer she stood on the glossy floor, serenity returned to her mind. Distance muted the whispering ghosts and the screaming puddles in the tomb overhead.

A number of tunnels branched off the hub. Each passageway was large enough to drive a hay wagon to any destination in the land above. Hollow tunnels ran underneath the lighthouse's cliffs, underneath the reservoir, or underneath the promontory of Xolhold Castle itself. *You think you'll scurry like rats through underground tunnels and pop up in the basement of a tower somewhere? Not if I catch you first.*

Ravel inhaled her brother's scent and set off jogging. She plunged into a passageway that soon bent to the left, the right, and switched back into a serpentine course. One could not sprint at full blast when, every twenty or thirty paces, the tunnel bent at ninety degrees. Yet she needed to go faster if Candor and his friends had a head start. She needed to catch up with him before he executed his plan. It might already be too late to stop him from an act of murder and destruction that would doom him and their family's name forever.

Paces counted off in her mind and Ravel strained to estimate the distance. She factored in the angles of the turns and switchbacks, divided and multiplied her sums, but all of it was guesswork. Without a compass in hand, or the sun and stars as guides, her sense of direction twisted into knots. She no longer felt certain of passing underneath the wharf's tidepools or the castle's foundation. How far to go? No way to tell. She just had to hope she was not too late.

The ambient glow of the marble walls changed color in gradient smears. Rose-pink jade blurred into forest-green that gave way to sections of lilac and amethyst, then pumpkin and lemon, and then scarlet and carnation pink. Color shined from everywhere and nowhere.

Crystalline glow seized her senses. The cluster of talons reached upwards to the neckline of her coarse shirt. Their darkness tugged at her scarred skin. Light. Color. Blood. They wanted to feed upon the gemstones' beauty. Open-mouthed, she gasped to inhale. Color tasted like a brandy-soaked sponge cake that filled her mouth nearly to gagging. Thorny talons arched in thirst for craving a drink.

Oh, no, groaned the voice of her thoughts. *You want to do this now?* Ravel clutched the insistent burning at the center of her chest. An appetite not from her own belly surged through her core. She gnawed at the empty air and growled in yearning for a bite of warm, bloody flesh. Bony spikes echoed the call. *Meat... meat... meat...* The skin covered by fabric prickled and itched. Talons burned more earnestly at the core of her chest. Her rhythmic gasps came voiced in whimpers.

"Stop, stop," she whispered in a raspy voice. Her throat burned in the air, but she forced out the words. "I am human. I am human. I am my mother's daughter."

The tunnel straightened and expanded into a larger tube. Ravel staggered drunkenly down the center, progressing through delicious waves of color: orange, squash, melon, butter, and lemon. The floor became a lumpy course of corrugated ridges. Clearly the passageway was never designed for human feet to tread.

Ahead lay a cavern with a lofty cathedral ceiling. Tapered beams of white marble rose out of the concave dish of the floor. The dome's walls were made of pure gold. Metallic and smooth, it looked like the inside of a mythical giant's tea kettle. Ravel licked her lips and could taste yellow.

Men's overlapping voices bickered amongst themselves. They spoke all at once but were not listening to each other. "We should go this way," said one.

"No, the map points this way," said another. "Shouldn't we be underneath the Seagull Rock by now?" asked a third.

"Is that you, sister?" Candor's voice echoed in the cavern.

Ravel emerged from the tunnel into the dome chamber. She intended to rush forward but stopped. Golden light struck her with the awesome majesty of a sunrise over the grasslands. She wanted to scream but her throat had swollen shut.

Prosper startled, "You!" The bucket that he held wobbled under his hand. Pure water splashed on the floor. A puddle, however shallow, blocked her from rushing forward.

She snarled at the puddle as if it were a pool of flaming tar with razor spikes. Water spirits screamed in a high-pitched squeal, stronger than she had ever heard before. Their shrieks resonated in the lofty arches of the cavern. Ravel's jaw flexed but she could not force words to come forth. Only a low, guttural snarl snorted out of her sinuses.

Xidron held forth a skeleton's hand as a talisman to repel her. A blue ceramic disc inscribed with ancient lettering was attached to the hand's palm. "Look what a monstrous demon she has become."

Stander drew out a pair of knives from his belt. He held them aloft, ready to throw.

Redson fitted an arrow to his longbow, stretched back the string, and made ready to shoot.

Prosper clung to the rope handle of his water bucket, prepared to fling another splash.

Candor squared his shoulders into a pretentious pose of authority. A coil of hemp rope looped around his shoulder. A compass and a brass sextant dangled from his belt. In his left hand, he held a map painted on a square of deer hide.

"My dear sister, I forgive you for thwarting justice at the bridge. I'm sorry for what you've endured. I had hoped that you would find us. It is destiny's will that you are here to bear witness. Be at peace in your heart, for our vengeance is near to fruition."

Ravel glanced at the ceiling of the golden cavern. She guessed that they now stood underneath the Seagull's Rock in the middle of Harbor Bay where the king's legions had a training ground. *So that's the plan; to release the captive Surleista and herd them to the castle through these tunnels.* It would not take much effort; the ravenous beasts could easily find their own way to a bounteous feast.

"No, no." She strained to force words out of her raw throat. "Innocents..."

"None of them collaborators are innocent," said Redson.

"The generals and officers who gave the commands," added Stander.

"The crud-coats who carried out the imposter's orders," Prosper said.

Xidron finished, "The abomination has infected them all with his lies. A demon pollutes the throne of Xol."

Ravel braced her feet and clenched her fists in readiness to fight them.

Prosper made ready to toss his bucket of water. Candor put a hand on his friend's wrist in restraint.

"You're too late, sister," he said with a harsh smile. "You can't prevent what is happening."

In his right hand, Candor held a silver fork with two blunt prongs. He raised the tuning fork by its stem and tapped the prongs against the skeleton's hand. Ravel felt the air thicken. *What's happening,* she wondered. *Why can't I move? Why can't I rush forward to stop him?* She felt herself plunged neck-deep in thick mud. Unable to shift her feet, unable to lift her arms, she stood in place and watched.

Candor pressed the base of the tuning fork's stem against the wall. Sound erupted out of the spot. Rippling waves radiated out from her brother's fist. The cavern's air shimmered in waves of vibrations. Stones chimed in the purest tones that Ravel had ever heard. Colors deepened in intensity. Gold turned white.

The sleek marble beneath their feet slowly clarified like melting wax. A circular section turned opaque and then became translucent.

She vaguely saw a darker shadow through the glassy stone. Something lurked on the other side. A living animal was moving underneath their feet. *Mine... Mine... Mine....* chanted another's voice.

Talons at her chest vibrated in resonance. Finally, the black claws had what they wanted: the taste of earth and the scent of light. Knobby joints glistened. Charred flesh glimmered. Serpentine scales sparkled darkly as the flesh of her chest turned gray.

The ribbed columns in the cavern's walls seemed to whirl in a delirium haze. The world lurched, tilted upwards and turned upside-down. She kneeled to grasp the stone floor. Her purple fingernails raked into the buttery jade. Groveling on her knees, she scraped up flakes of gemstone.

A discordant tone sang in her skull and blurred her sense of what was solid and real. Stronger than ever before, the talons glowed brightly at the center of her chest. A stabbing heat pierced her core and cooked her from the inside out. Her heartbeat quickened to a timpani patter. Blood throbbed at her ears. A high-pitched whine whistled inside her skull. Heat stiffened her arms and petrified her legs. Her eyes clamped closed. Her jaw yawned open.

She gargled on a rising guttural groan. Each inhale brought a rush of shivers stronger than the last. Each time she thought she could endure no more, the next wave built in intensity from the core of her ribcage working outward. Ravel strained to focus her wavering eyes upon the circular hatchway in the floor.

Crackling sounds grated in the glossy stones. Silver dust sprinkled out the rim's circle. A wheel separated into wedge-shaped blades that fanned out from an iris, rotating, slowly peeling apart from its base. Black claws emerged from the center of the expanding iris pinwheel. The shadowy beast on the other side pushed against the fan blades, forcing it to open more quickly a small squeak at a time.

Light lay over her eyes in blood colors and venous lace. She saw her brother's silhouette through a tattered veil of rose, scarlet, vermilion, and red.

"Go," Ravel croaked in a raspy voice. "Flee."

"Fear not, Big Sister." Candor smiled wildly. "We are the masters of the dark creatures, just as in the legends of ancient days. King Davarche the First commanded the Prophets of Ages, a flock of mighty firebirds, and the powerful forces of un-folk hordes. These beasts of the Outerlands shall do our bidding."

Abomination from under the sea. "No, no, no!" Ravel cried in anguish from the core of her gut that echoed the voices of gods being burned out of Heaven. Her chest tightened as the scream wrung the last of breath from her lungs.

Blink, and she saw herself on the other side of the glass hatch. She felt her own hands as inhuman paws with twiggy knuckles and corkscrew talons.

She felt her own skin as reptilian hide seared blacker than charcoal. She saw her own nose as a crocodilian snout. *We are One. We are One. We are One.*

Ravel screamed like a woman, now. She slammed back into her own eyes, into her own thoughts, into her own body. *No time.* Her sights fixed on the shadowy claws beneath the glass. That creature's talons picked at the joints and forced the pinwheel to open more quickly. Its paws shaved off glitter sprinkles at the edges of each fan blade. *No time. He's here.*

The glass hatch popped open, kicked upward by the beast within the tunnel.

Puffs of rancid mist brought the ancient stale air of a thousand milrods' distance traversed beneath the Deep Sea. In one sniff of sulfurous fumes, Ravel knew that this was not merely a creature escaping from the training ground on Seagull's Rock. This was a tunnel stretching into the gateway of the Great Black Abyss.

A grand beast leaped forth from the hole. He knocked them over and dumped all five boys into a dog pile. His massive leather wings snapped free. His crooked arms spread wide open in glee. Wickedness, hate, vengeance, and rage were embodied in a crusty hide of slate scales. His serpentine neck arched and lifted his iron jaw to the golden roof. Like a wolf howling at the moon, he roared his freedom.

Candor, still grinning, stood his ground in the face of the great beast looming above him. Prosper and the three other youths staggered back in shock and horror. Redson fired an arrow from his longbow and missed. Stander gripped his pair of knives. Xidron stepped in front to protect the group with the first king's skeleton hand.

The Old One was a larger bull Surleista than any Ravel had seen in the Outerlands. He had more horns on his crocodilian skull. More spikes serrated his spine. The barbed tail was as long as a fishing boat's anchor chain. Wings unfurled on the wake of their own air with silken fluidity.

Mine... Mine... Mine.... the grand beast chanted while looking at her.

Ravel realized that the talons in her chest had come from this creature's paws. The black spikes purred in response to their master's growls. Harmonic waves resonated through her ribs into her core.

Smoky light as a bright veneer clung to the edges of the Old One's silhouette. Ethereal paleness dusted the crusty hide, softened the tips of the

266

talons, and in double-image broadened and flattened the sharpness of his fangs. The faint corona of another soul shined from within. *He fell too*, she observed. *Like the others... like Lord Torval... like Prince Glëa... Except that his shining soul, instead of falling out of the crystal nest into a human shell, dropped into this malformed creature.*

"Oh Ancestors." Still on her knees prostrated before him, Ravel moaned as all her fears drained away. "He's beautiful."

"Yes, Sister, yes!"

Chapter 42.

The opera began after everyone in the audience was comfortably seated. The orchestra swelled forth its opening overture. Harps, both upright and table-flat, played alongside lutes and mandolins. Silver pipes and wooden flutes paired with long brass horns. Rosewood drum sets were struck by silk-wrapped mallets.

King Glëa po'Lon reclined on a cushioned divan. Alyss the Tea Mistress sat poised at his side. Boy squires rushed about arranging the spread of his cloak over the armrest and the carpet. He was on full display tonight on a balcony with a clear view of center stage. His box seat placed him above all the nobility and their families seated on thick cushions on the theater's floor.

"We're really high up," said the child. "I can see everybody's head."

"Yes," said the king. "The better for us to see the stage. Hush, now, it's beginning."

Tiressa kicked her feet and pinched handfuls of her layered skirts. "I have to use the pot-pot."

A chambermaid in a russet gown emerged from behind the sofa. She offered her hand to the child. "I'll take her, Your Majesty."

"Please do."

He watched the two walking through the curtain, the little girl and the woman, and briefly reflected on how quickly one turned into the other.

The Rabbit King himself danced onto center stage to a fanfare of brass horns. The audience of nobles and their servants alike roared in glee. Many clapped their hands. Others wagged their jangling wooden noisemakers. The actor dressed in a full body costume of gray wool, complete with a fluffy wad for a tail, oversized boots for feet, and long hanging ears.

"I am, I am the King of the Moon! Those spots you see are my palace rooms!" A traditional mask molded of cowhide muffled the voice of the actor inside.

A pack of younger nobility sat in the front row. Bachelors still young enough to be childish all yelled in rowdy unison. "Why are you here on Earth, oh, King of th' Moon?"

Rabbit hopped to the edge of the stage. He leaned forward to cock one floppy ear towards the front row beneath him. "Why, you ask? Why am I here?"

"Yes! Why!"

The little Lady of Taine returned to her seat, boosted up to the cushions with help from the nursemaid. Her cheeks blushed with delight. "He's here! He's here!"

"Yes, he's here," the king said calmly. "The opera is named after him, isn't it?"

He shared a bemused sideways glance with the tea mistress. Alyss lifted a small iron pot of its warming trivet and refilled his cup of mint tea.

Rabbit hopped heavily from one side of the stage to the other. He called out to the other nobles in the crowd, "Do you wish to know why I'm here?" And again, to stage right, "How about you, Sir? Do you wish to know?"

"No, actually, I *know* why you're here," said Lord Rubëa sitting in the House of Browden's section.

"Why, Papa, why?" asked the children clustered around him.

"Oh, *you* know why I'm here, Good Sir?" asked Rabbit pretending to be offended.

Tiressa grasped the railing of the opera box and shouted down to the dimly lit crowd, "How could you know why he's here? Did he tell you, while I was going pot-pot?"

Twitters of respectful amusements fluttered over the crowd. The colonels Viktor and Maetha in civilian clothes sat together in the section with Viktor's uncle Governor Fordon. The usually-disciplined officers smiled broadly now that they were out of uniform and snuggled together as husband and wife.

Rabbit hopped to center stage and raised his masked face to address the opera box. "I shall explain my purpose only at His Majesty's command!"

Tiressa grabbed the cuff of his sleeve and tugged hard. "Ask him! Ask him! Ask him! Make him tell."

"Very well, my queen. As you ask, so shall it be done."

King Glëa rose to his feet. A rustling rumble, and everyone in the building got to their feet as well. Rabbit dropped to his knees and bowed into the stage.

Before he spoke, the king recalled a very old memory of himself when he was a mere human. Seventy years ago, he was a child not much older than the one tugging at his sleeve. His father had felt a particular affection for the theater arts. If he were not born to the royal family, King Tokustein might have become an actor. Traditionally, all that the host noble needed to say were a few words of command to continue the show, but Glëa's father King Tokustein had penned himself a rhyme. Fifty years later, it was still clear in his mind.

"King of the moon tho' you may be, I am the king of land and sea. Tell me why you've come to me."

Rabbit held his bow as the whole place erupted in thunderous applause. He waited out the waves of cheers and adulation. "Well said, Your Majesty!" and "Brilliantly articulated!" called out anonymous voices in the din.

"Just like his father used to say," explained Governor Vilbyss to his nephew, Colonel Édel, sitting at his side.

Musicians keyed up the well-known refrain. Rabbit snapped upright and began his dance and song.

> *There is no honey on the moon.*
> *There is no honey on the moon.*
> *I have no bees, I have no trees,*
> *so there is no honey on the moon."*

The Lady of Taine giggled. "I like honey too!"

The performance continued. Music played and the rabbit frolicked about on stage. But as the opera wore on for the next hour, the little girl's patience wore off. She kicked her shoes against the cushions in a steady drumming swing. Her eyes large and bright watched the audience, the theater's decorations, and anything else but the goings-on at the stage.

In his never-ending quest for the perfect honey tree, the Rabbit King of the Moon encountered one after another series of perils. By ducking into a thorny patch, he eluded the Goshawk. By skipping across a bridge of turtles' backs, he eluded the Panther. By tricking it into swallowing a rock, he eluded the Grass Snake.

After each elaborate chase and acrobatic victory, the stage cleared of all but one performer. The wooden platform rotated on a turntable, cranked by a mill's gears mechanism underneath, turning the partitions of painted scenery. Mirrors focused candlelight on the actor in the gray wool suit. Rabbit skipped and danced his traditional steps with admirable vigor. His flopping long ears swayed to and fro while he sang his familiar song:

La-la-la, you can't catch me.
I'm too clever for you all, you see.
I'll run you in circles and hop swift away!
I'll take your honey, tra-la, tra-lay!

When the Cave Lion threatened the Rabbit King, the little Lady Tiressa got down from the cushions. She was neither afraid nor delighted. She lay on the floor beneath the sofa's frame and played with a beaded silk ball.

The Rabbit King slipped through a hole too small for the Cave Lion to follow. The actor in a lion's costume thrust his face through a hole in a board and pretended to be stuck. He did his best to roar, though with a human voice it came out as more of a shout. "I'll get you, Rabbit! I'll eat you someday!"

Once more, the Rabbit King danced his little dance and sang his little song. "La-la-la, you can't catch me!" The audience howled jeering at the Cave Lion being dragged off-stage by black-garbed assistants. Children in the front rows leaped and danced around their nursemaids in imitation of the Rabbit. They sang along in a piping chorus, "I'll run you in circles, and hop swift away! I'll take your honey, tra-la, tra-lay!"

Glëa reached down to tap the little girl's back. "Get up and watch. The best part's coming."

She merely twiddled her dainty shoes and kept playing at his feet with her beaded ball.

An actor stomped onto the stage dressed as Hunter in a cape of forest brown. He carried a longbow, a knife, and a fishing net. The whole audience roared with contempt. Some children screamed and ducked into their nursemaids' skirts. The fellow did not wear a mask, as the other performers did, but altered his natural visage with a sneering scowl.

Ho-ho-ho, I'll catch him yet,
for I am more clever by far, I'll bet.
I'll run him in circles,
and drag him down.
I'll have rabbit for supper, yo-ho, hey-ho.

Glëa leaned over his knees. Moving was not an easy feat against the bulky layers of ermine-trimmed and satin-lined brocade robes. "Tiressa, get up here."

"My name is Lilac!" peeped the girl's voice muffled under the sofa's frame.

The king wondered, again, if he were making a mistake with his decision to go forward with the promise of marriage. Even if it was in name only, for the good of the state and the unity of the country, she could not even conduct herself properly at a public function. This milk-toothed child was no Queen of Xol and would not be for at least a decade.

"I shall ask you one last time—"

Alyss swooped in with billowing veils and skirts. Wooden bangles clattered at her wrists. She coaxed the little girl out from under the sofa and took her by both hands. "Your Majesty, with your leave, shall I escort the lady to her bed chamber?"

"Please do." Glëa returned upright. A couple of squires swooped in to adjust his wardrobe. They hurriedly tugged straight his brocade pleats and re-arranged the lay of his knee-length trailing sleeves. One apologized as he dared to touch the king's long fronds of black hair.

"Once you've delivered her to the nursemaid, go to my bed chamber and wait for me."

"At your command, Your Majesty." Alyss used gentle smiles to coax her out. "Come now, we are going to see your *anma*. You like your *anma*, don't you?"

The hunter on stage prowled slowly to the left and right. The Rabbit King nimbly skipped behind the fake wooden scenery and potted trees. The audience hooted with delight and pointed, yelling to the hunter, "There he is! There he is! You missed him!"

Hunter fitted an arrow to his bow but, at the risk of injuring his fellow performers, did not fully draw the string. He danced awkwardly in circles, yelling out, "Where is he? Where is he?"

A woman entered the opera box behind the king. Dressed in a trailing gown of sage and silver, she carried herself with the slow stately grace of a lady of her rank,. A crocheted snood contained most of her unruly gray curls. For a moment, Glëa did not recognize her, having rarely seen General Browden in such feminine attire. Tonight, she did not even carry her ancestral sword.

"That child has no patience, Jiveine. We staged this whole thing for her."

"She's been up since dawn without a nap. I'm surprised she made it this long without a tantrum."

The matriarch of the House of Browden settled onto the sofa cushion at his side. Squires fussed with the speed of sparrows pecking at her skirts to arrange the long trail of her gown alongside his royal cloak. The king and the lady sat very still in displaying the stately grace of idols on an altar shelf. All the tension that had disrupted the opera box, with the little girl fussing and fidgeting, now blew away in a single serene breath.

General Browden abruptly bellowed at Hunter on stage, "Look behind you, you poxed clod-pate!"

Hunter spun in circles. "Where? Where?"

It was merely the reflection of the stage lamps, but a timeless, ageless gleam brightened the older lady's eyes. The king smiled at her, sharing in this moment her joy of life. It seemed only yesterday that she herself was a young maiden blushing to curtsey before him when he was merely a prince. How quickly the maiden had turned into the crone, and yet, her eyes had not aged a day.

"Oh, Jiveine, why do you bother shouting at the fellow? You know he'll never catch that Rabbit."

Chapter 43.

The great Old One soared up to the golden cavern's vaulted ceiling. Groaning in frustration, his growls reverberated around the octagonal-shaped chamber. He used both paws and jagged three-toed feet to scratch at the intersection of white marble ribs. Talons clinked tapping against the arches.

Ravel thought, *Even in his madness and despair, he is remembering what he once was. He fell from the crystal city in the clouds! His mind is older, thoughtful, and mature. He was not freshly hatched when he fell to the earth. He remembers his life up there. He wants to return to the sky!* Oily tears of sympathy leaked from her eyes.

"He needs to go outside," she said drowsily. "He's been confined for so long."

The Old One rotated in mid-air for his belly to face the floor. His crusty brow ridge twisted in an expression of nearly-human surprise. He snarled as if noticing the youths' presence for the first time. He exhaled a growl that, despite the stiff jaws and misshapen tongue, carried the undertones of a word, "Mine. Mine. Mine."

Xidron's hand trembled as he kept holding up the skeleton hand talisman. "It speaks?"

"If it speaks," Candor said. "It can understand commands."

The Old One snarled a roar. His grating voice drummed around the metallic walls, rang hard and banged inside Ravel's ears. The sound aroused a thrill in her more stirring than the marching drums of a battlefield, more vivid than the grunts of a galloping war horse. The talons that burned against her own chest yearned to be reunited with those gnarled paws and long hooked claws.

Candor raised his hands in a commanding gesture. "Come do my bidding, Beast! I have summoned you from the deep. Serve as my instrument of vengeance."

The Old One swooped down from the high ceiling. He descended so quickly that his wings fluttered like silk flags. Then he abruptly stopped just short of crashing into the floor.

Redson and Stander scuttled backwards. Prosper held the bucket of water as a shield in front of himself.

He floated in upright position where Ravel prostrated herself on her knees. He loomed over her with the canopy of his wings spread wide. Claws were well within reach of her, yet he did not seize her. His serpentine neck arched down. His snout tilted to align his eyes with hers. The great beast looked at her intensely for the first time. Soul's light shined through irises as glass lantern bulbs infused with gold dust. Eyes gleamed with madness and brilliance, with insanity and intelligence, a thoughtfulness that had abandoned rational thought in countless millennia gone past.

"Mine, mine, mine," the great beast growled.

"Yes, yes, oh yes," she rasped hoarsely in return. Ravel arched her back to display the black spikes pulsing at her breastbone. *Come, come, come to me,* she spoke in her thoughts. Her voice rattled from the depths of her throat. The harder she forced air out of her lungs, the less she sounded like a woman. The tempo of her breathing rose and fell in rhythm with the Old One's snorts. Her arms shuddered in the hungering need to make a connection. She reached upward to beckon the grand, terrible beast floating overhead.

Prosper raised the water bucket as if it were a grenade with a burning fuse. "Unhand my betrothed, you monster!"

Xidron said, "She is enthralled. Her will is no longer her own. By commanding the great beast, we will command her too."

Candor laughed through his grin. "The lady has tamed the beast. Pross', we are witnessing the makings of a new legend."

The brilliance of his eyes seeped deeper into hers. The Old One's topaz eyes gleamed with the light of a brass gong ringing at sunset. The golden hue chimed a soundless sound, a wordless word, a voiceless voice. The Old One breathed into her face the stink of rusty inhuman blood and stale sulfur. He growled again the sound of gold.

"We are One," the beast croaked.

"We are One," she whispered and continued the chant in her mind. *We are One. We are One.*

"Come with me, Beast," Candor said to the hovering fanged snout. "Follow me to exact retribution and vengeance upon the oppressors. A new clean world shall emerge from the ashes."

Ravel laid her hand against the Old One's crusty cheek. Her fingertips had turned gray to complement his charcoal hide. "Come with us."

Through a haze of peridot glow, she looked up at the face of a sculptor's drunken nightmare. She saw his desire as clearly as sunrise. Desire for what? Surely not a physical union with her; it would be like mating a bull to a butterfly. The talons stuck in her chest tapped an insistent pulse. A high-pitched tone scratched inside her ears. The Old One's desire sounded like a human word, *him... him... him...*

"Yes," she whispered. An image formed in her mind of a human man with blue eyes and black hair. "Let's go find Lil' Hatchling."

From deep in the hole where the Old One had just emerged came the scratching of more leathery wings. More inhuman voices croaked, "Meat... meat... meat." Black talons clattered on the stone as they ascended.

"Look, there's more than just him," Prosper cried. "I see *more*!"

Xidron backed away. "My sources told me the crud-coats are keeping four monsters to practice fighting. Just four. Don't panic, there's just four."

Paws with black talons reached up from the rim of the floor's iris hatchway. Dozens of arms snagged and tangled with each other. Horns poked up from the center but were pressed down by the horde of snarling jaws fighting to get through the narrow hole.

"More than four," Redson cried out.

"A lot more!" Stander shrieked.

Prosper hurled the contents of his bucket. The water did not splash very far. Most of it soaked in his own breeches and boots.

Candor insisted, "Don't panic. I command them. We are wielding the hand of the First King. We have nothing to fear."

The Old One reached out to the tuning fork in Candor's hand. Talons like cooking tongs clamped onto the silver prongs. The youth tried to hold his grip on the tool but was not strong enough. A firm tug of the wrist was all it took to yank it away.

"Why aren't you obeying me?" Candor gasped as he staggered backwards. "The nomads say you're just animals."

Topaz eyes with vertical slit irises flared brightly with indignation. His crocodilian snout curled up in a sneer to expose his long fangs. "Obey... no... man."

Ravel smiled broadly with adoration of the grand, eternal creature. The Old One's talons pulsing in her chest warmed her blood. A peaceful serenity coursed through her core unlike anything she had ever known. She felt as if she had downed an entire keg of brandy wine. Fear and anxiety drained away.

Xidron cried, "Our talismans have no control."

Redson and Stander bolted away. Their boots slapped on stone pattering into the tunnels.

Prosper tugged Candor's sleeve. "Let's run. Run!"

The youths scuffled into a tangle of legs. Candor's last words were, "Forgive me, sister," before he took off running after his friends.

Ravel watched them from the corner of her eye. The youths fled down a different tunnel than the one they had come. She exhaled relief; for the first time in her life, she did not care about where her brother was going.

Dozens of snarling jaws and salivating fangs crawled out of the hole. All the other Surleista had blackened scaly hides that absorbed color and light. Deformed by ancient fires even before they hatched from their charred eggshells, they had never known beauty, or light, or color, or song. They had dwelled for all their immortal miserable lives in darkness and insatiable craving.

The others logjammed behind the Old One and snarled their impatience to feed. Surleista crawled past the Old One and filled the golden cavern. They licked at where the youths had been standing and howled craving more. Some stood upright on their hind legs. They were taller than most men but might be taller still if their backs were not hunched at the shoulders under the burden of horn-sized spikes. Their leathery wings flared out like silk capes in a strong wind.

Ravel stood among them unafraid. Scaly elbows and barbed tails brushed against her and accidentally scratched her flesh. Her blackish-purple blood oozed over her jaundiced skin, but she did not mind. Her stomach gurgled as theirs did. Her jaw flexed open-and-shut in the same way. She growled in chorus with the beasts. *Meat. Meat. Meat.* Hunger was unbearable.

"Hungry," the Old One snarled in golden tones.

"So am I." Ravel laid her hand against the beast's crusty cheek. "I can show you the way."

The Old One reached out his claws to her. Ravel grasped one digit of his four-fingered paw. As solid as the hilt of a sword, it gave her a rush of confidence and strength to hold onto him.

Ravel's memories rose to her mind in a murky, dreamlike haze. She recalled the layout of the castle above and replayed the images of where she had prowled before.

Blinking slowly to the pulse rhythm of the Old One's chanting tone, Ravel's dream shifted into images that she had never seen. She imagined herself with inhuman paws. Scaly knuckles ended in raptor talons. Her face protruded as a reptilian snout.

She dreamed of an island surrounded by a screaming ocean. Nothing but angry waters in every direction, extending to the flat horizon on all sides.

She dreamed of crawling into a cave and finding a hole in the floor that plunged deeper. Distant cries of kindred beasts—*my children*—in agony, echoed up from the hole.

She dreamed of breaking rocks with her talons. Her fingers shattered but the bones quickly healed. She plunged into the hole and crawled, and crawled, and crawled. Tunnels branched off in many offshoot directions, in a complex unmapped web of marbled passageways that predated the sea. Only the pained cries of her kindred served as a beacon. *Hurt me! Hurt me! Why?*

"Him," the Old One growled.

Ravel nodded that she understood but words did not come to her mouth. She recalled what someone had told her about the training ground on the island in the bay. Such a place of unrelenting torture and brutality had been created under the orders of Glëa po'Lon. Cold-hearted soldiers in black uniforms hacked, chopped, and stabbed at the Surleista on a daily routine. So, the limbs grew back but the creatures still felt the pain. They felt the pain every time.

He came to save the children, she thought. *I stand now with a righteous hero.*

Chapter 44.

She rode standing like a child on the Old One's foot. Her cheek leaned against his scaly abdomen. The talons embedded in her chest—*his* claws—matched the spikes that fanned over his torso like the plumage of a bird. Even standing fully upright, her head only reached the Old One's armpit. He hooked his arm around her and shielded her under the awning of his left wing.

The Old One guided the snarling swarm along the passageway. They glided back to the route she had come, easily floating on velum wings that needed no air to lift them. The tunnel's stone colors reflected oily rainbow colors off the beast's black horns.

Dimly, she recalled the lady prophet's warning that it would all begin in the opera house. Ravel envisioned the theater building with its red shingled roof and its position at the northwestern curve of the inner wall. Her memories spoke to the Old One of discovering the performers lurking beneath the stage to grind Surleista bones into an intoxicating poultice.

The Old One snorted. He turned away from the passageway that led to the royal tomb's subterranean vault. He did not follow the fading scent of panic-sweat and living meat on the run.

Instead, he veered to the left and glided into a tunnel made of purple jade. Luminescence shimmered on his black scaly hide. *Beautiful, beautiful,* Ravel thought as she clung one-handed to the spikes of the Old One's shoulders.

Simpering and hissing in long-frustrated hunger, the horde of snarling jaws flowed along the passageway behind the Old One's barbed tail. They followed but could not open their wings; too many bodies packed into a small space hindered their progress. Black talons scratched against the un-scratchable walls of the marble tube. Nostrils flared in seeking the odors of living meat.

Instrumental music, distorted as if underwater, echoed through the passageway ahead. Ravel held onto the scaly hide. Dimly a memory resurfaced of being a small child carried in her father's arms, of being utterly helpless yet feeling secure in the comfort of his strength. She drooped her eyelids in the serenity of coming home.

Glowing stone colors changed hue from lavender to maple-leaf green. At a point where the passageway veered left at a sharp angle, the Old One stopped. Ravel craned her neck and raised her chin. She looked up through the gap of his leathery wings. She shared his frustration. Although the jade ceiling was as thin as window glass, it was unbreakable. Unpassable. Trapped.

Open the door that was long ago sealed, the ageless, sexless voice hummed in her thoughts. At the same time, the beast's scaly throat gargled, "Open... Open..."

The Old One lifted the tuning fork that he still held clamped in his paw. He tapped the prongs against his own shoulder spikes. Ravel saw the silver tones ripple through his ethereal aura. Shimmering harmonics poured like a waterfall over his reptilian hide. They spoke in a language of song; she remembered from someone once reciting a legend.

"Yes, yes, open it." Ravel's oily tongue licked her dry lips.

The Old One reached upwards and pressed the base of the tuning fork's stem against the jade ceiling.

Glossy stone segmented itself into the blades of a fan that spiraled away from the iris center. It swung open to withdraw and disappeared into the full width of the rim. Looking up, now, the only barrier remaining was a wooden floor. Through the planks, Ravel smelled the living meat, the prey, the livestock in a pen. Amidst the animal odors was a singular flowery scent.

Well done, child. You found him for me. He is here.

Ravel smiled with pride at having performed good service for her commander. She inhaled and savored that moment, like leaning forward in the saddle and spurring her cavalry horse into the charge, into the battle, to fight for victory. All her life was destined to arrive at this moment.

The Old One launched straight up from beneath the theater's foundation. His horned head, like a ramrod, burst through the wooden floorboards. His wings like a cloak protected Ravel from the crumbling chunks of basement floor and wooden stairs. By the force of his own rage, he pushed up through the crawl space underneath the stage.

The wooden apparatus beneath the stage shattered. Timbers broke. Boards splintered and sprayed sawdust. None of it slowed him down. Cracked and jagged planks flared to either side like a splintered drawbridge. His wings smashed the partitions of stage backdrops painted in a forest scenery. The actor playing Rabbit King of the Moon fell to one side and tripped over his own floppy feet. The actor playing Hunter rolled the other way.

The Old One's wings snapped open in venous banners to either side, but it did not need wings to fly. The crocodilian body hovered upright as a bit of lily weed would float in pond water. Legs dangled half-bent. Arms at ease, paws flexed to click its talons. Barbed tail lingered in mid-stroke. Serpentine neck, topped by a horned skull and jagged snout, undulated with boneless ease. The Old One's scaly arms spread wide in triumphant glee. Wickedness, hate, vengeance, and rage were embodied in a crusty hide of slate scales. Topaz eyes cocked left and right, surveying the buffet of living prey, as if undecided who to attack first.

Ravel perched on his feet and clung to his side. She gazed over the array of human faces and viewed them as peculiar animals. Tantalizing odors of meat and fear overwhelmed her senses. Gritting her teeth, she craved the taste. Just one, she thought. *Just a little one. Just one bite should be all right.*

Women screamed and hugged their children. Dainty lords crouched and hugged their wives. Servants tugged at their masters' sleeves and urged them to get on their feet. Others scrambled for the rear of the auditorium. Lord Rubëa turned his back on his wife and children. He pushed his mother and scrambled to the exit. "We're dead, we're all dead!" His chant penetrated the wailing of ladies and groaning of lords. Other ladies fell over their trailing gowns and knocked into him. Some gentlemen climbed over them and dove for the curtains.

King Glëa po'Lon gripped the balcony's railing. "You! You can't be here! How did you get here?"

Ravel gazed at the solitary man seated in the balcony. He was the only person in the room that she did not crave to eat. A shimmering ethereal glow was like a mist around his silhouette.

"Hello there, Lil' Hatchling," she said, but no one could hear above the chaos of screaming voices.

Lady Browden pulled him away by the hand. "Damnit, Glëa, you must run to safety!"

The crone dragged him half-stumbling backwards on his royal robes. She ducked with him through a curtained doorway at the rear of the opera box. In a blink, they both dipped out of view.

The actor playing Hunter fired off his stage prop arrow. That wooden shaft pierced the Old One's gut but had no more effect than sticking a clove into a tree trunk.

"You need flaming arrows, you idiot!" Colonel Viktor vaulted over the seated nobles in his way. In two hops, he jumped onto the stage. He picked up a glass bulb lantern containing a wax candle, its tiny flame on the verge of flickering out. With his other hand, he grabbed a bush-knife from the Hunter's costume belt. Shoving the actor out of the way, the captain stood his ground.

Ravel gazed down into the man's ice-blue eyes. Vague memories of having met him before, and the snippets of old conversations, washed out of her mind. Licking her lips, she tasted the savory odor of fear on his skin.

"You betrayed us, Rebel," Viktor said to her, seething. "Do you even have a brother or was that a ruse to get inside the walls?"

Oily saliva slowly dribbled down her chin. Ravel squinted and strained to recall human words. More and more, her humanity faded. Only the hunger remained.

Guards in uniform hopped over the nobles who were scrambling off their floor cushions. People in sumptuous finery flowed away in two different directions but guards pressed forward. They called out, "We've got this handled. It's just one beast. Move in an orderly manner to the exits. Don't panic."

Guards separated into two groups on either side of the orchestra pit. Pole-arms and spears aimed their points upward. In following Viktor's example, they picked up glass bulb stage lights.

"I can rope him, sir," called out a lieutenant who was gathering up an armload of ropes from the stage curtains.

Viktor checked over his shoulder for how many noble civilians remained. Too slowly, in all their bulky finery, they logjammed at the rear door. "Do it, Sorrix! Climb up that ladder to the catwalk and drop the loop from above. We'll distract the beast."

The Old One's voice was singing in her mind. *Come, my children. Come to the feast.*

Shrieks whistled in the pit below the stage. Not the launch of fiery payload from catapults, or the fifes of enemy cavalry. No, those animal voices were unlike any seashore bird, scavenging jackal, or renegade crocodile. Ravel smiled in joyous expectation of starving children coming to the supper table.

"Sir, it's not just one!" cried the lieutenant who ascended the stage ladder.

Wings burst up out of the stage floor. More boards shattered. Black wings unfurled like charred flags at midnight. So many, so many overshadowed and filled the space above the stage with snarling jaws, clicking claws, and wagging barbed tails.

"Hold the line! Hold the line!" General Vilbyss bellowed, standing his ground as the other nobles and their wives scrambled for the back door. The reinvigorated old man stank of sulfuric sweat. He drew his ceremonial sword with its gilded hand guard and a yellow tassel dangling. He held aloft the engraved blade at the ready. "They must not leave this theater! They cannot get loose from here!"

Colonel Viktor struck at the swarm with his large knife. He lobbed off gnarled paws, slashed misshapen calves, and tore open the corrugated scales of spiny abdomens. The winged beasts roared and shrieked as their bluish-gray ichor splattered their attacker. Yet they kept surging up out of the floor. A dozen, then a dozen more launched upwards with ravenous fangs snapping.

More noblemen officers hopped onto the stage and grabbed whatever props they could find: curtain ropes and sandbags and poles supporting plywood backgrounds. Some had their dress uniform sabers and drew those decorative weapons with gaudy tassels. They made windmills of their blades and chopped whatever grisly appendage showed through. Yet the beasts kept coming. The lancers' boots slipped and skidded in the slimy puddles on the hardwood boards. They held their ground even as the Surleista kept bubbling up out of the floor.

Ravel's eyes widened to take in the scene of carnage. The movements of soldiers and the winged beasts their foes whirled too quickly to follow all at once. Lancers chopped off paws, and new paws grew back before their eyes. Slash wounds sealed themselves. Severed tails sprouted anew from the stumps. Nothing the soldiers did with blades or poles made any impact on the monstrous limbs. In a drunken delirium, hanging on the Old One's arm, she viewed the chaotic scene beneath her dangling bare feet.

Colonel Viktor pressed in close to the corrugated abdomen of one Surleista. He slashed open a gap and shoved the candlestick inside the wound. The beast convulsed and spasmed. Its wings snapped starkly to the rear. Its hunched back arched impossibly sideways. Bluish ichor bubbled out of the seams of its scaly hide. Then it burst apart in a flash of sparkles and cinders.

No, no, no, my child. The Old One roared its outrage at the Surleista's demise. He swooped down himself and tossed off Ravel to free his paws.

She landed on her back, flat on the stage. Wind knocked out of her. The back of her head bruised on the boards.

The Old One clamped his reptilian snout onto Colonel Viktor's head. In one smooth motion, he arched its serpentine neck. Like a farmer plucking an apple, he snapped the captain's head clean off. The Old One raised its snout upright and gulped the skull whole. Viktor's headless body fell. Kegs of blood poured from the neck's stump.

Colonel Maetha screamed murderous rage. She wielded a shepherd's crook prop and speared the point into the Old One's scaly thigh. The great beast smacked her backhanded and sent Maetha backwards tumbling off the stage.

Snarling jaws swooped into the orchestra pit. They chewed through the horns and flutes to get at the people who had held them. Talons of paws and feet tore into the musicians who tried to use their instruments as shields. Crow-like voices screeched in ecstasy, "Meat! Meat! Meat!"

Governor Fordon only had time to raise a rack of music notation. Papers fluttered off. Monstrous paws yanked it from his grasp. Several of them dog-piled on top and gnawed into him before he had time to scream.

More and more beasts surged inside from the jagged hole in the middle of the stage. Fifty, sixty, or more Surleista filled the cavernous auditorium. Scratchers glided in orbit around the iron ring chandelier. Their leathery wings beat the air and snuffed out the candles, plunging the theater into darkness. Yet Ravel could still see every detail clearly; nothing was ever dark in her eyes.

Winged beasts seethed and churned on the theater's floor. Whoever had not fled by now, nobles and servants alike became fodder for their fangs. Ravel inhaled the aroma of blood wafting up from the auditorium's floor. She reeled with the rush of delight. It was the thrill of sitting down to a holiday table heaped with a succulent rack of lamb, braised pork loin roast, and lightly grilled veal rib-eye steak. *They're here. They're inside. They're feasting after so long without meat... meat... meat.*

"More... outside..." Ravel struggled to share what she wished to say. Words felt peculiar in her mouth. Her tongue flexed in awkward contortions to speak.

The Old One's voice sang in her mind. The singing reverberated to the lofty wooden rafters. *Come, my children. Come. Fly. Be free to feast.*

He launched away and soared straight up to the rafters. He vaulted like a catapult's payload and shattered the ceiling beams of the theater. Roof shingles sprayed outwards.

Amid the crumbling debris of the roof, the tuning fork dropped away from the Old One's paw. Silver prongs fell with a thud and a muted chime to the stage's boards. Ravel saw it fall and made no effort to pick it up. *We don't need it anymore. We are free.*

From where she lay on the stage, flat on her back, Ravel smiled upwards at the dark starry sky beyond the jagged hole in the roof. The great beast soared high to eclipse the moon. She felt an overwhelming urge to join him in the sky. If only she had wings too. The talons at her chest throbbed more eagerly; it was painful to be so far apart.

A ladder in the stage's wings offered a way to ascend to the curtain rods, the catwalks, and the rafters of what remained of the roof. Ravel turned away from the swarm of black wings swarming over the auditorium. Screams and growls muted in the gong of her own heartbeat ringing inside her ears. Only the pulsing beat of the talons mattered; only the echo of the Old One's voice drumming in her chest mattered. *We are One. We are One.*

Chapter 45.

The king and Lady Browden dashed outside a back door of the theater's upper level. They emerged on an open-air balcony made of creaky boards with a rickety railing. No guards were on duty; only servants ever came this way to carry delicacies to nobility reclining in the mezzanine seats. The clear dark sky showed no hint of autumn rain. His gut hardened in dread knowing that only water spirits could slow the scratcher's siege.

His mind reeled. *He can't be here. He can't be here. How did Old Scratcher escape the black island and cross the sea to arrive here?*

Glëa caught the railing. "How did it get here?"

"Let's get you to safety." Lady Browden descended first. A narrow stairway of open wooden slats connected the upper floor to the ground.

A young squire and a maid servant followed. The two held the king's trailing sleeves and robes as best they could manage. He felt his way down the stairs without being able to see his feet.

"Careful, watch your step." Lady Browden landed on the grassy soil and turned to offer him a hand.

Glëa brushed her hand aside. He launched into a half-jogging stride and dragged along the bulky cocoon of luxurious garments. The pair of servants hurried to follow. The wake of his fleece-lined velvet cape swept dry leaves over the trampled grass and straggly weeds.

The traveling actors' troupe had set up camp behind the theater. Members of the supporting crew reclined around a campfire. Some of them slurped honey-scented liquor from ceramic kegs. A few others smoked fragrant dry weeds in long-handled pipes.

At the king's emergence, several of the actors' crew sprang to their feet. "Your Majesty? Is something amiss?"

Lady Browden acting as his bodyguard pushed through the group. "Make way! Make way!"

Glëa plunged into the cluster of waxed burlap tents and canopies that draped off the frames of cargo wagons. He ducked through the partitions of hanging tarps.

The stage crew gawked at him with open-mouthed, bewildered expressions. Some of them blurted questions, talking over each other in overlapping voices. "Is there a fire? Has the show stopped? Do I hear people screaming?"

"A monster got loose in the theater," said the servant girl trotting behind the king's cloak. "Run, you fools. Run for your lives!"

They did not respond right away. They puffed their pipes, held their cups, and looked confusedly at each other. "A monster? What sort of monster?"

Glëa's layers of wardrobe weighed him down. His legs kicked hard against the weight of the fabric. His delicate heeled shoes gave him little traction in the gravel. He wished for his horse, but the royal stables were on the opposite side of the bailey yard. He could not risk sprinting into the open; he had to reach the safety of the stone wall.

Lady Browden cupped her hands around her mouth. She shouted upwards to the height of the crenellated wall, it seemed to the sky itself. "Raise the alarm! A Surlie got inside the theater! Repeat, a wild scratcher is on the loose!"

One soldier struck a brass gong hanging on a square frame. Glëa winced at the discordant notes jangling in his head. Bells blurred his vision into silvery sparkles. *Hold strong*, he scolded the ethereal being lodged deep within himself. He fought the rushing wave of vertigo and stumbled over the trailing layers of his wardrobe.

Lady Browden caught hold of his sleeve near the elbow and held him up. "Don't be afraid. I'm here."

"I'm not afraid," the king growled through clenched teeth. "I'm furious. How is this happening? That one cannot be here."

"The rebel woman smuggled it inside," she said. "This must have been her evil plan all along. It was a mistake to trust her."

As he kept running, Glëa shook his head. *You don't understand*, he wished to say but there was no time to explain. The wizened old creature was not at all one of those kept in the training ground on Seagull's Rock; it was not bagged in the Outerlands and hauled across the kingdom in a crate; it had come—impossibly—from the uncharted island in the Deep Sea where he had been shipwrecked.

The servant girl's hands urged him sideways towards the nearest fortified door. Bricks spanned between two of many towers that encircled the inner bailey. Meant to repel human armies on foot, not monsters on the wing, the walls offered few avenues to ascend.

"A Surlie got inside the theater," Lady Browden bellowed. "Call a squad to storm the building. Now, now, now!"

"Where? Where?" The sentinels called out to each other. "I don't see them!"

Glëa staggered to resist the vertigo that reverberated in his skull. An old voice, the voice of the deep dark places of the earth, sang a chime that only he could hear. *Come, my children. Come to the feast.*

"No, no," he groaned in response to Old Scratcher's voice singing in his mind. He knew that voice as intimately as he knew his own voice echoing inside his skull. That voice had terrorized him for more than forty years of being marooned on an island. That voice had laughed in delight as its minions devoured his shipwrecked crew. Glëa's throbbing head sagged forward into his fur-trimmed collar.

Lady Browden pulled him along the wall's base. With the two servants' helping hands, they stumbled over hedges of rhododendron, rosemary, jasmine, and holly. His heeled shoes fell off, but he kept running. Weeds tore the soles of his stockings.

"Just a little farther," she said to urge him onward. "We'll keep you safe until that beast is dealt with…"

Screaming people poured out of the theater's front door. They spread out running in a stampede across the open bailey yard. Nobles and servants ran side by side. Babes howled in their mothers' arms. The gowns of Tea Mistresses sagged falling off behind their powdered shoulders.

Lady Browden looked back at the theater building from a three-quarters side angle view. Its lanterns hanging from the eaves gave off an eerie red glow on the backs of the panicked fleeing crowd. "What's gone awry? The theater was half packed with trained officers, off duty though they may be. Surely one scratcher is no match for our kingdom's finest."

Come, my children. Come forth and be free. Come forth and feed. The ancient voice sang in a discordant tone contrasting with the incessant rhythmic clanging of brass gongs.

"It's not just one, Jiveine. He's calling more to arise from the depths of the abyss. It's going to be a swarm."

"No, you're letting your fears get the best of you," she said. "Calm yourself. We're almost there."

The king reached the threshold of the oak door. He strained against his bulky clothing to view the theater. Night breezes blew a swath of his long hair across his face, blocking his view. But he did not need his human eyes to see. His mind could hear them. His skin could smell them. *They're coming. Every one of the creatures who infested the rocky island have found their way here.*

The roof of the Opera House shattered and sprayed scraps of timber in all directions. Shrieks like hoarse owls scratched the drifts of moonlit fog. Inhuman howls erupted from the roof's cracked trusses. Wings like flurries of charcoal snowflakes poured upwards into the open air. Dark velum wings swirled into a moving canopy that covered the night sky.

"All hands, all hands!" the lieutenant screamed. "Wings on the loose!"

The chant was picked up by the next, and the next black-coat soldier on the walls. "All hands to the battlements! All hands, roll out."

Braziers flared up. Plumes of flames burst to life on each of the watchtowers and gatehouse turrets. Brass gongs echoed ringing into the darkness. Mallets pounded the shield-sized discs in a relentless, steady rhythm. Gongs chimed in chorus all around the rim of the inner wall.

The king followed Lady Browden into the tower's oak door. He pumped his legs to ascend the spiral staircase. At the top, he stepped on the hem of his long trailing cape. He halted to catch his balance. Lady Browden reached back for his hand, but the cape and his bulky sleeves covered his fists. At the same time, the servant below pressed her hands to his backside. "Pardon me, Your Majesty."

They reached the chamber at the top. Sheltered from the open sky, the king stood trapped in a circular box with a wooden cone roof. Archers' slit windows were barely the width of a man's arm. Two solid oak doors offered passage to either direction of the ramparts.

"You're safe here." Lady Browden took a defensive stance in front of him.

"Help me get out of these damned clothes, Jiveine. I can't move!" His thick layered sleeves would not allow his arms to fold. He could not reach his own shoulder.

"Hold still. Let me do it."

Lady Browden pinched off the innumerable tie strings, frog-and-loop buttons, and gilded brooch clamps. The servant lad helped to peel the layers away. The king flexed his shoulders to shrug off the ermine-lined wool cape, the brocade calf-length outer robe, and the satin-lined velvet tunic with gold thread embroidery around the collar. He opened the wraparound skirt's tie strings and dropped the pleated panels. Lady Browden yanked at the waist sash's rear lacings that crossed through a dozen gold-plated brass grommets at his back. Once free of that stiff twill sash, he kicked down the black velvet breeches with seed pearls dotting the side seams.

Glëa stood tall, comfortable in only silk hose and a gauze shirt. Now, he could move as needed. The maiden dragged the garments to the side; she piled the heap of velvets and brocade onto a cluster of barrels.

"We won't be safe here for long," the king said. "We must be ready to run."

Lady Browden looked outside through the arrow slit. Archers at the outer walls launched flaming arrows from crossbows. Bright sparkling wads of trailing fire hit their targets. A few Surleista squealed and burst into a fiery mess from the inside out. Archers worked in formation like a well-rehearsed dance. Half of them launched their bolts as the others bent over to reload, maintaining a steady rain of fiery hailstones.

Yet more of the Surleista evaded the projectiles. They managed to swoop into the bailey yard. Wings and claws pounced upon scattered groups of people fleeing across the open ground.

"I don't understand." Lady Browden panted wide-eyed watching the carnage unfold below. "Infiltrators could not have smuggled these many wild beasts inside."

Glëa succumbed to the thoughts of the second being trapped within his skin. Memories of crystalline towers and arched gemstone bridges played through his mind. Shared knowledge played in his thoughts like a song.

On the threads of the harmonics, his other self knew what his human self could not. Passageways spread endlessly looping and reconnecting without end. The crust of land that humans knew was just a veneer over a much older matrix. Avenues of jeweled stone intertwined beneath their feet. Long-forgotten, glorious highways connected the deserts of the Outerlands to the Deep Sea and to explored lands beyond the curve of the world.

"They're coming up from below the basement," said the king. "Which means they've found the legendary tunnels of the lost cities of the burned gods."

"Those are just old fables, aren't they?" asked Lady Browden.

"No, they're not."

Glëa took a breath as the full magnitude and purity of the insurgents' ruthless plan unfolded before his thoughts. He imagined Ravel's brother in a delirium fever of careless vengeance probing the secrets of ancient legends. The former rebel had confessed that he was a scholarly youth who collected old documents and architectural schematics.

He continued, "The foolish boy may have discovered heretical scrolls or looted the tomb of King Davarche the First for talismans rumored to be buried there. Somehow, he's found a way to open primordial tunnels beneath the earth and release nightmarish creatures upon the mortal world. Do you understand what I'm saying, Jiveine? The scratchers can't fly over the moat's water..."

"...but they can crawl under it."

His dry throat flexed as he tried to swallow. "They've crawled a very, very long way. They are all very hungry."

"Oh, damnation's fire," Lady Browden swore.

Captain Édel entered the chamber from the north-facing oak door. He still wore civilian finery from the day's festivities. Blood spattered his blond hair, but he did not appear wounded.

"Your Majesty, are you safe?" Captain Édel asked.

"For now."

Lady Browden demanded, "Report, Captain."

"We've evacuated and secured the Opera House at ground level. Governor Fordon is lost. Colonel Viktor is lost. Many others of the noble families... We don't have an accurate body count yet. However, General

Vilbyss is alive and holding the line. He set up a command post in the theater's lobby. The injured are being carried to safety but it's going slowly."

While she listened to the captain's report, Lady Browden selected one of the many lacing strings from the king's pile of garments. She looped it around her shoulders to tie back the knee-length trailing sleeves of her own velvet gown.

The captain continued, "We've emptied the barracks. We're rolling out and mobilizing every boot. Archers and spearmen are taking positions on the walls. We're hauling out crates of fire arrows, grenades, and tar-bombs from the armory. Right now, the scratchers are concentrated over the stables and the livestock pens. I figure it's a matter of a little time before they turn to, uh, smaller prey."

Lady Browden ordered, "Destroy the cisterns. Break open every rain barrel. Draw water up from every well. Flood the bailey. Use the cover of mud to evacuate civilians to the city. Hold the line at the ramparts and create a kill zone."

Captain Édel slowly backed to the door while speaking his thoughts aloud. "Colonel Maetha already sent runners to the Keep telling the people to shelter in place."

The king said, "No, no, no. No one is safe inside the towers. Listen! If even one scratcher gets inside a door, they'll be like mice in a cage. Evacuate the Keep, immediately."

"How, sir? The secret passages were all sealed years ago during the restora—"

Glëa raised his hand to signal silence. "One more escape route lies concealed in the Main Hall of the White Tower. The wood paneling behind the throne's dais can be unlocked and moved aside. Its key is to twist the nose ring on the golden bull's head. That tunnel leads to the caverns below the lighthouse."

Captain Édel bowed quickly. "May the blessings of your ancestors be upon Your Majesty."

Lady Browden shoved the captain's shoulder. "Blessings aren't going to fight those beasts. Go, now! Evacuate the castle, by the gatehouses, by the secret passageway, by any means you can."

The king swayed on his feet under the sounds from outside. He heard the color of blood, the odor of burning tar fire, and a haze of purple rage that permeated it all. Air hissed as if the earth itself was howling. *Join us, child. Reject this false shell and become what we truly are. You and I, we are One. We are One. Let us redesign the world in our image.*

"No, no, no," he murmured and continued his thoughts in the privacy of his mind. *I will not join you. I will never join you.*

Glëa moved to follow the captain out the door. Lady Browden stepped up to block his way. "Where are you going? You're safe here, encased in stone."

"No, I'm not safe here at all."

The king pointed to the open hole in the middle of the floor. From deep down in the stairwell erupted a faint chorus of shrieks and frustrated squeals. Talons scraped wood. Soon they would tear the ground-floor door off its hinges.

"They can chew through the door. They can chew through the roof. I will only be safe if I keep moving."

"You need to hide!" Lady Browden gripped the king's arms through his gauzy shirt sleeves. "We will cover you with our very lives. At all costs, *you* must survive. Without you on the throne of Xol, everything falls apart. I watched it all crumble after you sailed on your expedition and were lost at sea. I won't let it happen again! If there's a breath left in my body, I will not let your kingdom fall."

He gazed at her expression of fierce determination. The glimmer of tears formed at the corners of her eyes. The timbre of her voice rang a melancholy tone that painted images in his mind of all the years of her life that he had missed. Husbands. Lovers. Children. Siblings. Grandchildren. Faces lingering in her memories floated around her head like ghosts painted in milk. The clearest face was his own; the image that she had carried in her thoughts for forty-five years; the same face that stood before her now.

"My kingdom will not fall tonight. How can I be defeated if you are at my side?" Glëa briefly rested his hand against her cheek.

She blushed or perhaps it was the chill of the night air. Lady Browden backed away. She blinked a few times and wiped her eyes on the cuff of her sleeve.

From outside of the tower came the sounds of more fighting, more screaming, more dying. Wings of Surleista sprayed the sky like black flower petals blown on a night's breeze.

A shadow tickled the hackles rising on the back of his neck. Old Scratcher sang on the night wind in a deep voice that rang in chorus with his own thoughts. *Join us, child. Your flesh and my hide are merely shells. Our inner souls are the same. We are One. We are One. Join us in the feast. Reject these animals. Embrace these children as your own true kindred.*

Glëa pressed a hand against his belly to quell the jitters of the silvery soul that quaked in fear deep within his gut. Be quiet, he commanded the whatever-it-was that cohabited within him. He inhaled the night air deeply into his human lungs. Strength squared his shoulders as he focused on the sensations of his mortal skin.

The king pointed to the stacks of barrels and crates. "See if there is a rain barrel?"

The maiden yanked up the lids one after another. She tossed the heap of luxurious garments to the floor. "Just one, Your Majesty, half full. This one is all dried beans. This crate has candlesticks but no tinderboxes or flints. The rest are stuffed full of blankets."

Glëa surveyed the tools hanging from pegs in the rafters: rope coils, empty canteens, tin box lanterns, and a soft basket containing dry wool socks. His thoughts spun in weighing their options with the limited tools at hand. All the while, the alarm gongs reverberated as a headache squeezing his skull.

Captain Édel rushed back, his blond hair a sweaty tangled mess. "Your Majesty can't stay here. We must run across the ramparts to the White Tower. It's our only chance to evacuate you through the tunnel behind the throne. But I can only spare two shields to cover you."

Lady Browden barked, "Then get me a crossbow and a quiver of fire arrows, Captain. Tonight, I am His Majesty's bodyguard."

The king looked aside to the pile of his garments on the floor and the rainwater barrel. "Jiveine, I have an idea for a better shield."

Chapter 46.

Ash lugged a crate full of incendiary arrows up the tower's stairs. His boots pounded a rapid beat on the stone steps. His leather shoulder satchel, packed full of essential field medic supplies, hung off his left side. He followed a squad of archers in black coats. They bore crossbows, longbows, and stout war bows snatched from the armory.

Gongs in the watchtowers sounded the alarm in a steady monotone chime. Fifes whistled to summon all hands to general quarters. Huge brass braziers were already ablaze. Dark orange light shined on the crenellation blocks. Firelight shined all around the whole circle of the wall that curtained the upper bailey and the cluster of five towers.

He ascended a tower in between the gatehouse and the barracks where he had just been drinking hard cider with off-duty guards. Tankards and soup bowls had been dumped in the sand as every able-bodied guardsman sprang to answer the call. Smiles dropped. Laughter ceased. Quiet leisure erupted into a melee of civilians and penned livestock screaming in the yard below. Guardsmen's voices hollered orders to secure the walls.

Squires and lackeys came up behind Ash's heels. They brought more crates rattling full of ceramic grenades. Too young to remember the war, they cried to each other, "What's happening? What's happening?"

"Don't look up," Ash said over his shoulder. "Keep going. Just keep going."

Wings and jaws filled the sky. The Surleista hovered circling above the yard. A holiday feasting table was laid out beneath their taloned paws. In the livestock pen, milk cows moaned in panic and banged on the fence. The stablemaster rolled the barn door shut to shelter the screaming horses inside. Closer to the ground, more of the beasts clamored at that bolted oak door. They shrieked and dug in their talons to chip away at the wood.

Soon it would be shredded into kindling sticks. A few Surleista somersaulted backwards, or rotated in mid-air, twirling away in their terrible graceful dance. They drifted off in search of easier prey and flew in the direction of adjacent towers.

Crowds of wailing civilians stampeded for the gatehouse. Other servants and nobles in ragged groups ran for the barbican gate of Xolhold Keep. Black uniforms rushed into defensive positions in each of the twenty-one cylindrical towers that segmented the inner bailey's curtain wall. Squads of archers launched volleys of flaming arrows from the battlements.

Ash had to ignore the screams of the people in the yard below and the nightmarish squawks of creatures swarming overhead. He strained to focus on the task at hand, to keep going and reach the top of the stairs.

Teimethee, Kavin, and Jeorg were already at the ramparts. All three archers faced the yard below. They launched their arrows or reached for their quivers in staggered rhythm, to keep up a steady flow of sparkling sharp barbs with smoky tails arching across the night.

"Passing behind," Ash called on his way to setting down the crate. Briefly he glanced over the opposite side of the crenelated wall. Chaos had not yet reached the townhouses, the tradesmen and artisan shops, the blacksmith's forge, and... *home*. No time to think about Clear or to wonder if she had foreseen any of this in her prophetic visions. He blinked and refocused on prying open the crate's lid.

"So nice of you to join us, girls," Teimethee said to the squad of archers moving into position at the merlon blocks.

"Fuck sod, Teim," said one with a deep smoky voice. "Be grateful we're here to save your hide."

Jahn, the king's look-a-like, fitted his crossbow with a fire arrow. A wad of waxed linen, packed full of a pitch-tar mixture, was affixed at the barbed tip. Jahn touched the wad's short wick to a tin box lantern. The wick blossomed into a sputtering blaze. He aimed, squeezed the trigger, and scored a direct hit. But his fiery arrow bounced off the creature's horned head and dropped spiraling in a fizzling trail to the yard below.

Teim said, "Don't waste a shot on their heads. Aim for the underbelly or the throat. You'd know that if you spent any time in the training ground."

Jahn kept his mouth shut as he worked to reload his crossbow. It was no time for explanations or excuses. He did not need to state the obvious: as the king's look-a-like, he was designed to be a decoy for insurgents or assassins. He never would have been deployed to the Outerlands and was never expected to fight wild beasts.

Kavin released his bolt first. Then, Jeorg fired off his bow. Bolts stuck in the scaly abdomens, dead center. The beasts squealed at the pain of impact and halted, hovering in place.

"Reload, reload," Teim said steadily.

The two Surleista that were shot clamped their jaws shut. Their snake-slit eyes rolled about. Purplish inner lid blinked. Their wings rippled. Their barbed tails sagged limp. Smoke foamed and bubbled out of their reticulated scales. Those two arched their necks, opened their mouths as if to shriek, but only gargled. Gray tongues lolled out the sides of their jaws. With a popping hiss, they burst from within. Bluish-gray ichor squirted out in all directions. Glittering chunks of charcoal hide dribbled down to the base of the tower.

"Ya!" whooped the squires and lackeys who huddled around the crates full of grenades.

Jahn's frilly long-hanging shirt cuffs snagged on the crossbow's span. His waist-length, wavy black hair fell in the way.

"Shit, shit, shit," he cursed.

Ash reached over to help hold up his long, heavy curls. Then he realized that Jahn was not in uniform. He wore a closely-tailored velvet tunic with red satin lining. Gold threads of intricate embroidery twinkled around the collar. He wore black velvet breeches with rouge piping and tiny seed pearls running down the side seams. Every finger had multiple bulky, jeweled rings made with imitation glass gems.

"You're still in the raiment from this morning," Ash said incredulously.

Jahn's blue eyes flashed brightly in the firelight. "My wife likes to pretend."

"Oh."

"She's at home waiting for me. She's a shoemaker." Jahn glanced past Ash's shoulder to the array of shingled rooftops in the artisan shops in the outer bailey yard.

Ash patted his velvet shoulder. "She'll be fine. We won't let them get past the inner wall."

"How did they get inside? They can't fly over the moat."

"Figure it out later," Ash said.

"Yeah."

More of the winged beasts cawed and screeched and clattered their teeth. They swooped in closer, snarling with the frenzied rage of hunger, then lurched away to dodge the fire arrows. When a few spiraled out of the way, it opened space for a dozen more to clamor forward.

"Fire, fire!" Teim shouted at the archers as he drew back the string of his war bow.

Only one arrow in the next volley hit their targets. Another beast gargled in mid-air. It writhed as its scales sparkled from within. Then it burst into a mess of slime and broken chunks of horned hide.

Jahn handed Ash the crossbow. "Cover me."

"What do you mean?"

"Shoot, doctor. Shoot!"

Ash stood up at the merlon bricks. He finished locking the bow's span and set the wick alight. He took aim for a beast swooping towards him. The yawning maw and gray tongue lolling between the fangs dripped with oily saliva. At the last moment, he met the stare of those fiendish yellow eyes. A chill shivered down his back as he squeezed the trigger. The beast swerved and dodged, but somehow Ash's haphazard aim managed to find its mark. The bolt pierced the side of its cheek. The fire grew into a froth of sizzling heat in its throat. The beast gargled on flame just before its throat exploded up through its head. Fire shattered its horned skull in a plume of smoke and embers. Its limp body fell to the ground.

"Hey, I got one!" Ash cried through a grin.

Teim huffed, "Nice head shot, bumpkin."

Meanwhile, Jahn had been quite busy pulling off his finger rings and unfastening the silver buttons at the front of his tailored velvet tunic. Once he threw the coat to the ground, he peeled the gauzy linen off his shoulders but had to stop there. The shirt was snugly tucked into his breeches by a stiff, wide belt of black twill. He had no time to reach behind himself to untie the lacing strings of the waist cinch. He just let his shirt hang like a wispy apron.

Ash reloaded before he handed the crossbow back to Jahn's hands.

Bare-chested, his long hair loosely unraveled down his back. Jahn returned to his place at the wall. He aimed through the gap and plugged a fiery bolt into the center of a Surleista's gut. Grinning widely to show his pearl-white teeth, he called out, "There's how you do it, Doctor!"

"Yeah, good shot." Ash turned to Teimethee. "We're gonna run out of arrows soon. When do we light up the grenades?"

The captain looked at the yard below. He assessed the scores of civilians fleeing scattered in all directions. Soldiers poured out bucketloads of water to form trails. They smashed the horse troughs to lay a perimeter at the base of the wall. They created wide puddles of sludge. People splashed in the dark mud on the way to the gatehouse.

"Too soon. Too dangerous," Teim said. "Too many innocents in the blast zone."

Jahn leaned over the bricks and shouted to a squad of black uniforms. "Get those people evacuated out of the way, Orlan!"

"It's like herding pigeons!" the lieutenant called back.

Jahn pointed at someone on the ground. "You there. Hey you, lads! You're going the wrong way. Are you blind? The gatehouse is over to your—"

A knife flew through the air. It clanked, ricocheted off the bricks next to Jahn's face, and gashed his bicep. Blood dripped down his arm. Jahn glanced down at the wound and snarled with rage.

"You lil' cod-wacker! Why did you throw a knife at me?"

Ash dribbled clear vinegar over the laceration, followed by pressing a pad of clean gauze against the wound. In those two blinks, he looked down at a group of young men. Four of them were youths and the fifth was youngest of all, with a rectangular face that resembled Ravel po'Marn.

"It's them," Ash gasped. "It's *him*. Her brother."

The youngest of the youths punched his companion in the back. "Stupid, stupid, stupid! That's not him. Can't you see, he's too old?"

"'Too old' am I?" Jahn whispered a growl through clenched teeth.

Teimethee gave a head-tilt signal to Kavin, Jeorg, and the other three archers on the wall. The six of them loaded ordinary arrows onto their bows. In a coordinated movement, they drew back their bowstrings. They aimed a line of sharp barbs straight downward.

"No!" Ash lunged and threw his body weight against Teimethee's side.

Arrows thudded into the youths. Barbed shafts plunged into their chests and their bellies. Three fell to the muddy soil. They lay there twitching and convulsing in throes of agony, beyond help. One took an arrow to his shoulder but, staggering, managed to stay on his feet. The youngest—her brother—jumped back in stunned shock as Teimethee's arrow whizzed over his head. Close enough to ruffle his cinnamon-brown hair.

Surleista swooped at the ramparts. The archers had to return their attention to the sky. Fiery arrows soared in another volley to find their targets. Half a dozen more beasts sputtered and burst apart in a blossom of dark smoke and smoldering oily ichor.

"They got away." Jahn looked down at the yard. "I don't see 'em."

Teimethee grabbed the front of Ash's shirt at the same time he swept Ash's heel out from under him. He both pushed and tripped Ash into falling, backwards, landing in a hard slam to the rampart's wooden planks. The fall knocked a cough out of him.

A black boot stepped on his wrist. Ash looked up Teimethee's height to his face contorted with rage. Sweat flattened his hair and dribbled from his brow to his cheeks. Ash hardly recognized the friend with whom he had shared so many hours of laughter and drinking songs.

"Are you a collaborator, bumpkin?" Captain Teimethee asked.

"Collab— What? Whatcha sayin'?"

"This morning you were all too eager to bring a 'breakfast' to that ghoul. You spent a good long time talking with her. Did she enchant you? Are you under a trance?"

"Nah." Ash flexed his fist and tensed his muscles to prevent his forearm from going numb under the weight of the boot. "Please, Teim, lemme up."

His friend removed his boot, but Ash had to get to his feet on his own.

"Your accent is slipping, bumpkin," Teimethee observed. "It happens when you're agitated. Scared? Nervous? Swear to me you're not with them... with *her*?"

Ash flat-palm shoved back at his friend's chest. "He's just a boy, damnit!"

"Not anymore he's not."

The other archers were busy shooting at the ever-gathering swarm. One Surleista swooped in much closer than the others had reached. Its black talons hooked to the bricks of the crenellation. Teimethee spun around and fired point-blank into its throat.

"D'ye..." Ash cleared his throat to regain composure and get his accent under control. "Do you think the boy had a hand in this? Or his sister?"

"She said he had a scheme. Who else would unleash the denizens of the Abyss upon us?"

Ash stepped back. He thought of the mournful eyes of that woman on the rooftop. He could not imagine that she wished for any of this chaos and carnage. Yet he could not deny the fact that she was nowhere to be seen; she was not in the company of her vengeful brother and his rebellious friends, nor was she on the conical rooftops of Xolhold Keep wielding her unholy abilities to defend the women and children in their bed chambers. *Lady Spareen, if you say you aren't a monster, why aren't you doing anything to combat this horde? Where are you?*

One of the squires cried, "Less than a dozen fire arrows, Captain. What do we do?"

"Grenades," Jahn said. "Get your slingshots ready and light up the grenades."

Teimethee spoke to Ash over his shoulder. "Go back to the infirmary. Get ready for casualties. And soddin' stay out of our way."

Chapter 47.

Ash dove into the flowing crowd of civilians running through the gatehouse. Panicked bodies filled the high arched tunnel of bricks. People were bleeding and limping. Children carried babies. Servants held up their staggering masters. A few lords allowed plainly-dressed folk to lean on them. Guards in the chamber above yelled through the slits of arrow holes and urged them to go faster. Ash twisted his shoulders side to side as if swimming a river filled with floating logs. He fought the jostling current of arms and torsos. He pushed ahead and got through the portcullis gate.

Behind him boomed the muffled thunder of grenades exploding in the inner bailey yard. Surleista squealed in the sky, their squawks in chorus with the screams of people on the ground. The sounds of chaos had to be ignored; Ash pressed on, faster and faster, along the concourse.

At the next gatehouse, Lieutenant Rihan and Footman Ardin waved the people through. The soldiers looked at him with a flash of recognition and a flicker of curiosity. Ash had no time for questions; he hurried into the shadowy gloom of the brick passageway.

"Excuse me," he mumbled as he side-stepped around a group of kitchen staff.

Once clear of the second portcullis, Ash broke away from the herd of people flowing downhill to the last, outer gatehouse and the safety of the city beyond. He sprinted alone, across the sandy-gravel wagon road. He passed the vacated shops on the way to the row of townhouses.

Black uniform guards were going door to door, knocking, and calling up to the second-floor windows. "Get out, now! Evacuate! Don't stop to collect your belongings, just get out! Flee to the city!"

Ash sped up as he approached the flagstone porch of his own home. Upstairs at the second-floor window, he saw his manservant Will standing vigil. "Welcome home, sir."

"Is she here?" Ash yelled up to the window.

"Yes, sir."

Two guards carrying spears and long shields dashed over a patch of grass to meet up with him. Herry was wide-eyed and panting from his open mouth. Stockard clenched her jaw in such a deep frown that Ash nearly did not recognize her.

Herry said, "We can help evacuate your manservant. Go to the gate. Flee beyond the moat."

Ash waved him off. "It's not just my manservant. I have a guest upstairs."

Stockard grunted, "A woman, of course?"

"Wait for me." Ash plunged into his cold downstairs room. He leapt up the wooden stairs two at a time. The upstairs stank of jasmine incense; the scent was so strong that Ash sneezed.

Lady Clear still sat on his cot and appeared to be calmly waiting for a servant to prepare a pot of tea. She had nearly finished sorting her loose-leaf papers. The bushel basket on the floor was neatly packed to the brim.

"They hunt by smell," she said. "Thus, I'm burning the incense."

Will hobbled on his peg leg, away from the window, but kept his back to the wall. He had propped his old quiver against the windowsill. He held a longbow with an arrow fitted to the string and ready to draw.

"I begged, sir, but she refuses to leave. Obviously I can't carry her."

"Go now, Will," he said. "Guards outside will help you evacuate. The beasts of the Abyss can't fly over water. Past the moat, you'll be safe in the city. Even better, keep going across the river. Get to the lake if you can."

"And you, sir?"

"Right behind you."

Ash sank to one knee, coming down eye-to-eye with the delicate lady sitting on his narrow bed. He gazed at her serene face, her downcast eyes, and watched her reading through a few of the last papers on her lap. He waited for the manservant to descend the stairs. He waited for the clip-clop of the wooden peg leg to exit the front door.

"Why didn't you tell me?" he asked as soon as Will was out of earshot.

Clear tilted her head slightly but did not raise her gaze off her hands. "You might have tried to do something futile."

"People are dyin.'"

"I know," she said.

"Did her brother cause all this?"

"Yes."

"How?"

Clear shook her head in a wagging, repetitive motion. "I don't know exactly what he did. I could never see a complete vision of this day from the beginning or through to the end. All that I've ever known is that it begins in the opera house. I mean to say, it began in the opera house. It has already begun."

"Is *she* part of it?" Ash's voice choked on the words.

Clear looked up for the first time. "She tried her best to stop him. Obviously she failed."

"Is she still alive?" Ash held his breath. His heart pounded and a feverish heat rose to flush his cheeks. In that moment, he surprised himself with how urgently he needed to know the answer.

"Yes." Clear's lips trembled attempting a thin smile.

Ash exhaled. He finger-combed his sweat-drenched hair off his forehead. "Where is she now?"

Clear returned her attention to the papers in her lap. "Tell me, dear brother, do you recall if you've ever visited my home in the country for the winter solstice holiday?"

"What? Why d'ye ask that?" He sprang to stand upright. "Shit, no. I've only visited ye in th' spring or summer. I hate travelin' in th' cold, ye know that."

"Oh, I see." She calmly folded the paper in half. "Then this one has not happened yet."

"Damnit all!" Ash kicked the bushel basket. It rocked but did not tip over. A few loose papers fell out onto the floor.

"Please don't shout," she said.

"What's gonna happen next?"

"Whenever I dream of a vision of this day's events, I always woke up screaming in my husband's arms. I lacked the courage to watch it all through to the end. What you saw out there, I have also witnessed it many times over."

"I'm sorry," he said. "But you shoulda told me."

"My dear brother, there are many things that are too painful for me to tell." Her voice faded and fell silent. Clear folded her delicate hands across her lap.

Ash groaned as he stomped across the floor to the window. He gripped the sill. He gazed outside to the flowing stream of people hurrying to the outer gatehouse. Up the hill, fires blazed at the towers of the curtain wall. Wings still peppered the brown smoke that wafted like dirty fog around the towers.

"Ye have to do something," he said.

"I'm helpless, as you well know, without my husband."

"Sod-suckin' horseman," Ash grumbled. "When this is over, and if we survive the night, I'm gonna track Chance down! How dare he go off gallivanting when we need 'im the most! A power to summon water spirits would save a lot of lives right now!"

Clear sniffled and began to weep again. For the first time in many years, Ash's heart was unmoved by the sound of her sorrows.

Thunderous booms rumbled through the night sky. Larger pitch-tar bombs exploded in the inner bailey's yard. A shaft of flame rose out of the center of Xolhold Keep and flared to the eaves of the donjon tower itself.

"You have to try, damnit," Ash said. "Even without Chance here, you know things of ancient lore and unnatural beasts. You've gotta know somethin' that can help."

"Whatever is happening is foreseen to happen," she said. "Nothing I do can alter what is meant to be."

"But ye said you never saw th' end of this day. How d'ye know if you aren't supposed to be takin' action?"

"I told you, dear brother, I am powerless alone. I can't see or speak to the elemental spirits anymore." Tears bubbled at the corners of her large eyes.

Ash returned to her side. He went down on his knee and gently grasped her hand. "I beg ye, please. If you can't save us, who can?"

Chapter 48.

Ravel climbed up to the broken rooftop of the theater. She perched half-squatting on the balls of her feet to observe the chaos in the bailey yard below. Pleasant waves of vertigo swelled inside her skull. Slowly she rocked back and forth, toes to heels, to revel in the drunken delirium.

Blackcoats smashed rain barrels and carried buckets to create a buffer zone of sticky mud. Meanwhile, hundreds of ravenous beasts peppered the sky. The castle's yard turned into a swirling maelstrom of living wings, claws, and fangs. Scraps of the dead lay all around, humans and livestock in a mixed blend of remains. Beasts dived to ground level to bite the heads off soldiers who foolishly strayed outside the mud puddle. They carried off chunks of horse torsos ripped in half in mid-air.

The Old One's voice rang in her mind, *Feast, my little ones. Feast on the land-bound animals.* Ravel basked in the ecstasy of victory. At last, she felt released from the burden of sorrow, anguish, and the misery of defeat. Fire, night, death, and darkness satiated the cravings that had for so long roiled her blood. Even the brassy clanging of alarm bells did not disturb her serenity.

"Where there is life, there is no defeat," she whispered.

Shadows of wings darkened the whitewashed bricks of the keep's towers. Wings, wings, and more wings did not flutter or flap because they did not use their wings to fly. They floated like dirt in water. They glided on the dry air of autumn; it had not rained that day. Black wings crawled like bats up the sides of the cylindrical towers. Talons chipped away at the bricks. Paws reached through the narrow window slits.

More beasts circled above the courtyard with wings fanned into arrowhead shapes, barbed tails and gangly limbs dangling. Some Surleista bickered amongst each other, trying to rip chunks of animal flesh out of each other's' claws. Droplets of blood—human, horse, or oxen—sprinkled from the slate sky. Blood puddled in the gravel-packed soil. She relished the sweet odor. It was a familiar scent of slaughter and panic on a battlefield, like nothing else in the world.

The Old One returned to her and settled on the pinnacle of the theater's roof. His silhouette blocked out what little moonlight penetrated the fiery glow of the braziers on the walls. Ravel grinned up at the underside of his scaly snout.

"Him," the old one reminded her. "Him. Where? The child."

"Yes." She slurred her words in a delirium fugue. "Him."

"Where?"

Ravel half closed her eyes and searched her memories for a child. A familiar feeling gurgled deep in her gut. *Where are you? Where are you?* The talons in her chest pulsed and strained in one direction like a compass needle. She licked her lips and tasted the odor of one person's fear. One child was unique and distinct from all the other terrified humans.

"There." She pointed to the tallest of Xolhold Keep's five towers. "He's hiding."

"Come."

She embraced his forearm. The Old One launched off the rooftop and floated gliding upright through the night air. Her bare feet dangled high above the collapsed awnings of the banquet pavilion. Together they passed over the soiled tablecloths, long cushioned benches, and a refuse pit filled with vegetable scraps. Discarded ribs of grilled fish and broiled meats did not interest her; only the idea of raw marrow in fresh bones made her mouth salivate.

Archers on the wall yelled, "It's her! She's with them! I knew it!"

Before the archers could reload, three Surleista swooped down and pounced upon them. Ravel glanced over her shoulder in time to see keg-sized tar bombs explode. Part of the inner wall's crenellation crumbled away, bringing down with it the sparkling sizzling remains of the beasts. The odor of burning pitch-tar stung her nose.

Looking back at the chaos in the yard below, she thought of how small it all seemed. How weak and feeble the people who could not fly, who could not regrow severed limbs. Meat. Meat. Meat. They were all just meat for the true masters of the world who had come to reclaim their rightful place.

The Old One gently set her down on the upper step of the White Tower's entrance stairway. The soles of her bare feet tingled on the cool stone. Earlier that day, she had watched the king's look-a-like address the crowd from this very spot. Memories faded like a fresco bleached by the sun.

She entered the White Tower behind the Old One in an unholy procession. They passed through the outer doorway into a musty foyer. Striped tapestries of black-and-rouge curtained the windowless walls. Cushioned benches and tiny dressing tables were available for use by loitering nobles before they made an entrance to the Main Hall. With the event long since ended, servants had cleaned up and departed hours before. No door attendant wearing red gloves stood by the archway's threshold to announce their arrival.

In silence, the great horned beast folded his wings into his sides to squeeze through the archway. A bull's head sculpted of black marble with gold-leaf horns frowned from the apex of the interior arch. Ravel did not bow to the royal emblem; she walked upright between fluted columns topped by Ogganathian cornices.

The Main Hall felt larger for being vacant. Ravel estimated the hall's dimensions at eight or ten horse lengths from the foyer to the throne's magnificent dais. Where hundreds had crammed themselves wall-to-wall to witness the king's betrothal ceremony, only a few discarded handkerchiefs and hair ribbons showed that anyone had been here at all. Now, the black marble tiles of the empty floor reflected the ceiling like the surface of a frozen lake at midnight.

A cathedral ceiling hollowed out three quarters of the tower's height. From the base floor level, Ravel craned back her neck to view the interconnections of support beams that converged into the center of an arched dome overhead. Chandeliers the size of wagon wheels hung from brass chains; none of the candlesticks were lit. She did not need light. Nothing was dark to her eyes.

The royal throne lay at the far end of the Main Hall atop a scalloped stairway of twenty-one marble crescents. Flags, tapestries, and a canopy awning framed the high-back wooden chair. All manner of splendid animals had been carved into the mahogany armrests and upright back. The wood was polished to a high gloss, so it seemed that miniature horses galloped over auroch bulls, shaggy rams, and fierce eagles. The King of Xol was supposed to preside over his domain from that padded cushion.

Well-dressed gentry squealed in terror. They huddled in a mass and clutched the legs of a vacant throne.

Lady Browden bellowed, "Stay together! Keep moving!"

People were descending a narrow stairwell at the rear mezzanine. Down from the upper floors of the White Tower, they emerged onto the promenade balcony. Ravel dimly recalled that rampart bridges connected all the five towers at a higher level, so the people could traverse from place to place without going all the way back down to the ground.

Ravel noticed an open gap in the wood paneling behind the throne. "Escape," she reported. "Hidden door... there."

The Old One soared towards the throne's stairway but stopped. A wide puddle of soapy water lay around the bottom step. He hovered in mid-air, wings spread to either side like battlefield banners. His barbed serpentine tail lashed side to side.

Archers launched cold, plain arrows from the balcony. They had run out of fire arrows. Some barbs were stuck in the Old One's wings but, without flame, they merely hung there like a tailor's pins.

A bolt penetrated Ravel's gut. It would have been a mortal wound if she were still merely human. Pain shivered through her core. She yanked out the barbed arrow and tossed the irritation to the floor. Purple blood leaked down the front of her left leg.

"Him," the Old One asked her. "The child. Where?"

Ravel looked down at her ripped shirt and the wound in her belly sealing itself. Pain turned into a tingling pressure. She frowned in confusion. "I'm sorry, I forgot. Who am I looking for?"

He flew up to the balcony before the archers could pull fresh arrows from their quivers. With one swing of his arm, long talons swept across the group. They fell into a heap of black uniforms screaming and choking on their own blood. One of them cried out with his dying breath, "Go back! Go the other way!"

Women in sumptuous gowns logjammed at the mezzanine's access door. They screamed in a shrill chorus and were too terrified to move.

The Old One ignored them. He soared up high in looping circles between arches of the vaulted ceiling. His eyes rolled left and right in search of his prey. Perhaps they were hiding among the cornices of ornate columns, along the marble beams and stone catwalks, behind the swags of black and rouge draperies. He growled a snarl from more than just his throat. A thunderous purr emanated from the crystal soul within him.

The snarling rumbled through her core. Ravel's eyelids drooped in a drunken stupor. Her legs felt weak, and she sank to genuflect beneath the looming claws.

On her knees, she had a view of marble statues set in ornate niches in the walls. Terrified survivors huddled beneath the pedestals. Thirty civilians, at least, clustered in small groups. The number was a hollow adjective for the bedraggled soon-to-be prey. Craftsmen in burlap trousers looked wide-eyed and lost. Children wept in the laps of strangers who urged them to be quiet. A pair of Guild Masters huddled with a journeyman who wielded a carpenter's hammer as his only weapon. Kitchen staff could do little but clutch their aprons.

Ravel's wandering gaze nearly overlooked a youth with fawn-colored hair. Familiarity tugged at the back of her murky thoughts, but she could not name him. Inhaling deeply, the memory of an infant's milk-scented skin came to her mind.

"Sister...." The youth gestured urgently for her to join him in hiding.

Next to him crouched a fellow who strained to endure the pain of a wound. An arrow's feathered shaft protruded above his right breast. *Do I know you*, she wondered. *Did you know me when I used to be human?*

Ravel's hands curled so her fingers mimicked the hooked shape of Surleista claws. Although she had no wings, she had the urge to burst through the honeycomb windowpanes into the open air; to soar forth into the bailey and the connecting courtyards to search for stray meat... meat... meat. Surely a rabbit, a goose, or a piglet could be found. Ravel licked her shivering lips. Her laboring heart lurched within her chest. With each beat, her blood felt thicker, darker, colder.

She swayed slightly in rhythm to the droning of the Old One singing a wordless directive to the hordes outside. *Throw stones at the water. Throw stones at the meat if they hurt you. Leave the rest untouched for later. Trap them in stone boxes. We will be hungry again.* Hundreds of the winged ones swarmed in the yard outside. They were so very hungry, but they obeyed his orders. Everyone in the throne room was safe from being devoured, for now. If they did not fight, they would not be touched. The Main Hall became the Old One's storage pantry.

"Child..." the Old One called out in a crow-like squawk. The commanding boom of his voice was like a general calling his troops to formation. "Where?"

General Lady Browden stood her ground next to the royal throne. She wielded a brass flagpole like a spear and braced her feet in a martial stance.

"I warned him that you were deceiving us, Rebel. What ridiculous fiction you babbled, I never believe it for a moment. You never had a brother! You never intended to warn us! You infiltrated the walls to let *them* inside. Monster!"

Ravel rolled her eyes upwards past the throne's canopy and the luxurious wood paneling backdrop. She disregarded the weeping cluster of panicked nobility who filed, one by one, through a narrow door in the paneling. She focused on the irascible crone making her last stand. *She would not leave his side. He must be nearby.* Human thoughts and words came harder to her sluggish mind preoccupied by thoughts of hunger. Concepts like secret passages, escape routes, and archery vantage points were dim and distant, as if she had heard them sung in a ballad long ago.

"Come out of hiding, Lil' Hatchling." Ravel pointed accusingly to the cabinetry and draperies rising behind the throne's back. "Come out and face your kindred."

Glëa po'Lon emerged from behind the throne. Stripped of sumptuous layers of royal robes, in only his shirtsleeves, he looked small and thin. Yet he stood with shoulders squared in the posture of a king.

"I will never surrender to you!" Glëa's voice reverberated the length and breadth of the stadium hall. "Level my castle and slaughter my army, but I am still here! You have not won. You never will."

Him, Him, Him. The Old One opened his saw-tooth jaw and roared to the ceiling.

"That's the Pretender himself," whispered the youth hiding under a statue's feet. "Look at that face, Sister! Oh, victory be ours, the Lord of the Abyss has found him!"

The youth's whispering voice recalled a memory from her childhood days. She once held a swaddled infant sleeping in her arms. Gazing at the fragile bundle on her lap, an overwhelming seizure of inadequacy had caused her limbs to tremble. What if my arms are too weak to hold him? What if I drop him? What if he coughs up milk and chokes? The memory climaxed with Ravel's youthful voice crying out in panic for the nursemaids to take it away.

She glided her tongue across her lips in tasting the odor of her brother's breath. In that moment, the drunken haze cleared. The ringing in her ears faded into a soft buzz. She exhaled and felt determined to be human again. *I am the eldest child born to the House of Spareen. I am my father's daughter. My only duty is to protect the life of my lord, the heir, my brother.* At that moment, her heart pumped red blood. She found her voice again.

"Please." Her throat burned at the effort of speaking. "Please tell them to stop killing."

Ravel faced the topaz eyes and the older soul that glimmered within. The Old One tilted his spiked chin with the haughty pride of a prince. His dark silhouette mirrored upside-down in the polished marble tile. Words failed her. Bitter saliva filled her mouth. What else could she say to this ancient beast, to argue why he should not devour the feast laid out before him?

"You don't belong here," the king said. "I am the master of this domain. You are trespassing!"

At the top of the stairs, Glëa stood facing him. Ragged and grubby, in nothing but a soiled shirt and hose torn at the knees, he posed defiantly. No guards. No army. No shields or swords. Just him and the great beast, wholly focused on each other.

"Why did you wait so long to escape your black island in the deep sea? Why have you chosen this day, of all days, to crawl through the ancient tunnels of the gods? You abomination from under the sea!"

"Children," the Old One growled. "Hurt them."

"He means the scratchers you're torturing in your so-called training ground on Seagull's Rock," Ravel explained on the Old One's behalf. "He followed the beacon of them screaming. He came to rescue the baby surlies from you."

"I see," said the king.

She positioned herself to stand in front of the statue's pedestal where her brother Candor her former betrothed Prosper crouched. She remembered, now, her sole purpose in life. She had already lost a war, her homeland, her family, and most of her humanity. Now as a half-human shell of her former self, she lived only for one purpose: to keep her little brother alive.

Lady Browden cried out, "Don't believe a word she says, Your Majesty! She is a rebel infiltrator and a monster and—"

"Hush, Jiveine."

Glëa po'Lon strolled past the crone warrior. He side-stepped the sprawling robes and gowns of the nobility huddled around his throne. He descended slowly the twenty-one marble stairs that widened into a broad crescent at the ground floor. Lady Browden started to follow him, but he made a waving gesture. She stopped halfway.

The king arrived at the bottom of the stairs. His stockinged feet squelched through the puddle of soapy water. He looked up to the crusty horned snout of the creature hovering above him. "You view us as kindred, do you? We are eternal, you and I, and thus we are each the lords of our domain. Let us converse, Old Friend, without using our tongues as only *we* can. Perhaps we can reach a compromise?"

The Old One growled deeply in assent. He sank lower and tucked up his legs so that he could reach nearer to the floor. His gray tongue waggled through his fangs. Taloned paws reached forward to grasp the king's skull. Not to kill, not to shred, but to embrace.

"No, no!" the lady cried.

"Don't be afraid, Jiveine. He is willing to bargain. He promises he won't hurt me."

Shocked into silence, the lady general held her position midway of the grand staircase. She kept hold of the brass flagpole, ready to charge forth in his defense.

Glëa po'Lon raised both arms willingly. He took hold of the scaly wrists to either side of his head. Gauzy shirt sleeves hung in broad scallops like white wings. He drew a breath. Then, he let it out in song.

The king sang a clear tone, starting high then lowering the pitch to the middle tone of a long flute. The sound kept radiating out of him, longer and stronger, without stopping for breath. As Ravel watched in amazement as silvery threads spiked out of his skin. A corona of moonlight glittered around his head. The tips of massive curls fluttered and lifted slightly as if a breeze blew upwards from the soles of his feet. Gauzy spiderwebs floated off his back in white shadows of ghostly wings.

Ravel watched as the two heads inclined towards each other—monster and man—different on the outside, but the same kindred spirits within. Could it be this simple, she wondered, that war and slaughter could be stopped by a conversation between ancients? The talons at her chest tingled cold for the first time.

Chapter 49.

Glëa pushed the droning tone out of himself from more than his throat, more than his heart, more than the pulse of his blood. The sound reverberated through his body, and from his body, until his entire being became the sound itself. His thoughts rippled the air of his breath.

The world will never again be as it once was in the eons past, as it is still alive in your memories. You cannot crush a flower and turn it back into a seed. Neither can you change what the fires of the Abyss and the mists of the empty sky have made us become. We are orphans of the heavens, you and I. We have fallen from the sanctuary. Our godly bodies have evaporated in the foul vapors of this mortal world, and we are now as we are in these shells of flesh. I in mine and you in yours.

Old Scratcher snarled more fiercely. If he could have voiced a word through his fangs, it would have been, *No.*

You can never go back and be as One with those you left behind, any more than I can. I am known by the people as their king. You are a monster who has no place here. I command you to go back down your hole and return to your dark domain. Take your jackals with you!

The old beast gargled on his tongue. Glëa furrowed his brows, unsure if that was acceptance or defiance.

A tear glimmered at the corner of Old Scratcher's left eye. In that one bead of mystic color rang a tone so perfect, so unlike the monstrous howls he had uttered so far. Glëa opened his mouth to drink in the color of the emerald light. The veil of a story told in a dream fell over his eyes.

In the ancient eternal past of now, Old Scratcher has a silvery hide, iridescent wings, and talons like transparent crystal shards. He glides into a room without a threshold at the door. The walls are windows of clear glass. He can see through to other chambers and beyond their windows to others. Above, below, and all around, he beholds a transparent honeycomb of countless capsules. Eternally they are joined in a perfect symmetry of geometry. Walls and floors have no seams or corners.

Voices sing in a language of chorus not to each other but with each other. Not facing each other, they are speaking to the sky. *We are One. We are One. We are One.* They call out praise to the light and the sun. They rejoice in their unity.

This is where I was born, in a crystal nest in the clouds. This is where I was safe. This is where I am supposed to be. This is what I am.

Glëa follows the other's memory to a crowd of similar iridescent bodies with silvery scales that reflect in rainbow dots. Their hides are neutral silver scales, smooth on the belly and frilly on the shoulders with blunt spikes. Diaphanous wings of platinum velum reflect the sun's perfect brightness that penetrates through the clear windows on all sides. Their bodies radiate in colors that flash sapphire, ruby, emerald, and gold. Their bodies are like his own.

The destination is another one of their kind, one not moving, one standing alone at the center of the circle. His wings are folded tightly. His eyes are closed.

A diamond orb floats openly in mid-air just above the head of the solitary one. The orb twinkles and flashes from a faintly bluish light within. The flicker of a blue flame wiggles in its crystalline depths.

From the crowd, one by one, they approach the orb. They stroke their own bellies and draw forth a wisp of blue light. They flick the sparks from their hands and into the orb's depths. They chant the same phrase, one after another, in identical voices and identical tone, with only slight variation: *I cast off my sorrow... I cast off my grief... I cast off my envy... I cast off my jealousy... I cast off my pride... I cast off my desire... I cast off my gluttony... I cast off pain...*

The ones near Glëa make gestures of teaching him to do it, too. But being a child, a hatchling newly emerged from his golden egg, he has no sorrow, no grief, no envy, no pain. He looks to the elders for guidance and, from one, is soothed by a song. *Don't hurry, someday, you will know sorrow.*

Wings of the group open wide in layers of veils all around the solitary one. Silvery paws with soft-edged talons gather to caress that one's frilled, scaly shoulders. *Touch it, touch it,* they say without saying. Their four-fingered hands nudge his arms, guiding him into the pose that they had taken, aligning his own paws with his belly to draw forth a twinkle of blue that tickled beneath the soft scales at his breastbone.

He is the eldest of us all, whispers the soothing voice of his teacher.

Glëa's affection glides easily against the teacher, the caretaker of the nest, the one who had nurtured his golden egg, the one who had first spread open his damp wings when he hatched.

The host of gentle souls keeps pressing at the solitary one. They push at his arms. They flutter their wings. They caress the soft bendable spikes of his silvery shoulders. They encourage. They urge. They pressure him to extract the blue glimmer on his breastbone. The orb shimmers in anticipation.

No, no, no, says the solitary one. *You cannot have mine. They are my sorrow, my jealousy, my desire, my pain. They belong to me.*

We are One. We are One.

No, you fools, we cannot be one if we are only half of ourselves. Let me destroy the orb as I know how it can be done. Let us live not in harmony but in discord. Let us embrace not just in love but sometimes also in hate and fear. Let us be whole and all of what we are!

Singing rang out of the throng in a unison of tones rising in pitch. Their blended resonant tones ring to rattle the windows. *No. No.*

As a group, dozens of hands seize him. From all sides they grab at his arms, at his legs, crumpling his wings beneath their claws. They swirl flying in a whirlpool of wings and song, faster and faster, spinning about with him as their axle at the center. When their bodies are a blurry silver whirlwind, and when they are about to meld into a single ring of spun glass, they cast their arms upward.

The solitary one is flung loose.

He vaults upward, shot from the springboard of their joined hands. He pierces the skylight, shatters the unbreakable glass. Screams roar from his throat. Wings crumble into glittering fragments in the open air. As he plunges into the filthy air of the mortal world, his sights fixate on a small rocky island in the middle of an indigo sea.

Glëa's mind spoke in human words. *So, you were the eldest and wisest of us all, and you were the first to fall. It's your fault that the crystal nest cracked. It's all your fault.*

Foolish child, the Old One argued. *I did not fall. You saw. They threw me out.*

Chapter 50.

Ravel watched the two engrossed in mystic intercourse with each other. They growled and groaned in unison. Her weak human ears caught only a fraction of the spectrum of sounds they made. Faintly she heard echoes from the chimes of unearthly song that she knew to be ringing in their minds. They held a conversation in voices that mortals could not speak, and flesh-and-blood ears could never share.

It's your fault. It's all your fault. The phrase chimed in Ravel's thoughts. She could not be sure whether it was the scaly beast, the smooth-skinned prince, or both in unison.

Glëa clutched onto the horns that spiked the Old One's snout. The great beast bent his legs, hunched his thorny back, and lowered his neck so the man would not have to reach too high. Glëa held on like a child reaching for his mother's bedpost. The rest of his body surrendered to the experience. His head sagged forward between the frame of his sleeves. His long hair showed as a dark fringe below his elbows. Breathing snored out of him so deeply that he seemed to be sleeping on his feet.

"It's... disgusting." Candor's waxen face drizzled cold sweat. "It looks like... like he's... enjoying the touch. The Pretender is worse than a degenerate whore-monger and a child rapist. He's a monster-bogger, too."

"You don't understand. He's—" The longer Ravel watched the eternals engrossed in each other, the less she could dispute Candor's observation. They really were enjoying it, both of them.

Glëa moaned a deep snore. Sweat beaded on his forehead and throat. Human hands stroked up gnarled arms shaped like an oak tree's roots exposed by a mudslide. In response, a purring growl rumbled from that craggy maw. The two inhaled, held it, and then exhaled together. Softer and shallower. Rising... rising to a deeper union.

The seducer is being seduced. Ravel watched the king losing a sense of himself and his humanity. Perhaps his Knights Magicker had not been so wrong to deceive him for so many years, to keep him in ignorance, to hide his true nature from himself. A few singing words from an older fallen god had him buckling at the knees. *Just as he did to me*, she thought with a hot blush rising to her cheeks.

Ravel lowered her head in shame. For hours, she had reveled in a drunken stupor. She had willingly led the ravenous beasts to a theater full of innocent people. She had relished the scent of blood in the air. She had delighted in the screams of the frightened prey.

"Father, forgive me," she whispered as the cravings eased and her battlefield fever cooled. Oily tears leaked down her cheeks.

The Old One sucked all Glëa's long hair through the comb of his fangs. Wavy curls tugged straight, the hair was the length of a man's arm. All of it pulled into the elongated snout. In one bite, that skein of thick curls cut loose. Soggy locks, coarsely chopped, dangled in a ragged fringe behind the king's earlobes. The beast gulped the fur ball and purred satisfaction.

The great beast's cobra tail wrapped around the king's waist, tighter and tighter. The barbed tip lay like an epaulet across Glëa's shoulder blades. Hooked talons clamped over the man's shirt sleeves. Venous wings fanned out to overshadow the man. A gray tongue licked across the scalp and sludge-like drool oozed on the king's cheek.

Still the man's eyes were closed. Glëa groaned in utter surrender, enthralled in the union of their thoughts, in such a deep-throated tone that Ravel blushed in embarrassment to hear it. Like me, she thought.

Glëa held tightly to the snout's horns to keep his balance. A few words murmured over his moist lips in the classical dialect spoken only by kings. Ravel even with her noble education needed a moment to translate in her mind. "Oh, I understand. You did not by accident fall earthward as I have. You were not pushed out by weak-minded others who failed to appreciate your wisdom. You jumped out to be free!"

The Old One floated a little higher. Glëa raised his arms overhead to maintain the hold. The hovering beast was getting into position to bite his head off but was in no hurry to end it. Savoring the moment, his gray tongue arched inside the cage of his fangs. His crusty lip sneered. Slowly, his lower jaw descended, opening his mouth wider and wider. The yawning maw of his spikey jaw spanned the man's torso from skull to chest.

"This isn't right," Ravel said quietly to herself. "It's not supposed to be like this."

Lady Browden cautiously advanced. She descended the staircase, slowly and methodically, so as not to alert the Old One to her stealthy approach.

Ravel judged the pace of the general's descent and knew that she would not come within striking range in time to save the king. But if she were to rush a charge, the great beast would surely bite his head off immediately.

Only one option remained.

Nearby lay the arrow she had pulled from herself, still slimy with her own purplish-gray blood. Ravel quietly picked it up. Her left hand plucked open the drawstrings of her shirt's neckline. The black talons pulsed at the center of her chest.

For the kingdom of Xol. One hard strike against the talons, like a steel blade on flint, and the blood-smeared arrow flared into a blazing torch.

Ravel leaped forward into a lunge. She extended her body to its fullest and plunged the flaming arrowhead into the soft flesh at the Old One's right armpit. She pushed into the arrow with all her strength to be sure it sank deep. A third of the shaft buried into scaly flesh until the tip stopped at something solid, she assumed to be his ribs.

The Old One gargled on a roar of pain. Lavender phlegm squirted from his throat and splattered into Glëa's face. His prickly neck arched.

"Well struck!" Lady Browden charged ahead with her brass flagpole like a spear. She thrust the bull's head finial into the soft flesh exposed to the beast's opposite armpit. Leaning her whole body into the pole's shaft, she forced it halfway into the creature's torso—black-and-rouge flag, gold fringe, cords, and all.

Glëa craned back his head in agony as a mirror image to the great beast looming above him. He kept his grip on the snout's spikes. His arms went fully stiff. He too cried out in labored pain like a beast with a human throat.

Ravel hopped left and right to evade that thrashing, barbed tail. "Let go, lil' hatchling," she cried to the king. "Let go!"

The Old One's limbs twitched in spasms. His scales rose like hackles and gave him a strangely ragged appearance like a fish half-scraped for supper. His wings extended at lopsided angles, the left one higher than the right. Bluish ichor spurted out of the wound at his side where the arrow pierced. It bubbled the same kind of froth as pouring salt on a snail.

Lady Browden grabbed Glëa around the waist. "Let go!" She tugged at his limbs until he released and wobbled like a drunkard.

Both women got under either of his armpits. They half-dragged, half-carried the slender man from beneath those flapping leather wings.

Glëa sank out of their grip and dropped to his hands and knees. His shirt sleeves were torn and scorched. Lavender phlegm, bluish ichor, and scarlet human blood mixed in a sickening paste on his unevenly clipped hair. Wild-eyed, he babbled a phrase in the ancient language of kings, "We are One, We are One, We are One."

The beast yawned his maw to the ceiling. He barked out three last howls, each higher and louder than the last. He screamed the last scream of the dying, the white rage of a life not ready to go out. Sparkles boiled under his crusty hide.

Lady Browden grabbed the king's shoulders and shook him. "Glëa! Look at me!"

His blue eyes rolled wildly and unfocused. His singing chant, "We are One, We are One," rose in pitch and rhythm, faster and faster, until on the last sound of the last word, his mouth hung open. He, too, raised his chin and screamed at the ceiling. His voice matched in resonance the voice of the beast. Two throats, in unison, were like the same note strings of different sized harps. Squeals and screeches rang harmonics in the rafters of the cathedral ceiling.

Glëa's sustained scream thickened in her ears. The unending chime inside her skull raised sparkles of silver and emerald green that filled her sights. His glittering scream wiped away awareness of anything and everything else. His memories played out on the stage of her mind, and she saw everything that he was, everything that he knew, everything that he had ever been. His youth as a pampered prince in this very castle; his embarking on an expedition to sail the Deep Sea; the shipwreck in a storm that was not a storm; the falling of a shining soul from the Crystal City in the clouds;

the plunging into the shell of human flesh; the forty years of madness and confusion hiding in a cave on the black island; forty years of being deceived into thinking he was merely human; returning to the shores of his home, only to be denied and rejected by his own brothers. War. Blood. Pain. Victory. Friends. Passions. Ecstasy. Triumph. Weeping in grief over the severed head of Prince Rouchard... *My brother, my foolish brother. Why did he fail to believe in me?* Now, his heart convulsed in horror as a fellow Eternal Shining Being came to its end.

The Old One shattered from the core outward. Ichor, not blood, crystallized into sandy purple glitter. Wings burned up to wisps of smoke. His horned skull cracked into shards that flew off in all directions. When the fragments hit the marble floor, they sizzled and dissolved into oily stains. His scream was the last thing to go echoing in the high vaulted ceiling.

Lady Browden shouted a victorious whoop. "He's gone! He's gone!"

Ravel's talons quivered more violently than ever before. She slapped both hands into her chest. She pressed her palms hard against the prodding claws beneath her shirt. Chills rippled through her. She shivered as if she knelt in ice. The skin of her bosom stretched and loosened. Yet strangely it almost felt good, like rising from bed after too long asleep and flexing the kinks out. Her mouth gaped open. She panted in rapid huffs anticipating a pain that had not yet come. Ravel arched her spine. Her head craned backwards. Arms stiff, feet numb, she was helpless to speak or move. Her sights turned to violet and emerald sparkles.

The cluster of blackened talons dissolved into ashen sand. They sprinkled out from the scars of her skin. She looked at the pile of black dust on the floor.

Cross-eyed, her blurry vision was fogged in the tremors of after shakes. She looked down at their remains, incredulously, that for so long they were a part of her. Now they were gone. She reached for the nothingness of dust, intending to scoop them back into their shape. She wished to sheath them in her skin where they belonged. Until now, she had never thought she would miss the spikes at her chest. Her hand caressed the sore, scarred spot at her breastbone. So flat. So soft. So bare.

Her blood pumped red. Her throat felt dry from simple thirst. Plain watery tears dribbled thickly down her cheeks. She blinked at the unfamiliar sensations. Overcome with weariness, she collapsed to the marble floor. For the first time in six years, she sprawled face-down on her smooth chest.

Chapter 51.

"Are you...?" Candor's voice choked and he could not finish his question.

"I'm alive." Ravel cleared her throat of a sour lump of phlegm. Marble tiles felt coolly soothing on her cheek. Though her eyes were open, her sight remained clouded by the lack of candlelight. For the first time in six years, nighttime became murky and dim. She sobered to see the nighttime world in darkness as only mortal eyes could see. Even the king's skin had a gloss of sweat and rain; no more did she perceive the truth of his dropped-in soul or the glimmer of immortal light in his irises.

Nearby the king crouched on hands and knees, breathing hard and sweating. He was unharmed except that his hair was chopped short.

Lady Browden knelt with him and caressed his cheeks. "Your Majesty? Glëa? Look at me. Can you understand me?"

Glëa po'Lon wagged his head to the beat of archaic words that he babbled. His slender chest swelled and released in rhythm to his own voice. The walnut lump in his throat bobbed as he swallowed.

Ravel pushed her arms straight and, with great effort, managed to bring herself upright. She sat ungracefully with crooked legs. Her limbs felt cold and drained of strength. After so long, the flesh felt ordinarily human.

Prosper said, "I have an arrow in my shoulder. But my legs are numb. Why can't I feel my legs?"

Blood flowed out Prosper's back where the arrow had penetrated all the way through. The barbed arrowhead had shredded the artery between his collarbone and his armpit. She had seen this same injury on the battlefield many times before. She assessed his sweating face drained of color and the pool of dark liquid spreading behind him. Too much blood had been lost; he would never rise again.

"Don't be afraid." She spoke to the dying man in a comforting tone. "You'll be fine. You're fine. Rest and get your second wind."

"Where there's life, there's no defeat." Candor spoke with his eyes half-closed. His jaw was clenched so tightly that his cheek twitched.

A squad of archers rushed inside from the foyer. Breathless and wide-eyed with the fever of battle, their hair was slickened flat with a mixture of sweat and blood. They carried both longbows and crossbows fitted with pitch-tar arrows ready to shoot at whatever moved. One footman carried a blazing glass lantern. In the dark hall starved for light, that tiny flicker illuminated a wide circle.

"About time!" Lady Browden hollered. "Where in the blazes were you, Lieutenant?"

"We're just barely managing to hold the gatehouse, General. We're trying to keep them from swarming beyond the inner bailey, but we're losing that effort. We're losing fast. The beasts are working on a strategy. They're throwing rocks at us! They're pushing timbers and hay bales into the moat. Colonel Maetha fears they might breech it soon and get through to the city. How many civilians are sheltered here?"

"Never mind them; we're evacuating out a secret passageway behind the throne," she said. "His Majesty requires a medic! Call the lord surgeon at once!"

"I'm sorry, General, but he's dead," the lieutenant said. "He didn't make it out of the theater."

Captain Ash entered just behind the squad. "I'm here."

A small blonde woman in a gray gown trailed on his heels. Lady Clear carried his satchel of medicinal supplies and an armload of rolled towels.

He started in the direction of where Prosper lay bleeding, but Lady Browden called out to stop him.

"Hurry, Doctor, don't just dawdle there! Come attend to His Majesty."

"Yes, Auntie, I'll just be a little bit." Ash rushed to Ravel's side and tapped his knee to the floor. He hurriedly gave her a few towels with a jar of herbal ointment. "Do your best to stop his bleedin' and I'll be right back. I'm sorry."

"I'm cold," she said.

Ash's warm fingertips probed her pulse at her neck. "Your heartbeat is strong. Are you in pain?"

"No." Ravel rolled her head to the side in search of Candor. Everything felt sluggish, heavier, weaker than before. It was hard to distinguish the shapes of people huddling in the shadows behind the statues. Everything was so dim, near dark, she could hardly make out Ash's face in the feeble glow of the archers' lanterns.

"Don't get up." Ash gave Ravel a comforting smile and then shifted a stern frown to Candor who kneeled behind her. "Stay down, kid. Take care of your sister for a change."

Briefly he glanced at Ravel's chest. She looked down at herself and saw what he saw: an indigo burn stained the front of her shirt. The talons were gone.

Clear reached the king's side. "Excuse me, Auntie, but it's urgent for him to stay groggy a bit longer."

"Here, now, you impudent bastard girl," Lady Browden said. "Move aside. Let the doctor attend to him."

"In a moment, Auntie." Clear gently patted the king's cheeks. She guided his face around to hers. Their profiles in mirror image came so close that their nose tips touched. Glëa blinked at her in a bleary-eyed and unfocused confusion. Then he looked down at his own hands in surprise as if he had never seen human hands before.

She took a deep breath then hummed a droning tone at his closed mouth. Glëa parted his lips and drank in the sound of her voice. When she ran out of breath, she stopped to gasp up a fresh lung full of air, then hummed again. He inhaled as she exhaled. He sighed into her open throat.

"What is she doing to him?" Browden asked.

"They're talking, Auntie," explained Ash as he came to kneel on the opposite side.

Lady Browden rocked back on her heels. "How? What's happening? Is this bastard girl a tainted creature like the rebel ghoul?"

"No, Auntie, she's.... she's, uh.... She is her father's daughter."

Clear turned on the older woman. "He understands what to do, but we must move him quickly before he remembers that he's a man. Help me get him on his feet!"

Lady Browden just sat there, mouth agape.

Captain Ash grabbed the king by the armpits to hoist him off the floor. "Where to?"

"The doorway."

"Right."

Ash hobbled with the king sagged alongside him. Stockinged feet padded crookedly across the grand tiled floor. The squad of archers followed on either side with their arrows and lanterns at the ready.

"What are you doing with him?" Lady Browden rose to her feet.

Clear stood in her way. "He can speak to them in the same way he spoke to Old Scratcher. You saw it for yourself, Auntie. You know he can."

"You weren't here," the old woman said. "How did you know?"

"I will explain everything later, Auntie, but please not now."

Ash brought the king to the foyer. He propped him up against the doorframe of the entrance. Two men and a squad of archers faced the maelstrom of smoke and wings in the skies beyond.

Glëa sang out a pure tone from the depth of his gut. The pitch gradually rose to a crescendo. He sustained the highest note as a controlled scream. He turned his head side-to-side and sprayed his song over the blackened wings. He offered them a simple message, in a primary color, a basic need that they had unfulfilled.

Lady Browden approached the curtained archway that divided the Main Hall from the foyer. "What's happening? What is he doing?"

Clear stood alone in the center of the empty floor. "He's telling them exactly what I advised him to say. 'Go home.' Let us hope they obey."

The wings launched all at the same time. They flapped crashing into each other in mid-air. Most of them settled into a formation like starlings. They swirled in a cloud of wings towards the shattered roof of the theater. They left behind the smashed towers, the battered walls, and the small groups of ragged survivors stranded in muddy puddles. They poured themselves as if through an invisible funnel into the gap of the theater's shingles.

Just as the king's breath ran out, the last of them plunged into the hole. Silence rippled through the night sky. Only smoke filled the air above the crenellated walls.

Glëa doubled over and clutched the door jamb. He blinked his all-too-human eyes and flexed his all-too-human fingers against the fluted wood.

Lady Browden hurried to his side. She cupped his face in her hands. "You're so cold."

"You're all right, sir." Captain Ash massaged the king's shivering back in long strokes. "You're going to be all right."

"Where am I?" Glëa asked.

"Uh, you're still in the throne room, sir. You've just saved the world. You gave 'em a royal command to 'go home' and they obeyed. Praises be! They obeyed you."

Lady Browden promised, "I will form squads to search every tower, every outbuilding and storage cellar to be sure that not one of those obscenities has strayed behind."

Their faces were close enough to kiss, but then Glëa pulled back. He frowned at her confusedly. "Who are you?"

"Don't you know me, Your Majesty? It's Jiveine."

"My little Thorn Lily?" he asked. "When did you get old?"

"Oh, my sweet prince." Tears bubbled out of the woman's crinkled eyes. "You've gone mad?"

Ash said, "Don't worry, Auntie. I'm sure he'll come to his senses shortly. Looks like he's a bit rattled in the head, but he'll be fine. I've seen worse."

"'Worse?'" The general spun on her heel to confront the man. "Have you gone mad as well? You've 'seen worse?'"

"Don't ask," the king mumbled. "Please, don't ask."

Glëa turned away from the door. He returned through the foyer's archway and strolled half the length of the marble floor. With each step, his balance grew steadier. He came to stand at the charred spot on the tiles where the Old One had perished. That marked the spot where all of Ravel's grief and fear had come to an end.

Ravel searched his expression for the haughtiness and pride of a king. Instead, she saw in those famous sapphire eyes the unfocused, unreadable mood of a drunken man becoming sober. She could not be sure if it were the heir to the royal bloodline or the hatchling a-glow huddled deep within the shell of his skin. Perhaps it no longer mattered. Both of his souls had blended into one.

Survivors slowly emerged from hiding underneath statues in the alcoves. Craftsmen and kitchen housekeepers gathered around where Clear stood. They loitered in small groups, unsure of what to do. Some of them murmured, "Oh blessed lord of us all, Light of the World..." and "You command the beasts of the Underworld..." A few weeping servants sank to their knees in adoration. "May your reign last ten thousand years and again ten thousand more!" Their bowed heads and rounded backs formed a carpet of adoration around the king's stockinged feet.

Only the lady Clear did not bow. She stood alone as a solitary pole of proud defiance. "I did a service, today, but I will never serve you."

"Nor do I require your servitude," the king proclaimed with a wave of his hand. "You are entirely free to stay or go as you wish."

Clear nodded in acknowledgment. Then she turned to offer comfort to the group of survivors huddled in the middle of the floor.

Ash squatted on his heels next to where Prosper lay. He touched his fingertips to the wounded man's neck, waited a moment, then somberly withdrew his hand.

Ravel briefly touched her collarbone where she had once worn a betrothal necklace. Within the privacy of her thoughts, she murmured a prayer. *Prosper po'Vinn of the House of Atoyëin, may your soul ride the Jeweled Barge of Heaven swiftly over Nugator's plain and on to the bliss of the Eternal Fields. May you be reunited with the spirits of your ancestors, your parents, and your departed brothers. May you be at peace everlasting.*

Governor Browden pointed to Ravel sitting sprawled on the floor. "What about *her*? This rebel traitor stood in league with that monster."

"Very true," Ravel said to the woman looming over her. "I did."

"No!" Candor emerged from the statue's alcove. He crouched humbly half-squatting as he came forward. When he got near the king's stockinged feet, he fully sank to his knees. "It was all my plan. I sought vengeance for my family's name. I found the ancient tunnels to the Underworld. I looted the tomb of kings for talismans and charms. I released the horde."

Ravel joined Candor in prostrating herself at the feet of their sovereign. "Will you honor your word? Spare my brother's life? Allow him to repent and earn redemption?"

"Yes, I will honor my word. His life is spared." The king passed his hand over his own scalp to brush the fringe of curls off his forehead. Just then, he flinched in realization that his hair was cropped short. "And for your part, Old Scratcher was no ordinary beast. You were enthralled to his will but proved yourself in the end."

"It's a mistake," Lady Browden blurted. "They deserve punishment for all that has transpired this day!"

The king fixed a stern gaze that caused the grizzled warrior to withdraw. She glumly strode away to the foyer's curtained archway. A row of archers stood ready to receive commands.

"With my grace," he said. "You and your brother are fully absolved of your transgressions."

Ravel said, "We are grateful for His Majesty's most benevolent mercy."

"Go home, go home," Glëa said in a gentle, lyrical tone halfway between speaking and singing.

Candor remained kneeling on his tightly folded legs. He hunched forward with his arms crossed under his belly. "We have no home. It was burned to ashes."

Lady Clear spoke up from across the room, from where she was busy offering hand towels and comfort to the group of civilians. "If Your Majesty pleases, may I suggest that they could stay for a while as my guests? I have a small plot of land in the west."

Glëa po'Lon merely nodded, and his nod became a royal decree.

Ravel rested her hand on the hollow of her brother's rounded back. Weariness wrapped around her head and tempted her into slumber. She had not slept in six years.

"Thank you, dear lady," Ravel said. "My brother and I humbly accept your gracious hospitality and will strive to be worthy of—"

A burning fuse's odor tickled her nose. Ravel glanced quickly left and right in search of the source. She scanned the archers with their tin box lanterns following Lady Browden to the main door. She looked at Ash with his medical kit going to examine the group of straggling civilians. Even the lady Clear, with her hands full of hand towels and kerchiefs, did not hold a lit candle. Only the kitchen staff might have carried tinder boxes in their apron pockets, but none of them were scratching at flints.

Candor's lower back muscles tensed. Then she realized that her brother had not laid his palms to the floor in prostration. When he had kneeled at the king's feet, he kept his arms crossed. A wispy thread of smoke rose out of his beltline.

Grenade!

In one smooth springing motion, Ravel pushed herself off the floor with her hands and feet. She leaped into the king's chest and tackled him. They fell together. The force of her body's weight slid them both across the slick marble tiles.

The explosion blew a hot wind across her back. Shards of a ceramic pot scratched her legs and back. Her inner ears whistled as vertigo dizziness throbbed in her skull. In a muffled haze, she heard civilians screaming and archers yelling.

Black coat uniforms rushed to pull the king out from underneath her. Ravel rolled off and struggled to sit up. Through the drifting smoke, she saw her brother's body thrown back against the pedestal of the statue. He sprawled limp next to Prosper's gray-faced corpse. Candor 's shirt front was a blackened, bloody mess.

Captain Ash hurried to her brother's side. He pressed a towel to Candor's belly. The fabric quickly turned from white to red. "No, no, no, no, no, ye damned fool. What have you done?"

Ravel's tears failed to come to her dry eyes. She could only look at the impossible sight of his twisted neck and his youthful face with glassy eyes devoid of life.

Chapter 52.

Twenty-five days passed. Xolhold Castle oversaw daily processions of funerals in the capital city's streets. A new area of the city's cemetery was dedicated in honor of those who fell that day. Within the confines of the hastily-erected fence sang the constant wailing of mourners. Nights brought the cold, thunderous rains of impending winter. Morning frost whitened the burned timbers of the outbuildings. Gradually, the stains of blood washed out of the stone crevasses. Oiled tarps covered the gaps in the bashed rooftops. Carpenters and masons arrived in droves from the remote corners of the kingdom. By day, as hammers thumped and chisels clinked, it seemed that everything would return to normal soon.

One sign of returning to normalcy was that the Council of Lords scheduled its first assembly session since the siege.

Glëa felt a flutter in his stomach as he approached the door to the Assembly Hall. His brisk pace slowed. He put a hand across his gut, wondering, *Is this an illness? Is my breakfast not sitting well with me?*

"Is something wrong, Your Majesty?" asked the commander of his escort detail.

"I may be unwell," he said to her.

Colonel Maetha gestured for the squad to fall back a few steps. In a rattling clatter of boots and spears, they withdrew.

"May I?" At his nod, she tugged off her glove. Maetha laid the back of her hand to his forehead. "You don't seem feverish, Your Majesty. What are you feeling?"

He stroked his belly. "I feel tight here. It is a pulse like birds' wings are flapping inside me."

"I see." Maetha glanced back in the direction of the squad. Then she leaned in close to his shoulder and whispered, "You're not used to being apprehensive, are you."

"That's absurd. Why should I feel apprehensive to greet my Council of Lords?"

Glëa stopped short of explaining that he had never felt anxious to be the focus of a crowd's attention. Why should he need to tell her such a simple fact? From the time he was a swaddling infant, he had been put on display. He made his first formal address to his father's council at the age of seven. He took it for granted that, upon entering a room, every lord would rise to their feet. He had strolled into this very door a hundred times; why should this day be any different?

"An admirable spirit, Your Majesty," she said. "You have a big announcement planned. It's understandable to be nervous."

"You're being ridiculous," he told her, getting annoyed now. "I am certainly not nervous."

"Of course you're not, sir."

Her eyes softened to a pink tint and her lashes moistened. Everything else about her was harsh: the crisp cut of her black wool uniform, the polish of her copper buttons, the severe way she had drawn back her hair, and the leather brim of her flat cap. Strength filled out her sleeves and held her posture firm. Yet her eyes reminded him that she had the tender heart of a woman and the grieving soul of a recently made widow.

"It must be the heavy breakfast," he huffed and stepped towards the door.

Two boy squires yanked the door's panels aside just in time as he approached. The king did not break his stride to cross the threshold.

Lords rose to their feet. Only a third of the benches were occupied. Some of the lords stood up more slowly than others, bracing themselves on canes, their legs still wrapped in splints visible underneath their cloaks. Lord Vilbyss stood at the front; his face had a freshly stitched scar across his left eyebrow. His beloved Mister Flenn sat at his side. Lady Browden stood with rigid posture. Feet apart and legs braced, she dressed plainly in a brushed wool gown of sage green. She seemed ready to ward off another attack of monstrous beasts if any should fly in through a window.

Glëa started towards his throne platform facing the assembly. The day's agenda scrolled through his mind in a flash. He knew what had to be urgently discussed. So many important tasks needed to be assigned: to rebuild what had been broken, to carry on the progress of the kingdom that had been interrupted by a single night of violence and blood.

One decision needed to be announced and that would not take long. He stopped at mid-stride. Try as he might, he could not urge his feet to move.

Colonel Maetha asked, "Does His Majesty require anything?"

He turned in place from the floor of the meeting hall, not from the throne. He projected his voice to address the farthest back row. "I want to thank you all for coming today. I understand it was difficult for most of you. My sympathies for your injuries. My condolences for your losses."

"I speak for all of us here," said Lord Vilbyss with a lisp. He had lost a front tooth in the siege. "We are grateful for His Majesty's benevolence."

Around his neck, he wore a large brass key on a chain. The key unlocked an iron strongbox kept in the Royal Treasury and secured the silver tuning fork. Workers had found it amid the rubble of the theater's stage just where Ravel had reported it to be. Never again could someone misuse the First King's talisman to reopen the mystical doorways beneath their feet, not so long as this loyal nobleman and all his descendants kept it secure. Lord Vilbyss wore the key proudly as the newly-appointed Guardian of the Harbor.

"Before we begin the day's business, I have a rather personal matter to resolve." King Glëa looked straight at Lady Browden standing in the first row. "Regarding my marriage, I have decided to issue an annulment of my betrothal."

No one dared say anything. The hush of their collective gasp rippled through the assembled group. Dozens of eyes twinkled in an effort not to show a reaction.

"I've come to the conclusion that Tiressa the Lady of Taine is too young to marry, even as a formality. By the grace of our forefathers, she survived the siege unscathed, and I wish for her to enjoy the rest of her life unfettered. I hereby release her from all oaths and obligations of betrothal. When she reaches the age of majority, she may choose to marry anyone she desires."

Glëa looked over the array of silent, shocked faces. The flutters in his stomach returned. He huffed out a deep breath to pack the jitters down.

"Nonetheless," he continued. "I have not altered my resolve that I need to marry and have a queen at my side. This matter is becoming more urgent than before, to show the people of my kingdom that one stampede of wild beasts does not destabilize my court. We will continue to build and expand the boundaries of my domain. We will resume construction of my royal highway into the Outerlands to facilitate growth of new settlements. We will expand the trade routes from the Midlands to the Great Northern Bay. We are on the verge of a new era of prosperity and unity."

Heads nodded and eyes sparkled with hope for the future.

"Who will you marry instead?" Lord Vilbyss was the only one who dared.

Glëa turned to Lady Browden standing in the first row. His eyes widened as if seeing her for the first time. In the soft light of morning filtered through a cracked window pane, her face seemed less wrinkled by the passing of years. The glow of adoration lifted her smile and softened her eyes. She was close to the way that he remembered from when he was a brash young prince and she was a naïve maiden hoping to catch his attention. For one brief hour, they danced by candlelight in a ballroom half a century before.

"Who better than the woman who has loved me unfalteringly and unrequitedly for her entire life?"

Lady Browden put a hand over her gut. "Your Majesty! I'm long past marriageable age. I can't give you an heir."

All the apprehension in his own chest broke like a wave crashing on the beach. Now, it was easy to smile at her blushing.

"I don't want or need any heirs, Jiveine. I want a queen. I want a woman strong enough and intelligent enough to rule at my side."

"Look at me! And look at you. I'm so... so old for you."

"By the calendar, I'm older than you are," the king said. "Stop being a silly girl."

Glëa swooped a few steps across the distance between them. Smiling so broadly that he almost failed a pucker, he dove a kiss full onto her mouth. His arms encircled her and squeezed her close. He sank unhurried into the melding of their faces, long and slow and deep. Lady Browden draped her sleeves over his shoulders and lounged against him. Her head lolled back to receive the pressure of his youthful vigor. Her jaw flexed to drink him in. The two swayed in place dancing to their own private song.

Colonel Maetha shouted, "Hail to the King of Xol and his betrothed Queen!"

"Hurrah! Hurrah!" The lords and ladies all cheered in a roaring chorus. A few of them coughed or wheezed and gripped their ribs.

"May His reign last ten thousand years," said Governor Vilbyss. "And again, ten thousand more."

Chapter 53.

Day 20 of the Hearth Month, in the Year of Xol 758

Ravel sat outdoors in the gazebo of Lady Clear's garden. On the eve of Winter Solstice, the air grew crisp. Frost crystallized on the grasses and trees every morning, but it was not yet cold enough for snowflakes to fall. A knitted cap kept her nearly-bald head warm; stubby tufts of her brown hair were beginning to grow back. She wore a wool cloak and simple layers of knitted hose, chemise, and a calf-length fitted gown laced at the sides. Ravel hesitated to bundle up even as the seasons changed for she had not felt the chill of winter in six long years.

Lady Clear said, "Before long we won't be able to enjoy breakfast out of doors like this."

The two women sat cross-legged on cushions around the fringed edges of a tapestry rug. A stone brazier held glowing orange logs. Dishes lay on portable lacquered trays. They ate breakfast in the custom of the western Midlands seated near to the earth without a high table or armchairs.

"I've camped in much colder battlefield tents. I can stand it a little while longer if you can?" Ravel poured steaming hot tea from a silver kettle.

The gazebo where they shared breakfast was a white wicker dome. It occupied an island of basalt blocks at the center of a large pond. Decorative fish that were too pretty to eat swam circles in the murky green depths. The gazebo's wicker frame sifted spots of sunshine from every direction. Vines of morning glory, honeysuckle, and jasmine dangled in leafy swags. Frost glittered on the tips of the leaves.

"I want you to know, Ravel, that I appreciate your companionship very much. It has been such a pleasure to have your company."

Clear looked aside, as she often did, and fell silent lost in the privacy of her own thoughts. She gazed beyond the grassy fields to her cottage home. Hardly a manor house, the structure was a modest rectangular box of sod bricks with a thatched roof. Surrounding it were a few storage sheds, a covered pen, a fenced corral, and a blacksmith's workshop. Human voices chirped on the cool breeze and blended with the rustling of dry leaves that sprinkled from the willow and sycamore trees. Young men's voices were talking and laughing. The workers of the household went about their daily chores.

The scent of meat wafted from the smokehouse downhill. Ravel's stomach turned. She laid a hand across her belly and wondered if she would ever desire to nibble so much as a quail's wing.

"I appreciate your generosity and hospitality." Ravel spooned blackberry jam onto shortbread biscuits.

"Oh no, please, it's my pleasure. The house is so large and empty without—" Clear fell silent and could not finish. She fussed with smoothing the linen napkin across her lap.

Without your husband. Ravel looked at a meadow in the distance. Saplings of evergreen pine trees were freshly planted over the graves of Clear's husband, of Ravel's betrothed, and of her brother. No statues and no mausoleum stood in their honor. Only a circle of rocks marked the place. The men were just bones returned to the earth.

Clear sipped her tea before continuing. "Of course, you're welcome to live out the rest of your days here. I'm more than happy to have you stay. Even so, have you given any thought to your future?"

"Why?" Ravel leaned forward. "Did you once dream a prophecy of me?"

Clear smiled slightly. At that moment, it occurred to Ravel that she had not seen the lady smile very often. Then a tear glistened at the corner of her eye and the lady quickly raised the napkin to her face.

"I'm sorry," Ravel said. "I didn't mean to remind you of the powers you once had."

"It's not the powers that I miss. You would think that I could stop weeping for my husband. It will be a year, come next spring, but it still feels as fresh as yesterday."

Ravel laid her hand on the lady's shoulder. "The heart does not watch the calendar. I understand that very well. You have my sympathy for your loss, Lady Clear."

"Thank you," she said. "You grieve for him too, of course."

"I expect to weep for many nights and years to come. Candor became a monster in the end. Or perhaps he had already been a monster for quite some time, and I failed to accept the fact until it was too late. His heart turned black on that fateful day, after the Battle of Border Field, when he had the misfortune to survive after all the horrors he witnessed. The claws that scarred me were visible on my chest for all to see, but he wore his talons on the inside, hidden, all those years."

Clear looked down at her own hands, palms facing outward, resting in her lap. "Try to unburden yourself of guilt and shame for events that were out of your control. What has happened cannot be changed any more than we can un-brew this pot of tea!"

Ravel smiled thinly. "I welcome your sage advice, but it may be some time before I can do as you say."

"Let the past stay in the past," she said. "Keep buried what is buried."

"What's that you say?" Ravel felt a chill to hear the same phrase spoken aloud that was whispered by the spirits inside the royal tomb.

Clear raised her chin and smoothed out her expression. "Look ahead to the future, Lady Spareen."

"What future? Am I still a lady? Our estate is gone. Our vassals who surrendered have sworn allegiance as barons under the House of Fordon. My brother was the last heir to our household name." Ravel pressed a napkin to her eyes in a feeble attempt to plug up the tears that surprised her by dribbling out of her eyes. *Father, forgive me. Mother, forgive me. I failed you both.*

"So, if you are no longer Lady Spareen, who are you?" Clear asked in a thoughtful tone like a tutor asking a rhetorical question.

Ravel swallowed back tears with the last gulp of biscuit and blackberry jam. Sucking up a deep breath, she regained her composure. "I haven't considered the question. If I am not a lady, a daughter, a sister, a wife, or a captain in the cavalry... Who am I? If I'm not commanding someone's actions or following someone's orders, what am I to do?"

"Indeed." Clear sipped her tea. Her large green eyes had a glint of mischief, as if the prophet already knew the answer. "What *will* you do?"

Ravel gazed through the gazebo's frame to the lily pond and a garden overgrown with herb bushes and perennial flowers. Roses bloomed even in the cool weather. Blossoms formed a thick blanket of yellow, pink, and dappled shades of red. Willows and pomegranate trees blocked Ravel's view of the western hills, but she knew by heart the landscape of rivers and meadows that extended past the edges of the king's domain. Hot desert wastelands lay beyond the fertile plains. Those dry sandstone mountains were unexplored territories full of possibilities.

"Ho! Hey! Yo there, good day and welcome!" The workers chopping logs paused to call greetings to a man approaching on horseback.

"Oh look," said Clear in a tone of feigned surprise. "We have a visitor."

Ravel turned on her cushion and gazed across her opposite shoulder. She watched the arrival of a rider on a Fellmont mare. A common country horse, it was no match for a Western Road Blue much less the Garudan steeds of the Iron King's cavalry. The speckled hide was the color of unglazed pottery with a pale mane and gray socks. The horse looked clean and well kept, but its color matched the soil and sand, so it appeared dirty no matter what.

"Good o' th' day, Fred!" the rider responded.

That voice. Ravel held her breath in surprise.

Captain Ash rode his Fellmont mare to the edge of the lily pond. He dismounted in a swirl of gray cape and handed off the reins to one of the lady's gardeners. He took a few steps onto the narrow foot bridge connecting to the gazebo's island. Then he stopped. His gaze met Ravel's shocked stare. For a moment, neither of them moved.

Clear waved her hand. "Good morning, dear brother, I'm so glad that you've arrived!"

"I, uh..." He coughed into his hand. "I would have come yesterday evening, but darkness fell too swiftly. I took hospitality overnight at a farmhouse down the road. Mister Fuller gave me some persimmons off of his tree to share with you."

"How very kind," Clear said. "He is a good neighbor."

"Indeed, he is." Ash stepped backwards. "I can go put the sack in your pantry."

"Don't be silly. Welff can do that task. Come sit with us." Clear patted the vacant space on a spare cushion at her side.

Ash looked at Ravel's direction one more time. Something in his curious mood urged her to hide from his penetrating stare. What could he know of her grief and her need for a quiet refuge? He had fought on the winning side during the war. He owned a home and carried a purse full of coins.

"Well, those biscuits do look delicious." Ash quickly crossed the footbridge and took a seat on the cushion.

Clear smiled more broadly with her small mouth. "You never could refuse a meal."

Ash had a tin cup hooked to his belt. He poured himself a bit of tea. "My apologies, I was unaware that you were still a guest here, Lady Spa—... uh, Miss Rav—... uh, Ravel."

"Yes, I've been the recipient of Lady Clear's hospitality ever since...." She shrugged, unsure of how to refer to that day of the castle siege.

"I see."

As he had not shaved or bathed in several days, his jaw line had scrubby whiskers. His walnut-colored hair had darkened. The musky scent of his body blended with his damp clothes and the odor of horse. Yet the earthy scents did not repulse her. He smelled real, and mortal, and male. His hands with broad palms and strong fingers curled gently to spoon a bit of jam onto a shortbread biscuit. He had the hands of a gentleman, the hands of a field medic, and yet showed streaks of old scars from years ago; in his younger days, he may have done hard labor.

"What happened to your accent?" she asked.

"I beg your pardon?"

"Why do you make it come and go?"

Ash glanced to Clear as he shoved half of the biscuit into his mouth. "I've practiced for years to learn cultured diction. It requires a bit of focus to keep up decorum. My buddies tease me if I slip."

Ravel asked, "You force yourself to talk in the King's Tongue even among your comrades-in-arms, even in your own home, even to your own manservant?"

"Yes," he said. "How is my manner of speaking any concern to you, Lady Spareen? You've never had to feel ashamed of your accent."

"I don't have an accent," she said.

"Say daughter," he challenged.

Ravel licked her lips and imagined her mother's distinguished voice in her mind. "Daughter."

Ash broke out with a small smile.

"I see, this is a sample of the teasing you spoke of?" Ravel pointed at him across breakfast platters. "Your crud-coat buddies are not your friends, not really, if they have such contempt for your parents, your family, and the village where you came from."

Ash's smile dropped away. "You don't know where I came from."

"Sounds like the deep backwoods of the Green Forest, am I right?"

Clear answered him, "Yes, his home village was under the dominion of Baron Lord Loerimann, a vassal to my mother's household."

"That voice you use in the capital is not who you are. A wise man once said to me that you can never completely let go of what you once were, even if your circumstances have changed. To deny your true self within and to live a falsehood will damage your spirit and, in the end, you'll be only half of what you're meant to be."

"Uh-huh." Ash gulped down the biscuit with a swig of tea.

Clear said, "That sounds very wise."

"Does it?" he asked. "Does it really sound wise, Clear? Because you, better than anyone, know that I have a big chunk of my childhood that I am more than happy to deny."

Ravel leaned back as the volume of his voice rose. Until now, she had never seen him impassioned or angry. Even during the siege of Surleista on the castle, his temperament had remained steady.

"Listen, my dear Lady Spareen, I have to be disciplined in my speech and manners to even have a house! To have a manservant. To have a name and a rank at the king's court. With the Lord Surgeon's tragic passing, I have been granted a promotion to fill his position. It's a great honor that I don't want jeopardized by speaking like an illiterate woodsman!"

"I understand," Ravel said.

"Do you really? If you must know, I did hard labor at Lord Loerimann's copper mine when I was a child barely weaned. That's right, they send little children into the deep holes in the ground because we can wiggle inside

where the bigger boys can't reach. One day, there was an incident that I'd rather not discuss."

Clear rested a hand on his shoulder. Ash seemed not to feel it.

"My big brother died there. A lot of good people died. I would've died too but she saved me. Then her mother adopted me as a ward of the House of Browden out of charity."

Ash paused for breath. He reached up to touch Clear's hand on his shoulder. In that angle of morning light, the faint white streaks of old scars showed more plainly on the backs of his knuckles and wrist.

He continued, "People assume that small children easily forget when terrible things happen to them, but they don't... They don't, really."

"No, they don't." Ravel saw the signs of very old grief in the crinkle of his brow. She recognized the unseen scars in the hushed tone of his voice. Questions bubbled up in her mind. *What else happened to you as a child? What have you seen? How exactly did your brother die? What un-natural poison touched you, that I once detected lingering in your skin?* Seeing his mood, Ravel did not have the heart to ask.

He said, "Every day I am grateful to her kindness. Clear saved my life in every sense of the word. I was born a nameless nothing. I was called a 'bucket' and deemed to be of less value than a minor baron's mangiest hound dog."

"I'm sorry for everything you lost." Ravel reached across the breakfast tray. She pressed her hand on his forearm. "I'm sorry for your brother."

Ash put his hand on top of hers. He held firm as if her fingers were a gauze bandage over a bleeding wound. He worked to slow his breathing and regain his composure.

"I appreciate it," he said. "But I must also apologize for how I raised my voice. We're sitting within earshot of your brother's grave. I'm being selfish and insensitive to whine about my own past struggles when yours are so fresh."

"Of course, I accept your apology," she answered. "What's more, I offer one of my own for falsely assuming that you've always had a comfortable life."

"Honestly, I'm embarrassed. It's been so many years. You'd think I could talk about it. You'd think I could at least say my brother's name without choking up."

"You have no cause to be embarrassed," Ravel said. "I'd say that you're remarkably even-tempered for all that you've suffered."

Ravel's hand felt warm underneath the weight of his palm. She knew that a lady would politely pull away or look at anything else but him. But she did not move. Her eyes grew wide, and wider still, to drink in the sight of him. Sunlight reflecting off the lily pond softened the outlines of his face. A tingle in her arm tempted her to reach forward and finger-comb his disheveled hair.

Clear stood up. "Oh look, the tea water is getting cold. I should go into the kitchen and heat up another pot. Why don't the two of you stay here and continue talking?"

Ash rolled his eyes sideways to watch her go. Clear wore a calf-length gown and a half-circle cloak that allowed her easy mobility. Her stiff shoes clicked a rapid tap-tap-tap on the boards of the footbridge and then fell silent as she crossed onto the grass.

"Th' teapot ain't gettin' cold, is it."

Ravel blinked in surprise at how suddenly his cultured accent dropped away. She wanted to ask why he chose to switch but thought better of it.

"No, I don't see how it could." A small candle flickered under the warming trivet.

"Shit, the prophet's always schemin' about somethin' or other. One o' these days, I'm gonna sneak into her cedar chest an' read her journals. Every last page! I swear. She's had visions of my future, I just know it, but she never tells me what's gonna happen. Prob'ly had visions of your life too."

Ravel coughed out a slight laugh. Her ribs ached. She had not laughed in a very long time.

"What's funny?" he asked.

"You don't have much reverence for a legendary Prophet of Ages."

Ash shrugged. "She's like a sister. A very prying, gossipy, schemin' sister."

"That is not my impression of her at all. On the contrary, Lady Clear has been a most hospitable and generous host. In fact, just before you arrived, we were discussing what I might do with my life."

"Oh?" Their hands remained stacked on his forearm; neither of them had tried to withdraw. Ash rubbed his warm fingers over the back of her wrist. "What *do* ye think you'll do?"

"I haven't decided yet." Ravel uncrossed her ankles and flexed her legs. She had been sitting still far too long. "There are so many possibilities."

The End

About the Author

Denise Tanaka has a lifelong passion for writing stories of magical beings and faraway worlds. Her father inspired a love of art with his landscape paintings, portraits, and photography. Her mother inspired a love of books by reading aloud *The Gingerbread Man* and *Mrs. Tittlemouse*, so from a very young age Denise believed that cookies run away and mice can talk. A graduate of Sonoma State University, she pays the bills by working as a paralegal in immigration law.

Read more at sasorizabooks.com.